The Shining Country

THE
SHINING
COUNTRY

—— ● ——

Kate Alexander

ROWAN

A ROWAN BOOK

Published by Arrow Books Limited
20 Vauxhall Bridge Road, London SW1V 2SA

A division of Random House UK Ltd

London Melbourne Sydney Auckland Johannesburg
and agencies throughout the world

First published in Great Britain in 1991
by Century
Rowan edition 1992

1 3 5 7 9 10 8 6 4 2

Phototypeset by Intype, London

Printed and bound in Germany by
Elsnerdruck, Berlin

ISBN 0 09 986360 X

GLOSSARY

achkan	long, knee-length formal coat
anna	small coin, one-sixteenth of a rupee
ashram	community
ayah	native nurse, ladies' maid
babu	native clerk
badmash	bad man, rascal
bhang	hashish
Bhodisattva	lit. 'pure minded one' – devotee of Buddha
Bhodisattva Padmapani	the holder of the lotus; also known as Avalokiteshvana – the lord who looks down
box wallah	derogatory term for European businessman
burkha	hooded cloak worn by Muslim women (see also *chador*)
burradin	big day (i.e., Christmas)
burras sahib	important man
chador	hooded cloak worn by Muslim women (see also *burkha*)
charpoy	string bed
choti	blouse worn under sari
crore	one hundred lakhs (i.e., ten million)
dak bungalow	Government staging post
Dassera	Hindu festival celebrated in October
dastur	bribe or perk
dhobi	washerman
dhoti	loin cloth
Diwali	Hindu festival of lights, celebrated in autumn
durzi	tailor
ekka	two-wheeled pony cart
Ganpati	festival honouring Ganesh, the elephant-headed god

ghat	flight of steps or slope sometimes leading. as in Varanasi, to river or cremation ground
guru	teacher
hartal	strike
Holi	Hindu fertility festival, celebrated in spring
howdah	canopied seat on back of elephant
Jains	religious sect
ki jai	long live
kshatrias	warrior caste
kurta	long shirt
lakh	one hundred thousand
lathi	long wooden stave, tipped with metal
lingam	male fertility symbol
maharajah	great ruler
maharajkumari	daughter of maharajah
maharani	great queen
mali	gardener
memsahib	lady
mofussil	up-country, the provinces
naan	flat bread baked in N. India
nautch girl	dancing girl
paise	small coin, four to one anna
Parsis	minority community of ancient Persian extraction
peepul	Indian fig tree
pi-dog	mongrel
puja	worship
purdah	seclusion
Ramayana	Epic story of Rama
Ras Garba	Dance performed at Dassera
rupee	Indian currency; worth about 1s.6d. in 1920s. In today's terms 1s.6d. is worth about 90p.

sadhu	holy man
sahib	sir
sarpech	turban ornament
shashtra puja	religious rites related to weapons
shikara	Kashmiri boat
sweeper	native of untouchable class who cleans latrines
'Tahsa char, garumi garum'	'Fresh tea, hot, hot'
tikka-ghari	four-wheeled horse-drawn carriage
tonga	two-wheeled horse-drawn carriage
toshakhana	treasury
Victoria	horse-drawn carriage
zenana	women's quarters

CHAPTER ONE

I was born in India and might have lived there all my life if my father had not died in January 1913, just before my fifteenth birthday.

It was so sudden. One day Dadda was complaining of a stomach upset, from which we expected him to recover in a few hours, and the next it was obvious that he was far more ill than he had ever been before with similar ailments. There was no cholera in the city, that was the first thing Mumma thought of, and so she went on treating him for a touch of food poisoning, scolding him for eating snacks from a street vendor instead of coming home to our own good food.

I could tell from the shrillness of her voice that she was frightened. So was I when I saw Dadda grey-faced, sweating and doubled up in pain. That was when we sent for a doctor. Dadda was rushed to hospital, but it was too late. I thought when he said the pain had stopped that he was getting better; in fact, the abscess on his appendix had burst. We were told that peritonitis had set in, which meant nothing to us, but we understood at last that he was in danger. He died the next day.

My whole world fell apart. To an outsider it might have seemed that Mumma was the dominant one in our family, but I had always known, not consciously but somewhere deep inside of me, that it was Dadda's strength of character and quiet good sense which held us together. Without him Mumma was like a rudderless ship, and I was equally adrift.

Dadda's family belonged in India, but Mumma had come out from England as a girl and had allowed her exotic surroundings to go to her head. She had been maid to a young lady who had married a well-to-do Army officer. Since marriage was in the air, Mumma had looked around for a suitable match for herself and Harry Bullen, serious, handsome and settled in a steady job, must have seemed just right, though I doubt if she thought it out as rationally as that. More likely she saw him, wanted him and took him, disregarding any warnings she might have been given, and only after the wedding faced up to the realisation that she had committed herself to living in India for the rest of her life. Dadda always loved her and she, in her inconsequential, maddening way, loved him, but theirs was not exactly a marriage of true minds.

Now, casting around for relief from the despair that consumed her, the whole sub-continent of India became detestable to her. 'I've never liked it here, never!' she declared, discarding some sixteen years of happiness in a breath. 'We'll go home, Jessica, that's what we'll do.'

She was forgetting that to me home was half a low white house with a peepul tree outside and a dusty compound at the back. Half a house only, for we were not at all well off. Dadda's position in the Finishing Works of the great British-owned cotton mill of Arkady & Pershore had carried the title of Superintendent, but he was paid far less than a manager newly arrived from England, inexperienced, with no knowledge of the languages or the customs of the country, but born and educated 'at home', and, above all, untainted by Indian blood.

'What about my school?' I asked as I began to realise that although Dadda's death was the overwhelming grief there were going to be other losses which would also be heard to bear.

'You'd have to leave, anyway. I can't afford to keep a great girl like you sitting around doing nothing.'

'Dadda's pension . . .'

Mumma sniffed. 'Small enough in all conscience, not to be compared with the wage he was earning. We'll be hard put to it to manage, especially now the other money's stopped.'

'What other money?'

2

It was difficult to get it out of her, but eventually she told me that there had been an allowance of two hundred rupees a month which had been paid to my grandmother and then passed on to Dadda after her death. I understood then how they had managed to send me to a fee-paying school, which was something I had never queried before.

'Where did the allowance come from?' I asked. 'Can't we ask for it to be paid until I've finished my education?'

'Huh! Fat chance of getting anything extra out of *them*, though it's not a quarter, not a tenth, of what he ought to have had. If your father had had his rights he'd have been a rich man.'

That was a cry I had heard before, that and the myth that the Bullens came from the same family as one of the Queens of England. I had discounted both stories, but now I began to wonder whether there might not be something in at least one of them. I tried to get Mumma to explain, but she shut up like a clam, primming up her mouth in a way that made me suspect that there was something improper about the story.

'I'll put William on to it,' she said. 'Though I know it won't do any good.'

Cousin William was the person we all turned to when we were in trouble. He was the most highly educated of the Bullen clan and possessed of infinite patience with his tiresome relatives. Mumma sent for him when Dadda died and William put aside his own work and came. Not that that meant much to Mumma, since what William did was not her idea of work. He had the rare distinction of having been to Cambridge University in England, but having got his degree William had returned to India to do what Mumma called crawling round ruins. She could see no use in it, and I was doubtful myself.

Strictly speaking, William was Dadda's cousin, since he was the son of the youngest of Grandmother's six brothers, but William was nearer in age to me than he was to Dadda and I had always felt that he belonged to my generation. His archaeological work took him away from Bombay and we no longer met very often, but

William was still one of my best friends and now that I was getting older the nine-year gap between us seemed to be narrowing. William had the sense to treat me like an adult and tell me the truth.

'Your father was illegitimate.'

'No!'

I tried to conjure up a picture of my grandmother Sophia, who had died when I was ten. As I remembered her, she had been a graceful, silent woman, adept at making the sticky Indian sweets which at that age I had adored. All of a sudden, things I had never quite understood fell into place.

'That's why the rest of the family have always been stand-offish towards us,' I said slowly.

'Aunt Sophia's brothers, including, I'm afraid, my own father, felt that she had let them down.'

'A bit mean of them to take it out on Dadda.'

'Cousin Harry naturally took his mother's side and when she was criticised he could be very quarrelsome. What you have to bear in mind, Jessica, is that the Bullen children of Sophia's generation were particularly sensitive about their birth and standing in the world. They were half-Indian and half-English, the children of an Indian girl and a British soldier. Sophia was the only girl and her brothers were outraged that she should have lived with a man without marrying him.'

'Do you know who the man was? Yes, you do, I can see you do.'

'A man of wealth and power who was able to offer Aunt Sophia everything but marriage,' William said slowly.

'Come on, William. Now that you've told me so much you must give me his name.'

'I'm not sure I should. On the other hand, perhaps it's better for me to tell you than for you to be taken by surprise one day. Your grandfather is Matthew Arkady.'

'Arkady . . .' I said, not really taking it in at first. 'One of the cotton Arkadys?'

'The Chairman of Arkady & Pershore, the father of the present General Manager of the Bombay Mill.'

'Dadda was working for his own brother?'

'His half-brother.'

I was so incredulous that for a few minutes the revelation took my mind right off the terrible weight of misery I had carried around inside me since Dadda's death. ' "If Dadda had had his rights he would have been a rich man",' I quoted.

'There's some truth in that,' William admitted. 'Except that, of course, he had no legal right to anything beyond what Mr Matthew Arkady allowed him.'

'Two hundred miserable rupees a month.'

'And the house in which Aunt Sophia lived until she died.'

'Little enough. Has Mumma talked to you about this, William?'

'She wanted me to get in touch with Mr Steven Arkady, here in Bombay, but I thought that would be a grave mistake. Your father kept scrupulously to the bargain his mother made, not to communicate with any of the family, and I can see nothing to be gained by breaking that promise now. I've had a talk with a lawyer friend of mine and shown him the document – there was a proper agreement drawn up – by which Matthew Arkady agreed to maintain his mistress and their son, and he thinks there are no grounds for claiming an extension of the allowance. Unless, of course, Mr Arkady can be persuaded to be compassionate. It won't help to annoy him by approaching his son.'

'So what happens next?'

'I want to write on Nora's behalf direct to Matthew Arkady, but she won't let me do that.'

My heart sank. Far more clearly than William I saw what it was that had suddenly buoyed Mumma up since she had talked to him.

'Now I see why Mumma is so keen to get to England, quite apart from taking a dislike to India,' I said. 'She's going to take me to confront the old man and press her claim – my claim – to some of the money that would have been mine if Granny had worn a wedding ring.'

For once William looked disconcerted, but then he did not really understand the way Mumma's volatile imagination had carried her in a moment from a deprived widowhood in India to the life of a lady of means in England.

'I sympathise with her wanting to get some help for you, but not if that's the way she means to go about it,' he said. 'I wish I could persuade her to let me handle it.'

'Dadda was the only one who could get her to change her mind once she'd seized hold of something.'

My voice broke and I turned my head away, fighting back the tears, until suddenly William's arms were round me and I was held in the most comforting embrace I had known since Dadda died. I cried and cried and cried, until I was limp and lightheaded and could hardly see out of my swollen eyes, while William said nothing, just held me and rocked me in his arms as if I had been a little child.

'I'm sorry,' I whispered at last.

'My dear, dear Jessica.' William's lips gently brushed my hot forehead. 'My poor little girl.'

'I keep trying to remember him and all I can see is the way he turned his head and tried to smile at me as they carried him off to hospital. It hurts, William, it hurts and hurts, all the time.'

'Gently, darling. No more tears. Cousin Harry was a good, brave man and you're just like him.'

'He could have done so much more with his life than he did and now that I know about his father it makes me *angry*.'

'I understand, but what you have to remember is that Harry accepted his life.'

That was true. Dadda had been everything William had said, but he was not a fighter. I was, and so was Mumma. Perhaps after all there was something in her idea of claiming our rights.

I sounded her out about it and, sure enough, that was what she had in mind. I think she was relieved that William had told me the story.

'I suppose you're old enough to know,' she said. 'Of

6

course, it's not a thing to be talked about, especially not at that posh school of yours. It's an old story now, but I don't see why Mr High-and-Mighty Arkady should start saving money just because Harry died young.'

We sailed from Bombay towards the end of April on a day when the hard, bright blue sky was veiled in a mist of humidity. I tried to smile as we stood on the deck and waved goodbye to William on the quayside, but I had a lump in my throat that could not be swallowed. Dear William, in his crumpled suit, his black hair moving in the breeze of the ship's departure, his fine, thin face lifted towards us. I knew now what a valuable person he was to have around at a time of trouble and I would miss him more than anyone else I was leaving behind.

Mumma was in floods of tears, suddenly overcome by the thought of that solitary grave in the Christian burial ground. I hugged and kissed her and told her how much I was looking forward to seeing England until she dried her eyes and said gratefully, 'Oh, Jess, you're such a comfort to me,' which made me ashamed because until then I had been far more taken up with my own grief than with hers.

The voyage was uneventful as we ploughed our way across the empty ocean, with nothing to look at but a few flying fish and the occasional shark. It became more interesting when we went through the Suez Canal and then, after we had called at Port Said, all the old hands began to say that we had left the East behind.

To someone who had been taught as much ancient history as I had it was thrilling to sail through the Mediterranean. I enjoyed that part of the voyage. The weather was still warm, the sea was calm and I could see for myself that the ports in my school atlas were real places. Mumma's spirits improved, too. She allowed herself to be drawn into some of the social events on board and began to be popular, particularly amongst the unattached men, of whom there were quite a few travelling second-class like us.

I had never thought about her looks before, but now I saw that her pretty features, her mass of brown hair with only a strand or two of grey, and her big grey eyes were still appealing in spite of her forty years. She did not forget her widowed state, our loss was too recent for that, but she was used to having a man by her side and after nearly three months without Dadda she relished having someone to find her a chair and buy her a discreet drink.

For the first time it occurred to me that Mumma might well marry again, and that it would be a good thing if she did. As England drew nearer it became obvious that she did not relish returning to live in her parents' house, which we had to do because we could not afford to live anywhere else. Our voyage had taken all our spare cash and had swallowed Dadda's insurance. Unless Mr Matthew Arkady could be induced to stump up, we were probably both going to have to go out to work.

What could I do? Not a great deal. Dadda's ambition had been for me to become a teacher and I had been nerving myself before he died to tell him that the idea did not greatly appeal to me. All the same, it would have been preferable to ending up in a shop or a factory, which looked only too likely now.

Mumma remembered the Bay of Biscay from her voyage out and it was every bit as nasty as she had predicted. We tossed and heaved, sick and miserable, until I was ready to join Mumma in saying, 'Never again! I'll never cross this horrible ocean again.'

By the time we docked at Southampton I was thoroughly bored with the ship. I had been the only person of my age on board and I had hovered uncertainly between the children, who wanted me to play with them, and the adults, who overlooked me as if I were not there. I was glad to land: now the adventure would begin.

We travelled from Southampton by train, meandering through the countryside, which was gentle and green, just as I had expected it to be. It was not in the least like an

Indian train journey. The stations seemed amazingly quiet: no families camped out on the platforms, no bundles of possessions being passed through the windows, no beggars, no food-sellers – just a few passengers calmly alighting and joining the train and one man in a blue uniform who raised a hand and blew a whistle. Everyone seemed half-asleep.

We stayed one night in London, without any time at all for me to see the sights as I would have liked, and then went on again by train to Manchester. Manchester, of course, meant cotton, and cotton meant Arkady & Pershore. It also happened to be where Mumma's parents lived and I think that had influenced her in deciding to tackle Mr Arkady about our future; it gave her a base to work from.

'Will Grandma and Grandad be pleased to see us?' I asked, all guileless innocence.

'Of course they will,' Mumma snapped. 'Stands to reason, doesn't it? Their own daughter and the granddaughter they've never seen.'

I kept diplomatically silent and at last she added reluctantly, 'I can't say they ever liked me marrying Harry. There were harsh things said in some of the letters they wrote. Mum, in particular, was very down on me marrying someone who lived in India. She . . . she's a bit of a tartar, my Mum.'

'When do you mean to get in touch with my other grandfather?' I asked.

'I've not worked out how to do it yet,' Mumma said. She sounded uneasy and I suspected that her courage was failing now that the confrontation was drawing near. 'How much money have we got left, Jessica?'

I looked in the purse I had been keeping for her. 'Four pounds, two shillings and tenpence,' I said, carefully counting the unfamiliar notes and coins.

'That won't keep us for long so just you be nice to your Grandma and Grandad because we're going to be dependent on them to keep us until we can touch the old man.'

*

9

It appeared that Grandma and Grandad kept a boarding-house not far from the station. Grandad was a former mill-worker who had had an accident and received some compensation which had enabled him and his wife to set up in business. Not in a very big way, for they only had some half-dozen lodgers, and as I was quick to realise, the room occupied by Mumma and me meant money lost to them.

Grandma's greeting to the daughter she had not seen for over sixteen years was characteristic. 'So you're back, are you?'

She was a little woman, quick in all her movements, with a round, rosy face, very soft-skinned, but creased all over as if it needed ironing. Mumma gave a choke and bent down to kiss her, but Grandma did not prolong the embrace.

'Give over greetin',' she said, drawing back. 'So this is our Jessica.' She gave me a long, considering look. 'She's not as dark as I expected.'

I was outraged, having been brought up to take a pride in my light skin.

'Come away in,' Grandma said, oblivious to my reaction. 'You'll be fair clemmed after that train journey. I've got a good dinner in the oven. Come into the kitchen, sit down and get thi' feet under. Here's Dad to say hello to you.'

Grandad was also a small man, slightly bent, but with a very sweet smile. He said little, but his pleasure in seeing his daughter and granddaughter was more apparent than Grandma's had been. I warmed towards Grandad, which was more than I did towards Grandma.

The food lacked the spiciness to which I was accustomed, but it was good and hot and filling. There was a plum pie to follow, with pastry so light that it melted in the mouth.

'Plums o' my own bottling,' Grandma said. 'Eat up. I've the lodgers' tea to see to yet. Jessica, you can clear the table and wash up.'

I looked at Mumma, not quite believing what I heard.

10

She smiled uneasily, knowing that never in my life had I performed such tasks. True, we had lived on a very small scale in India, but I had always walked away from the uncleared table secure in the knowledge that the dirty work would be done by our servant. Now, faced with the necessity to boil kettles of water and slosh sudsy water over greasy plates, I could hardly believe the change that had taken place in my life.

'It'll be no good putting you into service, that's for sure,' Grandma commented, watching my unhandy performance.

'Our Jessica's been used to better things,' Grandad put in shyly.

Grandma's sniff was eloquent of her disapproval, but once that first difficult meeting was over I came to realise that her rough tongue disguised a warmer heart than she liked to reveal. She took us in and made room for us and filled us with all the food we could eat without once complaining that it was inconvenient. In return she asked for nothing more than some help with the work that filled her days.

I tried once to thank her, but all she said in reply was, 'Your own's your own, no matter what.'

In spite of which she could not put up with my idle ways for more than a fortnight, then she found me a job.

'Them as don't work don't eat,' she said. 'Nora knows her way around a kitchen, which is more than I can say for you, young madam. She can earn her keep giving me a hand, but I'd just as soon have you out from under my feet. Calthorpe's the bakers need a girl behind the counter and it's only a step down the road. It don't pay much, but it'll feed and clothe you till we see if you're capable of anything better.'

To my surprise, Mumma accepted the subservient role Grandma allotted her, sinking back into being the daughter of the house as if she had never been away. It seemed to me that for the time being she was glad to take orders and have decisions made for her, but I knew her too well to believe that it would last. There would be a rebellion

11

and a quarrel, because Mumma would be able to see no other way of breaking free, and we would be worse off than ever, unless we could get support from my other grandfather.

What dismayed me was my grandparents' reaction to the story of Dadda's birth, which Mumma now told them for the first time. They were appalled and, even worse, hostile to her wish to contact Matthew Arkady. I hoped that this opposition might make her defiant, but instead it weakened her already wavering resolution. Ever since we had arrived in Manchester she had been what Grandma called 'havering' and now Grandad's uneasiness about 'meddling wi' the big folks' shook her still further.

She had forgotten, all those long miles away, what a very important person Dadda's father was. She was at a loss to know how to make the first contact with him. A letter was ruled out because she did not trust herself to phrase it properly and my offer to write it was brushed aside. In her daydream Mumma had seen herself triumphantly confronting the great man, producing his granddaughter and winning him over to provide for her; she had not thought about how to get herself into the house in the first place.

I was on tenterhooks because I had been forming a plan for my own future which had nothing to do with working in a baker's shop. I was very much taken with the idea of learning business skills which would get me a job in an office. As the weeks slid by and Mumma did nothing except repeat what she was going to say to Mr Arkady when she saw him, without taking any steps to bring about the meeting, I saw that I was going to have to act for myself.

I had one afternoon off each week and was allowed to spend it as I pleased, even if it meant something as eccentric as visiting an art gallery, so no questions were asked when I washed and changed and left the house on my own one afternoon in July.

I had brushed the black skirt which the *durzi* had run up for me in Bombay and put on the clean white blouse

12

which I was rather proud of having washed and ironed myself. I tried putting up my hair, but the heavy knot was difficult to manage without help, so I twisted it into the long plait I usually wore, reaching down my back to below my waist. On my head I perched a straw boater with long black ribbons and then, because the effect was rather too much like a school uniform, helped myself to Mumma's best cameo brooch to pin at my neck, hoping to put it back before she noticed it was missing.

I took a tram to the outskirts of the city, which was all the few pennies in my purse would allow me to do, and then trudged along the dusty roads until I reached my unknown grandfather's house.

The approach was enough to daunt anyone. There was a lodge with big iron gates, which I had not expected, and grounds so extensive that they could properly be described as a park, with Stowbury House itself completely hidden. I was disconcerted to realise that I might have to state my business at the lodge gates before I even reached the front door, but then I saw that although the main gates were closed there was a smaller one at the side for pedestrians. I slipped through it and up the drive without being noticed.

When I reached the point where the drive swept round in a curve, I had my first view of Stowbury House. It had been built in the early years of the nineteenth century and added to some fifty years later in a manner which was more magnificent than harmonious, but that was something I learnt to recognise later. When I first saw it my taste had been formed in India, where size and display meant wealth, and I thought it splendid, as indeed it was. It stood on rising ground to the north of Manchester with views over the city which must have given the Arkadys a fine panorama of their mills thundering away in the distance.

Faced with such grandeur, I began to see some reason behind Mumma's hesitation. Before I could bring myself to walk up the flight of shallow steps which led to the portico over the great front door, I stepped into the shadow of a rhododendron bush and shook the dust off the hem of my skirt and wiped my shoes with my handkerchief.

The door was opened by a footman. I was still not used to seeing Europeans acting as servants and in my heart I despised them, so perhaps I spoke to him more imperiously than a girl of fifteen born in England would have done. At any rate, he let me into the house before turning, in some bewilderment I imagine, to his superior the butler for guidance.

The butler was everything a butler should be. In response to my reiterated request to see Mr Matthew Arkady he did not, as I had expected, ask if I had an appointment. He merely bowed his head politely and enquired my name.

'Miss Jessica Bullen.' I hesitated for a moment and then added, 'From Bombay.'

I had heard of visiting cards, but of course I had nothing of that sort to offer. Instead, I had written a little note. 'Perhaps you will give this to Mr Arkady,' I said in my grandest manner.

The note was brief. It merely said: '*I am the grand-daughter of Sophia Bullen by her son Harold.*' There were no claims, no innuendoes, nothing that could not be read by anybody in the world, but provided he remembered her name it would tell my grandfather precisely who I was and – if he had any imagination at all – why I was there.

I was offered a seat in the hall – a subtle indication, had I but known it, of the butler's doubts about my status. He took my note into a room to the right of the main door, leaving me to look about me in a way which I tried to keep careless, as if I had been accustomed all my life to black and white marble floors, polished mahogany doors, enormous paintings in gilded frames and sweeping staircases carpeted in red. *If Dadda had had his rights . . .*

I was just considering this when a third man appeared to look me over, a young man this time and goodlooking in a dark and florid way that would have been much

14

admired by my Indian girl-friends. He had my open note
in his hand. I gave him back look for look. This, I was
sure, was just another servant and I was not going to be
put down by a mere paid employee.

'Miss Bullen?' he said. 'I'm Edmond Fardale, Mr Arkady's confidential secretary. Perhaps I could help you?'

I did not care how confidential he was, I was not going
to state my business to anyone but my grandfather. 'I
would prefer to see Mr Arkady himself,' I said. 'Is he at
home?'

'I'm not sure if he's at liberty just at the moment. You
say you come from Bombay. Is your errand anything to
do with Mr Steven Arkady?'

'I've never seen Mr Steven Arkady. My business is with
his father.'

I was not particularly put out by this slow progress.
Much the same would have happened if I had tried to see
a high-up Indian official, except that there I would have
had to grease a few palms before reaching my goal. I had
been given to understand that bribery was not welcomed
in England and, in any case, I hadn't the means to attempt
it. Patience was all I had, and I was prepared to expend
a limitless amount of it in my determination to see the
man who owned the magnificence all round me.

In fact, it took no more than another quarter of an hour
before I was shown into the room off the hall from which
Mr Fardale had emerged and there, behind the great oak
desk, was a man who could only be my grandfather.

My first sight of him was a disappointment. Unconsciously, I had been expecting a replica of my father, but
there was little likeness between them. My father had
been of medium height and slim, whereas this man was
big and burly, with a shock of white hair. I had forgotten
that he would be old, seventy at least. One thing he had
in common with Dadda: the intensely blue eyes which I,
too, had inherited. With my honey-coloured skin and
thick black hair they were a striking feature, at that time
my only beauty, since I was still thin and undeveloped,

but they were equally sensational in my grandfather's craggy face.

He made a halfhearted gesture towards rising as I came in, but sank back immediately into his chair, staring at me, just as I was staring at him. 'So you're Jessica Bullen,' he said.

'Yes.'

I looked significantly at Edmond Fardale, but Mr Arkady said impatiently, 'Edmond knows all about you. You can speak in front of him.'

He might know the story now, but it was very recent information and I thought Mr Edmond Fardale had been surprised and perhaps shocked.

'What are you doing in England?' Mr Arkady asked.

'Dadda . . . my father died. You knew that?'

'Yes.' He must have seen I disapproved of that stark acknowledgement because he added, 'I never saw the boy after he was a few months old. You can't expect me to be moved by his death. What was the cause?'

'Peritonitis.'

'Sudden?'

'Very.' I looked down, afflicted just when I needed all my self-control by the desolation I had suffered when Dadda had left me.

'I'm sorry,' Mr Arkady said, but it seemed to cost him an effort.

'My mother wanted to come home. She was born in England.'

'And what do you want from me?'

'Money.'

I had surprised him into a brief bark of laughter. 'That's frank! I made provision for Sophia and the boy but I didn't even know you existed until today. My responsibility can't go on for ever, you know.'

'You can't have expected Dadda to die so young?'

'True. So you think I ought to extend the annuity to you?'

'Yes, please.' I took a deep breath and told him what I wanted. 'Enough to pay my fees at a commercial school

16

where I can learn shorthand and typewriting and book-keeping and something to live on until I'm earning.'

'You've got it all worked out, haven't you? How old are you?'

'I'll be sixteen in February.'

'This is July,' he pointed out.

'Yes, and if I'm to go to the school I've picked out I have to register and be ready to take my place at the beginning of next term.'

'Where does your mother come in all this? Why isn't she with you today?'

'She lost her nerve. In fact, she doesn't know I'm here.'

We sat and looked at one another in silence for a long moment and then he smiled with something like real friendliness.

'You're an Arkady all right,' he said. 'If you'd meant to sponge on me I'd have had you thrown out, but as long as you're prepared to work for a living I'll provide you with the means of learning your trade.'

I was dazed, not really believing that I had so easily achieved what I wanted. Before I could thank him, Mr Arkady went on, 'This mother of yours – will she find employment, or am I expected to keep her as well?'

'We're living in a lodging-house and Mumma is helping in the kitchen,' I said, not revealing how little Mumma liked the work and how necessary it was that she should stick to it if we were to have a roof over our heads.

'Hm. Ought to be able to do better than that.' He turned to Edmond Fardale, who appeared to have been struck dumb by this strange interview. 'Weren't you saying your father needed a housekeeper?'

'Er . . . yes. Yes, that's true, sir.' His look of horror nearly made me choke.

'I won't hold it against you if Mrs Bullen doesn't suit, but there's no harm in your father looking her over. He's got a decent-sized house and I dare say this young lady could be found a corner in it.'

'Yes, of course, if – as you say – Mrs Bullen proved suitable.'

I was beginning to see how my grandfather had made his fortune, or at any rate built on the money his forbears had left him. If he managed his business affairs as ruthlessly as he manipulated the lives of his dependants then he must indeed be formidable.

'There is one condition,' he said, turning back to me. 'Discretion. I don't want it all over Manchester that I'm keeping a bastard granddaughter in the city.'

'I'm not a . . . what you said,' I pointed out, deeply offended.

'You know what I mean. Edmond will manage the payment of the money – school fees and a hundred pounds a year – and as far as I'm concerned you cease to exist the minute you step outside the door. Agreed?'

'A hundred and fifty,' I said. 'I'll have books to buy, not to mention clothes.'

'Your mother ought to be able to see to that, especially if Fred Fardale takes her on. A hundred and twenty, take it or leave it.'

'For life?'

'Certainly not. Until you're eighteen and can keep yourself.'

'Twenty-one.'

He threw back his head and laughed out loud. 'I wish you were a boy! I could make something of you. No, madam, I'm not keeping you until you're twenty-one. One hundred and twenty pounds a year, paid quarterly, until you're eighteen, but I'll back-date it to your father's death. That's my final offer.'

He stood up and held out his hand, just as if I had been a man with whom he had struck a bargain and, deeply gratified, I put my hand in his. I suppose something of my pleasure must have showed in my face. I felt lit up and when that happened I sometimes looked quite different, almost as if I might be beautiful one day. Matthew Arkady's hold on my hand tightened.

'I thought I'd quite forgotten Sophia,' he said. 'But now, for the first time, I can see something of her in you.'

'Why didn't you marry her?' I asked.

18

'I was already married. Didn't anyone tell you that?'

'No one told me *anything* until after Dadda died,' I said feelingly.

'My wife – my late wife – had come home to England to settle our son in school. I was lonely. And I met Sophia. I set her up in a house of her own and for a couple of years we shared it whenever I could spare the time.'

'She bore you a son.'

'I made provision for them. Small enough, I admit, but her expectations weren't high.' He dropped my hand as if repudiating the criticism implied in my remark. 'It's not a thing I can expect a fifteen-year-old girl to understand,' he said.

'And you don't think it's suitable for me to talk about it,' I said. 'That's silly. If I'd been Indian I'd have been married by now and very likely with a baby of my own.'

'You're a precocious minx. What turned you into such a good businesswoman?'

'You've lived in India – you ought to know that the one thing you have to learn is how to bargain,' I pointed out, not wishing to reveal that it was my management which had kept Mumma and me with our heads above water so far, since I was afraid that might jeopardise her chances of working for Mr Fardale. She would cope all right once she had a proper budget and a house to look after and if I was on hand I could always go through the books with her and keep them straight.

'How did you get to Stowbury?' Mr Arkady asked, going off at a tangent.

'I walked a good part of the way.'

Mr Arkady turned to Edmond Fardale. 'Order the pony and trap and drive Miss Bullen home,' he said.

I could see that Edmond Fardale did not relish the errand but he obeyed and ten minutes later, having bidden my grandfather a somewhat incoherent farewell, I was bowling down the drive behind a smart little pony.

Just then two riders came cantering up the drive, a young man and a girl of about my own age. They were very alike and I guessed them to be brother and sister.

19

They were an attractive pair, as fine-drawn and elegant as their expensive horses. The girl in particular wore an outfit I deeply envied: a fawn riding habit with a flowing skirt, polished brown boots and a severe brown bowler hat with her hair drawn back in a net. The boy touched his hat with his whip as they passed us and the girl gave Edmond a half-smile and me a stare, not unfriendly, but curious.

'Who are they?' I asked.

'Mr Dominic and Miss Patricia Arkady,' Edmond Fardale replied. 'Mr Arkady's grandchildren.'

'Is their father the Mr Arkady who's in Bombay?'

'Yes, Mr Steven Arkady.'

'It's sad for English children to have to be separated from their parents,' I said, trying to make conversation like a grown-up young lady.

He agreed, but it seemed that what he really wanted was to find out more about me. 'Tell me about your life in India,' he said abruptly.

I chattered obligingly, all about Dadda's good job at the cotton mill and how happy we had been in our little house with our three servants – I emphasised that, but the truth was we would have had to be poor indeed to have been without a servant or two in India and the *mali* who tended the garden, such as it was, really belonged to our landlord. I described my school and how lucky I was to have been accepted for it and told him about Dadda's ambition for me to become a teacher.

Mumma longed to come back to England,' I said dramatically. 'She was so homesick.'

'After sixteen . . . seventeen years?'

'Oh, yes. Once Dadda had died she forgot all about being happy in India and wanted to return to her own people.'

'She has some family in this country then?'

That was a question I had hoped to avoid since I had rather skirted round it in my talk with Mr Matthew Arkady. I had thought that to reveal that the lodging-house where we were living was owned by Mumma's parents might make us sound better placed than we actually were.

'Mumma's parents are still living,' I said. Time enough for him to find out the truth when we had got Mumma settled as his father's housekeeper.

'Why didn't you ask Mr Arkady to subsidise your training as a teacher?' Mr Fardale asked. 'It's a good profession.'

'It would be years before I could start training and even longer before I was earning. Besides, I'm not sure I'm really suited to it,' I said, which was part of the truth, but not the whole of it. If I were really pushed I would have to admit that I was not sure that our Bombay standards actually fitted me for higher education in England.

Fortunately, Mr Fardale accepted what I said and went on to ask with a smile, 'What made you think of training for office work?'

'I've had a taste of serving in a shop and I don't like it – I'm too well educated to be a servant and I certainly don't want to go into a mill. I'm doubtful about teaching in a school and, of course, I'm not old enough to go as a governess in a private family. Besides, I've got a turn for business and I think there's a future for women in offices.'

'Arkady & Pershore do employ lady clerks,' he admitted. 'Their use is slightly limited . . .'

'Why? What is there about your job that I couldn't do as well as you?'

He was taken aback, but then so was I when he replied, 'For one thing, I'm a qualified accountant.'

'Is that really necessary?' I asked, feeling despondent.

'Only if you want to be confidential secretary to the head of a vast concern like Arkady & Pershore,' he replied with a smile.

I felt he was patronising me, but I let it go. We had left the pleasant area round Stowbury and were entering the city. I wondered whether he was as struck as I was by the contrast between the serenity we had left behind and the cluttered bustle all round us.

'I may as well have a word with your mother while

I'm here,' Mr Fardale said as we drew up outside my grandparents' house.

I had anticipated he might say that and I had been debating for the last mile whether or not to tell him that Mumma had gone out. On the whole I thought it might be as well to get it over. Mumma taken by surprise would be flustered but natural; given time to think it over she might rehearse herself into some role which would put Mr Fardale against her.

I jumped down from the trap and went in search of her. At four o'clock in the afternoon she would probably be sneaking a few minutes' rest. The house was very quiet; all the boarders were out, Grandad was reading the newspaper in his garden shed, Grandma was in the kitchen preparing vegetables for the evening meal and Mumma, as I had expected, was lying on her bed in the room we shared reading a penny novelette.

She looked up guiltily as I came in, expecting a reproof from her mother. There was no time for long explanations. I sat down on the edge of the bed and put the facts to her quickly.

'I've been to see Mr Matthew Arkady. No, I haven't got time to go into details, but he's going to help us. Quite apart from the money side, which I'll explain later, he's suggested you take a job as a housekeeper.'

'With him? Oh, Jess, I wouldn't dare!'

'And he wouldn't want it. He wants us safely provided for and out of his way. His secretary's father needs someone to look after his house. I've got the son downstairs and he'd like to see you. Will you come down!'

There was one thing you could count on with Mumma – the prospect of meeting someone new would always interest her. It took no more than five minutes to put on her shoes, change into a clean blouse and tuck a few wisps of hair behind her ears and she was ready: clean, bright, smart and eager.

I could see that Edmond Fardale was impressed. Her manner was exactly right – respectful but not subservient, very much the woman who had had a house with servants

22

of her own and knew how things should be run. I could only hope that our brief experience of helping in Grandma's boarding-house had reminded her of the way things were done in England.

It was a foregone conclusion that Mr Frederick Fardale would employ Mumma as his housekeeper and as soon as I set eyes on him, a well-set-up man in his late fifties, I knew that she would marry him. Not immediately, of course: Dadda had not been dead for a year and Mumma would certainly mourn him for that long; but once the anniversary was over and her tears of remembrance had been shed she would be ready to take a second husband and there he was, ready to hand and just what she needed.

As for me, I moved with the utmost thankfulness out of my grandparents' lodging-house. I was grateful to them for taking us in and I knew how difficult it had been for them to make room, not just in their house but in their lives, for a widowed daughter and a difficult, foreign-looking granddaughter, but I needed more space in which to grow than their narrow outlook allowed me.

The choice of a commercial course had been an excellent one. I was quick, neat, accurate and had a retentive memory. I was soon a star pupil at shorthand and my trial balances never failed to balance. I also studied the cotton industry and began to understand just how fortunately placed Arkady & Pershore had been with a foot both in England and on the Indian sub-continent.

There were no Pershores left in the firm now, but originally it had been a Pershore who had set up business as an importer of hand-woven cotton goods from India, way back in the eighteenth century. The Arkadys had come in with the new mechanical inventions which had increased the consumption of raw cotton in Britain and fed the growing demand for cotton yarn. At the beginning the United Kingdom had the advantage of being first in the field with the development of the mill system, but that had come to an end and the spread of mechanisation had been inevitable when the prohibition on the export of textile machinery from England was repealed in 1843.

The company, known from that time on as Arkady & Pershore Limited, established its first Indian mill in Bombay in the 1850s and expanded it some twenty years later. Their Manchester mills in Ancoats had also grown from an iron-framed building dating from 1820 to the latest twentieth-century spinning mill constructed of steel and concrete with redbrick walls and larger windows than had been thought necessary a hundred years earlier.

That new mill had been built at a time of boom between 1905 and 1907. It appeared that Arkady & Pershore were still prospering when I began to take an interest in the business, but I learnt that the British share in the world trade in cotton goods had fallen to fifty-eight per cent compared with eighty-two per cent in the early 1880s: it took no great head for figures to realise that the expanding Indian trade must be a boon to them. Rather a facer to a man like my grandfather to realise that the business which had been set up as a subsidiary was outpacing the home industry. Or perhaps he had always foreseen that, in which case I had to respect his vision.

I knew that Dadda had been a supervisor on the finishing side of the production of cloth in Bombay, but once I began to realise how much there was to know I was ashamed to think how little interest I had taken in his work. It had seemed remote from my world and since we had not lived in the compound of housing provided by the company for its convenanted employees, but had been outside the pale with the other country-born workers, I had had few friends amongst the children of his colleagues.

My new schoolfriends were far more knowledgeable and when I heard them glibly dropping expressions like singles and doubles, mule spinning and ring spinning, winding and beaming, shuttle-boxes and pirns I fretted over my ignorance.

The girls I met were prepared to be friendly, but they were suspicious of me as an in-comer who 'spoke queer'.

They did not think there was anything strange about their own broad Lancashire speech, but the unfortunate 'chi-chi' singsong I had picked up in India struck them as either comic or affected, they were not sure which. I could hear for myself that it was not acceptable in England and I struggled to change it, but the pattern of speech I set myself to copy was not the local dialect of my schoolmates but the cool, clipped cadences of Dominic and Patricia Arkady.

When Mr Arkady had first spoken of Edmond's father's need of a housekeeper I had assumed he was talking of someone else in the cotton trade, but Fred Fardale was a veterinary surgeon, a professional man. My interest had quickened when I realised that. Acting as his housekeeper would carry little social slur and once I had decided that Mumma should marry him I saw it as a definite step up for her.

He was a likeable man, broader in his speech than Edmond, with an open face and weatherbeaten complexion. He was deft and gentle with small animals, but he obviously had the strength to deal with farm beasts, and there was more call for his services in the countryside round Manchester than I had first realised when I had seen what looked like the endless development of the town. Mr Arkady, for one, kept a small herd of cows and a few sheep on the acres surrounding Stowbury and then, of course, there were the horses, which is what gave Dominic and Patricia an excuse to call and see me.

Mumma and I had been given rooms at the top of the house. As Mr Arkady had said, there was plenty of room for me to be stowed away without being noticed. For the first time I knew the luxury of privacy. I had had a room of my own in our house in Bombay, but there is little privacy in an Indian house. The doors stand perpetually open to catch any breeze that is going and even the windows had been covered by nothing more than rattan blinds. Now I had a room which was my own separate world. True it was small, and the ceiling sloped down on one side so that I could not stand upright at that end of the room, but it had a cupboard for hanging up my scanty wardrobe, a desk on which I could do my homework, a narrow bed with a white counterpane and, the thing I liked best of all, a wide windowsill on which I could perch and read for as long as the light lasted.

I was sitting there not long after we had moved in, basking like a cat in the pleasure of heat from the pale English sun, when I heard the clatter of hooves on the cobblestones of the yard below. I peered down and saw two riders – the young boy and girl I had last seen riding up the drive of my grandfather's house. I leaned out of the window and heard the girl's clear, carrying voice.

'Hello, Freddy dear. Would you take a look at Flock? She seems to be rather off her feed.'

She slid off the horse's back, not waiting to be helped, and her brother did the same. They were both looking round as if in expectation of seeing something.

'You're lucky to catch me in, Miss Patricia,' Mr Fardale said. 'But I've ten minutes to spare so I'll take a look.'

'Bless you. I say, you've got a new housekeeper, haven't you? Do you think she'd give us a cup of tea?'

'I dare say, if you ask her right, though it's not all my clients get that treatment.'

There was ink on my fingers, my black skirt was crumpled and my hair was untidy, but I was out of the attic and down the stairs in a flash.

In the kitchen Mumma, looking flustered, had already moved the kettle over to boil on the range and was standing clutching the teapot. 'Will you come through to the parlour?' she suggested nervously.

'Oh, don't let's be horribly formal,' the girl begged. 'We often had tea in the kitchen in old Mrs Firmin's time, didn't we, Dom?'

The boy she called Dom smiled at Mumma with enormous charm. 'It's what we'd really prefer, if you don't mind,' he said.

I was hovering in the doorway, listening with fascination to their assured manipulation of poor Mumma. Both heads turned towards me and I was inspected by two pairs of eyes as blue as my own. Patricia, as I had thought, was just my own age and Dominic perhaps two years older. Apart from the difference in age and sex they were as alike as two peas in a pod, slender and beautifully formed, with a look of breeding that must have come through the female line, since they certainly didn't get it from my thickset grandfather. Patricia, in particular, had the face of a cat, wide at the cheekbones and pointed at the chin, while Dominic's face was longer with heavier bones, but they both had the same chestnut hair and those vivid eyes.

Patricia got up from the kitchen chair on which she had perched herself and came over to me, holding out her hand. 'I do hope old Freddy doesn't do anything too drastic to poor Flock,' she said, 'because there isn't a thing wrong with her. We just wanted an excuse to come and see you. Grandfather told Dominic all about you and, of course, Dom told me because we tell one another *everything*. We just couldn't wait to meet our bastard cousin.'

Mumma dropped the teapot.

CHAPTER TWO

Patricia and Dominic shared another characteristic besides their looks and that was an implacable determination to have their own way. And charm, of course. The combination completely defeated poor Mumma. After a few incoherent protests she was cajoled into allowing me to sit down and drink tea with them.

'Of course we understand that our relationship is supposed to be utterly secret,' Dominic assured her.

'We won't talk about it to a soul,' Patricia said. 'You do see that we couldn't resist coming and meeting Jessica, don't you, dear Mrs Bullen?'

Mumma saw nothing of the sort, but she could hardly ask them to leave, not when her new employer had sent them in for tea.

'We'll buy a new teapot,' Patricia said.

'It was Pat's language that shocked you,' her brother added. 'She picks it up from the grooms, you know. I do apologise for her.'

We were still talking when Mr Fardale put his head round the door to say that he could find nothing wrong with Patricia's thoroughbred mare, except that she was overfed and under-exercised. 'If she's been holding back from stuffing herself it shows her good sense. Call me in if the problem goes on, of course.'

'The ground's been too hard for galloping,' Patricia said by way of excuse.

Mr Fardale went off on another call, but Patricia and Dominic and I went on with our talk.

'We were born in India, too,' Patricia informed me. 'We came home when I was five and Dominic was seven and we've never been back. Mother and Father are out there now, of course, and that's why we live with Grandfather. Mother will come home next year when I'm sixteen. She says I'll need grooming before she presents me. I can't imagine it'll take a whole year to lick me into shape and I do think it's hard on poor Father. Why can't I just make a quick curtsey and then go out to India? I long to see it again though I can't pretend I remember it at all.'

'Do you miss it?' Dominic asked me.

'Yes, I do,' I said, which was something I had not admitted before, not even to Mumma. 'I don't feel as much at home in England as I thought I would.'

'How old are you? Fifteen? The same as Pat. It's an awfully long time to live in one country and then uproot yourself and settle in another.'

I agreed, but he had not quite put his finger on the trouble. I had listened too much to the stories told by my father, who had never been to England, when I should have been learning about the reality of working-class life from my mother. The England in which I was living was not the England I had expected.

'Let's be friends, shall we?' Patricia said. 'Dom will be going back to school very soon and I'll be utterly bereft. Can I come and see you again?'

'You can come here, but I don't think Mr Arkady will want me visiting you,' I pointed out.

'True. Grandfather is very Victorian in his attitudes.'

'I must say it filled me with glee to hear that he'd misbehaved in his youth,' Dominic put in. 'We mustn't put Jessica and Mrs Bullen in an awkward position, Pat. If Grandfather hears you're visiting here regularly he might make Fred get rid of them. And don't think he wouldn't do it,' he added to me.

'I'm sure he would,' I agreed. I smiled at Patricia and suggested, 'Let's leave it to chance and see what happens,' serene in my conviction that Mumma was going to land Mr Fardale. A wife was less easily put away than a house-keeper and I had a suspicion that Mr Fardale thought sufficiently well of himself to expect his stepdaughter to be allowed to make friends with anyone, even an Arkady. Of course, he didn't know about the relationship, but no doubt Mumma would tell him in due course and I doubted it would shake his conviction that he and his were good enough to mix with the best in the land.

If I had settled more happily into my new life the friendship might not have flourished as it did, but even though I relished Mr Fardale's house and was doing well at school, I was restless. Talking to the Arkadys was an escape and once Dominic had gone back to his boarding school Patricia turned to me with even more eagerness.

I had persuaded Mumma that the most sensible thing to do with the first instalment of money from Mr Arkady was to buy me a bicycle. I was not yet wearing full-length skirts and so, once I had found my balance – and with my determination that did not take long – I rode sedately to school with my hat secured by an elastic band under my plait and, less sedately, out of the city to meet Patricia.

I began to learn more about the family. As I had suspected, my grandfather had married into the aristocracy.

'And is your father the only son?' I asked.

'The only child, apart from your own father,' Patricia said. 'Grandmother died young. I never knew her.'

The son, Steven, had followed his father's example. Patricia's mother was Lady Cynthia, the daughter of a duke, no less.

'That's why she thinks I've got to be presented at Court,' Patricia said gloomily. 'After that I'm to go to India, make another curtsey to the Viceroy and get married. Unless, of course, she manages to get me off her hands in my first Season in London.'

It was a Saturday afternoon in October, a fine autumn day with a nip in the air and all the leaves turning brown and gold, the sort of day I had hardly known in India. I had said I was going to the Public Library and by some hard riding had managed to combine this with a visit to the park surrounding Stowbury. Patricia and I were in one of our favourite haunts, a grove of trees on a little knoll covered with grass and moss.

'Do you want to get married?' I asked.

30

'Not much, but what else can I do? I mustn't be a drag on Dominic and he wants to go into the Army, where I can't follow.'

'The Army?'

I was startled, since I had never thought of the heir to the Arkadys doing anything but join the family firm.

'Mother's all in favour of it and Dom's been mad about the idea ever since she put her brothers on to him. I must say they look utterly magnificent in uniform, but they're much more stupid than Dom.'

'But what about the mills?'

'What indeed? Mother believes underlings should be employed to do the menial tasks. Grandfather thinks she's addled in the head.'

'Edmond Fardale?' I asked.

'Ah – that's very acute of you. Yes, Grandfather has one or two promising young men he's bringing on in case Dom really does disappoint him. Edmond is one of the best, but the trouble is no one but Dominic will really do for Grandfather and he doesn't like his young men to know all his secrets. I suspect the reason he told Dom about you is that he couldn't bear someone outside the family, like Edmond, knowing something that his own grandson didn't know.'

Patricia lived a strange, shut-away life, almost like being in *purdah*. She had a governess, of whom she seemed quite fond, but in a slightly exasperated way as if she had outgrown her. There were a few families with whom she was on visiting terms and her mother's family sometimes remembered her and asked her to stay, but on the whole while Dominic was away she was thrown very much on her own company. She lived for his holidays and I began to share her obsession even though I knew him less well than I knew Pat.

When winter arrived it became less easy for us to meet. Besides, Dominic and Patricia were to spend Christmas with their other grandfather, the Duke, an invitation Patricia treated with a disdain I rather admired.

'It'll be *so* dull,' she told me. 'I'll be expected to amuse

31

the children. Dom will get some shooting and I suppose we might hunt, but if we do there'll always be somebody making me hold back. Church on Christmas Day, of course – stone-flagged floors and no heating. A big tree and a present about two years too young for me. Dancing perhaps for the adults, but I'll be sent off to bed just as I start to enjoy myself. Dom will be allowed to stay up, but he'll have to do his duty by all the dreary cousins. He'll hate it.'

I hoped he would, but I suspected that Dominic might enjoy this country house visit more than his sister, perhaps because he was older and could join in the adult sports, perhaps because it would give him a chance to practise a power over women he was only just beginning to realise he possessed.

The cold that winter was almost beyond bearing. We had snow for Christmas, which in my ignorance I thought beautiful, until I had to go out in it. No doubt the fells were visions of loveliness, unless you were a farmer with sheep, but in the city the snow was transformed into brown slush which splashed over my skirt, seeped through my most serviceable boots and clogged the wheels of my bicycle. I skidded and slithered to my classes, frozen and miserable, and relieved my feelings by muttering some choice curses I had picked up in the Bombay bazaars.

Indoors, I huddled close to the fire and was glad of extra blankets and a hot brick in my bed at night. I got chilblains, too, hideous red bumps on my fingers and toes which itched and burned. I went out as little as possible, even though Mr Fardale assured me that exercise out of doors would improve my circulation, make me warmer and drive away my chilblains.

He was extremely busy, out day and night. Mumma coped very well and whenever he came in there was something hot ready for him. After all, she had been brought up in a Lancashire kitchen and in spite of the years spent doing little more than ordering a chicken for Sunday to be put in the oven by our cook-boy, she had not forgotten the value of a good hotpot.

I heard her stir one night quite late when he returned from a call. I had been hugging my heated brick wrapped in an old woolly vest and wishing miserably that my chilblains would stop throbbing, but when I heard her door open I sat up. I hesitated, wondering whether I should interfere, but my curiosity – and my misgivings – would not let me stay in bed.

I opened my door very quietly, still struggling into the thick dressing gown which had been a Christmas present, and a very welcome one, from Grandma. Mumma was going down the stairs. She had a fine woollen shawl from Kashmir thrown over her nightgown and her hair was hanging loose, so I knew that this was something she had planned because otherwise she would have plaited her hair up tightly for the night.

She went into the kitchen and I heard her say, 'Is there anything I can get you? Eh, you must be starved,' which I had learnt meant cold right through and not hungry as I had always thought.

I heard him answer. 'Nay, lass, you shouldn't have come down. I'll have a sup of your good broth and be off to my bed.'

'Is it hot? I left it on the hob thinking you'd be glad of it when you came in.'

'I am that. It's good an' hot and I'm grateful for it.'

'Well, then . . .'

'You go off back to your bed. I'd not know which way to turn if you got pneumonia.'

Mumma gave a pleased laugh and said in a coquettish way which had me gritting my teeth, 'I'd have to come to you for some embrocation.'

No, Mumma, no! I thought in an agony of apprehension. Don't say something vulgar about rubbing your chest, don't spoil everything now. Remember you're supposed to be a lady.

Fortunately, I think Mr Fardale was too tired and too cold to embark on a flirtation at one o'clock in the morning. 'I'd not trust myself to treat you,' he said and I realised he was not only tired but despondent. 'I lost the patient I went to see tonight.'

'Oh . . . I'm sorry,' Mumma said with just the right sympathetic note in her voice. 'Cheer up, it's not often one slips away from you.'

'Nay . . . I don't do so bad, but this was as fine a cow as you'd see . . . But I'm still keeping you out of your bed. You look right pretty with your hair hanging down like that.'

Again I heard Mumma's laugh, with a touch of excitement behind it. I tried to send my thoughts towards her. Come away now, Mumma, *now* before it's all spoilt. She came out of the kitchen then and saw me sitting at the bottom of the stairs. I put my finger to my lips and she did not speak, but followed me as I crept up to the attic. All the same, she was not pleased.

'You ought to be asleep, Jessica,' she said. 'What made you come downstairs after me?'

'I wanted to know what was happening,' I answered truthfully. I followed her into her room, which was larger than mine and without the sloping ceiling across one corner, and watched as she tossed off her shawl, got into bed and took hold of her hair to plait it. 'Mumma, do you like Mr Fardale?'

'Yes, of course. He's a very nice gentleman.'

'He likes you, too. He might want to marry you.'

'Jess! How can you say such a thing with your poor father only a year in his grave! I wouldn't . . . well, I'd need a lot of persuading before I considered another husband.'

'I think it would be a very good thing. I'd be pleased. Dadda would have wanted you to have someone to look after you.'

'Do you think so?' Her eyes filled with tears. 'Dear Harry . . . I do miss him, Jess.'

'So do I,' I said with a steadiness that had nothing to do with the agony of grief I had suffered the previous week on the anniversary of Dadda's death.

'Do you really think Mr Fardale likes me?'

'I'm sure he does. But, Mumma, you're always telling me I've got to start behaving like a young lady and that men don't respect girls who are fast. Is it . . . please don't mind me asking, it's only because I want to know . . . is it quite right to go down to see Mr Fardale in the middle of the night with only a shawl over your nightdress? I mean, if he doesn't respect you, he won't marry you, will he?'

'You know nothing about it,' she said crossly. 'I'm a widow and over forty. Of course there's nothing wrong in anything I've done.'

'I'm sorry,' I said. 'I just thought that our position being rather difficult . . .' – meaning that hers was – '. . . we have to be careful not to . . . to give the wrong impression.'

Mumma was looking at me with well-justified suspicion. 'Don't you worry about me,' she said. 'If I decide to marry Fred Fardale I'll nab him, don't you fret. A man needs a bit of a push. Well, I've given him one, showed him what's on offer if he's got the sense to take it, but he'll get no more than that without a ring on my finger. And I don't want any interference from a sixteen-year-old know-all with a mind like a sewer. Get you off to bed, Jess Bullen, before I take the flat of my hand to you.'

I liked her when she spoke her mind like that, straight and to the point. I kissed her before I left her and got a hug which showed me that she knew I'd not been entirely in the wrong. She might pretend that her sortie downstairs was part of a settled campaign, but we both knew that her craving for a bit of excitement had nearly got the better of her.

They were married in April, not long after Easter, when the pale sun was beginning to peep through the clouds on our more promising days. Mumma and 'Step', as I had drifted into calling him, went off to the Lake District for a week's honeymoon and I stayed with Grandma and

35

Grandad. I felt strangely light, as if a weight had been lifted from my shoulders.

In fact, now that the harsh winter was behind us I was like an animal coming out of hibernation or a chrysalis breaking out of its cocoon to find itself transformed. While I had been hunched over the fire during the winter months changes had taken place in me. Certainly I had grown taller and where I had once been straight up and down I was developing unexpectedly pleasing curves. I had a waist, a definite indentation, so that the skirt which had hung loosely on me now fitted snugly both round the middle and over my newly rounded hips. Best of all, the little buds of breasts which I had been anxiously scrutinising for years had developed at last, round and firm, though not as large as on all those Indian sculptures which had been my guide to the human body.

My colour, too, had improved. During the autumn the touch of gold in my skin had faded to an unattractive sallowness, but after the sunless winter my face was the colour of old ivory, pale and flawless. My cheekbones were better defined and even my eyebrows seemed to arch more attractively.

The only comment I got from Grandma was, 'Eh, you're shooting up like a beanpole, lass,' but other people were noticing my improved looks and one of them was my new stepbrother.

I was never quite sure whether Edmond had been as farseeing as I had when his father had taken on Mumma as his new housekeeper. Certainly he made no fuss about accepting her. Perhaps he, too, was relieved to see his parent settled. He called Mumma 'Nora' and took to visiting the house more frequently once she and Step were married.

He lived in at Stowbury House where, I presume, he made himself indispensable. He accompanied Mr Arkady to the mills every day, dealt with his correspondence, went with him to meetings and was the sort of factotum I saw myself being one day.

Edmond was darker than his father, but with the same

36

big bones, and considered handsome. I gathered that he had been a long-distance runner for his school and that he still played cricket rather well. His room was much the same as it had been when he left home, with school photographs of cricket teams and boys' books and two little silver cups standing on the shelves. There was a suggestion that I might take over that room, but I preferred to keep my attic. Gradually my possessions overflowed into the room Mumma had once occupied until it became a sort of sitting room for me, a place where I could be quiet and do my homework.

I am not sure when I first realised that Edmond was taking more notice of me. It must have been after the wedding because up to that time I had no thoughts of anything but getting Mumma safely up the aisle. Once the honeymoon was over and it was obvious that she and Step were happily settled into married life I had more time to think about myself and the way I had changed. I was hoping Dominic would notice, but in the meantime I did not mind at all when Edmond offered to give me tennis lessons.

I was right in thinking my status would change with Mumma's marriage. All of a sudden I was eligible for the tennis club, especially with Edmond as my tutor. There was money now for a white skirt and blouse and a tennis racket.

Patricia, hearing of my new prowess, challenged me to play against her at Stowbury and I accepted. It was a daring move, but Step saw nothing wrong in it and soothed Mumma's agitated murmurings by saying that if there was one person he was sorry for it was that young Patricia, cooped up like royalty in a castle, and in his opinion a friend like our Jess was just what she needed. So I went and played singles games against Patricia and drank tea or cold lemonade with her afterwards and Mr Arkady turned a blind eye, or perhaps he didn't know about it. He knew all right though when Edmond and I played a doubles match against Patricia and Dominic.

We were very equally matched. Edmond had a powerful

serve and we both had a long reach. Dominic played as he did everything, with effortless grace and a sort of inspired madness which pulled off the most unlikely returns, while Patricia was a born net player, very nippy and full of courage. Edmond and I might have won if Edmond had not caught sight of his employer watching us. He faltered, let past a ball that he should have reached, and Patricia threw up her racket in undisguised pleasure as she and Dominic clinched the match.

I noticed that when she and Dominic saw our grandfather watching them they instinctively moved closer together, whereas I felt no such impulse to turn to Edmond.

'I'd like a word with you,' Mr Arkady said to Edmond. Dominic took a step forward. 'You stay with your sister,' Mr Arkady said. He ignored me.

Dominic, Patricia and I went to the table where a pitcher of iced lemonade and four glasses had been put out for us.

'Trouble,' Dominic said. 'I hope he isn't taking it out on Edmond.'

'He's so unreasonable,' Patricia complained.

We all took it for granted that it was my presence that had upset him. As Patricia said, it was unreasonable. He must have known I'd been playing tennis with her for weeks.

'Edmond will kow-tow to him,' Patricia said. 'He always does.'

'He's got his job to consider,' I pointed out. I put my glass down with a crack on the metal table. 'If it's me he's complaining about then I'd rather he did it to my face. I'm going after them.'

Dominic caught me by the arm. 'Don't do that. Look, if he forbids you straight out to come here then you'll feel obliged to obey him, but if he just tells Edmond he'd rather there were no more tennis parties than we can go on meeting in other ways.'

It was not his deviousness that struck me, but the fact that Dominic wanted to go on seeing me. I hesitated and he smiled, his blue eyes very bright, and let his hand slip slowly down my arm.

I had ridden to Stowbury on my bicycle, unaccompanied, but Edmond was told to drive me home with the bicycle tied on behind. 'I'm afraid we've upset Mr Arkady,' he said. 'I'm very, very sorry, Jessica. Perhaps it was thoughtless of me. You see, I didn't realise that Miss Patricia and Mr Dominic knew about . . . your relationship. I took you up to Stowbury as my stepsister, that's all.'

I could hardly believe that he thought the three of us had never discussed our family background and surely he must have known that Dominic had been told? However, that was doubtless the excuse he had given to Mr Arkady and he meant to stick to it.

'No more tennis doubles?' I asked, making light of it because I was secure in the knowledge that Dominic wanted us to go on meeting.

'Not at Stowbury. You and I can play together at the club. Perhaps we should enter for the tournament as we make such a good pair.'

'If we win, can I have the cup to keep in my room?' I asked and he was so diverted by my eagerness that he failed to pass on any other embargo Mr Arkady might have issued.

The two Arkadys and I went on meeting, in secret now, which gave an added spice to the adventure. It was all very innocent. I never saw Dominic alone, only with his sister. We would lounge on the ground in the shade of the trees, talking, talking – and what we talked about was India.

'I don't really remember anything,' Patricia mourned. 'Except that sometimes I think I can recall being carried by someone dressed in bright pink, with a gold stud in her nose. Dom says it must have been our *ayah*.'

'I remember odd things,' Dominic said. 'Flowers in pots and the *mali* watering them and the smell of the wet earth; a tree with red flowers and monkeys swinging from branch to branch; riding my first pony towards a ruined building across a big empty space with the grass burned brown – I can't think where that can have been – and a great sweep of shoreline with waves rolling in. There was a big house all on one floor with all the doors standing open and a verandah all round. I had lessons at home with two other boys and I can recollect being cross because I wanted to go out to play cricket on the lawn and being told I must pay attention or I wouldn't grow up to be a *burra sahib*. It's like a lot of snapshots, but I can't put them together and make a proper story out of them.'

'Tell, Jess, go on tell,' Patricia urged. 'Bring back our memories.'

But my recollections were different from theirs. I told, and I was honest in my telling, but they did not really understand the gulf that lay between their world and mine, nor did I care to stress how hard we had tried to cross over to join them. They were amazed to hear that the other half of our house had been inhabited by an Indian family and even more surprised to learn that the head of that family had been our landlord.

'What about caste?' Dominic asked, showing off his knowledge.

'We never intruded on their part of the house,' I explained. 'They were Parsis.'

'Parsis!' Dominic exclaimed. 'That's something I remember. The Towers of Silence and the vultures eating the bodies. I told you about it, Pat.'

'Yes, you did, you ghoul. You were trying to frighten me. I must say it's utterly gruesome.'

'Quite practical,' I pointed out. 'And it's part of their religion no worse than the burning *ghats* or being shovelled into the ground.' I had spoken unthinkingly, but all three of us fell silent. It was unbelievable to us, but there was talk of Great Britain going to war.

Patricia shivered. 'We're being morbid,' she said. 'All this talk of death. The war won't happen, of course it won't.'

'If it does I'll have my chance of getting into the Army instead of the ghastly mills,' Dominic said.

'By the time you're trained the whole thing will be over – if it happens at all,' Patricia said, but we both knew she was trying to reassure herself.

We were ignorant, and selfish. All we really wanted was that our golden summer should go on. The assassination of an obscure Arch-Duke meant nothing to us, nor to most of our fellow countrymen, but gradually we began to realise that there were larger issues involved.

When war was declared on 4 August, the little world which Dominic and Patricia and I inhabited was changed for ever. The most immediate effect, as far as they were concerned, was that their parents' return to England was cancelled. For as long as the fighting lasted Mr Steven Arkady would remain in Bombay in charge of the firm's Indian interests and Lady Cynthia had elected to stay by his side. Indeed, it was thought too dangerous for civilians to venture on the long voyage to England. Matthew Arkady had to delay the retirement he insisted he wanted. According to Dominic, the realisation that he could go on dominating the Board of Arkady & Pershore at a time when the firm's goods were of national importance had given him a new lease of life.

'And he's forbidden me to join up without Father's permission, the old tyrant,' Dominic said. 'I've written to Father, of course, but it'll take weeks to get a reply.'

'You won't do something silly like running off and joining the ranks, will you?' I asked.

'It'd be good experience, but no . . . no, I don't want to do anything that will spoil my chances of getting into the right regiment.'

'What Dom means is that our beastly uncles have told him to wait,' Patricia said. 'They want him in the Guards, of course. Won't he look absolutely stupid in a bearskin?'

'Not many bearskins at the front,' Dominic said, unmoved by her scorn. 'What I've always really wanted is to join an Indian cavalry regiment, but that will have to wait.'

41

The early reverses of the British Army dismayed me, since I had thought it invincible. The retreat from Mons was a miserable saga of defeat and the early optimism about the war 'being over by Christmas' soon faded.

Dominic went up to Cambridge and I did not know how his father had responded to his request to be allowed to join up. Indeed, we were well into my second miserable winter in England before I heard what reply Dominic had received.

I was in the parlour, doing my shorthand homework, when Pat came to look for me. I knew, as soon as I saw her face, what had happened.

'He's j-joined up,' she said. 'He wrote to Father and Father – oh, dear God, I'll never forgive him! – said that if Dom felt it was his duty to fight then he wouldn't stop him. Duty! Stupid men! As if it could be anyone's duty to go out and get themselves shot.'

She was shaking from head to foot. I put my arm round her and drew her down to sit on the sofa by the fire.

'He's so p-pleased with himself,' she said. 'I could kill him . . . oh, no, no, I don't mean that!'

I heard voices in the hall and expected my mother to come in. Indeed, I would have welcomed her since I had no idea what to do beyond patting Patricia's shoulder and murmuring stupidly that Dominic would be all right, knowing very well that it meant nothing. Instead, it was Dominic himself who put his head round the door.

'Have you got my little sister . . . ? Oh, Pat, you are an idiot. I guessed you might come here. This isn't the way to send a soldier off to war. You're supposed to be proud of me.'

Patricia glared at him over the handkerchief I had managed to find for her. 'The trouble with you is you're too conceited to imagine we can win the war without your help,' she said.

'Pat, I must do my bit. Surely you can see that? What about when it's over and other men of my age talk about . . .'

' "Crispin Crispian's Day",' I said, quoting from *Henry V*.

'That's it. Jessica understands. ". . . *Shall think themselves accurs'd they were not here*". It makes me cringe to think of standing back and letting other people do my fighting for me.'

My feelings were more with Patricia than with Dominic, but I was stirred by his ardour. It was thrilling, this readiness to offer his life for his country. Dimly, I recognised the attraction of war for a man, the joining together in a common cause, the comradeship of shared danger. We were still arguing when Step came to find out what was going on.

'I could see you were in a state when you jumped off your horse and ran across the yard, Miss Patricia,' he said, looking at the three of us huddled together on the sofa. 'I suppose Mr Dominic's made up his mind to go for a soldier?'

'Mr Fardale, tell him what a fool he is,' Patricia implored.

'He'll not take note of owt I say, will he? When do you leave?' he asked Dominic.

'In the morning.'

'You can't volunteer one day and take it back the next. Be sensible, Miss Patricia. It was bound to happen and you're no worse off than plenty of other girls, aye and women too, with children to keep.'

'He'll be killed,' Patricia insisted.

'That's no way to talk. Dry your eyes and come into the kitchen. Nora'll make you a cup of tea.'

To my surprise, Pat let him put an arm round her shoulders and lead her away. Perhaps she felt the comfort, as I did sometimes, of his enormous kindness.

'Whew!' Dominic looked at me with a shamefaced grin. 'I knew Pat would cut up rough, but I didn't expect it to be quite so bad.'

'She's devoted to you,' I said inadequately.

'We've been everything to one another since she was a little thing of five. We've only seen Mother and Father once since then. Grandfather's been good, but . . . it's not the same.'

'No,' I said. I was grappling with a strong desire to burst into tears myself so I kept my answers short.

'You'll keep an eye on her? Not let her mope?'

'I'll do my best,' I agreed. 'Oh, Dom, I can't help it, but I do wish you weren't going.'

'Oh, come on, Jessica!' he said, slipping his arm round me. 'I was relying on you for a smile – and a kiss?'

I could hear the murmur of voices in the kitchen and with half my mind wondered whether Mumma was protesting that Miss Arkady should have been given her tea in the parlour. In the yard one of Step's dog patients barked persistently until Step went out to him. Dominic was so close that I could see a faint prickle of beard on his chin, the tiny mole on the side of his nose, his eyelashes, tipped with gold and impossibly long, veiling those bright blue eyes.

His lips touched mine and for a moment I was panic-stricken, not knowing what to do. Should I purse my lips or keep them straight? And how was I to breathe? He shifted his position so that he could hold me closer and suddenly it was all right. I took a deep breath and my chest expanded, pushing my breasts against him; his grip tightened and the tentative pressure on my mouth increased.

I let out my breath in a deep, voluptuous sigh as Dominic took his lips away, laughing, and Mumma called out, 'Jessica! Are you coming?'

I could hear the note of suspicion in her voice and drew back.

'Don't tell,' Dominic said in a whisper.

'Of course not.'

'Wish me well?'

'I do. Oh, Dominic, I do, I do.'

He took my hand as we left the parlour, but I drew it away, fearing my mother's sharp eyes. As for Patricia, I never gave her a thought. I was far too taken up with my new importance. I was still only sixteen and I had been

44

kissed by a man. I had known what to do. It had been easy. And I had enjoyed it, after the first few worried seconds. In fact, it had been just as thrilling as the romantic stories said it would be, but whether that was because it had been Dominic, or because kissing was enjoyable in itself, I could not know. I let the thought enter my mind that that was something I would have to find out . . . and then was shocked that I was already being unfaithful in my thoughts to my wonderful Dominic.

By 1916 there was no longer any pretence that the war could be won by volunteers alone.

'If conscription comes in then I'll be called up. I'd rather go of my own accord than be hauled in with a crowd of others,' Edmond said.

He did not enter into it in the same ardent spirit Dominic had shown, but I admired him in a grudging way when I heard that Mr Arkady had offered to try to get him exempted and Edmond had refused.

He looked well in uniform, that I had to admit. His were not exactly the sort of looks I admired, but I gathered that other girls disagreed with me. He was very dark and in later years would probably have the same red veins in his cheeks as his father, but now in his mid-twenties he had a fresh, well-coloured face, sleek black hair, thick eyebrows which could make him look more formidable than he really was, and dark, liquid eyes. Molly, my friend from school, sighed over those wonderful eyes and was outraged when I said they were cowlike, but to me they had just the same expression, soulful but opaque, as a cow chewing the cud. He was far from stupid; I gathered he had made himself extremely useful to Mr Arkady and my unofficial grandfather was not the man to tolerate a fool about him.

Edmond had his vulnerable points. He was emotional and sentimental. When he came to say goodbye before going off to the front he had tears in his eyes as he shook his father by the hand and kissed my mother. I felt

45

uncomfortable, as if there were something not quite true about it, although I could see that Edmond was completely sincere.

He took both my hands in his and said, 'Jessy, dear, you will write to me, won't you? It'll mean a lot to me.'

I promised, of course. I would probably have dropped him a line now and again anyway without the need to make a scene about it. He bent towards me and I turned my head so that his kiss fell on my cheek, most suitably I thought. After all, we were brother and sister, weren't we? Or very nearly.

The departure of young men like Edmond brought unexpected benefits to young women in offices, even youngsters like myself. I was seventeen, nearly eighteen, and as highly trained as the Secretarial College could make me. I was ready to start earning a living and from the first I had my sights set on working for Arkady & Pershore. Edmond would not have approved, but once he was out of the way I felt free to apply for a vacancy in the family firm. I thought it unlikely that Mr Matthew Arkady had anything to do with engaging junior office staff and, of course, I allowed no hint of my connection with him to escape me, but I did mention that Edmond was my step-brother and that went down well, Edmond being well thought of in the firm.

I made no secret of my ambitions either: one day I wanted to be a proper, confidential secretary like Edmond, I said, and that was well received, too, in spite of the indulgent smile I noticed on the face of the lady in charge of the Typing Pool. Two months later, after my compulsory training period in the Pool, she was more respectful and ready to recommend me for a position in the Accounts Department.

I went off to work each day wearing a neat navy blue two-piece and a prim white blouse, black silk stockings when I could get them and afford them, polished black shoes with heels as high as I could smuggle past my mother, and a wide-brimmed, wide-crowned hat. I had already grasped one thing: in fashion the silhouette was everything.

I saw less of Patricia than before. There was a shortage of servants at Stowbury and Patricia had taken up gardening. I was not exactly shocked, but jolted, the first time I saw her in breeches, and then envious of her freedom.

'I'm ruining my complexion, my hands are a disgrace and no man will ever want to marry me if he sees me looking like a boy – or so I'm told,' she said, laughing. 'But I'm doing something really useful, not growing flowers or stupid things like that, but vegetables for the house. And I'm thinking of going in for hens. Do you know anything about chickens, Jessica? Or pigs?'

'Nothing,' I said with a thankfulness that made Patricia laugh again. The next moment she was serious. 'Dom's still all right. It's like a miracle. He's hoping for leave soon.'

He came on leave and asked Pat to get me to meet them, which elated me. Patricia was right, his survival was like a miracle. He was thin and twitchy, but there was a new resolution about him.

'I hate it, but I'm sticking it out,' he said.

'You're different,' Patricia said and she spoke flatly, not liking and not altogether understanding the change in him.

'Of course he is,' I said. 'How could he be anything else? Dom's had experiences we couldn't even begin to share.'

She loathed the idea of that, but Dominic agreed with me. 'The sound of gunfire is never out of my head. Even now, here in this quietness, I think I can hear it. Those of us who've been out there will always be set apart from the ones who stayed at home.'

We were in our old haunt, the wood on the crown of the hill. As usual, they had ridden over. Their horses were quietly cropping the grass and we were all sprawled on the ground, looking out over the wide valley towards Stowbury.

'I hate the war, I hate it!' Patricia said. She jumped to

her feet. I thought she was going to ride off and leave us, but she only moved away and stood leaning against the trunk of a tree, and I knew she was fighting against tears.

I was surprised when Dominic made no attempt to go after her. 'You're much the same age, but sometimes Pat seems much younger than you,' he said in a low voice.

'I'm out in the world and she's still very sheltered,' I said. 'I've been working with people who've lost husbands, brothers, sweethearts. I've seen some of the men who've been broken by the war, in their minds as well as in their bodies. How do you stand it, Dominic?'

'I don't know. It goes on and on. Death all round you, all day and every day; the stench of it, the degradation. Filthy conditions. Lice and rats and endless mud. And always the possibility of being killed. I'm no hero – I'm afraid most of the time, but I know now that I can survive anything except a bullet with my name on it.'

'You're an officer . . .'

'A very lowly one,' he interrupted.

'But you have responsibility for other people, don't you?'

'In some ways that's the most rewarding part. I've got a good bunch of chaps. They're awfully decent to me. I'm . . . actually, Jess, I'm rather good at being a soldier, just as I always thought I would be. There are times when I almost enjoy it in spite of the killing.'

'That's what's upset Pat!' I exclaimed.

'Yes. She can't believe it and I don't think I've ever done anything she couldn't understand before.'

We sat quietly together, not talking, until Patricia came back. At that moment I felt closer to Dominic than I ever had before, closer even than when he had kissed me.

It was the only meeting I had with him during that leave and I was seeing less of Patricia. My chances of running up to Stowbury were fewer and we seemed to be growing apart.

I tried to remember some of the things Dominic had said when Edmond came on leave and to be sympathetic to his need for rest and recreation, but it was something of a shock to have him devoting himself exclusively to me. He, too, was marked by his experience of war, but he was not standing up to it as well as Dominic. It seemed strange to me. Edmond was older, more experienced and, I would have said, better balanced, and yet it was Dominic who had found an inner strength which Edmond seemed to lack.

When Edmond offered to take me to a dance which was being held to raise funds for the Red Cross, of course I accepted. I could hardly refuse. No one else had asked me and my mother took it for granted that I would welcome this small gaiety. It was good of Edmond to ask me, she said, when he could have had his pick of any of the girls.

Edmond danced well and he seemed to know all the latest steps. Where had he learnt them, I asked him.

'In Paris. We get up there occasionally for twenty-four hours, you know. Whenever we can wangle it, in fact.'

'I'd love to see Paris. In different circumstances, of course.'

'I'll take you, when the war's over. That's a promise.'

It was a promise I saw little chance of him keeping, but it seemed to please him and so I said nothing. Saying nothing was something I did rather a lot of with Edmond. He was in a very wrought-up state, I sensed that, and it all came bursting out after the dance as we walked home that night. If I had known more about men I might have seen it coming, but I was completely taken by surprise when he suddenly put his arm round me, turned me towards him and started kissing me all over my face.

I struggled out of his hold, startled and annoyed. 'Edmond! For goodness' sake! That's no way to behave. And in the street!'

'I thought you knew how I felt about you. You must do. I've spent practically the whole of my leave with you.'

'I didn't realise . . . we're *family*,' I said incoherently. Was he trying to say he was in love with me? Surely not. Edmond? There was a bit of me that was gratified, but on the whole I was more dismayed than pleased.

'You're beautiful, Jessy. I can't help thinking about you. Can't you be a little bit kind to me? I've got to go back to that hell tomorrow night.' It was an appeal that weakened me, as he must have known it would.

'I've only ever thought of you as a brother,' I said.

'There's no relationship. No reason why we shouldn't . . . I'm not asking you to do anything wrong. Just one little kiss, something to remember when I'm in the trenches.'

Of course I kissed him. How could I do anything else? He held me tightly and when I moved away, trying to indicate that the kiss was over, he buried his face in my hair just above my left ear. 'I don't want to go back,' he whispered. 'I don't know how I'm going to stand it.'

I was helpless in his convulsive grip and when he turned his head to find my lips again I stood passively, letting him take the solace he seemed to want.

'Put your arms round my neck,' Edmond commanded and I did as he asked.

It was not so bad, in fact it was definitely interesting, feeling the whole length of his body pressed against mine, but I was startled when I felt his tongue insinuating itself between my half-open lips. That kiss lasted a long time, but at last Edmond decided to let me go.

'I mustn't be naughty,' he said, and it sounded so incongruous that I gave an involuntary giggle. 'Are you laughing? Have I made you happy?' he asked.

'I don't know . . . it's all so surprising, I don't know how I feel,' I said, which was true.

'Little thing, you've been so good to me. I'll never forget it, never.'

He was sounding much too sentimental and I was not sure I could cope with another emotional outburst. 'I've not had much experience of this sort of thing,' I said.

'I know. I should be shot . . . oh, God, why did I say that? Another twenty-four hours . . .'

I thought he was going to make another grab at me so I moved away and started walking down the street. 'You'll be brave, just as you have been up till now,' I said, trying to put some heart into him.

'I'm not a coward,' Edmond said quickly. 'I put up a good show when I have to, but it's such a relief to be able to unburden myself to someone who understands. You won't throw me over? You'll go on writing to me?'

'I'll go on writing to you,' I promised.

CHAPTER THREE

The Manchester mills throbbed with activity. It seemed to me that the ground quivered with the pounding machinery and the air thrummed to the everlasting whirring of the spindles. There is nothing like a war for increasing demand: cotton yarn for sheets and bedticking, uniforms – all those starched aprons – endless yards of khaki drill, heavy webbing, shrouds (but we kept quiet about that use for our good cotton), canvas for tents, poplin for shirts . . . The only thing that limited production was an absence of raw cotton and Arkady & Pershore were well-placed, with their interest in the Indian market, to secure what was needed and to supplement piece goods from the British mills with imports from Bombay.

Women came into their own during the war years. More and more we replaced the men who had gone off to fight. Even I, with my limited experience, had moved up the ladder in my department at Arkady & Pershore.

Patricia, protesting all the way, had been dragged away from her gardening and pushed into the uniform of the Voluntary Aid Detachment. In one last fleeting meeting she told me that she was sure she had no talent for nursing, but her mother had insisted that to be a VAD was suitable war work for a girl, provided, of course, that she was properly supervised in a hospital set up in a grand house belonging to one of her own relatives.

With Pat's departure I lost my link with Dominic. I still thought about him, but it was difficult to sustain my romantic interest with nothing to feed it on. I would have liked to have written to him, but I waited for him to suggest it, which he never did, and a silly shyness held me back from asking Pat for his address. I knew that he was mentioned in despatches and I knew that he received a minor wound, not severe enough for him to be returned to England, but what I would really have liked to know was whether he remembered kissing me and what it had meant to him.

In the meantime, there was Edmond. Edmond, contrary to all my expectations, had become a war hero. In the offensive at Passchendaele he led an attack on an enemy post, acquitted himself well and was awarded a DSO. I must admit I was surprised, after his display of nerves earlier in the war, but perhaps he had become hardened to the horrors and it was certainly unworthy of me to feel let down that he had the medal and Dominic, who must surely be displaying his usual dash and courage, had a mere 'mention'.

Edmond continued to write to me whenever he could and because Mumma badgered me about it I wrote back. She never asked to see his letters, which was just as well because they were distinctly loverlike. I was not sure how I felt about this. On the one hand it was gratifying to have a 'boyfriend' at the front, though it would have been better if it had been someone outside the family, not a sort of brother. On the other hand, I was bothered by the arch way Edmond wrote, always dropping hints about a special understanding between us but not coming out in the open about it.

When he wrote and said, '*I still think about that Red Cross dance and walking home with you afterwards – you know what I mean, don't you?*' how could I write back and say, '*No, I've completely forgotten!*' Perhaps I would have been more forthright if he had been safe in England, but not when he might be lying wounded in a hospital bed by the time my letter reached him. Instead, I refrained from answering any questions like that and told him instead about the weather, his father's practice and how I was getting on in my job, nothing really that justified him writing back to say, '*Your letters are my lifeline. Keep them coming, won't you, little thing? You can guess where I keep them.*' In his breast-pocket, I presumed, but the idea made me uncomfortable. And his habit of calling me 'little thing' irritated me.

I was shocked to the depths when Mumma and Step sat down to talk to me one day. 'I've had a letter from Edmond,' Step said. 'It took me by surprise, but I dare say you can guess what he said.' I shook my head, completely unprepared for what was coming.

'No? I think you're being coy with us,' Step said with a smile. 'He tells me the pair of you want to get married when the war is over.'

I was too stunned to answer him immediately and Mumma chimed in encouragingly, 'It's all right, Jess. We don't mind. In fact, the more I think about it the better I like the idea.'

'Edmond's never said anything to me . . . we've never mentioned marriage,' I managed to get out. I saw them glance at one another, surprised and troubled by the way I had reacted.

'From the way he writes it sounds like a settled thing,' Step said.

'You must have encouraged him,' Mumma said.

'How could I when I haven't set eyes on him for months and months? We've written, you knew about that, and perhaps Edmond's letters have been more affectionate than mine . . .'

'I should have made you show them to me,' Mumma said.

'You're very welcome to see the last one, if I can find it,' I retorted, uneasily aware that that had been one of Edmond's more explicit outpourings. I knew very well that it was still upstairs in my writing case, but I made up my mind that it was going to be lost. 'I've never written anything to him to make him think I was expecting us to marry,' I insisted.

'Edmond seems to have taken too much for granted,' Step said. 'All the same, there must have been something . . .'

There had been something. Several kisses, some surreptitious handholding, expressions of sympathy which I had meant at the time and a reluctance to be unkind to a man in constant danger.

'You talk to her, Fred,' Mumma said. 'I'm disappointed, I admit. I'd have liked your son to marry my daughter. I dare say they'll come to it in the end. Jessica's been taken by surprise, that's all.'

Neither Step nor I could think of anything to say after she had gone out of the room. He was embarrassed and I was worried.

'All I really need to know is how you feel about the idea now that it's out in the open,' he said. 'From the way he writes Edmond obviously thinks a great deal of you. If he asked you properly would you take him?'

'We hardly know one another. Before Edmond went into the Army I was scarcely grown up. How can I marry a man who's a stranger to me?'

Step's face brightened. I could guess the way his mind was working and could have kicked myself for being so diplomatic. I had not rejected his son outright and if Edmond persisted, he might win me.

'I suggest you write to Edmond and say he's taken you by surprise,' he said. 'He must know he's never proposed to you in so many words. Tell him you'll need time to get to know him better when the war is over.'

Mumma came back into the room and with a sinking heart I recognised the letter she was holding. I gave her a fierce look and she smirked, acknowledging her cleverness in going to raid my writing desk while I was safely occupied. To my relief she did not read the letter out loud in front of Step. She let him tell her what he thought we had agreed and then said, 'I'll just have a word with Jessica myself.'

'No point in hounding the lass,' Step warned.

'Of course not!' Mumma said, opening her eyes very wide. 'Run along, luv. Jess and I will have a cosy talk. It's women's business, after all.'

I knew what was coming as soon as Step had left us alone. Mumma spread Edmond's letter out on the table.

' "*I still think about the touch of your soft red lips*",' she quoted. 'What does that mean? What's been going on between you two?'

'Nothing. How could there by anything when Edmond's not had leave for the last eight months?'

' *"Will you be kind to me again when at last I come home?"* Well, miss, will you?'

'It was *nothing*. Edmond kissed me, that's all.'

'How often?'

'Three or four times.'

'You must be quite a kisser for a grown man to remember it for months on end. I've half a mind take you to the doctor.'

'What on earth for?'

'To see if you're still a virgin.'

'Mumma! How could you think such a thing. We're not in India now! And of course I am. I've told you, it was just a few kisses.'

'You must have liked it. If you'd complained I'd soon have sorted him out, stepson or not.'

That silenced me. I had liked it, on the whole. Or at any rate I had been sufficiently curious not to want to put an end to it.

'You might as well marry him,' Mumma said. 'Edmond will do all right for himself. Look at the way he's come through the war, with a medal and all, and not a scratch on him.'

'So far.'

'The war'll end some day. There'll be a shortage of men for girls like you to marry. Be sensible and take Edmond.'

Of course Mumma was right, there were very few men around for a girl of nineteen, as I was now, to think of marrying. At work I saw boys of fourteen and married men in their fifties. Social life, apart from contact with soldiers and sailors on leave who were usually spoken for, was almost non-existent. I had no wish to be left on the shelf and although I was now a striking-looking young woman, I was not overwhelmingly popular. There was a cutting edge to me that put men off. I was too clever and far too ready with my tongue. I had taken over a job that had previously been done by a man and was making a success of it. I was allowed to handle correspondence and concoct my own replies, although I could never sign a letter. I had worked hard to rid myself of the tell-tale singsong in the way I spoke and had succeeded only too well. I 'talked posh' and it was held against me as a sign that I gave myself airs.

I wished I could believe that the work I had taken on was likely to be permanent, but there had already been murmurings about girls being demoted 'when the men come home'. Of course there would be vacancies because so many had been killed, but in Arkady & Pershore preference would always be given to a man with a family to support.

Matthew Arkady had said it himself – if I had been a boy he could have made something of me – but as a woman I had little hope of aspiring to the level that Edmond had reached before the war. I was not even paid the same wage as the man I had replaced because as a woman I was not the wage-earner of a family. In fact, by our standards I was not at all badly off. Mumma often exclaimed at my good fortune. I gave her half my wages, but the other ten shillings was all mine to spend as I liked and on it I kept myself looking smart. The money from Mr Arkady had ceased with my eighteenth birthday, but after Mumma's marriage we had not had to spend all of it every year and there was a pleasant little sum put away for me and earning interest.

After Edmond's bombshell I asked myself what I really wanted. I knew only too well. I wanted a house like Stowbury and the means to live in it comfortably. It was my private dream; a useless one. In my heart I knew the only way I could achieve it was to marry someone like Dominic.

Dominic. We had completely lost touch. If he came to Stowbury I was not aware of it. Patricia was no letter writer; a Christmas card with her name scrawled on it was all I had received from her in the last year. They were outside my world. Now that we were truly grown up I had to accept that our friendship had drifted away with our childhood. I was very sensible about it, but it cost me some heartache. That one kiss I had exchanged with Dominic lingered in my memory more than the passionate embraces I had received from Edmond.

The war must come to an end some time. When the Americans came in with us in April 1917 we thought that it would soon be over, but it dragged on. A telegram usually meant a young man killed or wounded. I was glad that I was the one to open the door when the boy delivered one to us.

Step was out and Mumma was in the kitchen. I decided I had better open it. Considering the way my hands shook it was an anti-climax when it proved to be from Edmond himself, announcing that he would be arriving on Friday for seven days' leave.

I was glad to see him, of course I was. I had a fondness for him and it was impossible not to be influenced by the fact that he was in love with me.

Mumma treated us as if we were an engaged couple and left us alone together. Edmond was not slow to make the most of the opportunities that gave him. I grew accustomed to his kisses and his fondling hands, even, in a shivery sort of way, to enjoy his caresses. My body was ready enough to respond, it was only something in my mind that stood obstinately on one side, knowing that this was not *right*, no matter how exciting it might be; there was something better.

'I've got something for you,' Edmond said, nuzzling his lips against my ear as we sat cuddled up together on the sofa.

He felt in his pocket and I took advantage of the slackening of his arm to sit up straighter. He held out the small jeweller's box and I took it, knowing what it was going to be. A ring, of course – but what a ring! A big dark ruby, surrounded by diamonds.

'It . . . it's magnificent,' I said, genuinely stunned.

'I knew it was right for you as soon as I saw it. It's not

new – you don't mind that, do you? It came from a first-class jeweller in Paris.'

Strangely enough, it did grate slightly, being offered a secondhand engagement ring. And not being given any choice.

'It must be worth a fortune,' I said weakly.

'Only a small fortune. I've had it valued since I got back to England and I certainly didn't pay through the nose for it.'

I sat with the ring in my hand, twisting it so that the splendid stone caught the light and glowed with deep fire, but when Edmond took it from me and tried to slip it on my finger I resisted. Quite simply, I coveted the ring, but I was unsure about the conditions that went with it.

'Darling Jess, you're not going to say no to me, are you?' Edmond said in his most caressing voice.

'I think I must.'

'But why? You've shown me you love me, over and over again.'

Had I? I'd certainly accepted his attentions, as the old novels put it. He'd be entitled to complain that I'd led him on and I could think of no way of explaining the mixture of curiosity and pleasurable sensation that had made me receptive to his lovemaking.

'It's the rest of our lives,' I pointed out, knowing that it sounded feeble.

'Of course it is. I've got plans for the future, Jess. With my good Army record and my experience before the war I can go right to the top.'

That was true. I had no intention of telling Edmond so, but I had made a few enquiries about his standing at Arkady & Pershore and had been impressed to hear that he was expected to end up with a seat on the Board.

'You're the sort of girl I need for my wife, Jess. You're beautiful – did you know that, little thing? – and you've worked hard to improve yourself. You'll always be a credit to me and I'll be able to see that you have everything you want in life.'

'That's a rash promise,' I said, but irony was wasted

on Edmond. He only laughed, especially when I went on: 'Suppose I wanted to go on working?'

'You won't do that,' he said, with all the confidence in the world. 'What! A dreary office job when I can offer you your own nice house with friends and neighbours to visit – our own sort of people, Jess – a servant or two, a motor car . . .' He put his mouth to my ear once more and whispered, 'A dear little baby. You'd like that, wouldn't you, Jess?'

'I'm not so sure. Babies are mucky things and I've no experience with them.'

That made him laugh again, but he was not pleased when I still refused to wear his ring. 'You've hurt me, dearest,' he said with that wounded expression that made his brown eyes look more bovine than ever.

It made me squirm, but I held out. In the end we compromised: I would keep the ring, but I would not wear it until the war was over.

'When the future seems safer . . .' I said weakly.

'Is that what's worrying you? It'd make me extra careful to keep myself safe if I knew for certain I'd got you to come home to.'

I leaned forward and kissed him just once on the lips. 'That's blackmail,' I said. 'And I won't give in to it. Ask me again when this ghastly war's over and I'll give you a straight answer, yes or no.'

'It'll be yes, I know it will,' Edmond assured me.

Mumma could make nothing of the strange state of affairs between us. 'Either you're engaged or you're not,' she said crossly.

'We're not,' I told her.

'Then what about that ring? My word, Jess, that's a lovely thing. How can you keep it shut away in a drawer? It ought to be on your finger.'

'Actually, it ought to be in the Bank, and that's where it's going as soon as Edmond goes back to the front. I don't want the responsibility of looking after it.'

'It must have cost him a pretty penny.'

'Yes . . . too much. I'm not worth that amount of money.'

'Strange way of looking at it. Most girls would be over the moon that their chaps thought so highly of them.'

'I'm not most girls and I'm not on offer in the market place.'

'Oh, that's a fine way of talking – now. I'll look forward to hearing you say it again when you're thirty. You'll be sorry one day, young madam, that you didn't take the best offer you're ever likely to get.'

Edmond went back to the fighting and his ring went to the Bank and I was still an unattached girl with her own way to make in the world, but I knew in my heart that there was no real escape from the shackles everyone was trying to fasten on me.

On 11 November 1918 I was at my desk in the office as usual, but we were all on tenterhooks, knowing that the war was as good as over. Old Mr Tenterby, who had come out of retirement to run our department, came into the room. Three times he tried to speak, but in the end he could manage only one word, '*Peace* . . .'

There was a moment's silence and then everyone went mad. One silly girl picked up the filing tray and threw it in the air so that we were surrounded by falling papers. They all ran out and I could hear the sound of cheering in the street. Only Mr Tenterby and I remained. Tears were running down his cheeks. I had to strain to hear what he was saying and when I did I felt my own tears start.

'My boy . . . my boy . . .'

He had lost his son, his only child, on the Somme. What could I say? What could anyone say to him and to all the other bereaved parents, the widows, the orphans, the crippled, the broken? I went and put my arms round him and we stood together, grieving for what could not be remedied by any armistice, no matter how welcome.

The Armistice brought changes, but not immediately. It took time to bring the boys home and Edmond was not demobbed for Christmas, as he had boasted he would be, which was a relief because I had still not made up my mind what answer I was going to give him.

I heard that Patricia was back at Stowbury and I sent her a Christmas card, hoping but not really expecting that she would reply. I was amazed by the way she responded. I was leaving the office building in the Mill one dark December evening when I heard an urgent tooting on a car hooter. I looked across the road and there was Patricia, waving to me.

'My own motor car!' she called. 'It's a Christmas present from Dom. Come on, Jessica, I'll run you home.'

I ran across to the small motor car, full of delight because she seemed to have taken up our old friendship just as if it had never been interrupted.

'Isn't this the most tremendous fun?' she asked. 'I learnt to drive an ambulance during the war, but I never *dreamed* . . . isn't Dom wonderful? Grandfather is furious. He says every time I go out he expects me to be brought back in little pieces, but really, of course, he can't bear to think of a woman having such freedom.'

'It's good to see you again,' I said. 'I was afraid we'd lost touch.'

'I know. I'm the world's worst letter writer . . . and there was so much happening . . . not all of it very nice. Mother thought when I became a VAD I'd be smoothing suitable brows with lavender water, but of course it wasn't like that at all. I've scrubbed floors and emptied bedpans, I've seen dreadful wounds and amputations and men dying . . . I'm not at all the blinkered little girl I was four years ago. How about you, Jess?'

'I suppose you could say I've kept the wheels of commerce turning,' I said. I felt vaguely ashamed, as if what I'd been doing had been less worthy than Patricia's service.

'I say! Working for the old firm! Does Grandfather know?'

'I don't think so. We haven't met since you and Dominic went away.'

'He's aged. I didn't realise it until the other day. Just as well Father will be home soon. He and Mother have already sailed.'

'Your presentation?' I asked with a smile.

'Oh, that farce! I suppose I'll have to go through with it. Perhaps I'll marry the Prince of Wales.'

'Can I be your lady-in-waiting if you do?'

'Certainly, but I think that's a fairly safe promise to make.'

'Dominic?' I asked carefully. 'Is he all right?'

'Very much so and longing to get home. He was wounded again, but not seriously. Oh, Jessica, can you believe it? It's over, it's over and we're all safe.'

'We won't be if you drive all over the road,' I said. 'Can you come in? Mumma and Step will be pleased to see you.'

'Better not. Another time. Au revoir, Jess.'

She drove off and I was left with a mingled feeling of pleasure and exasperation. Patricia was just the same and the old magic was still there. She dropped into my life for ten minutes, showed me, without in the least meaning to, that I had given little to the war effort, spoke inconsequentially about a way of life that was aeons away from my own – what had I to do with a girl who talked, even jokingly, about marrying the Prince of Wales? – and disappeared. Driving her own car, something I had never even considered. Why not? If Patricia Arkady could own and drive a motor car, why shouldn't I, too?

The next time she appeared to pick me up Dominic was with her. He got out of the small motor car and, just as Patricia had done, greeted me enthusiastically. 'Jessica, lovely to see you again! Not that I can see you in this miserable light. Let's go and have some tea.'

I could hardly see him either. All I had was an impression of a tall young man in a bulky British warm with a cap tilted at a dashing angle on his head. When we reached the tea rooms I watched him as he took off his

63

coat and cap and by the time he turned to me with equally frank curiosity I knew that Dominic had fulfilled all his earlier promise. As I remembered him, he had been thin for his height and his hands and feet had seemed too large, but now his body had settled into its proper proportions and he was no longer a gangling boy but a splendid young man. He must be about twenty-two, nearly twenty-three, I told myself, fixing my mind on mundane details. I would be twenty-one in February and Dominic was two years older. Looking up at him I saw that, he too had seen horrors. The memory lurked at the back of his eyes, as vividly blue as ever but curiously shadowed, as if Dominic had taken to veiling his thoughts.

'My word!' he said softly. 'Is this my little brown cousin from India?'

'You've turned into a beauty, Jessica,' Patricia said.

I was glad she was there, otherwise I might never have been able to look away from Dominic. I wished I could return her compliment, but Patricia was looking curiously diminished, almost shrivelled.

'Do you think my little sister looks well?' Dominic demanded, with that uncanny ability to read thoughts both he and Patricia sometimes displayed.

'No,' I said.

'I've been overworked for years,' Patricia said flatly. 'And now it's suddenly all over and I can't see the way ahead. What was it all *for*, Dom?'

'For us,' he said. 'For you and me, to make a better world.'

'Is that what we're going to do? When all you can think about is staying in the Army and going out to India? Dom, change your mind, please. It's not as if Mother and Father will be out there any more and I'll be stuck in England.'

He laid one long finger across her lips and she fell silent.

We had toasted tea cakes and a pot of tea and we chatted, just as we always had, but not with quite the former ease. I knew now that there was a strain between Dominic and Patricia because they disagreed about his

64

plans, while between Dominic and me there was enough tension to make the air vibrate.

For a long time I had cherished a secret romantic dream about him, but this was something quite different, an attraction so immediate and so strong that there was room for only one thought in my head: how soon could I be alone with him? I was scarcely aware of what I ate or what I said. I must have kept the conversation going because Patricia seemed to notice nothing. How was it possible that she did not know what was happening, she whose antennae constantly searched the air for signals from her brother? Suddenly I knew, and understood too why Patricia was looking so diminished: Dominic had learnt to hide his thoughts from her and she was bereft.

She drove me home and Dominic got out to see me to the door. It looked like politeness, but really he was seizing the only opportunity we had for a word alone.

'When shall I see you?'

'It's Saturday tomorrow. I only work until one o'clock.'

'Are you allowed to have lunch out with strange men?'

'Yes, of course. And you're not strange . . .'

'I'll meet you where we picked you up today.'

There was no suggestion that Patricia would be with him nor did I believe that he meant to tell her about our meeting. As for me, when I went in and was asked why I was so late home I talked eloquently about how delightful it was to have the Arkadys back again and told Mumma that I was being taken out for lunch the next day. If she got the impression that both brother and sister would be with me that was not my fault for I never said so. Already Dominic and I were tangling ourselves in a net of our own weaving.

We met and it was a delight beyond imagining. We stretched out the lunch to last more than two hours, while we talked and didn't talk. Dominic told me about the fighting, but lightly, as if it had been something to laugh about, and I watched his lips moving and failed to hear what he was saying. I told him about my own life, but I did not mention Edmond's wish to marry me.

By three o'clock we were desperate with our longing to touch. Dominic stretched his hand out across the table and I put mine in it and we looked at one another helplessly.

'I can't believe it,' Dominic said. 'What's happened to me? My little brown cousin . . . Jessica, what are we going to do?'

I shook my head, unable to speak for the joy that flooded me because he had admitted that he felt the same as I did.

Outside, the dim December day was darkening. Everyone else had finished eating and gone and the waitresses were giving us curious looks.

'I'll walk you home,' Dominic said.

We walked slowly, my arm tucked through his and our hands tightly clasped, and every now and again Dominic gave my hand a squeeze and I pressed his arm closer against my side. It was a long walk, since Step had his practice on the outskirts of the city, but it could not be too long for us. At last the crowded streets fell behind us and there were long oases in which we saw no people at all. We kissed then, long kisses which were both enchanting and unsatisfactory. Our lips met and there was a moment of solace and when I stirred restlessly in Dominic's arms and we were both conscious of our thick overcoats, all the layers of clothing that hampered us from the closer contact we so urgently desired.

Dominic drew a deep breath. 'The time has come to be sensible,' he said. 'I've got to take you home. For one thing, there's a nasty cold sleet falling . . .'

'I hadn't noticed.'

He laughed, a little throaty chuckle, and kissed me swiftly on the tip of my nose. 'Darling . . . darling . . . I don't know when we can meet again. There's Christmas to be got over. Not a hope of seeing you until after that. How am I going to live?'

'Or me?'

'It's so unexpected, like being hit by a sledgehammer. Of course, I always knew you were special. Do you remember I kissed you before I went off to the war?'

'I remember. I thought you would have forgotten.'

'It always lingered in my mind. A pleasant memory, but this . . . What did you do? You cast some subtle Eastern spell over me, didn't you?'

'No, I just looked up and there you were and I thought, "That's Dominic: I love him".'

'Darling . . .'

'We'll never get home at this rate,' I said, pulling away. 'My turn to be sensible. Let's accept that we can't meet again until after Christmas. After that . . .'

'I'll arrange something. Shall I buy you a present?'

'Better not.'

'I'll get something and keep it until we meet.'

There are certain practical difficulties about carrying on a secret love affair in Lancashire in midwinter, especially when the New Year is ushered in by a snowstorm. My bicycle was useless, Dominic could not ride his horse, Patricia's little car was laid up in the garage and even the telephone which Step had had installed was out of action because the wires were down. Not that it was wise to try to talk on the telephone. It was not meant for private conversation and it was almost always answered by Step or Mumma.

Dominic walked down to the Mill and met me from work and we snatched a few minutes over a cup of tea or even a drink in a public house, which was not at all the thing for a girl like me to do, and all the time we lived for the slow walk home and the snatched embraces on dark corners.

I was on tenterhooks, expecting any day to hear that Dominic had been recalled, but he told me that he was negotiating to exchange into another regiment and because of all the complications of demobilisation he had been put on one side 'to stagnate' as he said in disgust.

At last on a bright frosty January Sunday I announced that I was going to take one of those healthy winter walks Step had always urged on me.

'Mind how you go,' he said absentmindedly. 'There are deep drifts in some of the lanes.'

'I won't take any risks,' I promised, which was not strictly true, since I was in the mood to throw everything I had to the winds if that was what Dominic wanted.

We met in a little summerhouse in the grounds of Stowbury, a ridiculous pillared temple, a place for the ladies of the house to take their sewing and drink tea in the heat of the summer. Dominic was there first, which pleased me, and I went straight into his arms.

He removed the woollen hat I had pulled down over my ears and then his fingers plucked at the pins that held my hair in place. 'I've wanted so much to see you with your hair down . . . oh, Jessica!'

It was the first time we had achieved real solitude and I clung to him in a delirium of delight.

'I've brought blankets and a hot water bottle,' he said. 'So we shan't freeze to death. All the same, it's not exactly an ideal setting, my darling.'

We made ourselves a nest on the floor and I did not protest when Dominic's hands felt for the openings of my clothes. Why should I when it was what I wanted more than I had ever wanted anything in my life? No passing thought of morality or of what was to happen in the future came between me and my singleminded drive to get closer and closer to Dominic until he was swallowed up in me and I in him.

It would have happened. Beyond any doubt at all he would have taken me if we had not been interrupted. I think I did hear some barking, but it hardly registered with me. It was not until one of Matthew Arkady's black spaniels came snuffling at the two bodies twisted in blankets on the temple floor that we realised we were not alone.

Dominic lifted up his head and I heard him draw in his breath. As he moved away from me I sat up. Our grandfather was standing on the steps outside, leaning his hand against one of the pillars.

It was all spoilt. In place of a haven of love the summerhouse and our makeshift bed looked sordid. I burned with the realisation of my tumbled hair and bare shoulders and the rough blanket pulled up to hide my breasts. Dominic, too . . . I sensed the moment when desire died in him and he felt ashamed.

Matthew Arkady spoke and if he had thought about it for a hundred years he could hardly have said anything better calculated to wither our passion. He nodded in apparent affability to his grandson and said, 'If you can get it done in this temperature you're a better man than I am.'

He turned and left us, with the dog following him, and if there had been any justice in the world one of the icicles hanging from the portico would have fallen and pierced him through his cold heart.

I cried – I, who never cried. Angry, hurt, humiliated tears ran down my face as I scrambled into my clothes and Dominic, who ought to have consoled me, could only say helplessly, 'Don't, Jessica. Don't let him upset you. I'll sort something out . . .'

But, of course, there was little he could do. We had been living in a dream and now we had been woken up to a life in which cold practicality counted for more than the delirium of young love.

I was sent for the next day at work. Mr Arkady, I was told, had heard about the good work I had done during the war and wanted to consider me for permanent promotion. It was a wicked lie and it made me sufficiently angry to take me into his office with colour in my cheeks and my head held high.

'You want to see me . . . sir?' I asked.

'I do. I'll tell you what's going to happen. You'll not get this promotion you're supposed to be in line for and you'll be so incensed you'll up and take your services elsewhere.'

'I didn't think you knew I was employed by Arkady & Pershore.'

'Don't be daft, lass. I've known for years, but you were

discreet – then – and a good worker by all accounts so I let it lie.'

'I'd just as soon move on,' I said, but at the back of my mind I was uneasy. Jobs were not going to be all that plentiful now that the war was over.

'As for the other business . . .'

'Need we discuss that?' I asked, as haughtily as if my heart were not in my well-polished shoes.

'I think we should, for your sake as well as Dominic's. Lass, you've been living in a fool's paradise. How the devil did it happen? He's not been home five minutes.'

'As soon as we saw one another . . .'

'Aye, well, I've been young myself. There's no future in it, you know.'

'Why not? Can you give me one reason why I shouldn't marry Dominic? Blind prejudice, that's all that stands in our way.'

'There's another reason: he hasn't asked you.' That pulled me up short because, of course, it was true.

'There's been so little time,' I said.

'Long enough to get you down on the floor. According to Dominic I interrupted you in time yesterday?'

The memory of that ghastly moment made it impossible for me to go on looking at him. 'Yes,' I muttered.

'And it hadn't gone that far before?'

'No.'

'Aye . . . middle of winter. Good job it wasn't summer. Young rip, he ought to be ashamed of himself.'

'You make it sound so sordid!' I burst out. 'You don't understand! We're in love!'

'I dare say you are, but if it's marriage you have in mind you've not gone about it the right way. Think, lass; Dominic's over twenty-one and you're a respectable girl, the stepdaughter of a man he's known all his life, his own cousin even if it is on the wrong side of the blanket – so why did it have to be kept secret?'

There was no way I could describe the red-hot desire that had overwhelmed us, the craving of the flesh that had

70

blotted out all rational thought. 'We knew you'd be angry,' I said, but it sounded feeble.

'I am that! And if his mother and father knew they'd be fit to be tied, especially Lady Cynthia. But an obstinate young couple can always get their own way. There's more to it than that, lass. Dominic knew he couldn't have both the career he wants and you, too – not openly.'

'That's not true!'

'Isn't it? The Colonel of the regiment he wants to join wouldn't have him if he was married. Young married officers are frowned on, especially for service in India. And your background is too suspect for you to be readily accepted.'

'Whose fault is that?'

'Mine. That doesn't alter the facts. You're the daughter of the illegitimate son of a half-caste.'

'No! That's a wicked way of putting it.'

'But true.'

'How long does it have to go on, this paying for the sins of my ancestors? It's too ridiculous in this day and age.'

'I agree, but they're a hundred years behind the times in India and it's India Dominic has set his heart on.'

I fell silent, baffled by the reasonable tone he had adopted. There must be some way out of our predicament, but at that moment I couldn't see it. 'I must see Dominic,' I said.

'I thought you'd say that and I agree. He's a man and a soldier and he ought to face up to telling you himself. I'll send my motor car to pick you up from home this evening and you can tell your mother you're invited to spend an hour at Stowbury. I doubt it'll take longer than that.'

I got through the day by telling myself that Dominic would stand by me, but there was a terrible straight-forward practicality about the way Matthew Arkady had spoken that undermined my faith.

Mumma was delighted to hear that I was invited to the big house. She insisted I must change into the good wool

71

dress I had been given for Christmas and to please her I washed my face and re-did my hair. Once I was inside the motor car I pulled to the outside of my dress the heart-shaped gold pendant Dominic had given me for Christmas and which I had worn in secret round my neck ever since. Only now did I allow myself to admit that I had been disappointed that it was not a ring.

I was shown into the library, a splendid room lined from floor to ceiling with leather-bound books, their gilded spines catching the firelight. Mr Arkady and Dominic were both there, both wearing dinner jackets and black ties. I had never seen Dominic dressed like that before and my heart turned over at the sight of him. There was no sign of Patricia. Did she know, I wondered, and if so how had she taken the revelation that her brother was in love with me?

'I'll leave you two to sort yourselves out,' our grandfather said. 'Jessica, I've made Dominic an offer and it'd suit me fine if he accepted, but I doubt he will.'

He went out, leaving Dominic and me to face one another in front of the fire, both of us at a loss to know how to greet one another. In the end Dominic took both my hands in his and kissed first one and then the other. It was a nice gesture, but I would have appreciated something less courtly.

'Come and sit down on the sofa,' he said, and when we were seated side by side he still kept one of my hands in his.

'What offer?' I asked.

'If I choose to marry you Grandfather will support me provided I go into the Mill, at the bottom at first, to be trained to follow on after my father as the head of the firm one day.'

'And?'

'It's not what I want, Jessica. All my life I've had this burning ambition to serve in India.'

'You burned for me yesterday,' I said, taking my hand away.

'Darling, I still love you, but there's more than one side

72

to me. Cotton mills aren't my only inheritance. On the other side of my family there's a long Army tradition.'

'And a dukedom. Do I rank too far below you to be thought of as a wife?'

'No! But it's true I wouldn't be welcomed into the regiment I've chosen with a wife already in tow.'

'Why not? It seems heartless to me. "A good man married, is a good man marred" – is that the way your precious regiment thinks?'

'A young junior officer is expected to be a free agent. I telephoned my Uncle Bernard this morning and put the case to him.'

'You told him about me?'

'Not exactly, but he must have guessed. He had to tell me that an early marriage would be a mistake.'

I tried another tactic. 'Haven't you seen enough fighting? Everyone else wants to get out of the Army. Why are you different?'

'I can't explain it. I want the colour, the excitement, the opportunity to do things, not just sit at a desk watching the price of cotton go up and down. I can manage men. I enjoy doing it. I can plot logistics . . .'

'I don't even know what that is.'

'Oh, troop movements, getting supplies to the right place at the right time, ammunition, food . . . it has a fascination that's very special, especially when your life depends on it.'

'Peacetime soldiering, moving pins about on a map.'

'Not in India. There's always the chance of action though, of course, we're really there to keep the peace.'

'Did you ever think of marrying me?'

When he hesitated I knew I had lost him. He was bitterly honest and it cost him nearly as much as it did me. 'I never looked into the future at all. What happened to us was so sudden, so unexpected, that I could think of nothing except . . .'

'Getting me into bed,' I completed his sentence. 'We never even achieved a bed, did we?' For a moment I closed my eyes, shuddering in horror at the recollection

73

of the way we had lifted ourselves up and found Matthew Arkady watching us.

There was still one way of persuading him. I sighed deeply, as if acquiescing in everything he had said, and leaned towards him. Automatically, Dominic's arm went round me and I put my head down on his shoulder. My hand strayed forward and rested on his thigh, then I lifted my head. Our mouths were no more than an inch apart. I leaned forward and my lips parted. In the next breath we were clamped together in an embrace so fierce that my lips were bruised and my body ached. I sank back against the sofa and Dominic turned, half on top of me, his lips moving ceaselessly over my face and my throat.

'God, Jess, I can't let you go! It's not bearable!'

I opened my eyes, knowing I had got him where I wanted him, but not as triumphant as I might have been. Across the room, dimly lit by the firelight and the lamps which stood around the room, I saw an oil painting of a woman, tall and elegant in pale satin, the portrait of the wife Matthew Arkady had wronged when he made my grandmother his mistress. She stood very erect, one hand holding a fan and the other lightly touching it, every inch an aristocrat, her lips faintly smiling, her eyes watchful. The other side of Dominic's life. And I knew that this was my true enemy, not his longing for the Army, not his repugnance for commerce, but the cool, judgmental gaze which weighed me up and found me wanting, as he might come to do one day. What had I to offer beyond an ardent body which he desired? He would hate working for Arkady & Pershore and the day might come when he would blame me for the loss of the life for which he was designed.

I tried to free myself and sit up, but Dominic kept fast hold of me. 'There must be some way,' he said.

'Suppose you accept Mr Arkady's offer, but insist on going out to Bombay to learn the trade?' I suggested.

'As a *box wallah*? That would be worse than staying in Manchester.'

I knew then that, for all our love, we were poles apart.

To me, the opportunity of learning the family business, working a way up through the ranks to the highest position, was exciting, even challenging. If I had been in Dominic's shoes I would have seized the chance with both hands. But Dominic . . . ? The hold his mother's family had over him was stronger than I had realised. The poised aristocrat in the picture knew all about it.

'There's no way for you to keep your dream and have me as well,' I said.

'Then I'll give up the dream.'

'No. I'm making this decision. We'll part now and you'll go to India as soon as you can get a passage.'

'No!'

'It's what you'd decided before I came here tonight.'

'That was before I'd put my arms around you again,' he said, unconsciously confirming what I knew already.

'Yes, I could always keep a hold over you in that way, but I don't think it would be good for either of us.'

I would have been hard put to it to explain myself more clearly than that, but dimly I perceived that it would be ruination for Dominic to be in thrall to a woman who could persuade him to do what she wanted by using her body to tempt him. Like Merlin and Vivien in Tennyson's poem, I thought vaguely, remembering one of the 'Idylls of the King' which had not been included in my school studies, but which we had all read in secret. He'd end up weak and helpless and then, terrible thought, I might not love him any more: '. . . lost to life and use and name and fame.' No, that was not the Dominic I loved. The pain was so intense when I got up from that sofa and walked over to the fire that I had to hold myself upright by gripping the carved surround of the fireplace – a stupid marble woman with bulbous breasts and no legs. I stood looking down into the flames and they glared and dazzled in the tears I was holding back.

'I must go,' I said.

'Jessica, this can't be the end . . .'

'Yes, it is.' I mastered myself and turned to face him, adamant that I was doing the right thing. It was I who

75

rang the bell and asked for the motor car to be sent round to take me home. I felt strong, almost triumphant, as if I had won a victory, even though I knew, poor fool, that I was the loser and as soon as I was alone I was going to suffer for it even more than I did now.

In the hall I found Patricia hovering. 'Oh, Jessica! Jessica, I'm so *sorry*!' she whispered.

So she knew. Who had told her, I wondered? And she had not even bothered to ask the outcome of my talk with her brother. She had no doubt what he would choose to do if he were free. For one bitter moment I thought of telling her that I could have held her brother in England if I had chosen to do it, but in the end I said nothing. I kissed her, a cold little kiss on the cheek, and then I left.

CHAPTER FOUR

The strange thing was, no one close to me knew what had happened. Mumma was disappointed when my one visit to Stowbury led to nothing more and she was surprised when I threw up my job with Arkady & Pershore and found a post with a firm of solicitors, but she failed to notice that my heart was broken.

'I suppose it wouldn't do for you and Edmond to be working in the same place,' she said. 'Not as things are.'

I ought to have contradicted her, but I let it go. I spent my days alternating between exaltation and misery. Sometimes I was borne up by the feeling that I had been brave and true when I had freed Dominic, but mostly I knew I had been a fool. I ought to have held on to him. When it came to fighting for his happiness I could have been strong enough for two and surely some compromise could have been reached? But Dominic had not refused his freedom when I had handed it to him; that was the rock on which all my regrets foundered.

The new job was not a success. I had thought that I would have more freedom in a smaller office, but that was far from being the case, especially when the younger partner came back from the war and turned out to be a finicky fault-finder. I could see that I would never get any further ahead in that situation and I began to look round for something more satisfactory.

By leaving Arkady & Pershore I had cut myself off from gossip about the head of the firm and his family. Mr Steven and Lady Cynthia had landed in England, that I did know because it was reported in the local paper, and Patricia had been removed to London by her mother, but I heard nothing at all of Dominic.

By the time Edmond came home permanently I was in a rage of dissatisfaction with my life. He went back to Arkady & Pershore, but in a rather more advanced position, and I gathered that he had made a good impression on Mr Steven Arkady. Indeed, Edmond reported as much, with a certain amount of complacency.

To my surprise he did not immediately press me to agree to an engagement and the beautiful ring he had left with me remained in the Bank. I ought to have been relieved, but at the back of my mind there was a trace of annoyance that Edmond was not as ardent as he had been. I even began to wonder whether, now that he was no longer in danger, he had lost the urgency that had made him push the engagement on me in the past.

It was March before he came home one day and remarked casually that both Mr Matthew and Mr Steven Arkady would be away for a few days.

'They've gone down to Southampton, and Lady Cynthia and Patricia, too, of course, to see Dominic off to India. In my opinion that boy is mad to walk away from his place in the firm to go soldiering at the back of beyond.'

I slipped out of the room. Now that it had happened I was more shaken than I would have expected, but what made me curl up in a tight ball of misery on my bed was the realisation that while I had been imagining Dominic on the high seas or galloping across the sunbrowned plains of India he had still been in England, and he had made no attempt to get in touch with me.

It took me about a week to come to terms with my irrevocable loss. Mumma exclaimed over my pallor and worried in case I was infected with the influenza which had mown down people in hundreds, but I pleaded a minor stomach upset and went steadily on, grimly getting through my hopeless days.

Once again it was my grandfather who brought about a change in my life, though this time he did it involuntarily: he had a stroke which put him out of action. We heard about it from Edmond, of course.

'He's paralysed down one side,' Edmond reported. 'It was time, and more than time, that he retired, but we're all sorry it should have come about in this way.'

I thought of that hard, vigorous old man and pitied his helplessness. On the few occasions we had met we had liked one another and even when he had been intent on separating me from Dominic he had not, according to his lights, been unfair. He had offered us a choice and it was not his fault that the way we had taken had sent Dominic out to India and me . . . and me into marriage with Edmond.

I might have stood out against the solid provincial life Edmond had described to me, but everything changed when he came home one day alight with excitement.

'It's a tremendous responsibility,' he said. 'I never dreamed I'd be chosen, but Mr Steven says he must have a man in Bombay he can trust now that there's no question of him going back himself. He's offered me the post of Chief Accountant at the Bombay Mill. What do you think about that, little thing? You'll come with me, won't you? I know you've always hankered to go back and your knowledge of the country will be an asset to me.'

It was true that I had wanted to return to the land of my birth. Just as England had once been my far and shining country, now I saw India in a haze of remembered enchantment. The prospect of going out to Bombay threw an entirely new light on marrying Edmond. As for Dominic, we had the whole sub-continent to live in and it was unlikely that we would meet one another. Edmond would be one of the *box wallahs* Dominic had disparaged, far removed from the life of the Army, especially the swish regiment Dominic had joined.

Mumma wanted the wedding of her only daughter to be a big affair, but even she was taken aback when Edmond talked of the ceremony taking place in the Cathedral. Fortunately, it proved impossible to arrange that in the short time we had before Edmond was due to take up his new appointment and we fell back on the local Parish Church, with the wedding to be followed by our immediate departure for Bombay.

I was rushed off my feet, having fittings for my wedding gown, consulting my two bridesmaids about their dresses, sending out invitations, writing thank-you letters for presents and packing my trunks so that they could be shipped out to India. It felt unreal, as if I were doing it for someone else.

By the time I walked down the aisle I had surrendered completely to this dreamlike state. It was a beautiful day in June with sunlight streaming through the stained glass windows. With my hand on my stepfather's arm I moved slowly towards the altar. Edmond turned to watch, looking unexpectedly pale and far more tense than I was myself. It was a bizarre situation, the bride being given away by the bridegroom's father; that was what brought a faint smile to my lips, not pleasure at seeing Edmond waiting for me.

I wore a gown of figured satin, cut on mediaeval lines, with a long bodice and fullness from the hips, the skirt extended at the back to form a semi-train. My veil was of plain fine net, springing from a cap sewn with seed pearls, and I carried a sheaf of lilies and stephanotis. My bridesmaids, a schoolfriend and a girl from my office, wore pink taffeta frocks with pannièred skirts which they had chosen and I disliked.

There were more guests on the bridesgroom's side of the church than the bride's, mostly business colleagues from Arkady & Pershore. To my relief, although Edmond had insisted on sending them an invitation, the Arkady family had sent their regrets and a cut-glass vase. Edmond said it was handsome. I hoped it would get broken on the voyage.

Mumma looked charming in lilac crêpe with two dyed ostrich feathers on the brim of her hat, but she was in floods of tears. Later on, after the wedding breakfast, when she was helping me to change, I tried to reason with her, but she was inconsolable.

'It's all gone off very well and, of course, I wanted you to marry Edmond, but it's not at all the way I thought it would be,' she said. 'All done in a rush, no proper honeymoon . . .'

'We'll be three weeks on the voyage, that's going to be our honeymoon,' I pointed out.

'It's not the same. You'll probably be seasick half the time – remember me, coming home? I thought you'd settle down near at hand with a nice house and a garden and I'd be able to come to tea . . .'

'I don't know that I would have liked that kind of life,' I said.

'No, that's what worries me. You've taken Edmond because you think you'll have a high old time in India. You'll come down to earth with a thump, my girl, when you have to cope with running a house with two or three servants slithering around you, not understanding what you say – or pretending not to – and never, ever doing what you ask unless you're running behind them all the time checking up.'

'I'll manage,' I said, serene in the knowledge that I spoke Hindi far more fluently than Mumma had ever done even after seventeen years in the country, and a bit of Marathi and Gujarati when pressed.

'And all this trouble there's been lately – strikes and riots and that funny business in Amritsar. I'll never have a moment's peace worrying whether you're safe.'

'Amritsar is hundreds of miles from Bombay,' I pointed out.

'It's the beginning of the end, you mark my words. Your father always said the British would have to give up India one day.'

Dadda had been so fiercely British that I was sceptical about this, nor did I worry much about the reports of trouble in the Punjab. The information that had appeared in the English papers was sparse and noncommittal. It appeared that there had been an attempt at an uprising which had been suppressed with over-zealous violence, but I knew the volatile nature of an Indian mob on the rampage – easily incited and apt to protest the next day that their actions had been misunderstood. As far as I was concerned it was one of the hazards of life in the more excitable areas but unlikely to affect me living in a company compound in Bombay.

'And what about children?' Mumma persisted. 'I was going to be such a help to you!'

'I'm not disappearing for a lifetime. Four and a half years and then we'll be home for six months,' I said, putting my arm round her. 'The time will pass in a flash, you'll see.'

She let me dry her tears and roused herself to help me into the brown two-piece and gold-coloured satin blouse in which I was 'going away'.

'I suppose I ought to have talked to you,' she said. 'I don't know how much you know. Still . . . you're twenty-one and you must have some idea. Edmond will look after you. Just do your best to please him and you'll be all right.'

Strangely enough I had never considered whether I was sufficiently well-informed about the physical side of married life. With Dominic it had all seemed to be happening so naturally that I had needed no guidance. Standing in my bedroom while Mumma packed into my trunk the wedding gown I was taking with me to use as an evening dress, with my brand new wedding ring on my finger, I was shaken by a fierce regret that we had never reached the consummation of our love. Even if we had had to part I would have *known*. Damn Matthew Arkady. Why had he had to arrive on the scene at that precise critical moment? Another ten minutes . . . a quarter of an hour . . . and my entire life might have taken a different course.

Edmond and I had no great distance to travel since we were sailing from Liverpool on the Anchor Line and we went straight from Manchester to the ship. Our cabin was comfortable, but it was not large and it did occur to me that perhaps Mumma was right and it was not the ideal setting for a honeymoon.

Still, it was up to me to make the best of it. I had not married Edmond because he could give me an intense experience of romantic love, but because what he had to offer was a life which would be interesting, even exciting, and perhaps the chance to make myself useful in his career if I was not to have one of my own. I could not love him as I had loved Dominic during that brief, crazy interlude when we had been like two people struck by lightning, but taking Edmond was not like marrying a stranger. I was used to him; his caresses had never been entirely unwelcome – I could manage.

Except, of course, that we all marry strangers. I had thought I knew Edmond. Considering the way he had pressed himself on me over the years I had expected him to be an ardent lover. Indeed, I would have welcomed a bit of honest, unthinking lust which would have swept me past the difficult barrier of our first union.

Instead, he was just what Mumma had said he would be, he was careful with me. First of all we had to have a little talk into which he managed to introduce an embarrassment I had not previously felt. Edmond wanted to explain that he believed we should delay starting a family and he would, therefore, be taking precautions which he seemed to have the greatest difficulty in explaining.

In the end I put my fingers to his lips and said, with a sweetness that managed to conceal my growing impatience with him, 'Dear Edmond, you must do what you think is right. It would be nice, wouldn't it, if I could have a baby when we come home on leave?'

Four and a half years. I thought by that time I would be able to face the fright and worry of producing a child. After all, I was still only twenty-one. There was plenty of time.

'Dear little thing, I knew you'd understand,' he said gratefully.

After that we had to spend a long time getting me ready for the great event of losing my virginity. Edmond liked the slithery satin nightdress I was wearing. He liked what was inside it, too. I remembered Dominic groaning with delight as he cupped his hand round my naked breast. Edmond didn't groan, but he sighed a lot, almost as if he were suffering. It was not unpleasant, being stroked and patted and kissed, but it did seem to go on for rather a long time. In the end Edmond turned away and started fumbling around and I realised that what he had been trying to tell me was that he would have to wear something to stop his seed getting into me. It seemed very sensible and I couldn't see why he had made such a fuss about it.

When he turned back to me it seemed that we were at last ready. Edmond said in a husky voice, 'Be brave, little girl,' which had the wholly unexpected effect of making me want to burst into hysterical laughter, and then he entered me, which felt peculiar and not very comfortable, and began to move. I was just beginning to get the hang of it when he grabbed me even tighter, heaved convulsively and it was all over.

The only thing I was conscious of was complete disbelief. Was that all there was to it? This shattering event which was supposed to change a girl for ever, this sin for which men and women had defied the world down the ages, was there really nothing more to it than that?

'Lovely Jessica, now you're all mine,' Edmond whispered. He seemed pleased enough. I was the one who was left feeling cheated. 'Are you all right, dear?' he asked.

'Oh . . . yes,' I said. Why shouldn't I be all right? As far as I was concerned nothing much had happened. 'Edmond, is it always like that?'

'No, dear, it won't hurt you next time and, of course, you won't bleed.'

I was not aware that I had bled, but he was quite right – I had, very slightly. Since he assured me it was natural I didn't let it worry me. I turned and tucked myself into his side. 'I thought it would be more earthshaking,' I admitted.

Fortunately, Edmond did not take this as a criticism. 'Next time,' he promised. 'You're such an innocent little thing, aren't you?'

It seemed to please him that I was so unknowing.

Edmond always liked to have the upper hand. That was why he took it badly when he was seasick in the Bay of Biscay and I was not. Poor Edmond, he did suffer and he took it as a personal affront that I remained on my feet and managed to eat while he lay groaning on his bunk.

'I didn't expect to be ill on my honeymoon,' he complained.

'Poor darling, you'll soon be better,' I promised him. 'If I helped you to sit up do you think you could sip this nice lemon barley water?'

'I suppose so.'

He looked like a big sulky baby sitting up in bed with his pyjama jacket open and his hair untidy. I felt an amused affection for him, but also a touch of exasperation, especially when he grumbled that he was lonely on his own and wanted me to sit with him all the time.

'I don't know what you find to do with yourself without me,' he complained.

'I've made friends with several passengers.' Mostly men, but I thought it would not be diplomatic to let him know that I was one of the few women not stricken down.

'I hope they're the right sort of people. You know so little of the world and with this being a one-class vessel you have to be discreet about getting friendly with the wrong sort.'

'You horrid old snob!' I managed to laugh and even to kiss him before I removed myself and the barley water from the cabin, but inside I was furious. The right sort! Who did Edmond Fardale think he was? The son of a provincial vet, that's who! If he thought he was going to dictate who my friends were to be, using some arbitrary rule of thumb to decide their class, then he could think again.

It was several days before Edmond felt well enough to resume our honeymoon and by that time I was menstruating, which both fascinated and embarrassed him. By the time we were able to get together again we were both suffering from frustration, though not to the same degree nor for the same reason.

Edmond's tension was easily dissipated. One strenuous bout on the narrow bunk and he was his goodtempered complacent self again. My dissatisfaction was more persistent although it was true that I felt more pleasure in the sexual act now that I was used to it. In some ways I was happy. As the temperature rose my sense of wellbeing increased. This was what I had been missing all those sunless days in England. I felt myself opening out, blossoming in the warmth and light.

'You must always wear a hat,' Edmond ordered. 'And carry a parasol as well.'

'The sun doesn't bother me,' I said.

'You're getting very brown.' He did not need to spell out his meaning, I seized on it for myself. My attractive ivory skin was darkening into a more exotic shade. I rather liked the effect of my brilliant sapphire eyes against the golden tan, but I remembered how careful the Eurasian girls I had known in the past had been to shield their faces from the sun and I realised uneasily that I might do well to follow their example.

What irked me was that Edmond said I 'must' always wear a hat. I didn't like being given orders and, in fact, it was the loss of my independence that I found the most difficult thing to accept in my married state.

In other ways being married to Edmond had its good side. He was charmingly attentive, especially in public, and I had no objection to a little pampering. When Mumma and I had travelled to England we had done it on the cheap, and, of course, as two women alone we had had to fend for ourselves. It was delightful to have a man to look after all the details of the journey, to order me cool drinks and see that I had a comfortable place to sit, to be my escort when we went ashore and my partner when we danced in the evenings. Edmond liked me to be admired and he encouraged me to dress up and make the most of my striking looks. He was never so ardent as after an evening when I had been a social success.

By the time we docked at Ballard Pier in Bombay I was congratulating myself on the success of my marriage.

True, the physical side was no great event and there had been one ghastly moment at Port Said when I had looked over the side of the ship and seen on the quayside a young Army officer in uniform and been shaken by a return of my longing for Dominic. I had to hang on to the rail just as I had clung to the fireplace on that terrible evening at Stowbury. The man turned his head and, of course, it was not, and could not have been, Dominic.

Putting that on one side, I was not displeased with the bargain I had made, especially when I discovered that we were booked into the Taj Mahal Hotel for our first two nights in Bombay, to give us time to sort out our accommodation.

'Such a pity we had to arrive during the monsoon,' I said to Edmond, looking out of the streaming windows at the grey heaving sea. 'We might almost be in Manchester.'

'Hardly. It seems exotic enough to me. I must say I think the Company is doing us rather well, putting us up in the best hotel. Did you come here when you were living in Bombay?'

'Never! Darling, we were the lowest of the low. Well, not quite that perhaps, but definitely not on Taj Mahal Hotel level. Staying here, I've achieved an ambition.'

'Thanks to being the wife of Arkady & Pershore's Chief Accountant,' Edmond pointed out. 'Do I get thanked?'

'Certainly.' I put my arms round his neck, but Edmond had rather more than that in mind. Love in the afternoon . . . well, well. I think Edmond was as struck by the novelty of it as I was.

We went down to dinner feeling pleased with ourselves and our sleek good humour communicated itself to the waiters so that we seemed to receive particularly attentive service. Edmond tried to look as if he was taking it all in his stride, but I had learned to know him well enough to see that his self-esteem was being stroked. I felt amused and indulgent and once again I realised that I often thought of Edmond as a child. How strange. He was quite sure that he was the strong one, looking after me, while

I was aware of reservations about this act, as if I knew it could crumble if I really put it to the test.

The next day we went to inspect the accommodation the Company was providing for us. As we drove through the streets, running with water, Edmond looked with dismay at the Indians paddling through the muddy torrent.

'How long will it be like this?' he asked.

'Until September. I told you it was a pity we'd arrived during the monsoon.'

'I knew about the rain, but I didn't expect such inadequate drainage in a great city.'

'Bombay is very low-lying,' I said, resenting even this slight criticism of the city where I had been born. 'Until the British started doing land reclamation it was five separate islands.'

I was not really paying much attention because I was peering out through the raindrops at landmarks which had once been as familiar to me as Manchester Town Hall was to Edmond.

'Flora Fountain!' I exclaimed. 'Do look, Edmond. To us that's as important as Piccadilly Circus in London. And we'll be going past Crawford Market where I'll be able to buy fresh fruit and vegetables and fish and meat.'

'You won't be doing the marketing, will you, little thing?' Edmond said, taking my hand in his and squeezing it. 'We'll have servants to look after all that.'

Well, yes, but Mumma had often gone to the market herself and I was looking forward to some zestful bargaining, so much more interesting than the dull English shops where they looked at you as if you'd crawled out from under a stone if you suggested a penny or two off the fixed price. However, I let it go. Once we were settled Edmond would begin to understand how necessary it was to keep an eye on prices for oneself.

The mill compound for Arkady & Pershore employees was well outside the main part of the city, past the racecourse and the Buddhist Temple, overlooking the Arabian Sea at Worli. To my regret, we did not have a house, but an apartment in a block of flats. True, it was spacious and airy and we had a sea view, but I felt hemmed in, just as I had when Mumma and I had been forced to live in Grandma's lodging-house. The apartment had a sitting room and a dining room, with a balcony running the length of both of them, and two bedrooms, with another balcony for the main one. All these rooms opened off a square entrance hall. Then, at the back, there was the kitchen and kitchen balcony and two rooms for the servants.

There were some basic items of furniture which we had taken over from the outgoing tenants, but I could see that there was plenty of scope for me to try my hand at homemaking.

'A pity we didn't know beforehand exactly what was needed; we could have brought it all out with us from England,' Edmond said, looking round the sparsely furnished sitting room.

'I'll guarantee to buy what we want at half the cost from the Bombay markets. I know my way around, remember.'

Edmond agreed, but in a halfhearted way. I understood what was worrying him when he said, 'Darling, you probably don't realise it, but you've been talking about "the British" and "us" as if you were . . . well, one of the natives.'

'I have one-eighth Indian blood,' I said evenly. 'You knew that before you married me.'

'It doesn't show, not if you're careful to keep out of the sun,' Edmond said quickly.

'I was brought up to conceal it,' I said. 'Even Dadda pretended that he was all English. I know more than you do about the stigma attached to being classed as Eurasian, but I still can't turn my back on the fact that I was born and brought up in India.'

'There's no need to flaunt it,' Edmond muttered.

The trouble was, he was right. If I wanted to be accepted by his new colleagues and their wives (especially their wives) it would be far better not to draw attention to my Indian inheritance. It cost me something, but I managed to promise, 'I'll be discreet,' and was rewarded by the smile and hearty kiss I could always count on from Edmond when I was being a conforming little wife.

Edmond would have liked to have supervised all the details of our new life, but fortunately he was far too busy getting to grips with his appointment as Chief Accountant. It was not, as I had thought, quite the top financial post; Edmond reported to a Financial Director called Gilbert Hillson while I, as I very soon discovered, was accountable to Mrs Gilbert Hillson.

She descended on me long before I was ready to receive visitors, literally descended, since the Hillsons lived in a very grand flat on the top floor of our block.

'A totally informal call,' she said when, still lacking a bearer, I opened the door myself. 'I know how difficult it is for young wives just settling in. If there's any help I can give you, please don't hesitate to ask.'

I invited her in, hoping she would have the tact to refuse, but tact had been left out of Madge Hillson's character. She stepped inside, her eyes darting over the trunks I was still unpacking.

'I'm sorry for the mess,' I said, though I didn't really see why I should apologise when it was she who had insisted on foisting herself on me. 'Do let me get you some tea.'

She was standing in the middle of the sitting room, smiling indulgently. I removed a cut-glass rose bowl (a wedding present), a copy of Lawrence's *Sons and Lovers* which I had been reading on the voyage, and a framed photograph of Edmond's cricket team from an armchair and she sat down. She was in her early forties, I suppose, a thin woman who held herself very upright. She wore a mauve linen two-piece which was not kind to her sallow complexion and a straw hat pulled down low on her forehead so that she had to tilt her chin to talk to me as I stood in front of her.

I dashed into the kitchen and put the kettle on to boil. Fortunately, I had a tin of biscuits which we had brought out from England with us and when I wrenched it open and nibbled the corner of one I was relieved to find that the airtight tin had preserved them without a trace of mustiness. Another good point was that I had already unpacked our linen and could put my hands on a dainty traycloth and matching napkins (more wedding presents). On the whole I was not displeased when I carried the tray through into the sitting room.

Mrs Hillson put down the cricketing photograph she had been inspecting. 'Is your husband in this picture? I haven't met him yet.'

'Edmond's the one in the middle with the cup. He was the captain. He plays very good cricket.'

'Excellent! He'll find it so useful.' She watched me pour the tea and then said gently, 'I always take lemon with my tea.'

'Oh! I'm sorry . . . I didn't think. I'm afraid I don't have any lemons. I did boil the milk.'

'How clever of you. Most new arrivals don't realise that's necessary. All the same, I'll take mine plain.'

'I'm not exactly a newcomer,' I said. 'I was born in Bombay and lived here until I was fifteen.'

'Really?' Her eyes flickered over me, reassessing my status. 'Your father . . . ?'

'Was also employed by Arkady & Pershore, just like Edmond.'

'Gilbert and I have been here for more years than I care to remember so we must surely have known him. What was your maiden name?'

'Bullen.'

'Bullen . . .' She shook her head. 'How strange that I can't recall him. Did you live in the Company compound?'

'No, we had our own house.'

That stumped her. Either we were very grand indeed or we had been so far outside the pale that she could hardly contemplate our existence.

'When Father died we went back to England,' I said. Why had I called him 'Father'? He had always been 'Dadda' to me and yet now, talking to this supercilious woman, I suddenly adopted another title for him.

'So you went to school in Bombay?' Mrs Hillson asked, still trying to place me.

'Yes, indeed! I went to St Thomas's Cathedral School,' I said with an enthusiasm that owed less to my memories of the school than to the knowledge that I was giving her a real facer.

There was no need for her to know that my parents had made considerable sacrifices to send me to that school. True I was classed as British and my fees would have been half of those charged to the Indian pupils, but it must have been a drain on them, even with the small additional income from Matthew Arkady. Left to herself, I think Mumma would have let me go to a school more suitable to our level in life. It was Dadda who had been ambitious for me.

'So you were here in the Willingdons' time,' Mrs Hillson went on, still probing. 'Such lovely people. They're very much missed, you know, since Lord Willingdon was moved to Madras.'

I was reasonably certain that Mrs Hillson had no greater acquaintance with the former Governor of Bombay and his lady than I had myself – a smiling word at a school Open Day from Lady Willingdon and half a dozen glimpses of Lord Willingdon in ceremonial costume on formal occasions.

'They were very popular,' I agreed. 'Of course, I was too young to be invited to their functions.' Having achieved a degree of ascendancy over Mrs Hillson I turned the conversation before she could discover how false it was. 'Do have a biscuit. They've come straight from England,' I urged her.

'How delightful. Just one. So, having been brought up in the city, I suppose you know all the ropes and don't need any help?'

'Not at all,' I protested. 'As far as engaging servants and the day-to-day running of the household are concerned, I think I can manage, provided I haven't forgotten all my Hindi and Gujurati. Where I shall be glad of your guidance is in a social way. After all, as I said, I was only fifteen when I went home.'

Mrs Hillson might have no tact, but I felt that my speech was loaded with it. Certainly it seemed to please her.

'We must get you launched into our little community. I'll give a dinner party. We'll get together and sort out dates when you're more settled. And, of course, when the horrid rains stop there'll be many things to do. Do you play tennis?'

'Yes, I'm particularly fond of a game of tennis.'

Tennis at Stowbury, with Patricia and Dominic. I looked down at the dregs in my teacup to hide the bitterness of that memory.

'And do you ride?'

'No.'

Dominic and Patricia, clattering into the cobbled yard behind Step's house. Why had these recollections suddenly come back to haunt me?

'Golf?'

'I'd like to learn.'

'You and Mr Fardale will join the Club, of course. We *box wallahs* all belong to the Woodhouse Gymkhana, but the Willingdon is excellent for golf. Mixed, you know, which the Bombay Gymkhana is *not.*'

For one moment I thought she meant it was all male, then I realised that she was talking about the social mixing of the different races.

'Bombay is a completely cosmopolitan city and we pride ourselves on our tolerance,' she assured me. 'The Parsis, in particular, are quite emancipated. But I suppose you must know this, just as you'll know that not every Indian wants to mix with the British. They have their own clubs, too. Let me see, what haven't I mentioned?'

'The Yacht Club?' I suggested maliciously.

'Oh, my dear, one doesn't aspire to that! So very snobbish.'

'I must talk to Edmond about it,' I said, once again exercising the tact of which I was beginning to be proud.

'Of course. You haven't been married long, have you?'

'We came straight from our wedding to the ship.'

'How romantic. Quite the little love birds.' To my relief she was finally showing signs of departing, picking up her gloves and handbag and giving a last searching look round the cluttered room. 'Now don't tire yourself out with all this unpacking,' she said. 'Would you like to borrow my bearer to fetch and carry for you?'

'It's kind of you to suggest it, but I have very little left to do,' I said untruthfully. 'I plan to interview one or two servants tomorrow.'

'Do be careful. A bad servant is a nightmare. But, of course, you know all about that.'

I saw her to the door and we murmured politely about getting in touch to arrange a dinner date, but before she went Mrs Hillson said, 'Burrell, did you say?'

'Bullen.' A mischievous impulse made me add, 'We're supposed to be descended from the same family as Anne Boleyn. The Boleyns changed their name from Bullen, you know.'

It had been no more than a family joke, but she had to pause to assess its value before she murmured, 'How quaint.'

I laughed at the game we had been playing, one step forward and one step back, score one point to me, score one to Mrs Hillson, but Edmond took it more seriously.

'Gilbert Hillson's good opinion is important to me,' he pointed out. 'And, of course, I'd like his wife to approve of you.'

'At the moment she doesn't know what to make of me,' I said cheerfully. 'I'll try to keep on her good side, but I'll make no rash promises.'

'You'll be lonely if you don't make friends with the other ladies and Mrs Hillson is one of their leaders.' He looked round the apartment with a dissatisfied air. 'I wish you'd been more organised before she came to call.'

'I would have been if she hadn't arrived on the doorstep as soon as the trunks were delivered.'

'She meant it kindly.'

'Perhaps. I think it would have been more neighbourly to have been less proper. She said it was an informal call, but she was wearing a hat and gloves.'

'Presumably that's the correct thing to do.'

'Oh, Edmond, don't be so stiff! She only had to walk down two flights of stairs. I hooted when I realised she hadn't been outside the building and was dressed up as if she'd driven for miles to see me.'

'Little thing, you're not very old and you haven't had any experience in doing the right social thing. I do beg you not to start putting people's backs up by insisting on being different.'

I wrinkled my nose at him, but I was prepared to be cooperative, up to a point. 'I won't put you to shame,' I promised.

'I know you won't. This job means a lot to me, Jessica. If I do well I could be in line for Hillson's own job when he goes home and possibly even for a seat on the Board in Manchester one day. How would you like that?'

'Splendiferous. In the meantime, I have to break it to Your Highness that supper this evening consists of an omelette and some rather wizened apples. Unless you'd like to go out?'

'Not in this rain and not to a restaurant that hasn't been recommended to us. Is there any cheese?'

'Cheese is almost non-existent in this part of the world, my dear. Never mind, by this time tomorrow I promise you I'll have a cook installed.'

'One who understands European cookery, please. I don't want curry every night.'

'Proper Indian food is delicious,' I assured him, but Edmond frowned and shook his head and I made a mental note to order a very simple first dinner from our cook, lamb chops or something like that, which Edmond would consider real food.

We settled in and I was surprisingly contented, far

happier than Edmond, who developed a streaming cold and was a miserable and disgruntled patient, just as he had been when he was seasick.

'Unbearable weather,' he grumbled.

'At least it's predictable. Cheer up, darling, and don't grumble about a good monsoon. It means everything to the farmers in the hinterland.'

'This is a *good* monsoon?'

'Of course it is. Lots and lots of lovely water. When you've been into the *mofussil* you'll understand.'

'Of course, you've taken to it . . .'

'Like a duck to water?' I suggested and for once Edmond laughed and allowed himself to be cheered up.

'I can't get near you with this horrible cold,' he complained.

'Is that what's making you so grumpy? Never mind, we'll make up for it when you're feeling better.'

It was not a prospect I looked forward to very much. I relished having a room to myself while Edmond slept separately to spare me the possibility of catching his cold. However, I had married the man and I was prepared to pay my dues for being given a life I had to admit I was enjoying.

It would have been better still if Edmond had left all the running of the household to me, but with his accountant's mind he insisted on inspecting the books. 'You're being cheated,' he said, after totting up the week's expenses.

'I know.'

'You must put a stop to it immediately. Once this sort of thing gets out of hand there's no end to it.'

'I won't let it go too far.'

'There's no reason why you should do the nasty work, little thing. Have Moti in now and I'll send him packing.'

'You mustn't do that,' I exclaimed in alarm. 'He's a splendid cook.'

'He's a thief.'

'He doesn't think of it like that,' I explained patiently. 'Moti came to us at quite a low wage, though I could see he had doubts when he realised I was an old India hand, with a sort of tacit understanding between us that he would make what he could on the side, and because he thought I'd appreciate him. He's quite an artist in his way.'

'If he's not earning enough why doesn't he ask for a rise?'

'It's more fun for him and he probably does better by exercising a bit of ingenuity on the bills. If we pay him more he'll still go on doctoring them, probably for larger amounts because he'll think we can afford it.'

'It's dishonest.'

'Not really. He knows that I know, and I know that he knows that I know. Come the weekend I'll exclaim in horror that we appear to have used three dozen eggs and point out that the butcher is obviously a *badmash* who's been overcharging and the bills will go down drastically for a time.'

'It's like a silly game. Surely it would be far better to pay him a decent wage in the first place and put things on a straightforward footing?'

'You're right and I know you're right,' I admitted. 'The person you won't persuade is Moti. We're talking about generations of custom. Everyone expects to make their bit of *dastur*. Haven't you come across it in business?'

'I have,' he admitted reluctantly. 'But in our own home . . . can't you put your foot down – or let me do it?'

'Farewell Moti if you do.'

Poor Edmond, I was a sore trial to him, especially when I plunged into the bazaars and came out hours later with the piece of furniture or length of cloth I wanted at a bargain price.

'When you come to the bazaar, *mem*, I put up the shutters,' one shopkeeper said feelingly, but we both knew that he had still made a profit on the fine carved chest I had purchased and he liked me none the worse for having made the sale a social occasion by taking a cup of tea and looking at a photograph of his son, even though I had beaten down the price of the chest to something like a reasonable figure.

Edmond admired the chest, but he said uneasily, 'Darling, I don't like you walking about the native quarter on your own. There's been a lot of unrest. You could be robbed or beaten up, like that poor woman in Amritsar.'

'I always take Akbar with me,' I said, shying away from the mention of Amritsar.

Amritsar was one of the subjects on which Edmond and I differed. Now that more details had come out I was appalled by the massacre of innocent people who happened to be caught up in a crowd which might or might not have gathered together to indulge in political agitation, while Edmond saw it as a regrettable but necessary action by General Dyer to maintain law and order. It was true that there had been rioting and looting in the city before that terrible day and no one could condone the brutal beating of a totally blameless Englishwoman, a good well-meaning teacher, who just happened to be out on the street at the wrong moment, but how many lives did it take to avenge an assault on one white woman?

It was a subject that was better not discussed since many of our new friends agreed with Edmond. I still thought that General Dyer's actions had been not merely unnecessarily brutal, but a great and lasting mistake which had damaged the standing of the British community in places far removed from the troubled Punjab, but then my opinions came from what Mrs Hillson called 'bazaar talk' and naturally differed from the views of the English-language newspapers.

On the whole I had more than enough to do without involving myself in the politics of India. Mrs Hillson had given her dinner party, to which I wore my wedding gown with the sleeves cut short and the train reduced. I was very much admired, which was a great boost to my morale. I gave my own party in return and before long we were overwhelmed by invitations. New faces, especially belonging to a young, convivial couple, were a godsend in that restricted society.

We joined the club and as the rains began to subside into daily showers and Bombay's most delicious season approached I was asked if we would be playing in the tennis tournament.

'Yes, indeed! Edmond and I play a demon doubles game.' I looked round to make sure Edmond was not in earshot and added, 'We used to play at Stowbury with the Arkadys – Dominic and Patricia, you know – and they'd had professional tuition. It improved our game no end.'

Once again I saw the baffled look on Mrs Hillson's face. She had still not quite 'placed' me, but it seemed that back home I had the most unexceptionable friends and now here I was, charming, friendly, not as subservient as I might have been, but always polite and above all, popular. She continued to smile on me, which made life very much easier than if she had frowned.

I had always foreseen that I would have to augment my wardrobe. Edmond had been worried by my scanty luggage, but what I lacked in made-up dresses I supplied in dress lengths. With the aid of a good *durzi* I was soon one of the best dressed women in the Company compound. Poor man, I was quite ruthless with him. If the seams were not properly finished or the hem was uneven, back the garment went until I was satisfied. It took up quite a lot of my time.

The fashions were, for once, eminently suitable for wear in a hot climate: loose-fitting frocks with dropped waists, short sleeves and cutaway necks, worn at a sensible mid-calf length. It was bliss to throw away the stiff, hot corsets our mothers had endured. Another good point was that these unfitted garments were extremely quick and easy to make. My *durzi*'s sewing machine whirred unceasingly and he could turn out a new garment in a couple of days – less if I was prepared to accept a poor finish. I never went in for the bows and sashes and frills which some ladies affected. All my dresses were cut on simple lines with the minimum of trimming, but of fine cotton, rich silk or soft chiffon which clung and floated, hinting at the excellent figure underneath. I was young and thoughtless and enjoying myself, and my new tussore silk with guipure lace at the edges of the sleeves and hem meant far more to me than the news of Mr Ghandi's latest campaign of passive resistance.

I did take note when a *hartal* was called in the cotton mills and all the operatives stopped working, but more because of the worry it caused Edmond than because of any real understanding of their aims.

I was learning to be a proficient hostess and I became adept at turning aside difficult subjects at my dinner parties. Edmond did his part, too. He liked having people in and he enjoyed my success. I basked in his approval and altogether it was quite the best time of our marriage so far.

I had just finished dressing for one of these dinner parties one evening, fastening a long crystal necklace round the neck of a new gown I particularly liked, a pale pink silk with a tunic top and an ankle-length skirt banded with gold embroidery – made, in fact, from a sari length I had discovered in a new shop – when I heard the doorbell ring and voices in the hall. I frowned at my reflection in the looking glass, annoyed that anyone had been tactless enough to arrive exactly on the hour.

'Are you nearly ready, darling?' I called to Edmond. 'People are starting to arrive.'

'Two minutes,' he answered from the bathroom.

I took a last satisfied look at myself in the glass and went out to greet my guests just as Akbar came to find me bearing a card on a silver salver. A stranger, then, and come at a most inopportune time. Who on earth could be calling at eight o'clock in the evening?

I glanced at the card and shrieked in delight. William! My own dear William! We had never been great correspondents, mainly because William seemed to be forever disappearing into the most inaccessible places, but I had written to the last address I had for him giving him the news of my marriage and telling him I would be living in the Arkady & Pershore compound in Bombay. The last

100

thing I expected was that he would turn up unannounced to visit me. I nearly knocked Akbar over in my haste to get into the sitting room.

William was standing by one of the little tables I had had set out with dishes of nuts for drinks before dinner. He was taller than I remembered, and thinner, but otherwise exactly the same, even to the ill-fitting linen suit I could have sworn was the same one he was wearing when he waved goodbye to Mumma and me.

The joy I felt at seeing him again amazed me and the fervour with which I cast myself on him literally rocked him back on his heels, so that he had to clutch at a chair to steady us both. I lifted my face, with every intention of kissing him, but William drew back, staring down at me as if I were some importunate stranger.

'You've changed,' he said.

'Of course I have! It's been more than six years. Didn't you realise I'd grown up?'

'I knew you were married and I ought to have realised you'd look different, but the image I had of you in my mind was quite different.'

'You look *exactly* the same,' I assured him. Since he made no move towards me I reached up and kissed him firmly on the lips, which seemed to startle him.

'I can see I've come at an inconvenient time,' he said, looking round the room at my preparations for receiving guests.

'Of course you haven't. We've got one or two people coming in for dinner. No one important, just colleagues of Edmond's. You must stay.'

'And upset your table? I know better than to do that to a hostess.'

'As if that mattered. Edmond . . .' I turned to the door as Edmond came in, '. . . this is my dear cousin William, who's just blown in from . . . where have you come from, William?'

'I'm excavating in the Indus Valley.' He held out his hand to Edmond. 'May I congratulate you on your marriage? Though I have to say that I remember Jessica as a

101

most troublesome child and I doubt whether she's improved very much.'

'Except in looks,' I put in.

William inspected me with the small, amused smile on his lips that brought back all sorts of memories and a rush of affection for him.

'I grant you that,' he said at last. 'I would never have believed scrawny little Jessica could have turned into such a beauty.'

'Make him stay to dinner, Edmond,' I demanded.

'Of course you'll be most welcome,' Edmond said, but I thought he sounded rather stiff.

William shook his head and I could see he was adamant. No point in arguing with William when he turned mulish. He did accept a drink and stood talking to Edmond with it in his hand while I flitted round the room checking that everything I had asked for had been done. He was still there when the guests began to arrive and I introduced him all round.

Mr and Mrs Hillson were among the first. I always had the impression that Madge Hillson came early in the hope of catching me out – and some of the other girls had admitted to having the same suspicion. To have a dinner party without her was, of course, unthinkable.

She spoke graciously to William and I suppressed a smile at the sight of her rigid face as she took in his dreadful suit. 'Your cousin, did you say?' she asked me.

'The relationship is more remote than that, but William and I agreed long ago that we would call one another Cousin.'

'He's quite an original, isn't he?' she said, which was a remark I looked forward to sharing with William.

'William is a most distinguished archaeologist,' I said. 'He's been digging for history in the Indus Valley.'

'Ah, yes – out in the hot sun.' Mrs Hillson looked across the room to where William was talking quietly with his fine, distinguished head bent courteously towards one of the sillier young wives. 'I suppose that would explain why he's so . . . dark?'

CHAPTER FIVE

It was not William's fault that his visit ended the honeymoon period of both my marriage and my acceptance into the Company compound. For one thing, his extremely sunburnt appearance aroused Mrs Hillson's suspicions and spurred her on to look into my family background. She discovered, of course, that my father had not been covenanted staff, but country born, and holding quite a lowly position in the Finishing Works. Nothing was said, not openly, but a faint cold wind of disapproval, like a breath off the snowfields of the Himalayas, wafted towards me from the top floor of our apartment block.

Having boasted of her tolerance she could not admit that she resented having to mix with a girl who must have some Indian blood, but when she could put difficulties in my way she did. She did not refuse my invitations, nor did she fail to invite me to tea with the other Company wives, but all of a sudden it was difficult to find a date when both she and Mr Hillson were free and the girls I was invited to meet were the wives of the under-managers ranking well below Edmond in status.

Not everyone followed her lead. Several of my new friends went out of their way to tell me that they, too, had fallen foul of her at one time or another. It would blow over, they assured me, but I knew that Mrs Hillson felt a deep resentment because she had allowed herself to be deceived by me. She had swallowed the hint of my good connections and disregarded her original suspicions and now she was disgruntled.

William stayed in Bombay for a week and I saw as much of him as I could. He was there to confer with some archaeological colleagues and it seemed to take up a lot of this time, but I managed to see him every day, even if it was for no more than a cup of tea.

'We've got years and years to catch up,' I pointed out. 'You're a rotten correspondent, William.'

'Getting letters through was difficult during the war.'

'I know, but all the same . . . what did you *do* in the war?'

'I was in the Army.'

'Oh, very informative! Getting anything out of you is like digging up one of your tombs.'

'I was an Intelligence Officer.'

'William! A sort of spy?'

'I merely collected together a few interesting facts. My languages came in useful.'

'But the war was in Europe . . .'

'There was activity in other places,' William said drily.

'Yes, of course . . . Mesopotamia . . .'

'That wretched campaign is better not mentioned in India.'

I could see I was going to get nothing more out of him about his work in the war, which was a nuisance because I suspected William had an interesting story to tell. 'How many languages do you speak?' I asked.

'Depends what you mean by "speak". Eight fluently, I suppose. English and Urdu are my basics.'

'And which do you think of as your mother tongue?'

'That's a question I may be forced to think about seriously when India gains her independence.'

'*When* . . . ?'

'Yes, my dear, it's no longer a question of "if". It must come and when it does people like me with a foot in both camps will be forced into making a decision. Am I Indian or am I British?'

'You've lived all your life in India,' I said slowly.

'So did your father, but what would he have said if he had been asked to name his nationality?'

'He always insisted he was English.'

'And you?' William asked.

'I'm British, too, both by birth and by marriage, and yet . . . I never really felt at home in England, William. I tried, I really did, but since I've come back to Bombay

104

I've felt myself expanding like a plant put back into its native soil.'

'And yet you wouldn't want to live in India as an Indian woman, would you?'

'No . . . no, of course not. The restrictions would be too great. Oh, bother you, William! I don't like acknowledging it, but what I really want is to live in India still clinging to my privileged position. You wanted me to admit that, didn't you, you devious beast?'

William laughed as he got up to go. 'It's called having your cake and eating it and most of the British in India think they can go on doing it. At least you recognise the problem. By the way, I've left a parcel in the hall for you. It's your wedding present.'

Typical of William to have left an untidily wrapped brown paper parcel lying around to be discovered and even more typical that it contained an exquisite bronze of Sita, the wife of Rama. There was a note inside – *'She's a genuine antique, not a copy, so please cherish her. She's executing the three bends pose.'*

I carried her round the flat trying to find the ideal place for her. In our bedroom I paused in front of the full-length mirror and tried out the three bends pose. It was rather more difficult than it looked. When Edmond came home that evening I showed him the statue, which looked beautifully at home in the dining room. 'I think I'll take lessons in Indian dancing,' I told him.

'Whatever for?'

'Interest . . . pleasure. Wouldn't you like me to dance for you, my lord?' It was no use, I couldn't coax Edmond out of his sulky mood. 'I've asked William to come for a proper meal tomorrow evening, just the three of us,' I said. 'I do want you to get to know him better before he disappears again.'

Edmond did not look as if the idea gave him much pleasure, but I was totally unprepared when he burst out, 'I think you might have told me!'

'Told you what?'

'That some of your relations were half-castes.'

105

I could not have been more shocked if he had hit me. To have used that derogatory term of any of my family would have been hurtful, but to describe William in such a way was beyond belief. I think Edmond had no idea how deeply he had wounded me because, as I often did, I defended myself by speaking flippantly. 'My dear, the Bullens are an immense tribe and range in colour from milk-with-a-dash to the darkest mocca. William is the only one you've met, so I presume you must be talking about him. He has more Indian blood than I have because he belongs to the previous generation, but it still amounts to no more than a quarter.'

'A pity he had to turn up here just as we were settling in.'

'I can't agree. I'll always be pleased to see William, no matter when or where he may "turn up". Do have some sense, Edmond. William is a man of learning and culture and very highly regarded in his particular field. Quite apart from that, he's . . . he's the most valuable human being I've ever known.'

It was Edmond's failure to recognise William's quality that upset me. It showed up a weakness not in William, but in Edmond, that distressed me beyond all measure. How could anyone be in the same room with William for more than a few minutes and not be humbled by the goodness that shone out of him?

'William's the only person I know who could have a light turned on any part of his mind and not be shamed by what was on view,' I said.

'Really?' Edmond was sufficiently annoyed by my defence to snatch at a way of turning the tables on me. 'If he's so pure what was he thinking about when he gave you that extremely suggestive statue? We can't keep it in the dining room. It would put people off their food.'

I went out of the room without a word, stalked into the dining room and picked up the statue of Sita. It was about nine inches high, exquisitely moulded and very heavy. It was only the thought of its value that stopped me from braining Edmond with it. I held it in my hands and considered it. Sita stood with one leg bent, her hip extended to one side, her slender waist curved and one arm raised. True, her full round breasts were bare and, in fact, she wore nothing but a head dress, a necklace and some drapery indicated by flowing lines over her legs and buttocks, but I could see nothing suggestive in her pose or her dress. She was beautiful and natural. Only a prurient mind could have seen anything amiss in William's gift, which led me to an unfortunate conclusion.

'You have a nasty mind,' I informed Edmond when I could bring myself to go back and join him. 'She's a lovely example of Indian art. A connoisseur would envy us for possessing her. However, since you think she'll put our guests off Moti's curried prawns, I'll find another place for her.'

Outwardly I conformed, but inwardly I raged. I went on seeing William and I forced Edmond to be civil to him, but of course William was not deceived.

'I wish Edmond and I got on better together,' he said one day, bringing out in the open the thing I had been trying to keep hidden.

'Edmond's sensitive about my Indian background,' I said.

'And I've drawn attention to it by turning up burned nearly black by the sun. I feel indignant – on your behalf, not mine. Is Edmond really so blind to the treasure he got when he married you?'

'No, of course he's not, and thank you for the compliment. In the ordinary way we rub along together very well.'

'You've been married half a year and you "rub along together"? Do you love him, Jessica?'

'Of course I do,' I said, tilting my chin and looking anywhere but at William's intent face.

'I'm not sure that's true.'

Damn William, he was going to make me tell him the truth and it was the last thing I wanted to do. 'He wasn't my first choice,' I said carefully because I was afraid to talk about Dominic, even to William. Saying his name out loud was too much like letting the genie out of the bottle; once out it might be difficult to put the stopper back on the regrets I had stifled. 'I married Edmond . . . oh, why did I marry Edmond? Out of bravado, out of hurt pride, out of a need to make a change in my life and because . . . well, because he loved me.'

'And is that enough?'

'It has to be. William, please . . . I'm working hard to make a success of my marriage and, yes, I know that the fact that I have to work at it means that it isn't all it should be, but there it is: I've made my bed . . .'

I broke off, realising that the old tag was all too applicable, and William completed it, 'And you'll have to lie on it.'

He made a curious gesture with his hand as if he were pushing away from him the picture of me lying on a bed with Edmond. He knew now that he had been right when he sensed a hollow at the heart of our relationship and it displeased him, since he would never have committed such a sin himself.

It *was* a sin, against myself and against Edmond. We shared a bed, and found a certain amount of pleasure in it, more on Edmond's side than on mine; we had a lively social life, and there at least I gave satisfaction, in spite of the odd kick in my gallop; I was beautiful, popular and admired – Edmond took a pride in owning me. But that pride was lessened by the tarnishing breath of Mrs Hillson's coldness and it was a sign of the base metal of our marriage that so small a cause should dim its first brightness.

I carried out my threat to start learning the elements of Indian classical dancing though I might not have done if William had not helped me. I was just a little suspicious of the blandness with which he took up my idea when he heard about it. If it had been anyone else I would have suspected him of encouraging me to defy my husband, but surely William would not be so devious? He was amused when I told him of my ambition, but then he decided to take it seriously.

'I know someone who studies dance,' he said. 'She's in Bombay at present. I'll have a word with her and see if she can help you.'

This was interesting. I was exceedingly curious about the women in William's life – if any. He never so much as hinted at any romantic involvement and yet surely he was too complete a man to be wholly celibate? Why had William never married? He must be over thirty. I would have put the question to him, but since our talk about my own marriage it was a subject I avoided when speaking to him. I should have known that his mysterious female friend would turn out to be no ordinary woman.

'Are you free for an hour this morning?' he asked on the day before he was to leave Bombay. 'If so, I'm to take you to meet Her Highness the Maharani of Bhuredar. If she approves of you she may invite you to share her dancing lessons.'

He barely gave me time to pull on a hat before hustling me out of the flat to the taxi he had kept waiting. 'When I saw Her Highness an hour ago she was very taken with the idea of an Englishwoman who wanted to study Indian culture,' William explained. 'I want to get you there before she starts to have doubts about knowing you.'

'Who is she? How old is she? Surely it's unusual for a Maharani to take dancing lessons? For goodness sake, William, tell me *something* about her.'

'She's about twenty-four, I suppose. Quite emancipated and well-educated, definitely not in *purdah*, but not entirely Westernised. Married to the Maharajah of Bhuredar and daughter of the previous one.'

'Goodness, we are moving in high circles. How do you come to know her?'

'I excavated on their land. Rukmini . . . Her Highness . . . took an interest.'

I had not previously encountered an Indian princess and hardly knew what to expect. 'Is she fabulously wealthy? Why doesn't she live in a palace?' I asked as the taxi drew up outside a large, but not palatial, house.

'Yes, she is wealthy and the Maharajah has several

palaces,' William said patiently. 'This is just a pied-à-terre which Her Highness uses for short visits to Bombay.'

We were ushered through the cool hall, all white marble pillars and potted palms in brass pots, and up the stairs into a first-floor room, two sides of which were open to a balcony with a fretted wooden screen all round it. The room had a polished wooden floor and the walls were quite plain and painted white, but the ceiling was a miracle of intricate carving and there were two chandeliers and an immense mirror on the far wall which I guessed to be Venetian. Apart from that there were two sofas set at right angles to one another in a corner, with a fine silk carpet in front of them, a small table and a heavy carved chest and no other furnishings at all.

There was a flash of colour at the far end of the room and Rukmini Bhuredar was with us. By her standards, as I subsequently discovered, she was dressed simply, in a fashion suitable for a morning at home. Her sari was of cotton, but so finely woven that it floated like silk. She had tassels of pearls in her ears and nothing but pearls round her neck, though personally I did not consider six rows of pearls the size of marrowfat peas as unostentatious as she did.

In that first moment, after I had wrenched my eyes away from the lustrous jewellery, I did not consider her beautiful. She had a high-bred, fastidious face with a thin nose which old age would turn into a beak, and a thin-lipped mouth, but her eyes were magnificent, almost too large for her fine features and very expressive. She was small, far shorter than I was, but that fleeting impression was soon forgotten; she bore herself like a queen and expected to be treated like one. Her hands were lovely, long-fingered, supple and restless as a pair of birds. Above all, as she came closer and began to smile, I was struck by the great sweetness of her expression. Her head was covered and she held the edge of her sari slantwise across her face, but this was the merest apology for the seclusion I would have expected her to practise.

Did I imagine it, or was there a special gentleness in

William's manner as he presented me? He towered over her and I thought there was something protective, almost tender, in the way he bent towards her. The way they smiled at one another suggested deep understanding, but I knew that whatever there was between them – and certainly there was something – this was the nearest it would ever come to being expressed.

'Mrs Fardale, this is a very great pleasure,' the Maharani said, and if she had had no other beauty the music of her voice would have been a potent attraction. 'It is most unusual for an Englishwoman to be interested in Indian dance.'

'I have some Indian blood,' I said.

I thought I saw a faint quiver of distaste on that delicate face, then she glanced at William, remembering that he was my cousin, and her prejudice disappeared. 'You will forgive me if I say that I must first be sure that you intend to take it seriously before I agree to share my lessons with you.'

'Of course. To me it's not a religious rite, but I know the dance has been sacred in the past in India and I want to approach it in the right spirit.'

I thought I had surprised her by saying that, but she also looked amused.

'Sacred, yes, but in more recent decades the temple dancers have also been prostitutes. My aim is to rescue the dance from that slur. I intend founding a school of music and dancing for the girls of Bhuredar and to show that there is nothing immoral in learning to dance I am taking lessons myself. It has always been our tradition that the royal ladies perform certain ceremonial dances, so I do not come to it without any knowledge at all.'

She turned to William and added, 'Kesri will be here shortly. Will you stay and see him?'

William shook his head. 'I must go. This is my only chance to visit the Royal Asiatic Society's library. I leave in the morning.'

I was dismayed to realise that this would be my own last meeting with William before he left. 'Can you come round to the flat this evening?' I asked, but William could not be persuaded.

'I'll probably see you again before long, Jessica,' he said. 'We're not as far apart as we once were.'

I would have liked to have kissed him, but I knew that gesture would be misunderstood so I merely gave him a rather miserable smile and then had to watch him walk to the door with the Maharani. They said a few words to one another, their voices low, but they did not touch and when she turned back to me I could see no sadness on the Maharani's face.

'Now we must talk,' she said. 'Tell me about yourself. Chichibai will go and see if our teacher has arrived.'

I had already noticed the small white-clad figure of an elderly woman who had come in behind the Maharani and seated herself on the floor in an unobtrusive corner. Now, in response to her name and a slight turn of the Maharani's head she went to the door and spoke to the servant outside.

'My *ayah*,' the Maharani said. 'She would like to be *ayah* to my own children, but she is too old, and so she is my . . . companion.'

Her chaperone. I understood the situation perfectly. It could be taken for granted that the small, watchful figure would remain in its place all the time the dancing teacher and musicians were with the Maharani, just as she would have been when William called. It was highly unlikely that they had ever been alone together.

'Are your children here with you?' I asked politely. Questions about children were always acceptable.

'No, I left them in Bhuredar. It's more healthy than Bombay.'

'How many children do you have?'

'Three. Two boys and a girl. I was married at fourteen and had my first child a year later. There were such rejoicings when it was a boy. A fine, beautiful child. I am proud of him. You, of course, are not under such pressure as I was to provide an heir.' She looked me up and down, clearly wondering why I was not pregnant. 'It will happen soon,' she said encouragingly.

I sincerely hoped not, but that was not something to say to an orthodox lady who had done her duty so amply. 'Do you think your dancing teacher will accept me as a pupil?' I asked.

'I will command him.'

As simple as that. I wondered whether to offer to pay, but in the face of such obvious wealth it seemed superfluous.

A bearer in the white *achkan*, blue sash and blue and gold turban all her servants wore came in and murmured to the *ayah*. The teacher, it seemed, had arrived.

'Good! Now I must present you to Gopal. He is very strict and very badtempered and not at all respectful, for which I like him. I should explain that we have our own tradition of dance in Bhuredar, very lyrical and graceful, somewhat similar to the Manipuri school. Gopal is one of the few masters capable of teaching it. I hope when my school is established to persuade him to return to live in Bhuredar. At the moment he is obstinate and insists on remaining in Bombay.'

In the face of the Maharani's determination the dancing teacher did not refuse to accept his new pupil, but it was plain that he did not like the idea, nor would he allow me to wear European clothes, so I was whirled away to the Maharani's bedroom and a chest full of beautiful saris was thrown open. The Maharani tossed them about and they spilled over the floor until I seized on a length of grass green silk scattered with embroidered daisies.

With the aid of the ancient *ayah* I put on the most becoming dress ever devised for a woman, though anyone who thinks it is practical has never tried working with six yards of material wound round the body. In all the hurry my hair had started to come down, so I twisted it into the plait I wore at bedtime.

'You look quite Indian!' the Maharani cried. 'See, I am as pale as you. Except for your blue eyes we could be . . . cousins.'

113

Not quite. Her long, thin nose and high arched brows showed her race. My own features looked blurred by the side of that incisiveness. And, no matter what she said, her skin was darker than mine. I was the taller, but she was far more graceful. I hoped the lessons I was about to take would give me some of that fluid grace.

The *ayah* had pulled a pierced wooden screen across one corner of the room when we returned and the musicians sat behind that. Only the *ayah* and the dancing master were allowed to see the Maharani being schooled in the ancient art of the temple dancers.

The master was a wizened little man in a white *kurta* and *dhoti*, who carried a staff which he banged on the floor to mark time or to stop us when he was displeased. He had a very poor opinion of our ability and, as the Maharani had said, he was not backward in expressing himself. She bore with him patiently, even laughing at his strictures.

As for me, I caught a sideways look which made me suspect that Gopal took a subtle pleasure in watching a *memsahib* floundering about with two left feet and no ear for the intricate rhythms of the dance. I prided myself on my supple body and I had always enjoyed ballroom dancing, but this was something different and I had enough humility to admit that I needed to learn a great deal more about native music as well as the movements Gopal was trying to demonstrate.

We had finished and the musicians were filing out of the long room when we were joined by the Maharajah.

'Kesri, you are just too late. Only a few minutes earlier and you could have seen us dancing,' the Maharani said. 'I have a companion in my lessons now, you see.'

She introduced us and Kesri Bhuredar's face lit up. 'William's cousin? Have I missed him? Oh, what a pity. William visits us too rarely. So you've decided to learn to dance? How well our dress becomes you.'

'Your Highness is too kind,' I said, piling on the politeness.

'Call me Kesri – please. Tell me, Mrs Fardale, are you interested in the cinematograph?'

The Maharani put her hands over her ears. 'No, no, no! I will not listen to you talking about the cinematograph. Would you believe, Mrs Fardale, that my husband wishes to make cinema films, here in India?'

'My name is Jessica,' I said. 'Why not films in India?'

'That is what I say. We have the climate, we have the audience. We even have one or two people who are trying to get the industry started.'

'But for you yourself to be a director is not suitable. Float a company if you must, but do, I beg you, stay away from the cameras. Come, Jessica, we will change our clothes and then perhaps you would like a cool drink.'

I was given a bowl of rose-scented water and left alone to get back into my cotton frock. It seemed shapeless and ungraceful after the delicate sari, particularly when the Maharani came back dressed in drifting yellow georgette and a complete change of jewellery, citrines set in gold.

We sat on the verandah and I was served a delicious fruit drink made from pressed mangoes, and little crisp biscuits, but neither Kesri nor Rukmini had anything. I felt self-conscious, eating and drinking alone. To me it seemed strange that, emancipated and Westernised as they were, they would not defy the rules of their caste by eating with me, not under their own roof.

Kesri Bhuredar was a pleasant young man, more English than Indian in his manner, and very goodlooking. He was not exactly plump, but his skin fitted him rather well and he had a sleek, well-fed look. All the same, from the way he moved it was obvious that he was an athlete and I had a vague recollection that I had heard of him as a champion polo player.

He was obsessed with the cinema and I could see why his wife had protested about his overriding interest. Gradually it was borne in on me that they welcomed my presence. They talked eagerly, seizing on me as something new. It seemed to me that they were bored with one another and a stranger was a welcome change. I was sorry

115

for them, recognising something of my own need for distraction from a marriage that was not entirely successful.

Edmond was uneasy about the dancing lessons, but I was glad of this new interest. It had come at just the right moment, when the first excitement of our arrival had faded and Mrs Hillson's disapproval was beginning to make itself felt. It took me out of the compound, away from the round of tea-parties and gossip. It gave me a certain *cachet* to be able to say I was so sorry I would not be free for bridge because the Maharani was expecting me.

I counted Rukmini as a friend, but only within certain limits, and I think it was because I did not intrude into her reticence that she gradually began to unbend and to talk to me, very hesitantly at first, about the difficulties of her life.

She always offered me refreshment after our lesson and I would stay for perhaps half an hour, sipping tea out of a cup so fine that the light shone through it, or cool sherbert from a crystal goblet. We spoke about our lessons and about trivialities, such as the coming horse races and the social scene in Bombay.

'Ah, yes, the races! Kesri wishes me to attend, but I cannot bring myself to go so far. I am the first of my family to come out of *purdah*, but I still observe certain restraints, especially in Bhuredar. In Bombay or Delhi I am much freer than I am at home, but I would not travel on public transport, except in a train with my own compartment, and to appear in public before a crowd of people – no, Kesri must excuse me from attending the races.'

It was a week later that she asked me a question that made me realise we were on the verge of exchanging confidences.

'Your marriage . . . it was a love match?'

To my surprise I found myself answering her truthfully. 'There was another man I would have preferred to marry, but it was not possible. Edmond had been in love with me for a long time and had asked me to marry him more than once. In the end I accepted because he could give me a life that appealed to me and I was not indifferent to him.'

'Did your parents intervene?'

'My father is dead and my mother is married to Edmond's father. They were both anxious for me to take him.'

'So you allowed yourself to be swayed by your family, just like an Indian girl! Are you happy?'

'Most of the time. Edmond is good to me.' I hesitated and then added, 'I suppose there are always difficulties when one partner loves more than the other.'

'Yes . . . yes, that is true. My own marriage was arranged, of course.'

'Did you meet before the wedding?'

'Yes, I was allowed that privilege. It was quite modern; we were introduced and spoke to one another, but I knew before we met that marriage to Kesri was my destiny. I was the late Maharaja's only surviving child, but Kesri was his heir. Our alliance perpetuated the old family line.'

'I think you told me that you were only fourteen and Kesri can't have been much older.'

'We grew up together and, of course, the children have been a joy to both of us. I bore Kesri's first son, that cannot be taken away from me. Whatever happens I shall always be the senior wife.'

The way she said it startled me. 'Whatever . . . ?'

'Kesri wishes to take a second wife.'

I was surprised, although I had always suspected Kesri of having a roving eye. It had turned towards me in a speculative way, but I had been very much on my guard against giving him encouragement.

'I'm sorry,' I said inadequately.

'It is his right, especially since I cannot bring myself to be as modern as he wishes, but she is French and not of our religion. I am distressed because he is betraying the trust of my father by this marriage.'

There was really nothing I could say that would comfort her. Kesri was the master and he would do what he

117
117

wanted. If she accepted the situation he would give her as much of his attention as he could spare from his new love and perhaps one day he would turn to Rukmini once more.

'Does William know?' I asked.

'Yes, but we have not talked about it. With William, it is not necessary to speak. I know I have his sympathy.'

'Perhaps . . . more than sympathy?'

I was pushing against the barriers of her reserve and when she said, very quietly, 'We are friends – anything more is unthinkable,' I knew that the subject would never be mentioned between us again.

In the meantime, the lessons continued and suddenly it was Christmas. Edmond got very sentimental about it: our first married Christmas, our first Christmas in India. He regretted the traditional white Christmas we might have had in England, but I remembered the slushy snow and chilblains and was perfectly happy to substitute a visit to Breach Candy Swimming Baths and lunch at the Club for roast goose and plum pudding in the cold of an English winter.

We had already dealt with the servants, who had filed in to congratulate us on our *burradin*.

'I don't see why they get presents when they're not even Christian,' Edmond grumbled.

'It's the custom and Christmas is supposed to be about giving rather than receiving, isn't it?'

He did his part graciously enough when it came to it and they went off looking delighted, which made Edmond suspect that we had been over-generous.

'Just as you've been too generous to me,' I said quickly, fingering the gold pendant set with rubies and pearls around my neck. I shut out the memory of another pendant, much more modest, which lay at the bottom of my jewel box, never worn but never quite forgotten.

'Glad you like it,' Edmond said. 'I'm as pleased as Punch with my gramophone. Clever girl to have thought to order it so far in advance.'

With the Christmas spirit restored we went off to attend

the service at St Thomas's. That was more or less obligatory, and I enjoyed it, even though I was not wallowing in nostalgia like the rest of the congregation.

When we got back from the Club we put on one of the records I had bought as part of Edmond's Christmas present and began to dance. To tell the truth, we were both a little drunk and eventually we tripped over one another's feet and collapsed on the sofa in a laughing tangle.

Edmond began to get amorous, just as I had known he would. I ought to have felt the same way myself after our happy, festive day, but somehow I could feel nothing more than a slightly weary distaste for the whole boring business. I looked up at Edmond and saw that he had his eyes closed and his face was flushed and had the swollen look about it I had come to recognise, as if he were puffing himself up like a bullfrog seeking a mate. It came to me then, realising that he was quite unaware of my scrutiny, that when Edmond made love he went away inside himself, savouring his own sensations and oblivious to mine. All that patting and stroking was supposed to be for my benefit, but really it was prolonged to the point where I could have shrieked with impatience because Edmond enjoyed it.

He opened his eyes and whispered, 'We'd better go into the bedroom.'

It was the proper, decorous thing to do and I doubted whether Edmond would ever forget himself so far as to copulate in the sitting room. I led the way, but for once I did not allow him the pleasure of undressing me, lingering over the feel of my silk underwear and fine stockings in his hands. Instead, I tossed off my clothes and was in bed and waiting long before he was ready. We were joined and I did my part as well as I could, but all the time I lay beneath him I knew that I was alone, alone, alone.

I was deeply saddened in the New Year to learn that Kesri had announced his intention to marry a certain Madame

Antoinette Romains. I went to the house but, as I had expected, there was to be no dancing lesson.

'I'm leaving almost immediately for the palace of Arangapore,' Rukmini said. 'I wanted to go there for Christmas, but Kesri preferred to stay in Bombay and so the children came here. Would you like to meet them?'

'Very much. You don't observe Christmas, do you?'

'Not the religious rites, but the feast day, yes – why not? You told me you put out lamps for *Diwali*.'

'I've done that ever since I was a child,' I admitted. 'But this year I managed to stop myself from throwing coloured powder about for *Holi*!' I had managed to get her to smile and, indeed, there was a serenity about her that I had difficulty in understanding.

The children were enchanting, fine-boned replicas of Rukmini, but with a promise of Kesri's height. The oldest boy was ten, his brother was eight and the little girl, an adorable scrap with her mother's fine eyes, was four.

'And I have been granted a great joy,' Rukmini said as they filed out with their *ayah*. 'I am to bear another child.'

I was too astonished to speak. Another child? When her husband was about to marry a second wife?

'There have been many objections to Kesri's choice. The British Resident in Bhuredar – the representative of the Government, you know – has been strongly against the marriage. The new wife will not be given the title of "Highness". Kesri is furious about that and the marriage has been delayed while he argued. He has had to wait with great impatience for Madame Romains to be allowed to join him. He is a man and I am still his wife. Naturally he turned to me.'

It might seem natural to Rukmini, but I would have kicked him down the stairs.

'You don't understand do you?' Rukmini said with a slight smile. 'He is my husband and my lord. What he desires I give him, otherwise I do wrong in my own sight and by all the teaching of my culture.'

'I would be more rebellious,' I admitted.

120

'You have an independent spirit. I'm afraid it will not make you happy.'

There was no doubt about it, we simply breathed a different air. And I had been priding myself on my understanding of India and this, my Indian friend.

'About the dancing,' Rukmini said. 'Gopal will continue your lessons if you wish.'

I tried to imagine Gopal and his musicians installed in the flat and Mrs Hillson's reactions as what she called 'that native catawauling' wafted up to her superior apartment.

'He has a studio,' Rukmini went on. 'Not, perhaps, in a part of the city you would normally visit, but you will be perfectly safe.'

I went straight to Gopal after leaving Rukmini. I wanted to do something to keep my mind occupied. I was angry on her behalf and her smiling acceptance only fuelled my anger. Ghastly men! Would Edmond take a second wife if our laws allowed it? Like a shot he would, and much good it would do her if he gave her as little satisfaction as he gave me.

Gopal was his usual badtempered and uncompromising self. '*Memsahib*, you'll never be a dancer,' he said. 'You are old and your joints are set. If you had come to me ten . . . fifteen years ago then, yes, perhaps. You have an ear for the rhythm and you are beginning to understand a little, just a little, about the music. You have one thing Her Highness lacks, even though she is truly musical and her spirit is finer than yours. When you strike the earth with your foot you feel the earth respond. That is something that has been refined out of Her Highness. Because of that I will go on teaching you, if you wish it. The money will be useful and I can use it to take a pupil who can afford little.'

Up to then I had never paid for my lessons, but now I struck a bargain with him and went away feeling pleased, though Rukmini was right in saying that he lived in a most noisome part of the city.

I was surprised, indeed I was outraged, to receive some days later an invitation from Kesri to a reception he was

121

giving to introduce his new wife to Bombay society. Edmond was delighted and would not hear of our refusing it.

'A slap-up party at the Taj Mahal Hotel. We'll probably be the only *box wallahs* there,' he said. 'Well done, little thing.'

'Do you really think it's right to go, when Rukmini was so much my friend?'

'Why not? From what you say, she's accepted the second marriage, and it's not as if he's doing anything wrong, not according to his way of thinking.'

I allowed myself to be persuaded, though I was more than a little ashamed of myself. I knew I was going because, just like Edmond, I relished the chance to mix with high society and to mention the invitation – just in passing – in front of Mrs Hillson.

Edmond began to fret about what I would wear, but I had already decided. 'I shan't wear any jewellery, not even my pretty pendant,' I said. 'It's no use trying to compete with a Maharajah's store of jewels. I shall make my effect by being utterly simple.'

Edmond was appalled when he saw me on the night of the party, but I knew what I was doing. I had had a length of pure white silk crêpe made up into a pleated tunic which fell straight from the shoulders to my ankles. It was sleeveless, with a round neck, and pulled in loosely at the waist by a tied belt of plaited silver leather which matched the sandals on my feet. My feet were bare, which really shocked Edmond. In fact, I was wearing the minimum of underclothes since I knew that my unconfined breasts, pushing against the soft pleated fabric, would be more effective than anything a dressmaker could do for me. No jewellery, none at all, except that all through the elaborate knot in which my hair was dressed I had made the hairdresser twist and loop a long rope of artificial pearls. Amongst the parakeet crowd at the Taj Mahal I stood out like a statue descended from the Parthenon.

The new Maharani had decided to adopt Indian dress. She was a tall blonde woman with a very white skin. She had a fine body and, observing the way her splendid breasts strained against the tight *choti* she wore under her sari, I thought that Kesri was probably getting his money's worth. Her sari was a magnificent thing of shot silk, blue and green and gold, which changed colour with every movement, and the emeralds she wore must have seriously depleted the mine.

We were introduced and she spoke to me and to Edmond with vivacious charm. Her English was fluent but strongly accented. It was obvious that she had no idea who we were. She took note of my dress though, and I saw her eyes narrow for a moment as she registered the effect. She noticed, too, that Kesri greeted me by my Christian name and with a certain familiarity. She laid her hand on his arm for a moment, a fleeting, proprietorial gesture, and I realised she was showing me that he was hers and she would brook no rivals. I could hardly say so, but she was in no danger from me. I didn't want him, though he was a handsome creature, especially at that moment, arrogant with satisfaction at having won this new and lovely wife.

We knew almost nobody in the crowded room. There were plenty of Europeans there, but they were high officials from the Indian Civil Service – the 'heaven born' – or Army people, with whom we hardly ever mixed. This was obviously not the sort of party where anyone was introduced so I accepted a glass of champagne and smiled at the nearest man, who responded with pop-eyed pleasure.

'What a motley throng,' I remarked.

'Isn't it just? I've just got in from the *mofussil* and to be thrown into this – well! They tell me it's the new form of entertaining. Will it catch on, do you think?'

'Oh, surely! The maximum numbers with the minimum trouble – what hostess could resist it? What do you do up country?'

'District Officer.'

'Will the crops be good this year?' I was launched. Once ask a man about his job and you can safely let your mind wander, as I must admit mine did while my District Officer told me about the difficulties of his villagers. Edmond had fortunately run into a judge he knew, so I need not worry about him for the time being. I sipped my drink, listened with half an ear to a dissertation on irrigation and looked around me at the shifting, colourful gathering, coveting the jewels but knowing that it required more than a bazaar-made dress, however clever, to carry off the rivers of diamonds some of the ladies were wearing.

The next time I looked towards the Maharani Kesri had introduced her to a young Army officer and she was talking animatedly to him and her husband, using her hands in gestures that were at once expressive and graceful. I shifted slightly to get a better look at the new arrival. He was a splendid young man, tall and wide-shouldered. I could not see his face, but I did not need to. I knew that way he had of standing with one leg slightly forward and the knee bent, I knew the tilt of his head towards Antoinette as he listened to what she said. I knew the strong hands holding his glass and my fingers had played with that whorl of hair at the nape of his neck which would never lie down flat. He must have felt my gaze riveted on him because he turned his head and looked straight at me and there it was, the blue flash of the Arkadys: *Dominic*.

CHAPTER SIX

I thought I had got over it. I had told myself again and again that if ever Dominic and I ran across one another I would be able to greet him as an indifferent friend. It was not true. The shock of recognition was exactly the same as it had been when he had come home from the war. Something inside me said 'This is the man,' and I began to move towards him, leaving my District Officer in mid-sentence.

Dominic must have had sufficient command over himself to say something to the Maharajah because as I joined them Kesri turned towards me with a smile and said, 'You know one another? But, of course, I should have thought of the Arkady & Pershore connection. You look as surprised to see Dominic as I am myself, Jessica.'

'I was seconded to do some reconnaissance for the Prince of Wales' visit, but it's been postponed,' Dominic said. 'I had time on my hands so I gatecrashed Kes's party.'

'And I'm very glad you did,' Kesri said. His attention was claimed by another guest and he turned away with Antoinette, leaving the two of us isolated in the middle of that chattering throng.

'I didn't expect to see you,' Dominic said. 'I'm only passing through Bombay.'

'You found time to look up your old friend the Maharajah.'

'Kes and I were at school together.'

'Oh, don't tell me! You were his fag at Eton!'

'No, Kesri lived separately because of the caste thing, but we were friends even though he's older than me.'

'How nice for you. I expect you're wondering how little Jessica Bullen, twelve annas to the rupee, comes to be moving in such exalted circles? My friendship is with his wife – his real wife, not this blonde tart with her load of emeralds.'

'Don't talk like that, Jess, either about yourself or about the new Maharani. According to his way of thinking, Kesri has done no wrong. As for you . . . you take my breath away.'

He had taken my breath away, too, and not by making any special effort, just by putting on a uniform designed to be worn by a man with long legs, slim hips and a straight back, and standing about looking lordly. It was so unfair I could have burst into tears. He had done nothing except turn his head and look at me and I was hardly capable of standing up. Thank God for alcohol. I drained my glass of champagne and took another from a passing tray.

When Edmond came pushing his way towards us, his face beaming and his hand held out, I was completely astonished because I had quite forgotten that he, too, knew Dominic, had known him longer than I had.

'This is an unexpected pleasure, Dominic! How long will you be in Bombay?'

'I'm leaving tomorrow.'

Tomorrow! As he spoke, he turned towards me and I knew that he was as stricken as I was, though he was controlling it better.

'What a shame. I would have liked to have had a little party for you – an Arkady & Pershore party. Everyone would have been so delighted to meet you.' And what a feather in Edmond's cap it would have been to have flaunted his friendship with the son of the Chairman. 'Jessica has become a most accomplished hostess,' he added.

'I'm sure she has,' Dominic said, but he spoke automatically with his eyes fixed on me and we were both thinking, 'Tomorrow! What are we going to do?'

Edmond looked me over uneasily, still not reconciled to the way I had chosen to present myself that evening. 'I don't usually allow her to go around wearing fancy dress,' he said.

126

'She looks incredibly lovely,' Dominic said and then, very softly, he added, 'Aphrodite.'

It was the nearest he could come to a word of love. I smiled and blinked at him through a mist of tears, but I managed to save myself from a complete breakdown. Fortunately, Edmond was still asking questions. 'What news is there of Mr Matthew Arkady?'

'Very little. He stays much the same. He's able to hobble a few steps with the aid of sticks and he's got back his speech.'

'And Patricia?'

'Pat's been doing the Season and turning Mother's hair white. She appears to have had quite a success.'

'Is there a wedding in the offing?'

'I don't think so. Patricia has set her heart on coming out to India and I doubt whether she'll settle down until she's done that.' Dominic turned to me. 'She hasn't written?'

I shook my head.

'Pat's the world's worst correspondent,' Dominic agreed. 'She'll turn up on your doorstep one of these days and expect you to drop everything to show her around.'

'And she'll be very welcome,' Edmond said. 'Just as you would have been if you'd had time to visit us.'

'What time do you leave tomorrow?' I asked.

'My train goes at nine o'clock from Coloba.'

No time, there was no time. We were being forced away from one another and it meant as much to Dominic as it did to me, I was sure of it.

Edmond and I spent another hour at the party. An hour of circling the room watching Dominic moving from group to group, trying to get closer to him and constantly frustrated. It was both anguish and relief when Edmond decided he had had enough and wanted to leave. He insisted on saying goodbye to his host and on interrupting Dominic's conversation with the Maharani. Dominic responded with automatic good manners to Edmond's boisterous injunctions to look us up if ever he came to Bombay again, but it was me he looked at. Edmond shook hands with him, but I did not dare to touch him. We might both have disappeared in a flash of light and a puff of blue smoke.

We went home, Edmond delighted with his evening and very concerned when I said my own quieter reaction was due to an appalling headache. It made a good excuse to evade his pawing hands, but after he had humped himself off to sleep I lay beside him hour after hour rigid and wakeful.

By the next morning I had made up my mind. When Edmond left for the office I asked if the car could come back to take me into town as soon as he had been dropped.

'Don't overdo it, will you, little thing?' Edmond said. 'You still look a bit peaky. Not going down with anything, are you?'

'No, I'm all right. I'll go out while it's still cool and then take it easy for the rest of the day.'

'Do you call this cool?' Edmond eased his finger round the inside of his collar. 'It's the humidity I can't stand.'

I was on tenterhooks for him to go. As soon as he was out of the way I bathed and dressed in my coolest and smartest cotton dress. By the time the car returned I had already got my hat on. I caught up my gloves and handbag and ran down the stairs.

'Coloba Station.'

When we got to the station I told the driver to wait for me. If I could find Dominic, how long would we have? I had an uneasy feeling that he was one of those travellers who strolled on to the platform with a scant five minutes to spare. I walked the length of the train, but saw no signs of him. All round me the crowds which always thronged an Indian railway station swirled and eddied – businessmen in Western suits, villagers returning home with the spoils of their work in the city done up in striped cloth bundles, porters in soiled red jackets, anxious women with the ends of their saris pulled over their heads and held between their lips, one child on the hip and dragging another by the hand, water-sellers with clinking brass cups, tea-sellers shouting '*Tahsar char, garuni garum*', food trolleys selling vegetable curry and chapatis, a half-naked *sadhu* smeared with ash, Jains with masks over their mouths and a broom to sweep their path clear of insects, Sikhs in crimson turbans and Bengali *babus* in loose white shirts and trousers, three Muslim women shrouded in black *burkhas* escorting a little boy dressed in white satin like a prince – perhaps he *was* a prince – a Parsi lady who looked neither to left nor to right, and a sweeper in dusty pink cotton who cackled and put up her hand to hide her toothless gums. My head swam as the kaleidoscope broke and re-formed round me and then I saw him, towering over a group of small dark men from the South.

Just as we had at the reception the night before, we pushed our way through the crowd, but this time we were more desperate.

'I went to your flat,' Dominic said.

'I never thought of that. How long have we got?'

'Fifteen minutes. Get on the train with me.'

We found his compartment and collapsed on the seat in one another's arms, ignoring the curious crowds outside.

'I was wrong to let you go,' Dominic said. 'Wrong, wrong, wrong.'

'Does that mean your life in the Army hasn't come up to expectations?'

'No,' he admitted reluctantly. 'It's been everything I thought it would be. Until I saw you last night I thought I was happy. Oh, God, Jessica, why did you come to India?'

'Edmond's job . . .'

'You didn't wait long before marrying him, did you? When Pat wrote and told me I couldn't believe it.'

I pulled away from him, but half of me was pleased by his jealousy. 'That's not fair, Dom. You were married to the Army, why shouldn't I take Edmond? I couldn't see any other future for me. Grandfather chucked me out of the company and with jobs going to the men back from the war there wasn't much prospect of a career for me anywhere else. If I'd waited, dwindling away into an old maid, would you have married me some time in the future? I doubt it.'

'What are we going to do now?'

'Nothing. What can we do? If I stayed on this train and ran away with you there'd be no future for either of us.'

He had nothing to say to that, only pulled me closer and buried his face in my hair.

'We've been through this before,' I said. 'We parted then and we can do it again.'

'It's harder now.'

Indeed it was. Whatever I might think of Edmond's lovemaking, I had been educated. I knew now what I was giving up in sending Dominic away from me. My body raged for him and we had ten minutes . . . five minutes . . .

We were clamped together, his mouth devouring mine, when I heard a warning whistle. 'I must go . . .'

'Darling . . .'

'There's nothing to say. Let me go, Dominic.'

'If I come to Bombay again . . .'

'I don't know, I don't know. Let me go.'

Somehow I scrambled off the train. It began to move and I knew Dominic was hanging out of the window, but I didn't wait to see him being carried away from me. I walked out of the station and found my car.

'Where to, *mem*?'

I looked at the driver blankly, unable to think of any destination.

'Crawford Market?' he asked patiently. 'Club? Bazaar?'

'Breach Candy,' I said, coming to an arbitrary decision.

I swam myself into a state of exhaustion, drove home, collapsed on my bed and slept away the long, hot afternoon and only when I began to drift back to consciousness was I troubled by fevered dreams.

Edmond was convinced I had picked up some miserable Indian germ and was sickening for an illness. He wanted me to see the doctor, but no doctor could prescribe for my malady.

'You won't go to your dancing class, will you?' he asked the next day.

'I think it will do me good.'

'I don't like it, Jess. It was all very well when you were going to the Maharani's house, but going off to some obscure street to have a private lesson on your own, that's quite another thing.'

'I won't come to any harm.'

'I'm not so sure. In fact, I think I'll have to put an end to it.'

I stared at him, not believing at first that he meant it, but he did. 'You can't do that,' I said.

'I think I can. No more dancing lessons, little thing, and that's an order.'

I can't imagine what made me think I would obey him. Now, more than ever, I wanted this outside interest. I liked my dancing lessons. I was beginning to gain a certain proficiency. Even Gopal occasionally said a word of grudging approval. I had become intensely interested in the complex music, had even thought of starting to learn to play the sitar. Without a second's hesitation I decided to continue the lessons, paying the fees out of the housekeeping, and saying nothing to Edmond.

That same day I went out, wearing a discreet blouse and skirt, but carrying my neatly folded sari over my arm, and hailed a passing Victoria. Very reluctantly I had decided that it would be unwise to use the Company car since the driver was all too likely to tell Edmond where I had been and I had no wish to stoop to bribing him to keep quiet.

The Victoria driver was surprised when I told him where I wanted to go, as well he might be since Gopal's house was on the fringe of Kamatipura, which I had discovered was the red light district of Bombay, something which had been kept hidden from me when I was a child.

Although Gopal's own house was in a reasonably respectable street it was impossible to avoid passing some of the shabby houses with barred windows and girls lounging in the entrances. I felt angry and ashamed. Here we were, in the twentieth century, with women in the West shaking off the shackles men had imposed on them and these, my sisters, were still being sold into a sort of slavery by their families. But, of course, that was a very European way of looking at it. The trade was an ancient one and tolerated. There were more men than women in Bombay and men could not afford to marry young; the girls supplied a want and earned a living, even perhaps supported elderly relatives. Who was I to quibble when I had done much the same myself by marrying a man for the material advantages he could give me?

I had been to the house before, but then I had had the Company car. This was the first time I had had to linger on the pavement, paying off the Victoria. There was a small tea-house next door to Gopal's dwelling and the men sitting at the rickety tables and chairs which spilled out on to the pavement, drinking tea, smoking their foul cigarettes, talking endlessly, looked round in surprise at the sight of a European woman in the street. I kept my eyes down, conscious of their stares and of the fact that the narrow alleyway between the café and Gopal's house was in use as a urinal.

Gopal's house was surrounded by iron railings enclosing a few straggly shrubs and small trees. I pushed open the tall iron gate, rusting on its hinges. It was for all the world like entering the enclosure round some ancient and neglected mausoleum. I knew better than to go up the steps to the front door. Indeed, the steps were cracked and shoots of the shrubs had forced their way through the cracks. I went round to the side, past the living quarters and found the austere room where Gopal gave his lessons.

This was little more than a walled enclosure with a rattan roof, but it was clean and the polished floor was free of splinters and could be trodden on with bare feet. I went behind a screen in the corner of the room, donned my sari and was ready for my lesson.

I stayed for a full two hours, paid Gopal the fee we had agreed and left, only to realise once I was outside that I had no transport and there was not a carriage in sight.

There was an easy solution to that. I spoke to one of the loungers at the tea-shop and asked him to go and fetch me a Victoria. I took it for granted that he would be pleased to earn a few *paise* from this simple errand, but to my amazement the man replied in impeccable English, 'If you will take the trouble to walk to the end of the road you will find plenty of *tikka-gharis* in Foras Road.'

'Foras Road isn't respectable and I don't wish to go there.'

He rose from his seat and bowed. 'Madam, we did not ask you to visit this district. You came of your own accord.'

He sat down again and I thought I heard a subdued laugh. I turned away, furiously angry. It was the first time in the whole of my life that any Indian had treated me with less than courtesy. I would not have believed it possible that my simple request could have been refused, still less with an insolence that had come through the polite form of words.

I marched off down the road, picking my way through the debris of an Indian back street, avoiding a cringing dog, circling round a wandering cow, its ribs sticking out from its side, stepping fastidiously over what was all too likely to be human excrement, and inevitably attracting a following of wide-eyed children. The walls were daubed with slogans. My languages were spoken, not written, but I could make out *Hind Swaraj – Indian Home Rule* and beside it, in English, *India for the Indians*. Was that the reason for the man's antagonism? Had I stumbled on a centre for Nationalism?

There were, as he had said, plenty of carriages in Foras Road, but the first driver I spoke to said he was engaged to wait for his fare to emerge from one of the houses. I felt myself flushing with shame as I realised what he meant, but fortunately another driver spoke up and said he was free and would be happy to take the *memsahib*. Since he looked respectable and, indeed, even rather sorry for me, I collapsed into his ramshackle vehicle and was thankful to be taken home.

I was not going to allow a setback like that to put me off my classes, not when I had already taken the step of secretly defying Edmond. My treatment would have been different, I knew, if they had believed me to be a respectable Indian woman, but I could not leave home wearing native dress because of the risk of running into one of the other wives on my way out. Still, transport was cheap enough, goodness knows. For my next lesson, I hired a Victoria to take me to the Taj Mahal Hotel, changed out of my European dress in their luxurious cloakroom while it waited for me outside, then went on to Gopal's house. With the end of my sari over my head and my face concealed I did not attract so much as a curious glance. At the end of the lesson the same driver picked me up and I repeated the changing process in reverse. It lent a certain piquancy to my twice-weekly expeditions.

I got away with it for months. Edmond accepted without question my glib accounts of shopping expeditions and visits to other wives. Indeed, it was borne in on me that so long as Edmond had two clean shirts a day, enough to eat, comfortable living quarters and a companion in his bed he was not really interested in how I spent my days. He expected me to be at home when he returned from the office, he expected me to welcome him with a kiss and to have a drink ready for him, he liked me to look decorative and to be a good hostess, but as for opinions of my own or interests outside the home, he was pleased that I seemed to have dropped all that nonsense.

I went along with it. Buried deep inside of me was a hard core of misery and resentment, but it was not Edmond's fault that he was not the man I wanted. I had the sense to realise that Edmond was too set in his ways to be altered by anything I could do, and so I refrained from the chiselling away at their husbands that most wives seemed to indulge in and accepted him for what he was, a smug, goodhearted man with his head firmly buried in the sand.

Edmond had worries enough, without coping with an errant wife. There were labour troubles and *hartals* at the

134

mills, but when I tried to ask intelligent questions he told me not to trouble myself, so that I lost heart and gave him nothing but the mindless sympathy which was all he wanted.

The temperature began to climb and the humidity to increase. The exertion of my dancing classes had become increasingly tiring and I knew that the time was coming when I would have to take a rest.

When I walked out of the apartment block on a day in May it seemed as if I was having to push my way through the thick hot air and that it closed up behind me as I moved. The Victoria driver who had more or less adopted me was waiting. He knew the routine as well as I did. I only had to smile and nod and he set off for the hotel.

It was blissfully cool inside. For a moment I was tempted to order myself a drink and sit down in the lounge to enjoy it in comfort instead of driving myself into a lather of sweat with the strenuous exercises Gopal demanded. This would be my last lesson until after the rains, I decided. One more effort and then I would work at home to keep myself supple until the autumn.

Most unusually, when we were approaching Gopal's house the road was crowded with people. I could hear shouts and I saw a police vehicle. I remembered my suspicions about the Nationalists and wondered whether arrests were being made. It was impossible to get by so I told the Victoria driver to put me down so that I could walk the last few yards.

'Be sure to be outside Gopal's house in two hours' time,' I said to him. 'If there's going to be trouble I don't want to be left here without transport.'

'I will be here, *memsahib*.'

I was sure he would be, as I hadn't paid him for the outward journey, so I set out to edge my way round the excited crowd. As always, I kept my eyes down and my head covered. I was stopped, not by an Indian but by a British police officer.

'Just a moment, I'd like a word with you.' He had spoken in English and automatically I stopped and looked up, letting my head-covering slip back. 'I thought so. You're European. What are you doing here, dressed up like a Hindu?'

I began to frown, resenting his tone of voice. 'I'm going to a dancing lesson.'

'Not a very likely story, if I may say so, madam. We know you come here regularly. Your movements have been observed. I'll have to ask you to come with me for questioning. Get in the van, please.'

I looked in disbelief at the back of the van, already crowded with the men I had been accustomed to seeing sitting outside the tea-house.

'In there? With them?'

'Why not? You've turned yourself into one of them, haven't you?'

'You wouldn't dare put me in a van with men if I were really an Indian lady.'

'But you're not, are you? You've been associating with dissidents and acting suspiciously and I'm taking you in for questioning.'

I would have protested, produced proof of my identity, demanded to be allowed to send a message to Edmond, but the young man who had spoken to me so insolently on my earlier visit, who was already in the van, suddenly laughed and held out his hand to help me in. 'Come, sister,' he said. 'I'll give you my seat.'

As far as the policeman was concerned, that settled it. A known troublemaker had called me 'sister'. I was one of them.

I knew that there were Englishwomen who sympathised with the movement for independent India, but I had kept out of politics. I seethed with resentment at the injustice that was being done to me. I took the seat that the young man offered me, but I certainly didn't thank him for it.

He was standing over me, swaying with the movement of the vehicle as we drove off, and laughing. Laughing at me. 'Don't worry, they'll let you go,' he said. 'I'll tell them you aren't connected with the Movement.'

'Will they believe you?'

'Perhaps not,' he admitted.

'If they had only checked with Gopal,' I fumed.

'Ah, but old Gopal is in the thick of it with us. His testimony is not likely to do you any good.'

I was astounded and, for the first time, worried. Of course it was absurd. It would soon be established that I was a totally innocent passerby.

'You must admit you've been acting suspiciously,' the young man said. 'Turning up twice a week in disguise – why did you do that?'

'To deceive my husband.'

'With old Gopal? Now you really do surprise me.'

In an instant I felt myself transformed into an outraged *memsahib*. 'How dare you speak to me like that!'

'We are in the same boat, or rather van,' he pointed out. 'We are equals in the same predicament and I can say anything I like to you.'

'Not quite the same,' I pointed out. 'You're guilty, I'm not.'

'There is that,' he admitted. 'But the police have yet to be convinced.'

The van jolted on as I digested that unpalatable truth.

'How do you come to speak such good English?' I asked him.

'I am highly educated. In fact, I am a barrister-at-law.'

'Like Mr Ghandi!'

'Oh, you know that much, do you? I assumed you were completely ignorant. Yes, like the revered Mahatma, but unlike him I favour something more fullblooded than passive resistance.'

'If you admit that you'll be sent to prison.'

'Of course. That is what I want. By the time we take power every Indian politician worth his salt will have spent some time in jail. I shall be most disappointed if I am not confined.'

When we reached the police station I was separated from the other people and put in a room on my own, watched over by a scared-looking woman. I asked to be allowed to send a note to my husband and she pretended not to understand me. With such patience as I could muster I repeated the request in Hindi and then, when she still did not reply, in Gujerati. She was sufficiently surprised to answer, in English to my exasperation, that it would be allowed later.

I was beginning to be worried, but at first I was mostly concerned because this would mean that Edmond would discover my long deception. The room was insufferably hot. There was a ceiling fan, but it only turned languidly, scarcely moving the heavy air. I slumped in my chair, feeling sorry for myself, until it occurred to me that this long waiting period was a ploy to break my spirit, then I began to be indignant once more.

'I've been here over an hour,' I said to the woman. 'I'm a totally innocent person and the wife of a well-known businessman. Go and tell your superiors I demand to be set free.'

'Please, *mem*, door is locked,' she said, looking more frightened than ever.

'Do you mean they've locked us both in?'

'Please, *mem*, yes.'

'You haven't got the key?'

'No, *mem*.'

'Then the time has come for me to start making a nuisance of myself.'

The door was stout. I kicked it without making any impression or much noise, so I took my chair and hurled it at the door. To my great satisfaction one of the legs broke off. I picked it up and began beating a loud tattoo, at the same time shouting to be let out, to an accompanying chorus of 'No, *mem*, no,' from my little companion.

It took some time to get any result, but it was better than sitting around doing nothing. I was breathing heavily and perspiration was running down my forehead, but I kept up my persistent assault on the door until it opened. The policeman who had brought me in was outside.

'This has gone far enough,' I said. 'I demand my rights. I want a lawyer, I want a message sent to my husband . . .'

I broke off. The policeman had moved to one side and coming into the room behind him was Mrs Hillson.

'Is this woman Jessica Fardale, the wife of Mr Edmond Fardale?' he asked her.

'Yes.'

I think she was too shocked to say anything more. I must have been an extraordinary sight – hot, angry, wearing native dress and brandishing a chair leg. Poor Mrs Hillson, she had never had to deal with anything like it before in her life.

'Has Mrs Fardale been in the habit of taking lessons in Indian dancing?'

'She used to go to the Maharani of Bhuredar's house . . . but since the Maharani left Bombay . . . I thought she had given it up.'

'Well, I didn't,' I snapped. 'I've been taking private lessons, as I'm sure my teacher will confirm. I've had nothing, absolutely nothing, to do with politics. I saw a few slogans on the walls, but I took no notice; you can see them anywhere. I was going about my legitimate business, doing no harm to anyone, when this . . . this *officer* put me under arrest.'

'You're not under arrest,' he said. 'You've merely been invited to come in and answer a few questions.'

'Invited! That's rich. You force me into a van full of men – though I won't make any complaint about that because they treated me with rather more consideration than you did.'

'You've been in the habit of leaving Gopal's house in a sari and going to a hotel to change into European dress before going home. Why did you do that?' he demanded.

'Because I disliked being stared at in the street.'

Of course in the end I had to admit that my husband had not known what I was doing. The policeman looked triumphant, but only for a few minutes. He knew he had behaved arbitrarily and, reluctantly, he began to accept that he had been mistaken about my suspicious behaviour. He had to let me go.

As we were leaving I saw a disconsolate group of men

139

in one of the outer rooms. Amongst them was the young barrister – I did not even know his name – who had been picked up with me. Since I had last seen him he had collected a split lip and a nasty bruise over the temple from which a slow line of blood was running down his face. He caught my eye and made a rueful movement of his lips.

'How did that man get hurt?' I asked the policeman.

'Resisting arrest. Don't waste any sympathy over him. Perhaps you aren't aware that the reason for this round-up is that there's been an explosion in the city. There's not much doubt he was involved.'

'Resisting arrest? But he *wanted* to go to prison!'

'He may have said so. Reality is a different thing.'

I looked hard at the policeman and he met my gaze stolidly. 'See that he gets proper medical attention,' I said.

'Of course. Will you please leave now, madam.'

On the way home I discovered how Mrs Hillson had been dragged into it. My appalled Victoria driver had seen me being taken away and, with considerable intelligence, had gone to the apartment to tell my servants. They, knowing the hierarchy of the Company, had reported the story to the senior lady, Mrs Hillson. To do her justice, she had come immediately to my aid.

'I suppose it's no use asking you not to tell Edmond,' I said.

'I expect you to do that, Mrs Fardale,' she replied.

'I'm grateful for your help,' I said through gritted teeth.

'I did no more than my duty, though I can't say it was pleasant and certainly not what one expects of a Company wife. I can only hope you've learnt a lesson, Mrs Fardale. You've never really settled down and become one of us. I'm prepared to be your friend if you will let me, but these odd ways simply won't do, you know.'

Of course, I deserved everything I got from Edmond. I half-hoped some word of what had happened would have filtered through to him, but it was obvious as soon as he got inside the flat that he knew nothing. Reluctantly, I gave Mrs Hillson credit for not having sent a message to the Mill. No doubt she was making up for it now by spilling out the story to her husband . . . as I was going to have to tell mine.

'It's like a steam bath outside,' Edmond grumbled. 'The thermometer in my office registered ninety-eight, and that was with the fan going.'

'Go and have a bath and change. I'll have a nice cool drink waiting for you.'

I already had two bottles of beer standing in a bowl of cracked ice and I whipped one open and poured out the drink as soon as he came back through the door, his hair still damp and wearing a fresh shirt and light trousers since we were not going out that night.

'Ah, wonderful!' Edmond said. 'What a good little wife you are.'

'You won't think so when you hear what I've got to tell you.' I took a deep breath and plunged in. 'I got myself arrested this afternoon.'

I had expected him to be angry, but what was difficult to face was that Edmond was wounded, deeply and bitterly hurt, by my long deception.

'Aren't you indignant about the way the police treated me?' I demanded, trying to turn his mind away from my own wrongdoing.

'Yes, of course . . . that policeman obviously went too far and I'll make a protest about it, but he was right in saying you'd been acting suspiciously. Four months . . . you'd been doing this for four months without telling me?'

'Yes.'

'Every week . . . twice a week, I came home and asked what you'd been doing and you lied to me.'

'I never told a direct lie, I just left out the dancing lessons.'

'Don't quibble. It boils down to a lie. Why? Why did you do this to me? I thought . . . I thought there was a better understanding than that between us.'

141

'You forbade me to go on with my lessons. *Forbade* me, Edmond. As if I were a little child to be told what I could or couldn't do. You simply didn't understand how much I needed this outside interest, so there seemed no point in arguing with you.'

'When have I ever been unreasonable? I would have tried to see your point of view.' He might have tried, but he would not have succeeded. I bit back that retort and kept silent as he went on, 'If you wanted an interest outside the home surely there are plenty of worthwhile projects – charitable work, hospital visiting – other women seem to find plenty to do.'

'Endless committees run by amateurs. I wanted something more than that.'

'So you took up silly posturing to music no one can stand to listen to.'

'An ancient culture which you have to be educated to understand. Don't worry, I've given it up now.'

'You certainly have! And you had to call in Mrs Hillson to get you out of jail! Of all people!'

We were in accord about that, but for different reasons. Edmond had his mind fixed on his standing in the Company and he couldn't decide whether it was better for Mrs Hillson to believe that he had condoned what I was doing or for her to know that he had been ignorant of my goings on.

'This damned country,' he burst out. 'I thought it was a good move, coming out here, but I don't know . . . the heat, the filth, the unhealthiness, it's getting me down. I have endless trouble with my staff. If one of them makes a mistake he'll move heaven and earth to conceal it instead of owning up like a man. I wanted to clear a desk to lay out some papers today and the clerk I asked to move a typewriter out of the way sent for another man to lift the machine from one desk to another because moving typewriters wasn't his job. Getting work done on time means keeping up endless pressure. Yes, yes, they say – straight away, Mr Fardale, immediately today, Mr Fardale –

and we all know that when I ask again tomorrow nothing will have been done.'

It was more than my shortcomings that had caused this outburst. 'Do you want to go back to England?' I asked.

'I want . . . I'll tell you what I want. A cool day and soft rain on the dales. Green grass under my feet and primroses in the hedgerows – new lambs and a dog you can pat instead of a cringing *pi*-dog which may be carrying rabies. I'd even put up with the smoke and noise of Manchester for the sake of a man who'll look you in the eye and give you a straight answer to a straight question.'

He was homesick. I had never even thought of it, but then I was not similarly afflicted since coming back to India had been like coming home to me.

'You don't understand, do you?' Edmond asked, with a bitter little smile. 'Just now, you didn't say did I want to go home, you said "back to England". You don't feel yourself to be in exile like I do. And I can't give up. It would look like failure.'

'We've both been lacking in understanding,' I said, speaking slowly because I wanted to find the right words. 'I'm sorry. I didn't know you felt like that.'

I had not meant to apologise about the dancing lessons, but now I made myself go on, 'And I'm sorry about carrying on with the dancing when I knew you disapproved.'

'It's the deceit that sickens me. But there, I should have expected it. You're one of *them*, aren't you?'

For a moment I was so shaken by anger that I was unable to reply, which was just as well because it gave me time to recognise the bitterness behind his words, the wish to hurt to get his own back.

'I'm what I've always been. No better, no worse. Forgive me, Edmond, please.'

He made no reply except a futile gesture with his hand, but when I poured out his second bottle of beer he did not refuse to take it. I sat down on the floor by the side of his chair and after a moment I felt him touch the top of my head. I pulled down his hand and laid it against

143

my cheek and all the time something inside of me stood on one side and watched derisively. I was acting a part, just as I had always acted a part with Edmond, and in my own estimation I belonged in Foras Road.

We were reconciled, largely because of the way I abased myself. To show that I was forgiven Edmond wanted to make love that night and I lay still and let him enjoy himself. What did it matter whether I received him enthusiastically or not? He was not likely to notice.

What was unusual was that he wanted to talk afterwards. Usually he gave me a last hug, turned over and went to sleep. Tonight he said, 'I've been thinking. If you need another interest so badly perhaps we should change our minds about not having a family just yet. Would you like me to give you a baby, little thing?'

I was stiff with horror. Of all possible complications this was the last one I desired.

'I think I'd rather wait,' I said carefully.

'Why don't we just let things take their natural course? If it happens, well and good – I must say I'd like a son – if it doesn't we'll just be patient.'

That meant he was going to discontinue the precautions he had always insisted were necessary. Never mind, I could deal with that. I was no longer the ignorant girl he had married and the other young wives had gossiped. There were other methods and they had revealed that the Company doctor was sympathetic towards wives who wanted to delay their pregnancy until they returned to a less demanding climate and would supply what was necessary.

Not for the first time, I lay wakeful while Edmond slept. It seemed that no sooner had I repented of one deception than I was preparing to embark on another and the reason I was so determined not to bear a child, not here, not now, was because I still hoped, against all reason, that if I remained free of that tie then there might be a way for Dominic and me to be together. He had sent me no word since we parted. I told myself he was right to cut himself off completely, but even the smallest scrap of paper with his writing on it would have been some consolation. And now I was to lose the one thing that had given me an outlet for my frustration.

I thumped my pillow, angry once more at being deprived of what I had come to think of as my art, and in such a way. Unbidden, the face of the young agitator came into my mind and with it a disquieting question – how had he really come by that nasty wound on his head?

CHAPTER SEVEN

Inevitably, my brush with the police became known. I knew it would, even while I was agreeing with Edmond that we would say nothing to anyone about it. The Hillsons, I believe, kept quiet, but of course the servants talked. I knew better than Edmond how quickly a choice bit of gossip passed from one household to another and I was braced and ready the first time someone twitted me on my criminal record.

'Quite the most interesting thing that's happened since I came to Bombay,' I said, borrowing the offhand, airy lightness I had learnt from the Arkadys. 'From now on I'm a marked woman. I won't even dare to walk on the grass in the wrong place. I mean, I'm *known*. And, of course, I did break one of their chairs. I'm surprised they haven't sent a bill for the damage.'

Fortunately, since Edmond failed to see that this was by far the best way of dealing with it, we were able to get away for a holiday. We went to Ootacamund for three weeks and celebrated our first wedding anniversary there, though not, as Edmond hoped, by conceiving the son and heir he had decided he wanted.

On the whole the holiday was a success. I liked being in Ooti and Edmond had made up his mind to be forbearing which, while it was sometimes difficult to accept, was better than the reproaches he had loaded on me in Bombay. The new faces, the better climate, the pleasant surroundings all helped. I became the sociable little wife who gave good dinner parties once more and we had several convivial evenings with our new acquaintances. I flirted discreetly with the young men and Edmond pretended to be jealous, knowing full well that there was nothing in the smiles and hand squeezes.

By working hard at it I kept myself from thinking about

Dominic. It was difficult because many of these tall young men with time on their hands who looked at me with longing eyes were just like him, nonchalant and assured and immensely attractive, with a charming diffidence in their manner which stopped them seeming arrogant.

By the time we returned to Bombay the Hillsons had left for their own holiday and we were spared Mrs Hillson's heavy silence about my misdemeanours. That left Edmond in charge of the Finance Department for the first time, something he took very seriously. He was rather put out when the sudden death of the Maratha Nationalist leader, Bal Gangadhar Tilkar, brought a renewal of the trouble which had simmered in the city throughout the year. The funeral was held on 31 July, right in the middle of the rainy season, and the city was paralysed by a shut-down as near total as made no odds.

'Better not go out today, little thing,' Edmond said, though he insisted on trying to get to the office himself. For once I had no wish to disobey him.

'Where is it going to end?' I asked him. 'When people are determined to gain independence, half-measures won't satisfy them.'

'Have you ever come across an Indian politician who was fit to govern?'

'I haven't met any politicians at all – and neither have you,' I pointed out.

'I haven't been impressed by the petty officials I've talked to. There may be one or two at the top . . .'

'Mr Ghandi?'

'He doesn't want power, or so he says.'

'He must be enormously impressive,' I said thought-fully. 'I'd like to hear him speak.'

'Please, Jessica, I don't want to come home to find you've been picked up for joining in one of the demon-strations round Ghandi.'

'Don't worry, I won't get into trouble,' I promised.

I was thinking again about the young barrister who had been so determined to get himself into prison in order to prove his credentials. Was he out there taking part in the mourning for his dead leader or was he still shut up?

The strike petered out and everything seemed to return to normal. The rains ended, to Edmond's relief, and the Hillsons returned, which he regretted. The winter social round would soon be on us and this time, because I knew what to expect, the prospect bored me.

I was yawning my way through a novel one day after a solitary lunch when the doorbell rang. I took my feet off the sofa where I had been sprawling, shook up the cushions, put down my book and went to look in the mirror to smooth my hair. It was probably only one of the wives come to talk about a picnic on the beach or a sale of work, but any diversion would be welcome.

The card on the silver salver which the bearer presented to me was such a surprise that I ran out into the hall without waiting for him to show my visitor in. 'Patricia!'

'Hello, Jess. Yes, it's me. Are you "at home"?'

'Of course I am. You wretch, why didn't you let me know you were coming?'

'You know me. By the time I got round to writing the letter would have come out on the same ship so it hardly seemed worth bothering. I say, you look stunning. If that's what marriage does for you maybe I should try it.'

I passed over that. For the time being I had no wish to indulge in confidences with Patricia Arkady about my marriage.

'I presume your father isn't with you or Edmond would have known,' I said.

'Quite right. Father has stayed in England to mind the shop and Mother has brought me out to make my curtsey to the Viceroy. I'm one of the fishing fleet.'

She pursed up her lips, mocking the idea that she needed to come all the way to India in search of an eligible young man. She was looking wonderful, and incredibly smart, with skirts far shorter than anything we had yet seen in Bombay and a close-fitting cloche hat which I would never have been able to fit over my mass of hair.

With a twist of her hand Patricia pulled off her hat and threw it on a chair.

'You've cut your hair!'

'Of course.' She patted her short, thick bob. 'Do you like it.'

'On you, yes.' With her neat, slim figure and her gamine charm, Patricia was everything a nineteen-twenties girl should be. The new fashions might have been made for her and she knew it. 'Poor old me,' I said. 'I can see bosoms and long hair are out.'

'Oh, absolutely! You'll have to wear a flat bodice and get your hair bobbed. Rather a pity, really, because you look marvellous, in your sweet, old-fashioned way.'

'Viper. Oh, Pat, it is good to see you. No one here laughs like we used to. How long are you staying?'

'Only a few days in Bombay. I told you, I've got to go to Delhi. Mother made it a condition of coming out here. After that, of course, we're planning to visit Dominic.'

'Yes,' I said. 'Of course.'

There was a moment's tense silence and then Patricia plunged into speech. 'Dom wrote and said he'd been here in Bombay and caught a fleeting glimpse of you. Looking ravishing, he said, which I can see is true. I say, Jessica, it is all right, isn't it? I mean, you and Dominic . . . You are happy, married to Edmond?'

So Dominic had not told her about our desperate realisation that we were still in love. I was glad about that.

'Edmond and I get along very well,' I said steadily. 'At least, we do when I'm not being madly disobedient and getting myself arrested.' I told her the story and Patricia rocked with laughter.

'Oh, you are lucky!' she said. 'Real adventures while I've just been dancing and dining in dreary old London.'

'What about the Prince of Wales? I was expecting to hear you'd landed him.'

'I danced with him several times, but to no avail. I think he's only interested in older women, and married ones at that.'

'And is there no one else?'

'No one who matters. Not now. During the war . . . I never told you, but there was someone. That's all over and done with and forgotten now, but I seem to have lost the knack of falling in love. I do try, but I'm awfully easily put off. Mother favours me getting hitched to my cousin, the dook's son, but I couldn't marry a man who parted his hair in the middle, could you?'

'Not easily,' I agreed. 'I suspect you'll fall for one of Dominic's friends. The uniform is most enticing.'

'Mm, possibly. It would be rather nice to marry into Dom's regiment.'

'Provided the Colonel doesn't think your young man's *too* young.'

'Oh, I'm sure we could get round that,' Patricia said and then caught herself up short, realising what she had said.

'Don't worry,' I said. 'I always knew Dominic's age was only one of the reasons why my marriage to him couldn't be permitted. I came out of the wrong class with the wrong blood mix, didn't I? Don't look so stricken, Pat. It's water under the bridge and I've learnt to accept it.'

'Have you really? When I first heard you were going to marry Edmond I couldn't believe it. I mean, dear old Edmond's been around for ever and no doubt he's the salt of the earth, but after *Dom* . . . How could you, Jess?'

'If any other solution had been offered to me, even if it had been an engagement lasting for years, then I would have waited for Dominic. As it was, he was lost to me and I had to do something with my life. Edmond had been pestering me to marry him. My mother and his father both wanted it. An arranged marriage can work quite well, you know.'

'If you really don't regret it then it's a great weight off my mind,' Patricia said. 'I've always been afraid it was something I let slip that made Grandfather realise you and Dom were meeting.'

'He was bound to find out,' I said.

The memory of that snowy day came back with the

familiar shame and anger. Damn Patricia! Had she really given us away by accident? She had been jealous of me, but that seemed to be forgotten now. I was glad when she went on in her inconsequential way to beg me to show her the sights of Bombay.

'Mother is talking about a duty dinner party for the élite of the Company. Will it be quite terrible?'

'Awful,' I said mechanically. I pulled myself together and went on, 'No, I shouldn't say that. They're quite nice people.'

'Dull, but worthy,' Patricia guessed.

'They'll love meeting you, the little princess,' I said unkindly.

'Ugh! I shall insist on you and Edmond being invited.'

'No need. Edmond is quite grand enough to be invited for his own sake.'

And he was dull but worthy, but that was not something I was going to admit to Patricia Arkady, any more than I was going to let her suspect how useless it had been to separate myself from Dominic.

Lady Cynthia gave her dinner party and Edmond was on tenterhooks until he was sure that we were on the invitation list.

'You must have a new frock,' he said. 'Nothing too striking,' he added nervously.

For once we were in agreement and I went to Lady Cynthia's party most decorously dressed in dark red silk, wearing the ruby pendant Edmond had given me. I thought of adding a red silk rose to the knot of hair I had dressed rather lower on my neck than usual, aiming at a look more Spanish than Indian, but Edmond looked uneasy, as if he might start murmuring about 'fancy dress', so I discarded it.

Patricia was wearing pale pink chiffon sewn with crystal beads, the skirt hanging in handkerchief points which swung and glinted as she walked.

'You look like the Sugar Plum Fairy,' I told her.

'Sweetly girlish, isn't it? I say, I've made the most marvellous plan. Better not tell you about it now or

Mother will start frowning because I'm not doing my duty amongst the serfs. Will you be in tomorrow?'

The serfs. So that was how Patricia thought of her father's employees. It grated on me, having been one of them myself, but I promised to be at home the next afternoon.

Lady Cynthia, in grey chiffon and pearls, looked younger than I had expected. She had a mass of ash blonde hair of the shade that edges imperceptibly into grey so that the gradual fading goes unnoticed. She was tall, with the straight back of someone who was never allowed to slump as a girl. She could never have been beautiful, her face was too long and narrow, but she had an air about her, I had to give her that. She gave no sign at all of being aware that in meeting me she was shaking hands with her father-in-law's granddaughter by his bastard son, nor did she betray by so much as the flicker of an eyelid that she knew I might have been her own daughter-in-law. To her, it seemed, I was just Mrs Edmond Fardale, the wife of a valued employee, but by no means the most important one present that evening.

Edmond was in ecstasies as we drove home. He said Lady Cynthia had been 'gracious'. I thought she had looked as if she was thinking about something else most of the evening.

I picked up the discarded silk rose from my dressing table while Edmond was in the bathroom and stuck it between my teeth, striking an attitude with one hand on my hip and the other raised above my head like a Spanish dancer. I had behaved like a tame rabbit that evening, and everyone had approved of me but I was not, I was *not* tame – and one of these days this wild rebellion in my blood was going to burst out.

'You know the Maharajah of Bhuredar, don't you?' Patricia demanded the next day. 'You must do because Dom said he saw you at his party.'

'I know his wife – his first wife – better,' I said.

'She's quite discarded now, isn't she? Holed up in some minor palace having a baby.' Fortunately, she did not give me time to say what I thought about the way Rukmini had been treated, but hurried on, 'Mother and Father know him well, of course, and he was at school with Dominic. I remember meeting him once or twice. Very handsome.'

'He's put on weight,' I said unkindly.

'Really? Alas for my girlhood dreams. I saw some pictures of him and his new wife when they got married and naturally they concentrated on her. The thing is, he's invited us to go to Bhuredar and stay in the palace at Arangapore and he says we must give him a list of friends we'd like to be invited, so will you come? And Edmond, of course.'

'I doubt whether Edmond could get away. We've had our annual holiday,' I said.

My mind was working furiously. It was enormously exciting to be asked to go and stay in a Maharajah's palace and I knew from the pictures I had seen of Arangapore that it was very beautiful, but what I really wanted to know was whether Dominic was likely to be there.

'If Edmond is chained to his desk can't you come without him?' Patricia asked.

'Lady Cynthia might not think it was quite the thing.'

'Mother isn't at all stuffy about that sort of thing, surprisingly enough. I've been on lots of house parties with her where there were wives without husbands – and with lovers, but I'm not supposed to know about that. Do come.'

'It's not as easy as you think. There'd be raging jealousy amongst the Company wives if I was invited to stay at Arangapore Palace.'

'You don't care what that parcel of dowds think, do you?'

'I have to live amongst them.'

'Poor you. I've divided them into dullards and gigglers. I'm not surprised you took up with the Nationalists. "Down with the *memsahibs*" would be my slogan if I lived in India. You don't actually know Mr Ghandi, do you? I die to meet him.'

'Patricia, stick to the point. No, I don't know Ghandi and if I did I wouldn't introduce him to you; you'd make his poor head whirl.' I had still not discovered the only thing which really interested me, and yet I could not bring myself to ask the bald question.

'I'd like to have a friend of my own in the party,' Patricia said. 'And you know so much about India. You can tell me all the history and everything.'

'My cousin William is the one you need for that.'

'Will he come? If Edmond can't?'

'William's somewhere in the wilds doing an excavation.' And the last thing I would want if Dominic was going to be in the party was William acting as a chaperone.

'Please come,' Patricia coaxed. 'I've written to Dominic and told him he's got to move heaven and earth to get his leave at the right time so that he can come and join us.'

'I thought he'd be joining you in Delhi to escort you to Ferozepore,' I said as casually as if my heart had not stopped beating.

'That was the original plan, but think what fun it'll be if he can be at Arangapore. You must come, Jessica.'

I made one half-hearted attempt to be sensible. 'I'll talk to Edmond,' I said.

I was not sure what I would do if Edmond refused to countenance my going to Arangapore without him. Part of me, I think, would be relieved at having the decision taken out of my hands, but the other part would have raged at being thwarted. I need not have worried. Edmond's face brightened as I outlined Patricia's plan.

'Can you get away?' I asked, knowing what the answer would be.

'Not a chance. I've had my holiday and if I take any more it'll jeopardise our home leave later on. Besides, it'd look a bit odd for the Chief Accountant to go off in the Chairman's wife's party to stay in a Maharajah's palace when higher-ranking staff are left behind. But you're known to have been Patricia's friend in England and I think you ought to go. It'll completely wipe out the memory of that other tiresome business with the police.'

'Won't you miss me?' I asked, still struggling.

'Of course I will. It'll be the first time we've been apart and you know I'm still crazy about you.'

Edmond was so pleased by my apparent reluctance to leave him that he came across the room to give me a hug and a kiss. As he held me in his arms he whispered, 'Don't you want to go?'

There is always a moment when it is possible to say 'No' to any temptation. I looked mine in the face and found it irresistible.

'Yes,' I said. 'I want to go.'

How to describe the beauty of Arangapore? It stood on top of a hill, at first sight more fortress than palace, with walls rising out of the sheer rock. The town clung to the foot of the hill, thronging with people dressed in more vivid colours than we saw in Bombay, who stopped to stare at the Maharajah's limousines which drove us from the railway station to the palace.

The road swept up in a great ramp, twisting round in a semi-circle to arrive at the platform where once the Maharajahs had alighted from their elephants. From there we walked through an open archway into the first courtyard. It was paved in white marble and in the middle there was a pool of water in which a fountain played. Then I saw that running diagonally from each corner of the courtyard were shallow channels lined with glittering blue tiles through which water ran to slide into the pool.

The courtyard was arcaded all round with white marble pillars supporting a carved wooden balcony above, but it seemed that there were no rooms behind this façade – it was merely an elaborate reception area, open to the sky.

Two servants in the blue, white and gold uniforms I recognised stood on either side of the great wooden doors on the far side. They swept the doors open and Kesri and Antoinette were waiting to greet us inside.

Patricia gave a surreptitious tug to my hand to get my attention. 'Much grander than Buckingham Palace,' she hissed.

I had a confused impression of richness and colour, of a mosaic on the wall of blue and gold and mirror glass which sparkled as the light changed, of furniture in the European style upholstered in yellow silk brocade and heavily gilded, of low tables of carved teak, and a floor patterned in subtle shades of marble and strewn with Kashmiri rugs. In his palace, I discovered, Kesri preferred to wear Indian dress, a close-fitting, high-necked tunic closed down the front by gold buttons, white silk jodhpurs, and slippers on his feet of gilded leather. By his side Antoinette shimmered in blue with a barbaric necklace of turquoises set in silver round her neck. She looked lovely, but my heart ached for Rukmini, who must be near her time, exiled to a minor palace to make way for this blonde beauty.

They were not alone. As Kesri introduced his new wife to Lady Cynthia I saw Dominic behind them, waiting to greet his mother. As she offered him her cheek to kiss I thought there was more duty than affection in the way he bent towards her and it occurred to me that they could hardly know one another. If Lady Cynthia's greeting to her son was cool, Patricia made up for it.

'Heaven to see you again, Dom! Isn't this the greatest fun? I never in all my life saw anything as thrilling as this place. Kesri, I don't know how to thank you for inviting us. Dom, isn't it beautiful? I always knew I'd enjoy India, but it's much, much better than I thought it would be and – look – we've brought Jessica with us.'

'Jessica.'

Dominic took my hand and it was there again, the instantaneous attraction that held us helplessly in thrall to one another. I thought he had gone slightly pale. Had he not expected to see me?

I suppose I said something, but the next few moments are a blank. Antoinette, I discovered, was suggesting that we should all go to our rooms and then, when we had had a chance to freshen ourselves after our long train journey, we could join her for afternoon tea.

'*Thé anglais,*' she said. 'But we have adopted it for many years in France and I find now that it is an institution in India.'

There were other guests, some of them French like Antoinette, some Indians from amongst the princely caste, three other English couples and two unattached young men. Because of this Patricia and I were to share a room. It was a very palatial room and we had our own Western-style bathroom, as well as other amenities.

'Just look at this ducky little balcony,' Patricia said, opening the doors on to a semi-circle of fretted stone jutting out from the wall. 'Real Romeo and Juliet stuff, except that Romeo would need a pretty good head for heights to climb up here.'

My Romeo would have climbed any wall to get at me, I knew that, but not with his sister sharing my room. I realised, as the thought sped through my mind, that already I had passed from the fear that I might be tempted to commit adultery to the realisation that it was almost inevitable.

I went out on the balcony, restless and disturbed. Far below on the plain, beyond the teeming little town, I saw the glint of water. There was a lake and in the piercing clarity of the afternoon light I could just make out the white marble Lake Palace, small as a toy, where Rukmini was waiting for the birth of her child.

We had our tea in the cool shade of a pavilion on the roof where the stone walls, pierced to catch every breeze that blew, made patterns of shadow and light on the floor. It was intensely civilised, from the choice of three different kinds of tea to the wafer-thin cucumber sandwiches and tiny macaroons handed round by silent, attentive servants. Kesri, I noticed, and some of his Indian guests were served from a separate table and by their own individual servant. It made me feel that I was taking part in an elaborate, and to me unnecessary, ritual.

'This is the first large party I've entertained at Arangapore,' Antoinette said. 'I hope you will all find something to amuse you. There are tennis courts, but not on this rock. Kesri had them built down in the town, which means that they are rather hot; tennis, I think, is an early-morning amusement. Riding, of course; we are planning to visit some of the old ruins, with horsedrawn vehicles for those who don't ride. There is to be a polo match and hunting for the men . . .'

'She means shooting,' Kesri said with a smile.

Antoinette grimaced at him. '*Bien sûr,*' she agreed. 'If the ladies wish to go shopping they have only to ask for a motor car. The silks are excellent and, of course, Arangapore is famous for its jewellery.'

'May one visit the *Palais du Lac*?' one of her French guests asked.

There was a barely perceptible hesitation and then Antoinette replied, '*En ce moment, non. Je le regrette.*'

I was sorry, too, but I was more anxious to see the woman who had been my friend than to visit her beautiful island home.

'It is hardly possible to have gardens here,' Antoinette went on, 'but the terraces are worth visiting, especially if the fountains are playing. Tomorrow, for anyone who wishes it, Kesri's secretary, who is very knowledgeable, will take you round the Palace and tell you the family history.'

'Very bloody,' Kesri put in. 'We've always been war-riors and the family feuds have been horrendous.'

We sat around talking idly in twos or threes until some people began to stir and move around. Dominic came and stood behind my chair.

'Shall we go and look at the terrace gardens?' he suggested.

Lady Cynthia was talking to Antoinette in a slightly laboured way. I suspected that her opinion of the new wife was much the same as mine. Patricia was laughing with the two bachelors, who had certainly been invited for her entertainment. Very sedately, Dominic and I saun-tered towards the door.

'Down this staircase,' he said.

The terraces were behind the Palace, each one a long length of stone paving with a carved balustrade and great pots of flowers and climbing plants rioting over the edge. Shallow flights of steps led down from one level to the next and on either side water tumbled in channels beside the steps to feed a pool and a fountain below.

'I suppose it's a miracle of engineering,' I said.

'Darling, I didn't bring you out here to talk about mechanics. There must be somewhere we can be alone for five minutes.'

'This is India. A gardener behind every bush.'

But two determined lovers can always find seclusion. On the lowest terrace, to which few guests ever descended because of the long climb back, the vegetation was rather more unkempt than it was higher up. There we found a stone bench in a corner behind a tiny pool, deep in the shadow, with bourgainvillea cascading all round it. We collapsed on to the seat with our arms round one another and kissed like two travellers in the desert finding water.

'I nearly died when I saw you walk in with Mother and Patricia,' Dominic said at last. 'That's twice you've done that to me, my pest, my angel.'

'Didn't you know I'd been invited? Didn't Patricia tell you?'

'Not her.'

'She thinks it's all over between us and I'm happily married to Edmond.'

'Don't mention Edmond,' Dominic said. 'When I saw him with you in Bombay, acting as if he owned you . . .'

'He does.'

'Don't say that!' Dominic set his lips to the hollow at the base of my throat. 'Don't say it,' he repeated with his lips moving against my skin.

I held him in my arms until he raised his head and found my lips again for a kiss so long and sweet that I felt my head swim. 'Dom, I'm not sure if it's love or lack of oxygen, but I'm afraid I may dissolve in bliss and float away,' I said.

159

Dominic gave a smothered chuckle. 'It's definitely love. Darling, it's going to be terrible, being under the same roof, if this is all we can have. Can I . . . will you let me come to you – tonight . . . any night?'

'I'm sharing a room with your sister.'

'Dear God.' In his perturbation Dominic got up and went to the edge of the balustrade, staring out blindly over the landscape shimmering in the late afternoon sun. I went and joined him and we stood shoulder to shoulder.

'When I accepted this invitation I didn't admit it to myself in so many words, but the truth is I expected that before the end of it we would have become lovers,' I said. 'It's not going to be possible, is it?'

'We could confide in Pat, make some arrangement . . .'

'No!' I shuddered away in horror at the idea of Patricia conniving to make opportunities for us to go to bed together.

'She'd be our friend,' Dominic said. 'If you don't like the idea . . . I don't know.'

He cupped his hand round my cheek and I closed my eyes, savouring the gentleness of his touch.

'I can't tell you how I suffered that time in England when Mr Arkady interrupted us. If it happened a second time I think I'd die.'

'No, we must have peace and security. But if I can contrive something . . . you are willing?'

'Willing? My dear, I'd give everything I have for one night in your arms.'

When Dominic spoke he had a strange, rough edge to his voice. 'I didn't believe this happened. Not in real life, not to reasonable people like us. Ever since we met in Bombay I've known there's no hope of getting over it. I've got to have you. Come to my room – now.'

'Where is it?'

'In the East Tower. What Kesri calls the bachelors' quarters,' Dominic answered reluctantly.

We both fell silent, knowing that for me to be seen with Dominic in the East Tower would be an open admission that we were lovers.

160

'There'll be nobody about,' Dominic urged. 'You're not worried about servants' chatter, are you?'

I was not worried what anyone might say, provided that our liaison was going to lead to something permanent, but we had not given ourselves the chance to discuss that.

'If we ran into the other men . . .'

'They wouldn't give us away.'

'Your friends might not, but I wouldn't put it past one of Antoinette's French guests to pass on a choice bit of gossip,' I retorted.

'If you can't come to me there I don't know what to suggest.'

The idea of a divorce came into my mind, but for the time being I suppressed it. Edmond would certainly insist on Dominic being named and what would that do to Dominic's career?

We wandered back up the terraces and as far as I could see no one had remarked on our absence. In the days that followed we became more daring. It was like a game of hide-and-seek with our fellow guests, with snatched embraces and smothered laughter as our prize for eluding them. To me it seemed as if oxygen had got into my veins so that my blood fizzed and bubbled and my feet hardly touched the floor as I skimmed towards another meeting with Dominic. As for Dominic, half the women in the party were in love with him and who could blame them? Dominic on horseback in jodhpurs and a silk shirt was like a young god, gilded by the sun.

We went to visit the ruins of an ancient temple and I chafed at my inability to ride by his side. Instead, I sat in a light carriage with his mother and we both kept our eyes on him as we jolted over the rough ground.

'This is where your cousin William excavated,' Kesri told me. 'His work has pushed back the knowledge of our culture by thousands of years. What he found here was a revelation. You must be very proud of him.'

'Yes . . . yes, I am,' I said, humbled – and not for the first time – by the realisation that William was a far greater man than he was given credit for in the family.

161

We picnicked in the shadow of the old carved stones and wandered afterwards among the courtyards which had been lost until William had rediscovered them. Dominic would have pulled me into the inner sanctum where the great black granite *lingam* still stood, a silent symbol of our own overwhelming desire, but for the only time in those foolish, reckless days I resisted him and I knew that it was because I could feel William's quiet presence in that haunted place, not judging me, that was not William's way, but not accepting either that what I was doing was right.

As well as the torment and the bliss of my love for Dominic I was also having to cope with not being quite at ease in the party Kesri and Antoinette has assembled. They all seemed to know the ropes so much better than I did, accepting their entertainment as if they had a right to it whereas I had to bite my lip to stop myself saying thank you all the time. They talked easily together, too, in a mixture of French and English, and my knowledge of Hindi was not required, except when speaking to the servants. Even Patricia seemed to know who they were talking about when they spoke of 'Theo' or 'Marcia' or 'Bob's little problem'. Presumably it would come to me, too, this careless social manner, if I ever joined the world they inhabited as something more than a visitor.

Kesri had not forgotten his obsession with the cinema and one of the projects he had thought up to entertain his guests was to rig up a camera and take moving pictures of us. He had a man to carry the heavy camera and tripod and two more to scurry round doing his bidding, but it was Kesri who actually peered at us through the lens and turned the handle.

We moved self-consciously about the terraces and through the courtyards and a couple of nights later he showed us the results. There were shrieks of laughter as well as groans and protests that 'No, no, one did not look like that! *Pas possible!*' My appearance came as a shock to me, too. I knew what I looked like in the mirror, but to see myself in motion was something different. Was

162

that really me, that siren with the undulating walk and seductive smile?

It must have been because Kesri remarked, 'You are a natural for the camera, Jessica. If I had my way and I could establish an Indian film industry I could turn you into our Theda Bara.'

'But surely there have already been Indian films?' someone asked.

'Yes, but to me it seems that there's an immense audience waiting for entertaining films. We've had news reports – the film of the 1911 Durbah was a great success – and D. G. Phalke made *Raja Harischandra* before the war and showed it round the villages. He hauled the screen and projector and reels of film on bullock carts. One of the great difficulties, of course, is that we don't like our women to appear on the screen and although we have male actors who can take the roles on stage it's difficult to sustain the illusion in front of the camera.'

I was amused by his regrets about the difficulties of finding Indian actresses because it had been quite obvious that Kesri had not really liked Antoinette being filmed and had tried to discourage her from taking part. I was interested in Kesri's belief in the potential audience for films, especially in the villages. It would not even be necessary to erect special buildings. In the long hot nights a simple screen and a projector would be all that was necessary. As for the making of the films, the brilliant light and reliable weather would be as conducive to film-making as they were in California. All that was lacking was someone with money and enthusiasm to make a start. Someone like Kesri, except that he was probably too grand to involve himself.

In the face of Antoinette's definite refusal of a visit to the Lake Palace I had dropped my half-formed plan of asking if I might see Rukmini, but Lady Cynthia had no such inhibitions.

'I knew her well when Steven and I were living in Bombay,' she said. 'I'd be sorry to be so near and miss the chance of seeing her. Kesri is arranging it and I'd like you to accompany me.'

It meant a whole day away from Dominic and the way she put it made me feel like a lady-in-waiting, but I agreed immediately.

One of Kesri's luxurious limousines took us to the lake-side and Lady Cynthia kept up a steady stream of comment about the passing scene. It was the first time we had been alone together for any period and I had thought I might find it awkward, but Lady Cynthia's social manners were equal to any situation and, to my surprise, I found myself enjoying our journey.

There was a small boat waiting for us at the quayside with servants in the usual blue, white and gold. We rowed out until they could find the semblance of a breeze and then they hauled up a sail and we tacked and glided towards the white marble palace which seemed to float on the water. It was a place of enchantment. Arangapore Palace, I saw now, was masculine, but the Lake Palace was feminine, all rounded curves and delicate carving, garnished with mirror mosaic and intricate tracery.

Rukmini was touchingly pleased to see us. She embraced us both, a most unusual gesture. She was obviously very near her time, her belly swollen under the folds of her sari, and for the time being she had lost the grace which had once distinguished her. She seemed glad to sit down once she had greeted us and I noticed that her fine-spun wrists and ankles were disfigured by swelling.

She scolded me when she discovered that I had given up my dancing lessons. 'As for me, I think my dancing days are over,' she said. 'But you should go on, Jessica.'

I suppressed the story of my brush with the police. I thought it might distress her and at that moment I wanted to save Rukmini from any upset. When I told her instead that I had visited the ruins William had excavated, her face lit up.

'Those months when William was with us were very happy,' she said. 'I'm ashamed to say that I had never before known very much about India's past; now it is one of my great interests. Have you seen our Ashoka pillar? That, I think, is one of the real wonders, that a decree inscribed on a pillar two thousand years ago should have survived and been deciphered by an Englishman and that it should have led us to understand our own forgotten history.'

We stayed until the heat of the day began to diminish.

'I would have liked you to have seen the sunset over the lake,' Rukmini said.

'Another time,' I suggested.

'I hope so.'

Lady Cynthia had something else to say to her, very quietly on their own, before we left. I thought it was probably to do with the imminent birth and I did not intrude. As we sailed away in our little boat I looked back with regretful eyes. In spite of what I had said to Rukmini I doubted whether I would ever visit the Lake Palace again.

'She's a fine person,' I said. 'I can't understand how Kesri could have put her away in favour of . . . of anyone else.'

'Perhaps she was *too* fine for him,' Lady Cynthia suggested. 'Naturally it was an arranged marriage. Rukmini comes from the true nobility, a very old line, but Kesri was merely adopted.'

'I had heard that.'

'It's very often done, of course, when the succession has failed. The old Maharajah chose Kesri almost at random from a selection of boys with some slight connection with the family and he was brought up and educated to become Maharajah in his turn.'

'An English education. Do you think that is a good thing?'

'On the whole, no. We've applied a veneer instead of polishing the natural wood. Still, Kesri has done well and Rukmini has already given him two sons and a daughter.'

'So now he can be allowed to please himself?'

'He still has a great affection for Rukmini.'

'Otherwise she wouldn't be expecting another baby,' I

agreed with a touch of bitterness. 'Do you think she looks well?'

'Far from it. In fact, as soon as we get back I shall tell Kesri he must get her off that island and into a proper hospital.'

'Good, he'll listen to you.'

'I hope so and now, child, will you listen to me?'

The breeze had failed us and the boatman had taken to the oars. Obviously it was going to be a slow return journey. Short of jumping in the water there was no way I could avoid what Lady Cynthia wanted to say to me.

'Are you in love with my son?'

It was impossible to lie to her. 'Yes.'

'Yes . . . I knew it, of course. I'm deeply troubled for you. What are you going to do?'

'I don't know. We just live from day to day.'

'The whole affair has been grossly mismanaged. If only I had been in England when it first began.'

'What could you have done? Dominic understood quite clearly that he couldn't have both me and the career he wanted.'

'Nonsense! He consulted my brothers. Boneheaded, both of them, and fifty years behind the times. As for my father-in-law, he's a fine businessman, but he doesn't understand what good connections can do. Dominic would have done better to have gone to his other grandfather.'

'The dook,' I said stupidly.

'Precisely. My dear girl, we're one of the oldest and grandest families in the country. If we had countenanced your marriage no pip-squeak colonel would have stood out against it.'

'If . . .' I said. 'But you didn't countenance it, did you?'

'When I came home I was told it was all over. What's more, the matter was presented to me as if you had been some ill-conditioned servant girl. When I met you I saw immediately that you were of a different quality altogether.

I stared out over the shimmering water, determined not

166

to cry, but almost blinded by the tears I was holding back. 'What am I to do?' I whispered.

'My advice is hard, and all the harder because of the reasoning behind it.'

'Don't tell me to give him up! Please, please, don't say that!'

She put her hand over mine and I was surprised by the warmth and firmness of her clasp. 'You think I don't understand, but I do. I know what it is to love a man. I was thought to have married beneath me, in spite of the Arkady fortune, and I had to fight a long fight to get my way. It's been a good marriage, too good perhaps; I stayed in India with my husband when I should have been at home with my children.'

'Why did you send them away? Bombay's climate is not so trying as in other parts of the country.'

'I know, I know. It was the custom and I conformed. Being with Steven was all that was important. Of course, the war prolonged the time we spent apart beyond what was reasonable. Since I have seen them as adults and got to know them better I've been overwhelmed by guilt for what I did to my children.'

'But they're wonderful. Beautiful, clever, interesting – more alive than most people.'

'All those things. And hollow. Inside these beautiful people there's a terrible emptiness.'

'No! Dominic loves me with all his heart and soul.'

'Dominic loves himself. And Patricia loves herself. Possibly they love one another. Certainly on Patricia's side there's an obsession with her brother. Dominic, I think, has shaken himself clear of it. I hope so, because it is far from healthy.'

'You're the one who isn't healthy! You make me feel sick.'

Lady Cynthia's ability to call a spade a spade was like a douche of cold water.

'I'm not talking about incest, not physical incest, but you can't have known Dominic and Patricia for so many

167

years without realising that they're far too taken up with one another.'

It was true, especially on Patricia's side, but that didn't mean anything else Lady Cynthia had said was true. Dominic did love me, as tenderly and truly as a man could. That I would hold to no matter what anyone might say.

'We love one another and I won't be separated from him, not again,' I said obstinately.

'Have you talked about a divorce?'

'No,' I admitted unwillingly. 'I've thought of it, naturally.'

'But Dominic hasn't suggested it?'

'No, but of course . . .'

'There's no "of course" about it,' Lady Cynthia said grimly. 'I doubt whether Dominic has thought any farther than getting you into bed at the first opportunity. If you have any future with him it'll be for you to plan it.'

She shifted her seat in the rocking boat so that she could look at me more directly. Her eyes were very shrewd and not unkind. All the same, I was convinced that her forthright speech was just another ploy to keep Dominic and me apart and when she spoke again I thought that her words confirmed my suspicions.

'Jessica, I beg you to face up to reality. Go back to your husband, work at making your marriage a success, have a family. You'll find more happiness that way than by pursuing the fairy tale you think my son can offer you.'

'You've been happy in your marriage. You don't understand what torture it is to live with a man you don't love. Edmond isn't . . . I want something *more*! Don't tell me to take up outside interests. I've tried that and it failed. What I want is to be with Dominic for the rest of my life – on any terms.'

We had arrived at the landing place. The boatman helped us out and we walked to where the Palace car was waiting for us without speaking to one another again. I turned and took a last look at the Lake Palace, floating on the water like some insubstantial dream, like the dream

Lady Cynthia thought the love between Dominic and me to be.

When we were settled in the limousine Lady Cynthia said, 'I blame myself for allowing Patricia to include you in this invitation to visit Arangapore. I thought your marriage had removed the danger, and nothing I observed in Dominic made me think he was hopelessly in love. I should have remembered that with Dominic it's always out of sight, out of mind. As soon as he saw you again he remembered.'

That was not an observation I liked, but I discounted it because I thought she was angry with me.

'We'd already met again in Bombay,' I said. 'It was too late to stop us admitting we still loved one another.'

'But not too late to stop this dangerous game you've been playing this last week. It's beginning to be noticed. Is it any use asking you to be more discreet – for Dominic's sake if not for your own?'

'I'll try.'

The truth was I knew that our snatched moments together were beginning to torment Dominic unbearably. Edmond would have been titillated by the long pursuit, but Dominic wanted the right true end of love and he wanted it quickly.

'I've got a plan, and if Mother's on to us then we'll have to be pretty clever in the way we carry it out,' Dominic said when I repeated the gist of my talk with Lady Cynthia.

I thought he meant a plan for our future and my heart lightened, but Dominic's idea was more short-term than that.

'Fraser is leaving today, you know. He's going to send me a telegram from Delhi ordering me to interrupt my leave for seven days. I'll ask Kesri if Mother and Patricia can stay on here until I'm free to escort them to my station in Ferozepore for the rest of their visit, as we planned. He won't mind.'

Jim Fraser was one of the young officers invited to amuse Patricia. I was not pleased to hear that Dominic had involved him in our plotting.

'Fraser won't talk,' Dominic said impatiently. 'He knows I'd do the same for him in a similar emergency.'

'Suppose Lady Cynthia and Patricia decide to come with you?'

'They won't. It'd add hundreds of miles to our journey to Ferozepore.'

'But *why* are you to go to Delhi! Surely someone will ask that?'

'Darling, in the Army you don't ask why, you just go. I'll come up with some piffling excuse – just the sort of thing our cockeyed administration would think of.'

'And when your mother gets to Ferozepore she'll complain about it to your superior officers.'

For a moment Dominic looked nonplussed. 'I hadn't thought of that,' he admitted. 'I'm not usually so stupid, Jess. Wanting you has got me all twisted up inside so that I can't think straight. It's a half-baked idea, I know, but can you come up with anything better?'

'We could come out in the open and tell everyone and then just go off and live together with no further fuss.'

I hoped I imagined the tiny pause before Dominic said, 'Sounds lovely, but what would we live on?'

'Dominic, you must have money. The Arkady fortune is immense.'

'It's not mine, not yet. Father makes me an allowance, but cavalry regiments are expensive and, in fact, I'm in debt. Even Pat's better off than I am because when she was twenty-one she came into money left to her by Grandmother Arkady. I suppose she might lend us . . .'

'No.'

'No, I suppose not. Of course, I've got expectations – if Grandfather Arkady kicks the bucket I should be quite rich – but if Father disapproves of what I do he might try to get me back into line by stopping my allowance. Darling, it's not just that. We're in the throes of being reorganised; regiments are being amalgamated – there's a

170

surplus of officers commissioned during the war. If I put a foot wrong I could find myself kicked out and shipped back to England. Once I'm back in Ferozepore I'll come clean and put the whole case to Colonel Newton. He'll appreciate that and perhaps try to help us, but he'll never forgive me if he hears about it via some scandalous gossip.'

It seemed odd to me, the way Dominic treated his regiment like part of his family and was prepared to bow to the judgement of a man who had never met me.

'All right, you go to Ferozepore and I'll go to Bombay and we won't meet again until you've made some arrangement that satisfies you,' I said.

'I couldn't stand that! Darling, you haven't heard the rest of my plan.'

I might not have heard it, but I was way ahead of him. Dominic would go to Delhi, leaving his mother and sister behind, and I would depart, ostensibly for Bombay, and join him there.

'Not in Delhi,' he said. 'I want to take you to Agra. We'll go and visit the Taj Mahal together.'

I hardly knew whether to laugh or cry. 'Dom, Agra will be full of English. We're bound to see someone who knows you.'

'I don't think so. If Mother were with us, yes, her acquaintances are all over the place, but I'm hardly known outside the regiment and it'll be damned bad luck if we run into any of your *box wallah* friends.'

We were in our favourite corner of the lowest of the garden terraces, huddled together in a tight embrace on the stone bench. Dominic, knowing that he was failing to convince me with words, began to kiss me, gentle, persistent kisses that had me sobbing with pleasure. And frustration. He was right, we couldn't go on like this. Against my better judgement, knowing that it was a mistake, I allowed myself to be persuaded into his mad plan.

CHAPTER EIGHT

'We're Mr and Mrs Pershore,' Dominic said. 'As in "Arkady & Pershore".'

'Crazy,' I said, but everything was crazy and dangerous and exciting.

We had got away with it. Everyone had appeared to be hoodwinked. Kesri said he would be delighted to keep Lady Cynthia and Patricia for an extra week when Dominic was apparently called away. Patricia wanted me to stay, too, but I protested that my husband was expecting me home. I could not look her in the eye when I said that, knowing that I had written a lying letter to Edmond to say I would be returning a week late.

I shut my mind to the possibility that Edmond might get to hear of my deception. Patricia and Lady Cynthia would not be going back to Bombay and the only connection Edmond had with Kesri and Antoinette was through me. He was not acquainted with any of the other guests and was not likely to meet them since they moved on a higher social level than we aspired to. I thought I was safe.

Since I was supposed to be benefiting from his escort for the first part of my journey, Dominic and I were able to leave together, sitting side by side in the enormous palace limousine with a foot of space between us and turning to one another in incredulous, delighted laughter as soon as we were alone.

Dominic had organised an hotel in Agra. He signed the register with a flourish and gave me a surreptitious wink when the clerk was not looking. It might have seemed furtive, but Dominic carried it off with the light touch that was the speciality of the Arkadys.

Our room was spacious. Dominic could raise enough money to pay for his comforts, it seemed.

'What a nice big bed,' he said approvingly, with another mischievous look at me.

I was afraid he might want to make use of it immediately and I was feeling travel-weary, grimy and sweaty, but it seemed that Dominic, too, felt in need of a bath, a rest and some food.

'And after that . . . no, not what you're thinking, Mrs Pershore . . . I'm going to take you to visit the Taj Mahal by moonlight and we'll find out whether it really is as beautiful as it's made out to be.'

I began to relax. Unconsciously, I realised, I had been expecting Dominic to pounce on me as soon as there was a suitable opportunity and I was not altogether looking forward to it. Secretly, I feared that the actual consummation of our love might be an anticlimax.

The Taj was no more than ten minutes' walk from our hotel, but that night we took a little horsedrawn *tonga* twined with ribbons and tinsel, and clopped along the road behind the underfed little horse and wizened driver. He tried to overcharge Dominic when we arrived, but I dealt with that in one crisp sentence that reduced him to openmouthed astonishment.

There were stalls set out along the side of the path leading up to the great red sandstone gates. They were lit by flares which cast an orange glare over the dark faces of the vendors and their wares: silk scarves embroidered with gold and sequins, ropes of necklaces, glass bangles, carved replicas of the Taj, ivory elephants, brass bowls and inlaid boxes. They clamoured for our attention, but Dominic smiled and shook his head and I walked straight by since I was too well acquainted with bazaar trash to be tempted by anything on offer here.

There were beggars, too, some of them mutilated by their families as children, some of them merely poor beyond the comprehension of our soft living. I knew it was a mistake for Dominic to feel in his pocket for his loose change, but I was glad when he did it, even though it unleashed a torrent of demand. We were glad to escape inside the gates where the beggars were not allowed.

I had seen many pictures of the Taj Mahal, but all were taken from inside the enclosing walls and I had not expected the vast portico through which we entered. Immediately there were murmurs all round us.

'I am torch boy, *sahib*, I show you steps. Careful *mem-sahib*, I light the way for you.'

We paid them off and took a few steps forward and immediately turned to one another in astonished delight. The truth was, we had neither of us really believed the stories of the beauty of the Taj Mahal. It was too trite, too obvious, too hackneyed – no building could really be as lovely as the Taj was made out to be. But it was. It was everything everyone had ever said about it, and more.

We held hands as we slowly walked towards the building which glowed as if the moon were inside it, instead of high above us in the dark blue sky. We would have to wait for daylight to appreciate all the fine detail, the inlaid work and bas-reliefs and the delicate carving. Tonight we could drink in the perfect proportions and the way that, for all its size, the tomb seemed to float, hardly anchored to the earth at all.

We walked on the black and white marble terrace and looked out over the Jumna River. The water was low and the moon glittered on the wet sand-bars stretching out from the shore. A thin wisp of white smoke drifted up into the air from an abandoned fire. Nothing else was stirring.

The inside of the building was dark and we left it unvisited. At every step some fresh delight surprised us, an arch through which a pool of moonlight fell, the outline of a minaret against the sky, a sudden view of the curve of the great dome, a reflection in the long pool of water in the middle of the garden.

There was a mosque on one side, which we are not allowed to enter, but on the other side, to balance it, was an empty building. We went and sat on the steps with our arms round one another and our eyes fixed unceasingly on the beauty in front of us. From behind us in the darkness someone was playing an Indian flute, gentle music, haunting and melancholy. I felt my eyes fill with tears.

'I could cry myself,' Dominic said when he realised I was feeling for a handkerchief. 'It was built for us, you know, just for us, so that we could sit here and take in this beauty and love one another.'

There was a note in his voice I had never heard before, deep and full of feeling. I turned to him and we kissed, one long sweet kiss, with no thought of the eyes that might be watching. We were alone in the world, just us and the magic night all round us.

As we walked slowly back along a path lined with trees I pointed to the sparks of light in the bushes. 'Look, fireflies.'

'The last perfect touch,' Dominic said. 'Is it real? Are we real?'

Nothing happened to disturb the dreaming mood we had fallen into, not even the walk back through the urgent hucksters and their brilliant torches. We went back to the hotel in silence, up to our room, and almost absentmindedly we laid aside our clothes and prepared ourselves for bed.

An anticlimax? Nothing, no, nothing in all my experience had prepared me for the glory of that night. To feel so much, to be joined with the man I loved in mutual delight, to know that he had not gone away from me, but was there speaking my name, murmuring love words, understanding the pleasure he was giving me and wanting more and more and more.

It was over too soon. I would have liked it to have gone on for ever, even though when Dominic withdrew from me I was so replete with love that I could not find strength in my slack hands to caress him.

'We were made for one another,' Dominic said in the same deep voice he had used earlier.

'Never before – never!' I said, my voice a mere whisper of sound. 'For me, it could have been the first time.'

He gathered me close and I drifted into a half-doze in which confused dreams chased across my mind until I realised that my vision of the curved dome of the Taj Mahal was linked to the sensation of Dominic's hand smoothing over the contours of my hips.

In astonished delight I discovered that our first union had not been unique and ecstasy could be repeated.

We were insatiable. Only the limits of our bodies put a stop to our lovemaking. Every day we visited the Taj, leaving the bed still hot with our early-morning love to view it at dawn, braving the midday sun to see it under a blaze of light, journeying to the far bank of the Jumna to see it from a distance and to the Red Fort to see it as sad Shah Jehan had seen it from his prison window.

It was terrible to bring our idyll to an end, but our week was nearly up and all we had settled was that we were perfect lovers and could not contemplate living without one another.

'I must tell Edmond,' I said.

'Delay it until I've had a chance to fix things at my end,' Dominic said.

'I've been away from him for three weeks. He'll expect to make love to me and I *can't*.'

In spite of being fathoms deep in love I felt a momentary exasperation at the expression on Dominic's face. It was all very well for him to feel such distaste – *he* was not the one who had to put up with it.

'Surely you can make some excuse . . . wrong time of the month or something.'

If Dominic had ever been married he would have known that husbands were better informed than that about their wives' menstrual cycles, but I let it go. He was right, I could invent some excuse. An upset stomach, perhaps – only too likely after train meals. What I was *not* sure about was how long I could keep my distance. If the worst came to the worst I would have to submit. It would not be first time I had gritted my teeth while Edmond made love to me, only previously, I had not known what I was missing. Now I knew, and my attitude to my marriage had changed and hardened.

We parted at Agra, since I was going south and Dominic

176

north, back to Arangapore. At the last moment Dominic was distracted by the realisation that I had no bearer with me to see to my comfort on the journey, while I could think of nothing but the pain of our parting.

I managed the journey with no great difficulty in spite of the inconvenience of travelling with no one to fetch and carry for me. It was long, boring and uncomfortable. I had plenty to think about and my thoughts were troubling.

I had written to Edmond to say that my visit to Arangapore had been extended for a week, so he would not have been worrying about my failure to return at the expected time, though he might be annoyed that I had stayed away from him longer than we had agreed. How was I to face him with my body still bruised from the ardour of my last night of love with Dominic?

The small, niggling thought crept into my mind that Dominic ought not to have put me into the position of having to keep up the deceit until he was ready to claim me. A clean, final break – that would have been honest – but it gave me a slimy feeling to be crawling home to Edmond on my own, to have to smile at him and pretend that all was well except, of course, that I was supposed to be too ill to sleep with him.

Edmond was going to be hurt, dreadfully hurt, and I was the one who was going to have to deliver that blow. I did not look forward to it, even though it would mean my freedom.

I was so reluctant to pick up the threads of my normal life that when we reached Bombay I sat in the train for a few moments steadying myself before I plunged into my distasteful deception. That was a mistake because by the time I roused myself to move, the usual array of porters had disappeared. It would only be a minute or two, I knew, before a porter saw me and rushed up to earn his fee, but in the meantime I was left standing alone, feeling helpless and foolish. Looking round, I saw someone watching me, a young man whose face was familiar though for a moment I could not think why. He smiled faintly and my memory came rushing back. Of course! It was the young barrister who had been picked up with me outside Gopal's house.

I beckoned and he came towards me, reluctantly I thought. 'I've often wondered what happened to you,' I said.

'There was nothing to connect me with the explosion so the police had to let me go. I've kept out of trouble since then. Do you want a porter?'

'I've stupidly let them all go.'

'I'll find one for you.' He put down his own suitcase and I glanced idly at the label. His name, it seemed, was Hari Chand and he was going to Ferozepore. Ferozepore! Just the sight of the name set up a longing for Dominic that almost felled me.

When Hari Chand came back I said, trying to appear normal, 'That was more than you would do for me the first time we met.'

'Ah, we've been to prison together since then. Did you get into trouble with your husband?'

Nothing like the trouble that was brewing now. I managed to make some sort of answer and changed the subject. I asked as we watched the porter collecting my suitcases, 'Are you going away?'

A stupid question. Obviously he was going away. What did arouse me to a momentary curiosity was his answer.

'Yes . . . yes. For a short time only. I am going to . . . Delhi.' He turned away as if anxious to part from me and I had to follow the porter. Perhaps the label on his suitcase was an old one. Still, it was nothing to me whether Hari Chand went to Ferozepore or Delhi or Timbuctoo so I put it out of my mind.

Everything seemed the same as usual when I got back to the flat, except that the servants were curiously subdued. I wondered whether Edmond had been too curt with them while I was away, but that could hardly be the trouble because then they would have been more pleased to see me. I had a good look round, suspecting I had caught them out in some neglect, but they seemed to have been

178

doing the work, apart from some skimping on the dusting which I was quick to point out.

I did not bother to let Edmond know I was home. Time enough to face him when he got back from the office. I heard him at the door at his usual time and braced myself to greet him with a smile and, God help me, a wifely kiss.

He came through the door and I saw immediately that something was wrong. His face was drawn and he looked faintly dishevelled, not at all the sleek, well turned-out Edmond I was used to.

I got up and took a step towards him, ready to play the part I had allotted myself, but something in Edmond's expression stopped me in my tracks. When he spoke, his voice was hoarse with strain. 'Where the hell have you been?'

At first I misunderstood. 'I wrote,' I protested. 'I told you I was staying an extra week. Surely you got my letter?'

Edmond's violent gesture disposed of my letter. 'That! You said you were staying at the Palace, but you left, you weren't there, and you certainly weren't here. Nothing's been seen of you since you got on a train with Dominic Arkady. So where have you been?'

'In Agra.'

'With Dominic?'

'Yes.'

It was out. Just like that. All our careful concealment had been for nothing. But how had Edmond known I was no longer at Arangapore?'

'The party broke up early,' he said. 'Patricia sent a telegram to the office asking me to break it to you that your friend the Maharani had died in childbirth. Naturally there had to be a period of mourning, so all the guests left, those of them who hadn't already gone, like you and Dominic.'

Rukmini was dead. Sweet Rukmini, who had borne her husband three children and carried a fourth for him when she had known that she had already been supplanted. Submissive Rukmini. Faithful Rukmini, who might perhaps have loved my cousin William, but who had never allowed herself to swerve from the path of her duty.

'The child?' I asked.

'Stillborn.'

I bowed my head. Not even my own dilemma could diminish my sense of loss, but Edmond had no such feelings and he was not to be diverted from his interrogation.

'You and Dominic,' he said. 'How long has that been going on?'

'We were in love before I married you, but we parted – I thought for ever. We realised we were still in love when we met at that party. You remember?'

'I remember you tarting yourself up like a Greek goddess and Dominic looking as if he could eat you, but so did every other man in the room. You weren't alone with one another, not once the whole evening.'

'I went to the station to see him off the following morning. It still seemed hopeless. I meant to stay faithful to you, truly I did, Edmond. Then I was invited to Arangapore and we spent two weeks under the same roof and it was unbearable. He's only been my lover for the past week.'

Only one week. I looked back at it in disbelief. One week of enchantment. There had been nothing sordid about it, but then we had not been living in the real world at all. This was the real world – an angry husband, red in the face with grief and jealousy; a man who was hurt and would lash out in revenge. There was something about Edmond's stance, his head sunk into his heavy shoulders and turning from side to side in baffled fury, that reminded me of a goaded bull. I shivered and, indeed, I think he would have struck me if Akbar had not appeared in the doorway with the drinks tray.

He kept his eyes down as he put the tray on the table. Usually he poured our drinks for us, but today in response to Edmond's furious, dismissing gesture he left us alone. He knew, of course. All the servants knew. That was why they had been so strange with me.

180

Akbar had scarcely left the room before Edmond said, 'Why have you come back?'

Why indeed? Now more than ever I longed for that clean break. 'To give Dominic time to . . . to arrange things,' I said.

'So you mean to leave me?'

'Yes.'

Edmond turned away and poured himself out a large whisky. I could have done with something to sustain me, but he did not offer it and I felt strangely inhibited about helping myself, as if the food and drink in this apartment no longer belonged to me.

That, it seemed, was Edmond's attitude, too. 'Right. Then you can go.'

'Go?'

'Now, this minute. Get out and don't come back.'

'But where . . .' I stopped. That was stupid, asking Edmond where I should go. Why should he care? If he meant it then I must cope for myself. After all, it was what I wanted, wasn't it?

My mind raced. I had unpacked and sent my clothes to the *dhobi* for washing, but that was unimportant. I would need little enough to begin with. Money . . . that was going to be a problem. I had very little in my purse and I could hardly expect Edmond to pay my hotel bill.

I was shaken by the suddenness with which events had moved and I had a real compassion for Edmond and his obvious suffering. Poor Edmond, his only fault was that he was the wrong man for me.

Haltingly, I tried to express my regret. 'I'm sorry . . .'

'It's a bit late for that,' he interrupted me. 'I've spent the best part of a week facing the fact that you must be off somewhere with another man. I made up my mind what I'd do if you had the nerve to come back here and I won't be budged from it.'

For the first time he looked me full in the face, his eyes holding mine as if he would probe into my mind. 'Was it always a lie? Didn't you ever love me?'

'You were always second-best. I did try to love you and

181

when I married you I meant it to be for ever. If I hadn't met Dominic again . . .'

'Don't mention his name. Damn him. Hasn't he got enough without taking my wife as well?'

To my horror, Edmond's voice broke. His eyes filled with tears and he turned away, his face crimson with the effort he was making to hold them back. I laid a tentative hand on his arm. 'I'm sorry,' I said. 'Truly, I'm sorry.'

Edmond flinched away from my touch. 'Get out of my sight.'

I went, shaken by the rawness of his hurt. It had been horrible and what was worse, it had been genuine. Edmond was stricken to the heart by my infidelity. As for me, I was overwhelmed by guilt and distress, but in this horrid contest I was the winner; I could look forward to a future with the man I loved and, if I were to be entirely truthful, I was relieved that I did not have to live under the same roof as Edmond, inventing excuses to evade his embraces, living a lie. It had been bad, but it had always been going to be bad. The fact that it had come sooner than expected made it neither better nor worse.

I packed and went to a small hotel near the railway station, the sort of place anyone passing through Bombay might use for a few days. As for money, there was no point in being sentimental. I sold my beautiful ruby engagement ring and the pendant Edmond had given me for Christmas.

I wrote to Dominic, of course, and it was a relief to get a reply from him within a few days, although the tone of his letter was not as satisfactory as it might have been.

'Darling,' he wrote, 'what foul luck being found out like that. Mother and Patricia scoured Delhi for me and Mother was distinctly frosty when I finally surfaced, having, of course, been all the way back to Arangapore to collect them, only to discover that they had already departed. I pleaded the exigencies of the service and she was civilised enough to pretend to believe me. Not Pat, though – she knew I'd been with you. Still, we might have got away with it if only she hadn't tried to get in touch with you about the Maharani's death. I suppose *you had to confess when Edmond taxed you with it? Silly question, of course you did. Now we're properly in the soup.*

'Listen, *darling, I've arranged to have a man-to-man talk with the CO and as soon as I've done that I'll come out in the open and tell Mother the truth, but the thing is at the moment we've got a bit of bother up here. Nothing serious, don't worry, just the usual agitators stirring up trouble and we're standing by to quell riot and insurrection. It infuriates me what a few hotheads can do with a crowd of ignorant peasants and they always end up the losers. Naturally, from the Army's point of view this is more important than private difficulties and so our affairs will have to wait until things quieten down again.*

'Darling Jessica, *I am missing you. Our wonderful time in Agra seems like a dream. I worry about you all on your own in an hotel. I suppose money is a bit tight? It is with me, too, but I enclose a tiny contribution, a token of my intention to look after you properly in the future, my own girl. With all my love, Dominic.'*

I looked at the enclosure and hardly knew whether to laugh or cry at the monumental inadequacy of it. He had sent me a cheque for two hundred and fifty rupees, about twenty pounds.

I read the letter through again and then again, trying to discover why I was disappointed with it. In the end I thought that it was not because of anything Dominic had said about us, but his passing mention of Rukmini's death. Perhaps he had never met her, since Kesri had already married Antoinette before he and Dominic renewed their friendship in Bombay, but he knew that I had valued her and so had his mother, and she had been the wife of his friend. It grated that he never referred to our loss except as a piece of foul luck that had led to our adultery being discovered prematurely.

As for the delay in sorting out our affairs, after a moment of rebellion I was forced to accept that a soldier was under command and could not drop everything for the sake of a woman at a time of emergency. It was not easy to be patient, particularly since I was extremely bored all by myself with no domestic duties, no friends, no one to talk to. I took to doing some of the things that visitors might do, going to the museums and studying Indian art. At least it was a cheap way of passing the time.

I scanned the newspapers for reports of trouble in the North and, sure enough, there was a cautious mention of 'disorders'. There was something about casualties, too, which made my heart skip a beat. If Dominic were to be wounded would anyone let me know?

Stupidly, I was more worried about this than about his own actual hurt. I had a vision of myself waiting, perhaps for weeks, while Dominic lay in a hospital bed unable to get a message to me. I told myself not to be morbid, but the idea persisted until one day I remembered my talk with Lady Cynthia. As Dominic had said himself, she was a civilised woman. She would not leave me in suspense if any harm came to her son.

Because of this, it was Lady Cynthia I was expecting to hear from if – but, of course, it was unthinkable – if Dominic should be injured. I went about my dull daily round, avoiding places where I might meet my former European contacts. I even went out to Elephanta Island one day to gaze in awe at the vast carvings hewn out of the solid rock. That was quite a good day. I found myself enjoying the tour of the caves, the sight of the quick little brown Koli people who fished along the coast and the boat trip across the bay. I returned to the hotel feeling more optimistic. Perhaps there would be a letter from Dominic, some news about when we could be together again.

It was Patricia who was waiting for me. She was in the foyer, huddled in a wicker chair, her new short hair hanging lankly round her white face, her body shrunken like that of an old woman. She looked at me and tried to speak. It was hardly necessary. The message she had come to deliver was there to be read in the terrible pain in her eyes.

'Dom . . .' she said at last. 'Dom . . .'

I wanted to ask if he was wounded, but instead I went

184

straight to the final question, knowing how she would answer it. 'Dead?'

'Yes,' she said and slid off her chair unconscious.

A girl who faints has to be dealt with even when the world is falling apart. The hotel staff were too alarmed by the inert body of an Englishwoman on the floor of their lobby to be of any great help. I was the one who brought her round, sent for a doctor and ordered a room to be made ready for her. Not my room. As soon as I could leave Patricia my need would be for solitude. Until then one part of me stood aside and watched my cool and competent handling of the situation, waiting for the time when I could bring my two halves together again and face what had happened.

Patricia looked very small as she lay on top of the big bed, part child and part old, old woman with a wizened face and hands like claws plucking ceaselessly at the white cotton counterpane.

'When did you last eat?' I asked.

'Eat?' Patricia moved her head and twisted her mouth as if the idea was nauseous to her. I guessed that she had taken hardly anything on the long train journey. No wonder she had fainted.

I sent for tea and thin bread and butter. Patricia protested, but I made her swallow the good, hot Indian tea and although she made a repugnant face I noticed that once she had started she got through the bread and butter without difficulty.

'I didn't think I could,' she said.

'The body insists on living.'

'What is there left to live for? How can you be so calm? You don't seem to understand . . .'

'I understand.'

Fortunately, because her voice was rising and I feared an hysterical outburst, the doctor arrived at that point. He approved of everything I had done, but he could see that Patricia was in a dangerous state and to my relief he prescribed a powerful sleeping draught.

I saw him to the door and he said, with the pedantic precision of the highly-educated Indian, 'One must not underestimate the effect of profound emotional shock. Miss Arkady was most unwise to undertake this long journey and, as you quite rightly saw, she is dehydrated. That matters more than the effect of going without food, which can be withstood for far longer. Make her drink, even if she will not eat.' He looked at me curiously. 'You are a relative?'

'A friend. I . . . I was going to marry Miss Arkady's brother, the man who's been killed.'

'Then you, too . . .'

'I can cope. I'll have to. But I must have time. If I can be sure that Patricia is sleeping, not needing me . . .'

'Once she has taken the sleeping draught she will not awaken for at least eight hours. But you will need sleep yourself. Let me give you something.'

I accepted the potion he gave me, but knew I would not use it. After he had gone I leaned against the wall for a moment with my eyes closed, rallying my strength. Speaking to the doctor about my own loss I had come close to losing my detachment and I must hang on to that until it was safe to let go.

I made Patricia get up and undress, I took her to the bathroom and washed her, I put her into one of my own nightdresses, since she had brought no luggage with her, and I made her swallow every drop of the doctor's powerful medicine. Then, at last, I went to my own room.

I went inside and locked the door behind me. It was the last co-ordinated action I was able to take. I tried to walk across the room, but my legs buckled under me. I crouched on my knees with my head resting on the side of the bed, almost as if I were praying, except that my hands were clenched into tight fists, not clasped in supplication. From out of the depths of my body a sound was wrenched from me with such pain that I might have been bearing his child instead of saying his name.

'Dominic . . . ! My dear, my dear. Dominic, Dominic, my love . . .'

Nothing came to me. No comfort, no feeling of his presence, nothing but the whisper of the fan revolving on the ceiling and the heartless sounds of life in the street outside. Dominic had gone. I was alone.

CHAPTER NINE

'I'm not going home,' Patricia said, 'I'm staying with Dom.'

'Here in Bombay you're hundreds of miles away from his grave. You might just as well be in England.'

'I thought you'd sympathise. But you're so hard, as if you don't feel anything at all.'

Hard! Every day I walked the tightrope of sanity, knowing that if I faltered the abyss was waiting to swallow me up.

'If only I could understand,' Patricia went on. 'Why did they shoot Dom? Why? You know these people, Jessica. Find me someone who can explain. What do they want?'

'Independence.'

'What does that mean for most ordinary Indians? Exchanging one set of masters for another. I want to hear it from their side.'

I thought of the young barrister, Hari Chand, and shuddered. He had been travelling to Ferozepore and he was a known agitator. Had he played any part in Dominic's death?

It was more for my own satisfaction than to quieten Patricia that I went back to Gopal's house and questioned him. At first he refused to admit that he knew who I was seeking.

'A barrister who fights for independence! There are many such. I cannot help you, *memsahib*.'

'I could go to the police,' I said thoughtfully. 'They took him into custody at the time they picked me up and I'm sure they'd be interested to hear that I saw him *en route* for Ferozepore just before the trouble there.'

Gopal was sulky about it, but he gave me a possible address and I went straight to it. The tenement house was crowded and ramshackle, but in a fairly respectable neighbourhood, and I had no qualms about visiting it. Nowhere is a woman who behaves modestly more safe than in India and I had taken the precaution of wearing native dress as I had when I went to my dancing lessons. I might have been robbed, but I was carrying little money and wearing no jewellery, not even the heart-shaped pendant Dominic had given me and which I now usually wore day and night.

I was fortunate in finding Hari Chand at home. There was another young man lounging on the *charpoy* in the corner, but Hari Chand dismissed him with a quick word. Besides that string bed the room contained a wooden table, strewn with papers, some books stacked on the floor, two chairs, a washstand with a basin and ewer, incongruously patterned with violets, and a rail on which hung Hari Chand's one Western-style suit.

'When we met on the railway station you were on your way to Ferozepore, though you said you were going to Delhi,' I began.

'Perhaps I was. Even under British rule a man is free to travel where he wishes on the train.'

'Without the British you wouldn't have any trains,' I retorted.

'Possibly not. What do you want from me?'

'An act of mercy.' That had him puzzled. I pressed on with my explanation. 'There was rioting in the area near Ferozepore. No, I'm not going to ask if you were involved, although I suspect you were. A young British officer, Dominic Arkady, was killed.'

'Ah, yes, one of the cotton Arkadys. I heard about that,' he admitted.

'I'm sure you did. His sister is here in Bombay. She wants . . .' I paused, trying to get it clear to myself what it was that Patricia wanted. 'She wants to understand the . . . the motivation behind the agitation that led to the fighting.'

'The trouble was not premeditated.'

'Perhaps not, though your experience in the past must have told you that if you stir up a mob someone will get hurt. It wasn't the British Army who fired the first shots, not this time.'

'As to that, the evidence is biased.'

'Oh, come on! You preached sedition and the men who listened to you took it all too literally. Freedom! They don't want freedom, they want bread in their mouths and some comfort in their lives, so they took the chance to snatch at what they could get. Heads were broken, old grievances were aired, shops were looted, it all got out of hand and the Army was called out because the police couldn't cope. That was when someone saw the chance of making real trouble. I'll acquit you because I don't think that's your line, but firearms were brought out and Dominic . . . Dominic was killed.' My voice broke and I turned away, fighting for the control that was essential if I was to go on living.

'What was he to you?'

'I was going to marry him, my own husband having put me away. But it's his sister who needs you, not me. She seems to think that if she could talk to a really committed Nationalist and understand your cause then she could reconcile herself to her brother's death. I don't know, it might work. Something's got to be done; her mind is so troubled that I'm afraid for her sanity.'

'But surely I'm not the man? If she knows I was in Ferozepore – I admit nothing, I merely mean, if she suspects . . .'

'That mustn't be mentioned. You're educated and you speak excellent English. You're capable of putting a lucid case to her. Please, I beg of you, come and talk to her.'

How could I explain to him the desperate need I had to get Patricia away from Bombay and out of my life so that I could mourn in peace? I pitied her, God knows, but the demands she made sapped me of energy, so that by the end of each day I could hardly move or speak. I longed for Lady Cynthia to come and take her daughter away, but she too was ill, poor woman, and for the time being Patricia was left in my care.

In the end Hari agreed to come with me. I saw him glance at the suit hanging in the corner and guessed that he wished to appear at his best when visiting our hotel.

'I'll find a *gharri* and wait for you downstairs,' I said.

When he emerged to join me he was wearing a clean white shirt, a tie, the lightweight grey suit, well-pressed, and polished black leather shoes, and I marvelled at the ability of the professional Indian to keep up the appearance of being fresh and smart in such spartan surroundings.

I could see Patricia was surprised. Presumably she had been expecting a white-clad *guru*, not a handsome young man. Hari Chand had the clean-cut good looks of many young Indians of his type, with a spare body, good features, fine eyes and wavy black hair. His manner was impressive, too; I had been struck by that even when we had been riding in the police van. If he could manage to keep himself out of trouble, which I doubted, and if he could keep his mind fixed on the law, which I doubted even more, he might have a good career in the courts.

I wanted to leave them alone, longing for the respite of an hour to myself, but I could see that would alarm Hari and so I stayed and listened. I had chosen well – he was a good advocate for his cause. Patricia was impressed and so, against my will, was I.

'But advances have been made,' I said, entering reluctantly into the discussion. 'There are more Indian officers in the Army, for instance.'

His smile was derisive. 'A token gesture. The only thing that will satisfy us is self-government.'

'By whom? Hindu or Moslem? It was when the two religions started massacring each other that Dominic's unit was ordered out to keep them apart. Without that impartial element won't the two sides slit one another's throats?'

'That's a tired old argument and something at which

191

the British are adept: divide and rule. Leave us to our-selves and we'll work out a suitable compromise.'

'I suppose in the end people have to be allowed to run their own country,' Patricia said.

'We'll make mistakes, but they'll be our own mistakes. As for our ability, you might remember that it is we, not the British, who control the greater part of the cotton industry.'

'The Parsis run it,' I said sourly. 'And they're nearly as European as the British. Will you admit them to your government?'

'Of course. A place for everybody who can get elected.'

'Which will leave the minorities out in the cold,' I pointed out. 'India is such a hotch-potch. And what about the princely States?'

'They can continue as they are for the time being, but eventually they will have to go.'

Patricia exclaimed and Hari turned his fine eyes on her.

'Why should one man enjoy limitless wealth at the expense of the poor peasants who live in his State?' he asked. 'The princes are an anomaly in this day and age.'

I could see that this was rather more than Patricia, with her own inheritance of wealth and family, could swallow.

'Are you a Communist?' I asked.

'I'm a good Hindu,' he answered with a smile.

'Are you married?' Patricia asked.

'Unfortunately, I am unable to afford a wife.'

'But you do have some family?' she persisted.

I stirred uneasily, aware that these personal questions would not be welcome, but Hari answered without hesi-tation, 'I have a father and a mother, two brothers and a sister. My parents and my elder brother and his wife and family live on the family farm; my second brother is in the railway office here in Bombay, and my sister is married and living in the next village to our parents.'

'If you died, your sister would grieve for you?'

'Of course.' Hari Chand hesitated and then he said carefully, 'After the allotted span of mourning she would continue with her life.'

I knew that what he said was right, but Patricia did not have the fatalism of an Indian woman and neither did I.

'We rage against our loss,' I said, thinking aloud.

'I regret it,' Hari Chand said, his face troubled. 'It should not have happened. Please accept my condolences.'

'That's enough, I think,' I said, getting up. 'Patricia, we mustn't trespass on Mr Chand's time any longer. It was good of him to come.'

'You'll come again?' Patricia said, taking his hand and clinging to it, to his embarrassment.

Hari Chand glanced at me and I nodded. 'Once more,' I said. 'That should be enough, I think.'

As I walked with him to the outer door of the hotel I asked, 'If it were offered to you, would you accept a fee for this consultation?'

'While the money would be welcome the truth is you haven't taken me away from my work because I haven't any. No, on the whole I think not. I was in Ferozepore and although I had no direct hand in Dominic Arkady's death I hold myself in some part responsible.' He paused and then added, just as he had before, 'It should not have happened.'

My hope was that this talk would give Patricia's thoughts a new turn, but I was not prepared for the energy with which she took up the cause of Indian Home Rule.

'Why did I never see it before?' she demanded. 'I always took it for granted that we had a right to be here.'

'If you'd sampled Indian bureaucracy you'd be thankful for a few straightforward British to keep things running,' I snapped, even though in my heart I knew that the time would have to come when, as Hari Chand had said, the Indians would be left to make their own mistakes.

'If we'd *known*, if Dom had gone into it instead of accepting what he was told . . . perhaps he wouldn't ever have gone into the Army.'

Dominic had given me up rather than spoil his chances of getting a commission in the regiment he had wanted, but I bit back the bitter rejoinder I might have made. Let her have her delusions if they were any comfort to her.

193

'As soon as I mention his name you close up and shut me out,' Patricia said. 'I thought when I came to you that we'd be able to comfort one another, but you're so hard, so cold!'

How could I tell her that I had to cover my bedside clock with a pillow because it said '*Dom-i-nic, Dom-i-nic*', all night. Every stroke of my blood repeated the refrain '*Dom – dead, Dom – dead.*' I was never free day or night from the realisation of what I had lost. But Patricia was right, I had resisted sharing that loss with her. Dominic would have expected me to be more generous.

'I loved him differently from you,' I said, speaking uncertainly because of the terrible difficulty of saying anything at all. 'I think I'm afraid that sharing my grief would make my . . . my experience of him less than it was.'

She turned to me with tears in her eyes once more. 'It was my fault that your stay in Agra was discovered.'

'You couldn't help it. It was natural for you to let me know that Rukmini had died.'

'No, I did it on purpose. I knew you wouldn't be at home.'

'Dominic *told* you?'

'He didn't need to. I guessed, just by looking at you, the way you went off together, so polite and careful, and shining with anticipation. I'd kept you apart for two weeks by telling Antoinette you were my friend and I wanted to share a room with you, but when I saw how crazy about one another you were I knew Dom would find a way.'

I was too choked to say anything. The memory of our magical week together swept over me and I found myself rocking backwards and forwards in an agony of sorrow.

'Jessica . . . forgive me,' Patricia said in a frightened whisper.

'We went to the Taj Mahal every day. Foolish of us . . . we should have remembered it was a tomb we were adoring.'

For the first time I turned to Patricia for comfort instead of the other way round and we clung together, both of us in tears, hugging one another tightly. At last I freed myself and found a handkerchief to wipe my streaming eyes and snuffling nose. My head ached and I felt dull and listless, as if I were coming down with a fever. Patricia, I thought, had benefited from our mutual outburst. Presumably she thought I had forgiven her. Perhaps I did. After all, what did it matter that she had allowed her jealousy to alert Edmond to my infidelity? It had only precipitated the outcome. She had been responsible for Matthew Arkady knowing that Dom and I were meeting in England, too, but there was no point in dwelling on that now. Dominic was dead. Beside that fact everything else was insignificant.

Patricia had taken a liking to Hari Chand. She admired the honest way he had talked to her. She also thought him handsome and said so after their second meeting.

'Don't think about him like that,' I said. 'You two are totally *tabu* to one another.'

'Jessica, you are horrid. Surely I can remark on a man's looks without being suspected of falling in love with him?'

'I hope so.'

'It's his mind I admire.'

'Good.'

'You're as friendly with him as I am.'

'But Hari Chand and I both understand the limits of that friendship. We both know the boundaries whereas you don't even know they exist.'

'There ought not to be any barriers like that between people who respect one another.'

'I'm not talking about race, but culture. Hari is a Hindu and, for all his free thinking, a devout one. It would take you a lifetime to begin to understand the way he thinks.'

'He's very Western in his way of thinking.'

'On the surface. Underneath he's what his ancestry and upbringing have made him. He's neither liberal nor tolerant, not when it comes to other religions. Oh, Pat, Pat, you've been here five minutes and you think you're an authority. I've lived here most of my life and I'm just beginning to understand my ignorance. Go home, back to your own people. Get married, have a family, be happy. Leave India to sort out her own problems.'

I was in tears again, as I so often was in those weak, despairing days and although Patricia did not realise it, it was partly because I saw a future for her and none for myself. Where was I to go, what was I to do? How lightly I had left Edmond, thinking that I could rely on a life for myself with Dominic.

I would go back to England. There at least I could earn a living. Here, in Bombay, the talents I possessed were useless. I was a good, competent secretary, but all the clerical posts were filled by men. It was unthinkable for a woman, particularly an Englishwoman, to appropriate such a position. If I had been qualified I could have taught, or if I had followed Patricia's example in the war I could have nursed, but apart from that I could think of no other way to earn a living.

My intention was to ask Lady Cynthia to lend me the money for a passage home. Surely she would do that? Her son had meant to marry me and even though she might not like the idea, surely she would help me for his sake? Besides, I was a member of the family; on the wrong side of the blanket, but acknowledged. If my grandfather had been fit enough to approach he would have done this small thing for me.

Against my wishes, Patricia and Hari Chand continued to meet. I insisted on being present at every meeting, not because I feared for Patricia but because I knew how easy it would be for Hari to misunderstand her persistence.

'I want to hear Mahatma Ghandi speak,' she announced one day.

'You won't understand what he says,' I pointed out.

'He often talks in English and if he doesn't, you and Hari can interpret for me. Would he see me if I wrote and asked him, do you think?'

'I doubt it and, besides, the journey would be too difficult and you can't leave Bombay when your mother will be arriving any day.'

'I won't go back to England,' Patricia muttered, just as

she had, day after day, ever since she got it into her head that to leave India would be a desertion of her brother.

Lady Cynthia had been ill with malaria, something she had contracted many years before and which recurred from time to time, especially when, as now, she was in a low state of health because of the shock of Dominic's death. Her recovery was slow and once she was reassured that Patricia was safe with me, she took time to build up her strength before attempting the long journey to Bombay. Now she was on her way and I, for one, was distinctly relieved. This 'India for the Indians' craze had taken too much of a hold on Patricia and I wanted her out of the country and, above all, to hand over responsibility for her to her mother.

At first Lady Cynthia was gracious to me. She was looking far from well, much too gaunt, with a greyness in her face that I hoped the voyage home would cure. She spoke to me of Dominic only once.

'We've both suffered a great loss,' she said. 'I hardly knew him. That's perhaps the most difficult thing to bear, that just as I was given the chance to get to know my son he was snatched away from me.'

It was not quite the moment to bring up the subject of a loan to pay my passage home, particularly since Lady Cynthia passed on with scarcely a pause to speak about Patricia.

'As for my other child . . . she's a great anxiety to me.'

'She must go back to England.'

'Of course.' Lady Cynthia looked surprised, but she did not know then about Patricia's obstinate determination to stay in India. When she did, she was extremely annoyed about it.

'I understand you introduced her to this Mr Chand?' she asked.

'I meant it for the best. I didn't expect Pat to get so obsessed with the Indian question.'

'There would be no "Indian question" if people like

197

your friend would accept that everything possible is being done to prepare his country for self-government. He should agitate less and do a little more towards earning a living.'

There was no point in arguing with her. I knew how difficult it was for young men like Hari to get work and I had sympathy for his aspirations, in spite of my misgivings.

I ought to have kept a better eye on Patricia, but once her mother arrived I relaxed the watch I had kept over her. I thought I could trust Hari, out of self-preservation as much as out of friendship, to stop her from doing anything too wild, but I was wrong. I had overlooked what a feather in his cap it would be to produce a British convert to the cause.

One day Lady Cynthia burst into my bedroom without even knocking. 'Patricia's gone off with your Indian friend!' she cried.

I took the sheet of paper she was flourishing and read Pat's note. 'She wants to hear Mr Ghandi speak,' I said.

'They'll be gone for *days*. How could she do such a thing?'

'Hari won't touch her,' I said quickly. 'You needn't be afraid of . . . of anything like that. He'll treat her like a sister.'

When I said it I believed it, but when Patricia and Hari returned a week later I was not so sure. I could not reconcile Patricia's suppressed excitement with anything so mundane as listening to political speeches and I did not like the way Hari avoided my eye. And yet . . . I could not quite bring myself to believe that a British girl of Patricia's standing would indulge in a love affair with an Indian. Hari was intelligent and likeable and goodlooking, but everything in my upbringing recoiled in horror at the idea. The one thing we country-born girls, especially those with a touch of native blood, had had drummed into us was that we must move heaven and earth to ally ourselves to one of our own sort. Amongst us, marriage to an Indian was to be deplored, an illicit affair unthinkable.

Whatever had happened, Patricia, of course, was unrepentant.

'It was an absolutely *ghastly* journey,' she said. 'Second-class! Ugh! You've no idea.'

Had I not! I knew only too well what it was like to travel out of the comfortable carriages Patricia had previously taken for granted.

'The people I met couldn't have been sweeter, especially when they heard I was going to meet the Mahatma.'

'And did you meet him?' I asked.

'Well, not actually face to face, but I went to two of his meetings and Hari told me what he said. Such a funny little man, but terribly impressive. Sort of childlike and wise at the same time.'

'Mr Ghandi is an astute politician and full of guile,' I said.

'That, too,' Patricia agreed. 'He'd have to be, wouldn't he, to have achieved as much as he has? But it's only a beginning and it's terribly exciting to be a part of a whole new world.'

Lady Cynthia had listened to this in grim-faced silence, but now she turned to me and said, 'I'd like to talk to Patricia alone, if you wouldn't mind, Jessica.'

I left them, guessing that what was pressing on Lady Cynthia's mind was the matter of Patricia's relations with Hari. I could have told her she had no chance of finding out the truth.

'She won't go home,' Lady Cynthia reported after this interview. I could see that she was stupefied by her daughter's obstinacy.

'Would you like me to talk to her?' I asked.

'What good will that do? I blame you, Jessica, for this whole sorry mess.'

All the same, I did talk to Patricia and found, as I had feared, that nothing would move her.

'How will you live?' I asked.

'I'll take an apartment or a little house. Not here, but in Delhi, nearer the government and the seat of action. There are other people, you know, who feel the way I do. British people, I mean. I'll get together with the other sympathisers and we'll lobby for changes.'

It seemed she saw herself as a sort of suffragette, chained to the railings of Viceregal Lodge. It was a wild, romantic dream and it had very little to do with the reality of the situation. Patricia, unless I was mistaken, was due for a heartbreak which would make the loss of her brother look small.

Since Lady Cynthia and I were in agreement it was hard that she held me responsible for her daughter's foolishness. I think it was the fact that she was powerless that made her particularly angry.

'Patricia has money of her own and she's over twenty-one,' she said. 'It seems I have no way of forcing her to return to England and I certainly have no intention of spending months in Bombay waiting for her to come to her senses.'

'The first hot weather in Delhi may change her mind,' I said.

'I refuse to wait for that. My husband needs me in England. He has lost a son, which is something that seems to have been overlooked in all this brouhaha.'

'Not by me.'

I opened my mouth to bring up the difficult subject of my passage to England, but Lady Cynthia forestalled me.

'As for you, Jessica, you should return to your husband.'

'He won't have me.'

'Yes, he will. I've spoken to him and Edmond has been most reasonable. He had the sense not to discuss your adultery with anyone except a lawyer who, I presume, can be trusted to keep his mouth shut. Most people seem to believe you quarrelled over your protracted visit to Arangapore and that in recent weeks you've remained unreconciled because you've been taking care of Patricia

200

following her bereavement. There's no obstacle to taking up your married life again.'

Except my own overwhelming desire to remain free. She had spoken to Edmond. How dared she? I tried to keep my anger within bounds, but my voice trembled as I said, 'I don't think you had any right to discuss me with my husband.'

'I'm extremely anxious to get you settled. You may not think it, but I have your interests at heart.'

'I won't go back to Edmond. It's unthinkable.'

'Then I wash my hands of you. I have quite enough to worry about over Patricia. The thought of leaving her here alone, unprotected . . .'

'You only have to tell the Viceroy that your daughter is living in Delhi and every ADC on his staff will descend on her to see that she's all right,' I said wearily.

'No one in Society will receive her, living the way she intends.'

'These are the nineteen-twenties, Lady Cynthia, and Patricia is not a child, she's an adult woman. A silly one, I agree, but not without resources. She might be thought eccentric and her views certainly won't be popular, but she'll survive. I don't think you can do anything but go home and leave her to it.'

It was not a particularly tactful way of putting it, but it made sense, as Lady Cynthia was forced to admit. As for me, I was going to take my own advice and leave Patricia to work out her own fate. I was more concerned with my own predicament. If I were to return to Edmond I would have to do it now, immediately. I could see what that would mean. Me, humble and contrite, suing for forgiveness and submitting once again to his unwelcome embraces. As I had already told Lady Cynthia, it was not to be thought of.

Obviously there was no point now in asking her to provide me with a passage to England. Patricia was going off to Delhi and although she might be prepared to offer me a refuge I would certainly not accept it. Somehow I had to think of a way of making a life for myself, without

201

training, without money and, because of my actions, with very few friends.

CHAPTER TEN

Commonsense dictated that I should go back to my husband, but commonsense had nothing to do with the way I felt and when Edmond, obedient to Lady Cynthia's wishes, tried to bring about a reconciliation I turned him down.

I was haunted by his look of hurt bewilderment, but when he tried to talk me round he made the mistake of attempting a clumsy embrace and I felt myself shudder from head to foot. Feeling like that, how could I take up married life with him again?

He shied away from me, knowing that I had rejected him before he had had a chance to speak.

'The trouble with you is, you've been living out of touch with reality,' he said. 'All this mixing with Maharajahs and staying in palaces, it's just make-believe, fairyland. Even this idea you've got of being in love with Dominic, it's more like acting than real life. People like us don't mess up their lives for a romantic hero, especially a dead one. Face facts, Jessica. What you need is a steady home life and a husband to look after you. I ought to have insisted on starting a family, that would have put an end to your silly goings-on.'

I was scarcely listening. Something he had said had put an idea into my head so startling that I needed to go away and think it out.

'How are you going to manage?' Edmond persisted. 'I'm not going to keep you if you aren't living with me.'

'I'll find a job,' I said absently. 'It's no use, Edmond, I've moved too far away from you to come back now.'

I looked round the apartment, where I had agreed to meet him. It had a faint air of neglect, the appearance of an establishment where there was no longer a mistress. 'Tell the *hamal* he must dust more often; he's always been slack about it,' I said. 'And those flowers should be thrown out and replaced. Are they feeding you properly?'

'Do you care?'

The truthful answer would have been no, not particularly, but I still felt a certain responsibility for Edmond's well-being. He made me feel guilty and because I knew his resentment was justified I was anxious to get away.

'If you're clearing out then I'd be glad if you'd take all your belongings,' Edmond said. 'I don't want your clothes cluttering up the bedroom, reminding me . . .'

His voice broke and once again I was overwhelmed by pity, but I was also repulsed by the raw emotion he displayed.

'I'll take everything,' I said. 'And, if you don't mind, I'd like the statue of Sita that William gave me for a wedding present.'

Edmond shrugged. 'Take it. You know I never liked it.'

As I returned to the hotel, which I was beginning to think I might not be able to afford for much longer, with two suitcases full of clothes and the heavy statue balanced on my lap, I was turning over in my mind the idea which had come to me while Edmond was speaking. Play-acting! Could I possibly take Kesri up on his offer of starring me in a film? Had he really meant it? No, probably not, but he could be made to mean it. The trouble was, how soon could I write to a presumably mourning widower to suggest that he should divert his mind by going into the film industry?

It was a difficult letter to write, but in the end I got it off. I put in a crafty bit about wanting the film to be a memorial to Rukmini, who had nurtured my interest in Indian music and dancing. That might work, especially if he, like me, was feeling guilty about the way he had treated his spouse.

While I was waiting for a reply I counted up my resources and found them scanty enough. Living was cheap in India and I had got a good price for my ring and ruby pendant, but every day my funds diminished and even if Kesri took the bait I had offered him I could not expect filming to start straight away. If the worse came to the worst, I supposed I could throw myself on the mercy of the Bullen tribe, even though I was not well acquainted with my many 'cousins' and had kept out of their way since my arrival in Bombay. Not William, though. I drew the line at sponging on him.

I was lightheaded with relief when I had a note from Kesri inviting me to lunch with him at the Taj 'to discuss my idea'. Surely this meant that he was thinking about it favourably?

I dressed with enormous care, but conventionally: hat and gloves, polished glacé kid shoes, pale stockings and a tussore silk two-piece with a pink chiffon blouse to match the pink silk rose on my hat. It was a demure outfit, but I had always known how to put on my clothes and I thought that one or two heads turned as I walked across the restaurant. I knew then what I had suspected already, that loving Dominic had given me an assurance over my body I had lacked before. I walked now like a woman who knew what it was to give and receive passion and the latent promise was there for those who had eyes to see it.

Kesri was appreciative, I knew that by the glint in his eyes, but I kept the talk on a business level, apart from murmuring my condolences once more.

'It was a sad loss,' he agreed. 'And followed so quickly by another. Dominic was my friend. His death was a great blow.'

'To me, too,' I said. There was no need to say any more. He knew all about it. 'I've separated from my husband,' I added.

'And that leaves you free to become my leading lady?'

'If you're serious about making a film. Are you?' I was being too forceful. Kesri was not ready to commit himself, not just like that.

'I'm interested,' he admitted. 'I've always wanted to be involved in cinematography. I've talked about it a great deal; perhaps now is the time for me to put my theories into practice.'

'Would you direct it yourself?'

'It would be difficult to resist . . . but one has so many calls on one's time.'

'Your princely duties must leave you little opportunity to develop a second career,' I agreed.

Since I had not noticed Kesri's duties stopping him from doing anything he wished by way of amusing himself this was sycophantic, to say the least, but he received it complacently and I saw that I had struck the right note.

After that I concentrated on the extremely good meal. Sharing food in a restaurant was permissible, it seemed, or had Kesri dropped his orthodox rules since parting with Rukmini? I could hardly ask him, since it was essential to keep him in a good mood. Gradually, with a little help from me, Kesri talked himself into a decision – as definite as any decision from such a creature of whims could be – to set up a film-making company in Bombay.

'Of course, I have to attend the new Assembly of Princes in Delhi in the spring,' he said.

'I think we ought to have completed our first film by then, don't you?' I asked.

I had at that time no idea how long it took to make a film. As far as I was concerned, you decided on a story, told the actors what to do and pointed the camera at them. Then, as soon as the film was developed, it could be shown to the public.

Kesri laughed at my ignorance, but it pleased him to enlighten me. It was all rather more complicated than I had thought, but one thing he had in abundance was money so there was none of the looking around for finance which hampered other directors.

Christmas was almost on us. Not a time I enjoyed spending alone in an hotel, especially since the news of my separation from Edmond had got through to England and I received reproachful letters from my mother instead of seasonable cards.

I tried going to church on Christmas Day, but it was a

206

mistake because no one spoke to me and I felt lonelier than ever. Everyone else seemed to be going off to a family party or to one club or another, but I had no family and even if my membership had not lapsed, which presumably it had, I could hardly show my face in the Club. I went back to the hotel, reminding myself that I was a film star, very nearly, and found two nice things waiting for me.

One was a card from Patricia, late as usual, with a scrawled message inside to say that she was utterly immersed in Independence. It was a typical Pat message – no mention of Hari, no mention of Dominic. Did she still miss him as much as ever? As much as I did?

The other was a small parcel from William, badly wrapped like all his parcels, which Edmond had had the grace to send round to me. Obviously the news of our split had not filtered through to William, which was unsurprising considering how far off the beaten track his expedition had taken him. He had sent me a small carving of Ganesh, the elephant-headed god, very fat and cheerful. Appropriate, too, since one was supposed to invoke Ganesh to remove obstacles.

My supplications to Ganesh must have got through, because in the New Year we suddenly began to make progress. A camera team was assembled, Kesri engaged an assistant director, who knew something about making films and could take over when his own expertise failed him, we decided on a story and a cast of actors was engaged.

The story was part myth, part fairy tale, and concerned a beautiful and virtuous princess whose parents offended the gods. Because of this her newly married husband was made to believe that she was unchaste and she had to prove her virtue by performing a series of tasks, after which the gods relented and opened his eyes to her goodness. The film was unusual in that these 'task-performing' epics were usually about men, but it was a wonderful vehicle for my talents, such as they were.

207

My fluent Hindi was useful in dealing with the rest of the cast, but since the film was silent I could have been speaking gibberish for all it mattered. I was worried about my blue eyes, but Kesri assured me they were by no means unknown in northern India and, in any case, on the black and white film my eyes were dark enough to pass muster.

I was not at that time a particularly good actress, but we had already discovered that the camera was kind to me. I could look pure when necessary, but my strong appeal lay in suggesting banked fires so that there was just a possibility that my film husband's suspicions might be correct after all, thus giving a vicarious thrill to the audience.

One of my tasks was to perform a dance on a floor of knives, treading a maze between the blades, which were made of rubber painted silver. We called in old Gopal to choreograph the dance. He was outraged by its unclassical nature, but we showed him the money and he arranged a dance which was both exciting and sensual. There were some interesting shots of my bare feet and ankles moving in intricate steps between the upturned blades and when I finally collapsed in front of the camera for a close-up of my closed eyes and heaving breasts there was a spontaneous burst of applause from the crew.

Another day I discovered the miserable side of movie-making. The princess was supposed to be searching for a stolen cup of great value and beauty, which she cleverly discovered had been hidden in a recess behind a waterfall. I emerged brandishing the cup in triumph, my hair streaming with water and my sari plastered to my body, an effect which has since been copied many, many times. I was uneasy about this, thinking it rather too revealing, but Kesri said it was artistic and I had to admit that the effect as I lifted the cup to the light and the sunshine glittered on my face was stunning. Fortunately we had finished filming for the day before I started sneezing.

We worked at speed with nothing to hold us up except the building of the sets and the delays caused by the

Indian genius for splitting a job into many small parts, each one to be performed by a different worker, none of whom would do anything but his own allotted task. Everything was done out of doors and the light, of course, never failed us. Kesri was in his element, turning up day after day, full of enthusiasm. I was surprised how much he really knew; most of the better ideas came from him.

There was no lovemaking in the story. At least, no overt lovemaking. We respected the scruples of our audience and never let the hero and heroine do more than cast languishing glances at one another, but my leading man very cleverly suggested the tension of a man unwillingly in love with a woman he believed to be beneath him.

'Quite in the best tradition of Ethel M. Dell,' I said to Kesri in amusement, but he looked at me blankly so that I had to explain that she was a writer of romances in England, which he did not appreciate. Kesri had elevated ideas about the value of his work.

The film absorbed him to such an extent that I was not surprised when Antoinette turned up on the set one day to see what was going on. She looked very lovely, but I thought she had put on weight. There was a softness about her that had not been there before and this blurring of the voluptuous lines of her body was not becoming to her. She was annoyed when Kesri would not break off from what he was doing to pay attention to her. I could have told her that it never did to get between a man and his work, but of course she did not recognise what we were doing as work.

'Jessica, *ma chère*, I had no idea you were so talented,' she said. 'But I mustn't call you that now, must I? You have a new identity.'

There had been considerable discussion about my name. I had said that if I were to retain a European name it must be Jessica Bullen. The advantage of that was that it would have made it clear that the shameless lady appearing on the screen was not Hindu or Moslem or any other variety of religion which would be offended by her antics. On the other hand, Kesri thought that since I was

209

playing an Indian role I ought not to use such an obviously un-Indian name. In the end I came up with the idea of calling myself simply Jasmina. It looked very well when we finally got it up on a billboard – 'Jasmina in *The Story of Princess Sushila*'.

Kesri would have liked the film to be finished in time for the arrival of the new Viceroy on 2 April, although since Lord and Lady Reading only spent two days in Bombay and their time was filled up with official engagements, it was hardly likely that they would have spared the time to see a film made by an amateur enthusiast, in spite of his princely status. Kesri had to reconcile himself to a first night in Bombay in May, followed by a second première in Delhi later, with a vague promise of Viceregal interest on that occasion.

The first night in Bombay was a triumph. I have to admit that was partly due to Kesri's contacts. A feature film made by a Maharajah was obviously going to be one of the highlights of the Bombay social season. Everyone who was anyone turned up, both to the showing of the film and to the party Kesri gave at the Taj afterwards. He invited me and my leading man, but not the rest of the cast nor the film crew, which I thought rather mean of him, even though I knew that the man who turned the camera might not have mixed too happily with Kesri's high-class social friends.

They were very kind to me. Kinder, in fact, than I expected. One or two of them I knew already from my visit to Arangapore, but that did not entirely explain the compliments that rained down on me. The truth was, I had expected this crowd of sophisticates to be more patronising about our little fairy story, even though the acting was not too bad and some of the effects were striking.

Quite apart from that, amongst these high-caste aristocrats an actress was a thing to be looked down on. No properly brought-up Indian lady would have allowed her face to be seen on the screen and the fact that I was British only made it marginally more respectable. I could only assume that Kesri's patronage made me not only acceptable, but remarkably popular, and as the party progressed I began to see how right that was.

I had chosen to wear European evening dress, very plain and simple and quite modestly cut, with little fluting cape sleeves hiding the upper part of my arms, in a lovely clear blue crêpe, to bring out the colour of my eyes. No jewellery, because I owned none. Antoinette was wearing her spectacular emeralds. I told myself that they were a little too heavy, but really I would have given my eye teeth for them, as would every other woman in the room.

'Jessica . . . or should I say Jasmina? . . . how charming you look,' one of the ladies cooed. 'So . . . unpretentious, when you are the star of the evening.'

I looked at the rubies glowing round her own neck. 'Alas, I have no husband with a treasury full of jewels,' I said.

'But surely Kesri . . . ? You must speak to him, darling. There are sapphires in the Arangapore *toshakhana* which would be just the thing for you.'

She drifted away, leaving me to grapple with the realisation that she thought I was on such terms with Kesri that it would be natural for him to supply me with jewels. It was borne in on me that most of this tinselly crowd believed I was his mistress. They almost took it for granted. Now I understood the speculative looks that had been coming my way. They were wondering whether there was a possibility of my becoming wife number three. I was Kesri's latest fancy, they thought, and if he was prepared to go to the lengths of making a film to satisfy my ambition then I must have a power over him which made me worth cultivating.

They underestimated Kesri's obsession with the process of film-making. That was what had absorbed him in the past months. Now, during the course of the evening I saw him, too, beginning to take in the idea that his friends were congratulating him not only on the success of his film, but also on possessing something he did not, in fact, have.

211

A sulky look began to come over his face. Instead of staying by Antoinette's side he began to spend more time hovering near me, while I took every possible opportunity to turn away to speak to someone else.

It was a troubling situation, but with Antoinette keeping a watchful eye on him I did not think that Kesri's attentions would get out of hand. The thing that worried me was that we were due to travel to Delhi together for the opening of the film there and Antoinette was not intending to come with us . . .

The journey to Delhi was the first time I had ever travelled in the luxury of a private railway coach and it was a revelation. The seats were upholstered in red cut velvet, there was a carpet on the floor and the light fittings were solid silver. There was a saloon, three sleeping compartments, elaborate toilet arrangements, a kitchen and accommodation for the servants. We travelled, in fact, in our own little world, cocooned from the hardships outside and knowing nothing of the trials of a railway journey in the packed carriages behind us.

Our party consisted of Kesri, myself, my leading man and Kesri's secretary, a sharp-faced young man who looked at me in a way which showed that he, too, shared the common delusion about my status.

I had assumed that we would be staying at one of the leading hotels, but it seemed that Kesri had recently acquired a house in Delhi because, as he said, he would need somewhere to live while he was attending the Assembly of Princes. I would not have thought that this body was going to meet often enough to warrant buying a house, but Kesri seemed to consider it essential.

It was not a palace, any more than his house in Bombay could be called a palace, but it felt palatial enough to someone who had been living in a cramped hotel room. I had a suite of rooms: a bedroom, a bathroom, a dressing room and a sitting room. I would have preferred a lighter and more modern style of decoration, but if one had a taste for blue damask and gilt then the rooms were certainly opulent. Another thing I would have liked was a good strong lock on the bedroom door, but when I examined it I was not particularly surprised to find that there was none. Nor was I surprised when the sharp-faced secretary came to enquire whether I would receive His Highness for a few minutes before dinner. Sooner or later Kesri was going to make a move to secure the prize everyone believed he already possessed.

He came into my sitting room, smiling and sure of his welcome and looking, one had to admit, extremely handsome in his silk *achkan* and tight-legged breeches.

'I have something to give you, with my apologies,' he said, holding out a box covered in green velvet. 'You should have had it in time for the first night in Bombay, to congratulate you on your splendid performance, but the fool of a jeweller delivered it late.'

A lie if ever I heard one because no jeweller would have risked a delay in selling the necklace that was displayed inside the box. It was a circle of opals and diamonds, a modern piece, set in pale gold. I lifted it out and the colour in the stones shifted and glinted with hidden fires.

'I'm overwhelmed,' I said.

'Will you wear it tonight?'

'The only reward I really want is the chance to make another film and repeat our success.'

A look of slight impatience passed over his face. 'Will you let me put it on for you?' he asked.

With the necklace in my hand I moved towards a looking glass. 'I can manage.'

I fastened the necklace round my neck and looked at it in the glass. It looked wonderful and it must have cost a fortune. Kesri was watching me and in our reflected images our eyes met. This was no reward for good acting, we both knew that; it was payment in advance for favours expected.

He was waiting to be thanked and he began to frown when I took the necklace off without saying anything.

'Doesn't it please you?' he asked.

'Of course it does. It's one of the most beautiful necklaces I've ever seen. I'm a little troubled, I must admit. Will you sit down for a moment?'

He sat on one of the blue damask sofas and watched me putting the necklace back in its box.

'I'm not sure I should accept such a costly gift,' I said. I was trying to move cautiously, but it was difficult.

'If I choose to give it to you . . .'

'You are generous and kind and I appreciate your wonderful gesture more than I can say. What worries me is that I think that our relations have already been misunderstood and if people see me wearing beautiful jewellery which you have given me. . . . I wouldn't for the world do anything which would distress dear Antoinette.'

'Antoinette isn't in Delhi.'

'Word will get back. You are fairly newly married and you know, I think, how deeply I have mourned for Dominic.'

I was proud of the artistry with which I allowed my voice to break and the way my eyes filled with tears as I turned my head away. Not that I was entirely acting. Speaking Dominic's name still caused me a pain that time had done nothing to diminish.

There was silence from the sofa. At least I had made Kesri stop to think. I put the jeweller's box down on the table, with considerable regret, and the little noise it made seemed to goad him into speech.

'If you make me take back that trumpery necklace I shall be very annoyed.'

Trumpery! It must have cost thousands.

'I'd like to keep it,' I said truthfully, 'if I may do so as a sign of our continuing friendship and a pledge of more successful films together in the future.'

Kesri got up, looking discontented and sulky. 'As to another film, I'll have to think about it. One can't spend all one's time chasing round a film set with a camera.'

That was something I was anxious about. He had made his film and achieved his ambition. Essentially, Kesri was an amateur, not a professional, and that single success

214

might be enough for him, whereas I felt I needed at least one more good role to establish myself as an actress.

'It would need careful consideration,' I agreed. 'Perhaps something more historical . . . an episode from your own interesting family history.'

That caught his fancy and for the moment his amorous intentions were forgotten.

'I might do that,' he said.

I was suspicious of the sidelong look he gave me and sure enough he went on: 'But not necessarily with you in the title role, Jessica. An episode from history needs a truly Indian heroine.'

'If you can find one,' I said sweetly.

I could have hit him. I had worked myself to a standstill for him during the making of *Princess Sushila* and now, just because he was being balked of a night in bed, he was thinking of dropping me.

'That is the difficulty,' Kesri agreed. 'Wear my necklace, Jessica.'

'On my terms.'

'Of course. Did I ever hint at anything else?'

So I went to our Delhi première wearing a fortune in opals and diamonds round my neck. Again the film was well received and Kesri's party afterwards was even more glittering than it had been in Bombay because the Viceroy and Vicereine kept their promise and came. I made my curtsey, accepted a few words of congratulation, and was glad that their presence gave a formality to the party which made it necessary for Kesri to behave himself. For the first time I wondered whether Antoinette's absence had been a matter of diplomacy, since I knew that her marriage to Kesri had been very unpopular indeed in official circles. So what about me? Were all these courtly ADCs and their ladies under the illusion that I was sleeping with him? If so, they hid it very well, far better than Kesri's princely friends in Bombay had done.

The person I was looking out for was Patricia. I had made sure she was sent an invitation, both to the première and to the party, and had followed it up with a letter urging her to come. Of course I had not heard from her in reply. I asked one of the ADCs if he had seen her and was not surprised when a pained look flitted across his face.

'Has she been making a nuisance of herself?' I asked sympathetically.

'Well . . . let's say that if you could persuade her to go back to England we'd be infinitely obliged,' he admitted. 'No, she's not here this evening. In fact, I can't remember seeing her for several weeks and I must admit it's been a relief. I was afraid the arrival of a new Viceroy would stir her up all over again.'

I was mildly annoyed with Patricia because I thought she might have made the effort to come and see my début as a film star, but I had plenty of other things to think about that evening and I put her out of my mind. I was still not quite sure if I had been successful in staving off Kesri. I spent a restless night, half expecting him to come visiting in spite of the brush-off I had given him. Nothing happened, so then I started worrying about that. If I had been too successful and he had taken a dislike to me then I could say farewell to my promising film career.

What would I do then? I had made enough money to pay my fare back to England, but I was no longer sure that a return to a secretarial job would satisfy me and I had no illusions about my chances of breaking into the film industry in England or America, not on the strength of one Bombay picture.

I only had one day in Delhi after the first night and the party, but I made the effort to go and seek out Patricia. I half expected to discover that she was away on some propaganda trip, though what use she could be when she spoke not one word of the language was more than I could imagine, in which case I think I would have washed my hands of her and left her to run her own life.

She had managed to take quite a pleasant little house, but not in an area favoured by the British. In fact, it was not dissimilar to the house in which I had grown up in Bombay. I was relieved to see that Patricia's money was sufficient to allow her to live in a reasonably civilised way. I wondered whether she was sharing her quarters with other devotees of the Mahatma, running a sort of *ashram*. The idea amused me, since I could not see Patricia running a chicken coop, let alone a house full of people.

I sent in my name and waited for the bearer to come back, but it was Patricia herself who came out to me on the verandah. She moved slowly, with none of the impetuosity of the past. As she came out of the shadow of the house, I saw why.

'You're pregnant,' I said.

'Oh, Jess, is it so obvious? I was afraid it was, that's why I didn't come to your film. I mean, it's a bit embarrassing, having to admit there's a little brown baby on the way.'

'Hari's the father, I take it?'

'Of course.'

'Pat, how could you?'

'Oh, ducky, you know how these things happen. We were together such a lot, I was miserable and he's a kind soul. And frightfully goodlooking, don't you think? We were both on fire for the cause so we had a lot in common and, of course, he's got no money so I had him to live here and . . . we sort of drifted into sleeping together. Poor Hari, he's in a frightful stew. He says he can't marry me.'

'Of course he can't.'

'I've offered to convert or whatever one does to become a Hindu, but he doesn't seem to think it would take.'

'His family would be outraged.'

Just as I was, by her ignorance and her silliness, but I was also desperately sorry for her. I could see only too easily how it had happened. She had been lonely, lonelier than she had expected once she had cut herself off from her natural friends. She was still grieving for Dominic and the love she had lavished on him had been going begging. As for Hari, he had all a young man's appetite for sex and, being an Indian, few outlets for it. Patricia had no doubt led him on – I was pretty sure they had slept together on their first expedition – and he had probably been swept away by the hungry way she had turned to him for the affection she was getting from no one else.

The fact that I understood the way it could have happened did not mean that I condoned what Patricia had done.

'Don't make that disapproving face,' she said. 'After all, you slept with Dominic.'

'I loved Dominic.'

'I loved Hari – sort of,' Patricia said.

'What are you going to do?'

'I wish I knew. I don't want this beastly baby, Jessica. I thought I might be able to shift it. I heard things when I was a nurse which ought to have worked, but it seems determined to stay with me.'

'No wonder you look so ill.'

She grimaced. 'I feel fairly awful. Perhaps I'll die. Rukmini did. I don't really want to live.'

'Don't say that!'

Patricia shrugged, but then her lips trembled and she said in a fierce whisper, 'Jess, I want to go home!'

So Patricia's love affair with India was over. It was no more than I expected. The great pity was it had not come to an end before she made this other dreadful mistake. I was angry until I saw the terror in her eyes, but what frightened me was when she started to look at me with hope. She was going to pass her burden on to me and I had no idea how to deal with it.

CHAPTER ELEVEN

I moved Patricia to Bombay as soon as I could. With the money from *Princess Sushila* I was able to take a small bungalow. Patricia shared the expenses and we managed very well as far as money was concerned. In every other way things could scarcely have been worse.

I tracked down Hari, expecting him to be remorseful, but instead he was full of resentment at what he saw as the way Patricia had led him on and then turned against him.

'She found out that I had been in Ferozepore at the time of her brother's death,' he said.

'Oh, Lord! I did so hope that would never come out.'

'But, really . . . to put the blame on me as she does! Not only for that but for the child as well. Did I make the baby alone?'

'Of course not. Patricia has been very foolish and very wrong.'

I could see that he agreed with me about that and I had an uneasy suspicion that he thought I was not much better myself.

'I have been covered in shame,' he said.

For a moment I did not understand him and then I realised what he meant. He had captured a young English-woman from a rich and influential family as a convert to the cause of Home Rule and he had lost her because he had not been able to suppress his carnal desires. His friends might have admired him, in a grudging sort of way, if he and Patricia had stayed together and she had kept him on her money, but once she rejected him and his cause they blamed him for his bad behaviour.

'It is quite impossible for me to support a child,' Hari said.

'There's no question of that,' I told him.

Patricia had refused to see him. She was now in head-long retreat from her obsession with all things Indian and 'I want to go home' was her constant cry.

'There's nothing to stop you booking a passage on the next boat to England,' I said in exasperation. 'You've still got time to get there before the baby arrives and no doubt your mother will see you get the best medical attention.'

'I can't do that. Jess, don't be so heartless. You know I can't go home until I've shed my little burden. Oh, Jess, what am I going to do?'

I was frightened by the way she depended on me. Hadn't I got enough problems without taking on Patricia and her unwanted child? What worried me, and what I could not get Patricia to face, was what was going to happen once the baby was born.

'I'll go home to England,' she said.

'Taking the baby with you?'

'No, of course not. The whole point of going into hiding is to keep it a secret. I'll just have to give it up for adoption, that's all.'

'In *India*? Do you know how many surplus children there are already? Who do you think will take on a half-caste bastard? No Indian family, that's for sure, and no British one either.'

'There must be places . . . orphanages, or something.'

'Precious few. You've seen the beggars in the streets. Could you abandon a child of yours to live like that?'

'You are horrid to me, Jess. I don't feel well. Be kind to me.'

Her pregnancy was not an easy one and I had to spend precious money on medical attention for her. At my insistence she dropped the name of Arkady, which would cause too much interest in Bombay, and was known as Mrs Harold, a desperate invention on my part because 'Hari' was in my mind and I was taken by surprise when her doctor asked for the name of his patient. I said she was a widow, which deceived nobody, least of all Dr Rao.

We were enduring the rains, which Patricia disliked as much as Edmond had done, but gradually they subsided and I was able to persuade her to take short walks in the glimpses of watery sunshine that filtered through the clouds for short periods each day.

To my relief, her health improved as her pregnancy advanced and as the birth drew near she became more placid. Together we sewed clothes for the baby and I surprised Patricia by my proficiency with the needle.

'I never thought of you as domesticated,' she said.

'We were all taught to sew at school. I've been lazy about it in the past, but I quite like making these little things.'

It was one of the better periods of the day and we had taken chairs out on the verandah of the small bungalow. The ladies of the Indian family next door had done the same thing and we exchanged polite smiles and bows. I would have liked to have known them better, but Patricia shrank from any contact with the rest of the world. They must have been curious about us, two Englishwomen living so simply, with one cook-bearer and a sweeper, and no visitors at all.

'Did you know Hari was in Ferozepore when Dominic was killed?' Patricia asked with a suddenness that made me stick my needle in my finger.

'Yes, I knew,' I admitted. 'He always insisted he wasn't involved in the trouble.'

'You ought to have told me.'

'Would it have made any difference?'

'I might not have got so deeply involved with him. Once I knew I felt such a revulsion towards him I couldn't bear him near me.'

'And out of the window went all your fine ideals about "India for the Indians",' I said, sucking my finger.

'Oh, that! I just wanted to have something to love.'

'So you took on the whole Indian sub-continent?'

'Something like that. Losing Dom threw me completely off-balance. It happened during the war, too. Hari wasn't my first lover. There was a Major in the hospital . . .'

'Did he get killed?' I asked, ready to be sympathetic.

'No, he just went back to his wife. I didn't really love him. I've never loved anyone but Dominic.'

'Perhaps the baby . . .' I suggested helplessly.

'It's hardly likely, is it?' She shifted uncomfortably in her chair. 'My legs ache if I stand up, my back aches if I sit down and my beastly incubus kicks me if I lie on my bed,' she complained. 'It can't be *much* longer, can it, Jess?'

Patricia's child was born two weeks later.

'I've seen a mare foal so I know what happens, more or less,' Patricia said when her pains started. 'You'll stay with me, won't you, Jess?'

I was there all through her labour, holding her twisting hands, wiping her sweating forehead, murmuring words of encouragement and only giving way to Dr Rao when at last the child began to appear.

He and the nurse pushed me out of the way into a corner of the room. I had no part in the messy business of delivery, but I heard the first thin, indignant wail of the newborn infant and found myself smiling, though I could hardly have said why. That foolish smile was the only welcome the child received. Certainly her mother had nothing good to say about her.

'You've got a lovely baby girl,' I said, bending over Patricia after they had cleaned her up.

'Do you think so? She looks like a screwed-up monkey and hideously dark.'

'You're tired,' I said.

'Yes, I am, and I ache all over, but it's wonderful to have my body to myself again. Don't look like that, Jessica. You always knew I didn't want her.'

Because I bullied her, Patricia reluctantly agreed to feed the infant.

'We're surrounded by infection,' I said. 'You must give her the protection of your own milk.'

It was about the only bit of baby lore I knew, but because I had heard it often my insistence carried conviction and Patricia put the baby to her breast with a grimace. To my relief she fed greedily and began to thrive.

It was true that she was dark, but that first dusky tinge faded until she was no darker than many Europeans. She was born with a shock of black hair, but she had inherited her mother's eyes – the Arkady eyes, the blue flash.

It caught me entirely off-guard a few days after the baby was born when I bent over her cot and she fixed her sweet, unfocused gaze on me with Dominic's eyes. My knees gave way and I sank down with my head pressed against the bars of the cot. From behind my closed eyelids the tears ran down my cheeks. How gladly I would have borne this child if it could have been Dominic's. I would have loved her and cherished her, no matter what it cost me. It was unfair, miserably unfair, that Patricia should have been given a baby from an affair of which she was ashamed and I was left alone with nothing to show for a love that had torn me apart.

We had an *ayah* for the baby, a Goanese Christian who spoke English. I watched her closely for the first few weeks, having been brought up on stories of *ayahs* who kept their charges quiet by putting opium on their fingers to suck, but it was soon obvious that Maria Gonzalez D'Souza was far too conscientious to do anything so discreditable.

'You do fuss,' Patricia said. 'Maria Gonzalez D'Souza is a treasure. Top marks to you for finding her. She does everything for the baby. My only job is to stick a nipple in her greedy little mouth when she cries.'

'Pat, don't you have any feeling for her at all?' I asked.

'Not much. She's quite sweet, in a way, like a puppy or something, and I wouldn't want any harm to come to her, but she's ruined my life. I'm trapped. I can't go home and I don't suppose anyone will ever want to marry me.'

'I do wish you'd think of a name for her. How about your own name?'

'No! I don't want anything that will connect her with me.'

In the end, because it was the plainest and most ordinary of names, we called her Jane. Jane Harold. It sounded unconvincing, but that was the name with which the poor little scrap was stuck.

I was not quite sure how much money Patricia actually had at her disposal. When we first moved into the bungalow I asked whether she could afford to pay half the rent and the bills and she agreed readily. Expenses were higher now and perhaps it was not quite fair that I should be paying half the *ayah's* wages, but I was too relieved to have her competent assistance to quibble. But what about the future? What about school fees and uniforms and clothes which were quickly outgrown? Sometimes my head swam with the realisation of what I had taken on when I allowed Patricia and her baby to join up with me.

I had to get some more work. I wrote to Kesri enquiring whether he had any fresh project in mind. To my relief he sent me a letter, obviously written by his secretary, but at least he had the grace the sign it himself, saying that he would be in Bombay in ten days' time and suggesting a meeting.

'Tea at the Taj,' Patricia said. 'Lucky you. I wish I could come with you. You won't tell him about me, will you?'

'Of course not. He thinks you're still in Delhi. I must look out something decent to wear and make sure it hasn't gone mildewed in this horrid damp.'

'It doesn't matter what you wear, you always look scrumptious,' Patricia said. 'I've gone all to pot since having the baby. Nothing seems to fit me any more.'

'Get the *durzi* round to make you something new,' I suggested.

'Maria Gonzalez D'Souza sews like a dream. Perhaps I'll get her to run something up for me.'

'You must pay her extra if she does.'

'Oh, you're always on the side of the workers.'

I was about to say that was because I was a worker myself, but I bit it back in case Pat thought I was complaining.

Instead, I remarked quite lightly, 'I do hope Kesri is serious about making another picture. I could really do with the money.'

'You could always hock the opals,' Patricia said with all the carelessness of someone with a regular income paid into the bank every month.

I wished she had not reminded me about the necklace. I still had the feeling that Kesri meant to demand payment for it one day, but tea at the Taj Mahal Hotel did not sound like a seduction scene and when the day came I put on my newly washed and pressed blue linen dress and jacket and went off with a fairly easy mind.

Right at the last moment, just as I was about to leave, Patricia came out of her bedroom to see me off and fastened a little turquoise and pearl brooch to my lapel.

'To wish you luck,' she said. 'It belonged to Grandmother.'

I was touched and pleased. 'I'll take great care of it,' I promised.

'It's for you to keep. I . . . I am grateful for all you've done, Jess, honestly I am.'

Kesri, to my relief, was very much on his best behaviour. Not that he could very well be anything else surrounded by the tinkling tea cups of the ladies of Bombay, most of whom knew very well who he was. In that feminine crowd he drew more attention than I did. He was goodlooking, of course, though a little too sleek for my taste, but there was something else about him that caused a *frisson* of excitement amongst the saris and the Paris frocks, and even affected me to a certain extent. His dark suit was a miracle of understated British tailoring, his silk shirt was plain, his tie was discreet and he wore no jewellery apart from a handsome wristwatch, and yet everything about him suggested money and power. No doubt, if he had chosen to do so (and if Mr Tata had been prepared to sell) he could have bought up the Taj Mahal Hotel and used it as another spare house; and, of course, one had to remember that a couple of hundred thousand of his subjects looked upon Kesri as not much less than a god.

With this thought in mind I began to feel dejected about the likelihood of Kesri wanting to go on with his career as a film director, but he had a pleasant surprise for me.

'I'm being encouraged to make another film,' he said. '*Princess Sushila* has had a very good reception. I'm dedicating the profits towards a hospital for women in Arangapore and even my tiresome British Resident approves.'

'How very generous of you,' I said.

'I never went into film-making for commercial reasons, I'm not a merchant.'

I was not sure whether this was a reference to his *kshatrias* caste or just an aristocratic distaste for trade, so I murmured, 'Of course not,' soothingly and waited to be told about the new film.

'An incident out of my own family history,' Kesri said. 'I have to give you credit for that suggestion, Jessica.'

It seemed that I was really in his good books. I only hoped his goodwill would extend to a substantial increase in my salary.

'One of my family was a Maharani who took up arms and defended Arangapore Palace in the seventeenth century. Her story is most interesting and heroic. I wish you to play this part.'

'It sounds wonderful. When do you hope to start?'

'We must press ahead with it as quickly as possible. If it's finished and as good as I hope it will be then it will be shown to the Prince of Wales during his visit.'

'He really is coming this time?'

'He's due to arrive in Bombay in the middle of November. He has, of course, many visits to make, but he'll be coming to Arangapore for some polo and my film will be shown for his entertainment one evening.'

I began to get excited. This was a chance for real fame. If I became sufficiently well known I might be able to break away from Kesri's Indian films and get myself an opening in California.

As if he had read my thoughts, Kesri went on: 'I want

to take personal control of this film because of the Prince's interest, but after that I shall retire.'

That was exactly what I had been afraid of. 'Perhaps you could form a company to carry on your work even though you are unable to direct yourself?' I suggested.

'Possibly. You'd like that, wouldn't you, Jessica?'

'It would mean continuing work for me – I hope.'

'It would be a rather more substantial investment than an opal necklace,' Kesri said with a smile.

And he would expect a better return on it than he had gained from the necklace? Was that what he meant?

'I hope Antoinette is well?' I asked in a crude attempt to remind him that he had a wife.

'Not quite well. She's in Switzerland at the moment undergoing treatment at a clinic.'

'I'm sorry to hear that. Nothing too serious, I hope?'

'Not in the least. A minor operation to improve her chance of giving me a child. She'll be back in time to entertain the Prince of Wales.'

And in the meantime Kesri was free and looking for adventure. Unless I was very much mistaken, life was about to become difficult. His next question gave me a jolt.

'Have you heard from Patricia Arkady? She seems to have quite dropped out of the world and no one knows where she is.'

'I haven't had any letters from her,' I said truthfully. 'Pat is the world's worst correspondent.'

'Perhaps one should start making enquiries.'

'If her family are worried I'm sure they'll ask for that to be done,' I said.

To my relief he did not pursue the subject and I made a mental note that I must goad Patricia into writing home, if only to ward off the enquiries Kesri had suggested.

'Tell me, Jessica, what exactly is your own matrimonial position?' he asked.

'My husband is divorcing me, but I've no idea what progress he's made.'

'Because of Dominic?'

227

'There's been no one else.'

'No . . . one has to applaud your discretion, tiresome though it is. So you've been living quite alone and unoccupied. How very boring for you.'

'I have a . . . a lady companion,' I said.

Kesri's shoulders shook with laughter. 'A chaperone! I said you were discreet, but that's more than I expected. Don't, I beg of you, bring her to Arangapore.'

'Arangapore?'

'Oh, yes, did I forget to mention that? A large part of the picture will be shot on location at the Palace. Naturally you will be my guest.'

'And the rest of the cast?'

'I don't think so. They can be perfectly adequately housed in the town.'

So I was to be given special treatment – in the palace where Dominic and I had played our silly, ecstatic game of hide-and-seek.

'Being in the Palace will bring back painful memories,' I said. 'I might be happier in an hotel with the rest of the cast.'

'But I want you with me.' Kesri spoke very softly, but when he fixed his eyes on mine I was unable to look away. 'Otherwise, dear Jessica, there will be no more films, either now or in the future.'

An ultimatum. I was furious and frightened. Of course, Kesri had no idea how badly I needed this work, but he must have some idea that money was running low – though what would that mean to him, a man who never in his life had to think twice about putting his hand in his pocket? Perhaps because of that he did not realise the cruelty of the blackmailing tactics he was employing.

'I've become too much of a professional actress to commit myself before I've seen the script,' I said. 'Send it to me and when I've read it I'll give you my answer.'

I think he rather admired my resistance. At any rate, he made no further attempt to win me over. The only thing he said when we parted was, 'I'd like a decision soon. Otherwise I'll have to look elsewhere.'

It was foolhardy, but I could not resist looking him straight in the eye and asking, 'Am I so easy to replace?'

'No,' he said curtly. 'If you were, I wouldn't be bidding for you.'

I went back to the bungalow in a very worried frame of mind. I told myself there were alternatives – there must be! – but it was difficult to think what they were. Patricia's money was certain, at least we had that to fall back on. There might be someone in India who would like a female British secretary. Or perhaps I could train for something, if Pat would keep me while I did so. None of it felt very attractive, not compared with doing the one thing I had discovered that I did well, which was acting in films.

I ought to have been more despondent than I was. Thinking it over, I realised that deep down I was exhilarated by Kesri's desire for me. After all, he was, as I had seen that afternoon, a man of charm, wealth and influence. He could have anything he wanted, but what he wanted was me and I was frustrating him. It ought not have given me a thrill, but it did.

Maria was on the verandah with the baby in her arms when I got back, but Patricia did not seem to be about.

'Mrs Harold is not here, *memsahib*,' the *ayah* said.

I was rather glad to hear it. Patricia had started to get out of the house occasionally and I was encouraging her, though she rarely did more than walk to the end of the street and back. It was hopeless to think of launching her into Bombay society again, especially while she was still feeding the baby, but in time I hoped to arrange some sort of life for her outside the bungalow.

'Did she say when she would be back?' I asked, idly tickling Jane under the chin and enchanted when she smiled at me.'

'Mrs Harold not here, *memsahib*. She has gone.'

'*Gone?*'

'There is a letter for you, *memsahib*.'

There was indeed a letter, propped up on my dressing

229

table: *Darling Jessica, Don't blame me too much. I do so long to go home and what future is there for me here? I booked my passage as soon as you heard from Kesri and I'm sailing today. I know you'll see Jane's looked after; you're much fonder of her than I am. I've put some money into your account at the bank. Not enough, I know, but you'll make lots when you're filming again, won't you? Thank you for everything and forgive me, please forgive me. Patricia.*

I had been left, quite literally, holding the baby. For one blinding moment I could have killed Patricia Arkady. How dared she do this to me? And the baby. How could she walk out of Jane's life after giving birth to her? A nasty memory came back to me of Lady Cynthia saying of her children, 'They are empty inside . . .' and I shivered. It had not been true of Dominic and nor was it, I was sure, of Patricia. She had been off-balance, even a little out of her mind, when Jane was conceived and I suspected she had taken the child in dislike because Jane represented her time of chaos.

So, what was I going to do? Take up my burden, of course. It was impossible to allow a child who looked at me with Dominic's eyes to be thrown on the scrap heap. I thought of the children who begged on the streets and shuddered. I was trapped by the helplessness of a small half-Indian girl with blue eyes. My blue eyes. Had Patricia thought of that? Everyone would assume that the child was mine. She had achieved the perfect escape and I was left to deal with the problem she had left behind.

CHAPTER TWELVE

My career as a concubine was short, but eventful. It helped, of course, that Kesri was young, attractive and a skilful lover. I went to him the first time seething with resentment both at the hold he had over me and because I had to keep silent about the motives that had driven me to accept the bargain he offered, but it was by no means as bad as I had expected.

'I've pleased you?' he asked complacently, sure of my response. 'I'm very well-educated in the art of love. I was given a couple of *nautch* girls to teach me when I was fourteen.'

'*Fourteen?*'

'I matured early.'

'But surely you were away at school, in England?'

'You can imagine how I looked forward to the holidays.'

'All the same . . . fourteen.'

'It's a custom which is less frequently followed in modern times,' he admitted. 'But I hadn't been brought up in the Palace and my great-uncle, who adopted me, thought that I should be handed over to the girls to learn manners and protocol and, as I have said, the way to give and receive pleasure.'

'You were an apt pupil,' I said drily. I propped myself up on my elbow to look down at him, his black hair ruffled and his brown limbs sprawling on the white sheets. 'After all that expert tuition, I must seem awkward to you.'

'Yes, but there's a freshness about you which I find attractive. It'll be better when you stop being angry with yourself for giving in to me.'

'How can I help being angry?' I said in a low voice. 'If you understood the necessity that drove me . . .' I pulled myself up, but something made me go on obstinately, 'I

231

don't understand how you can want me, knowing you've blackmailed me into it.' I was annoyed with him for looking amused.

'I've watched you closely,' he said. 'You are a woman with a deeply sensual nature. Your clumsy husband didn't satisfy you . . .'

'I don't see how you can possibly know that.'

'It was obvious. As soon as I saw you together I was sure of it. You had one short love affair . . .'

'Don't speak about that.'

'Dominic touched your heart. It may never happen to you again, but does that mean you are to live the rest of your life like one of your Catholic nuns?'

'Like a Hindu widow,' I said spitefully.

'As you say,' he agreed calmly. 'That's not the life for you, Jessica. I will be your teacher, your *guru*. It will amuse me.'

That was in Bombay, in the house where I had once gone to join Rukmini for dancing lessons, but shortly after that first night together we departed for Arangapore. I had to leave Jane behind in the care of her *ayah*. It worried me, but Maria assured me that she could manage. She promised to write every week and to call in the doctor if Jane showed the slightest sign of ailing and I tore myself away. Until Jane was born I had had little contact with small children and it was a revelation to me to see her growing at such a pace and, above all, to watch her awakening intelligence. When she began to laugh, not just the milky smile of a wellfilled stomach, but a real chortle, I was reduced to grovelling worship.

As Kesri had promised I was installed in the Palace at Arangapore. I felt prickly and on the defensive, but to my surprise the servants were as deferential as if I had been the première Maharani.

'My great-uncle had women in his *zenana* who were not his wives,' Kesri said. 'Everyone is accustomed to the idea. And, of course, while you enjoy my favour you are thought to be a powerful woman.'

'Am I? Powerful? Can I command you to do anything?'

'You can try. What would please you, my lady?'

I thought about it, but nothing came into my head. 'The trouble is, I've had no practice at this business of being kept,' I said. 'My salary for the new film is more than generous and you've promised to set up a company so that I can carry on working when it's finished. That's all I really need.'

'I said you were refreshing,' Kesri commented. He looked round the bedroom where he had come to join me shortly after my arrival at Arangapore. 'I was carrying a jeweller's box when I came in. Where did I put it down?'

'Is this it?'

'Look inside.'

The box contained a triple row of matched pearls, lustrous and beautiful. I fastened the catch and went to look at myself in the mirror.

'The fact that you are wearing nothing else makes the effect particularly pleasing,' Kesri said. 'Come back to bed.'

'Are they from your treasury?' I asked.

'The jewels in the *toshakhana* belong to the State and I have to return them each time after they've been worn. These pearls have been bought for you.'

'Thank you.'

'That's not how I want to be thanked. Come here.' He caught hold of my arm and yanked me towards him and I went, if not gladly, at least with none of the reluctance I ought to have been feeling. I told myself that it was despicable to be influenced by the present, but the pearls were very beautiful and I couldn't help being gratified. Oh, the truth was, dress it up as I may, that he gave me a very good time and I was beginning to enjoy it.

'We must make the most of our time together for the next day or two,' Kesri remarked. 'The *Dassera* begins next week and I shall be required to separate myself from you.'

I knew about the ten-day religious festival which was celebrated by the *kshatria* warrior caste to which Kesri belonged, but in Bombay the main Hindu festival had

233

been the *Ganpati*, honouring Ganesh, and so I was vague about the details and it was certainly news to me that he would be expected to remain celibate while it lasted.

'Customs vary from one place to another,' Kesri said. 'Here in Arangapore it has always been the tradition that the ruler refrains from women during the *Dassera*.'

'Does that mean filming will also be held up for ten days?'

'Certainly not. I shall be too occupied to do more than give instructions, but I wish the public part of the festival – the processions, the dancing and so on – to be put on film as part of the background to our story.'

'The "warrior queen" lived in the seventeenth century,' I pointed out.

'The ceremonies have changed very little,' Kesri said impatiently. 'I can edit out any tiresome things like motor cars and telegraph poles. I've asked William to come and advise me on the historical background and I shall rely on him to notice anything I've missed.'

I sat up, the ropes of pearls still swinging between my breasts. 'You've asked William to come here? My cousin William?'

'Yes, of course. Do you know anyone better qualified to be our adviser?'

'William's interest is in earlier periods.'

'His knowledge is encyclopaedic.'

I was deeply disturbed by this news. William knew that I had separated from Edmond, because I had written to tell him so, but he knew nothing of the rest of my story. It was going to be very difficult indeed to meet him here, installed in the Palace as Kesri's mistress and enjoying all the trappings and status of that dubious situation.

He did not arrive until the *Dassera* was well under way. It was an interesting, but also a frustrating time for me. There was very little to do since Kesri kept himself rigidly apart from me and the film crew were absorbed in chasing round taking shots of all the ceremonies as directed by Kesri.

I was asked to perform a few scenes, such as looking

out of the palace window and registering interest in the spectacle below, but I was not allowed to take any part in the real festival, not even when the women performed their *Ras Garba* dance in the courtyard. I was watching this when I heard someone come into the room behind me and, turning my head, discovered that, as usual, William had arrived out of nowhere.

I think that just for a moment he did not recognise me. Because Kesri liked it, I habitually wore Indian dress these days. Today, my sari was of deep blue silk, my hair was drawn back into a tight knot circled by jasmine flowers and I had the triple row of pearls round my neck.

'Jessica, my dear! I was just about to apologise for stumbling into the retreat of some unknown Maharani.'

He looked at me with his slight, amused smile and I held out my hands in spontaneous pleasure at seeing him again and finding him unchanged. As soon as I set eyes on him I knew that I had been worrying foolishly. I could tell William everything and he would understand.

He touched the flowers in my hair delicately. 'Jasmina,' he said. 'You've no idea how surprised I was to discover that the celebrated film star was my little cousin Jessica.'

'Hardly celebrated, on the strength of one film,' I protested. 'I'm hoping that this new one we're doing may really make a name for me.'

'Ah, yes: *The Warrior Queen*. Has Kesri overlooked the fact that at the time of her exploits she was over forty and rather fat?'

'That's exactly the sort of historical fact he doesn't want you to uncover,' I retorted. 'William, why did you come? You must know that Kesri is far more interested in turning out an entertaining story than in historical accuracy. Why did you let him drag you away from your real work?'

'I'm taking time off from what you call my real work to write a book. Kesri has generously offered me the use of his houses in Bombay and Delhi until it's finished. It would have been churlish to refuse to vet his film even though I agree with you that my usefulness will be limited.'

Again his amused smile invited me to share the joke, but I was grappling with the realisation that William was going to be around for longer than I had anticipated.

'There are things I have to tell you,' I said. 'Let's get away from this noise.'

William glanced out at the courtyard below. 'The men are performing their stick dance,' he said.

The sound of the drums was making my head throb. I led the way through the Palace to the terrace gardens at the back where the sound did not penetrate. I slipped my hand through William's arm and there, walking up and down the upper terrace, I told him about Dominic, about leaving Edmond, about Patricia and about Jane. I told him the truth about Jane's birth. No one was safer with the secret than William.

'My poor girl,' he said.

'I love her,' I said. 'Funny, isn't it? I never wanted a child of my own and yet here I am, desperate with love for someone else's baby.'

I took my hand away from his arm and went to look out over the plain to where the white marble Lake Palace glimmered like a toy in the distance.

'I'm Kesri's mistress,' I said. 'You must have suspected that? Antoinette in Europe and me installed in the Palace and wearing *lakhs* of rupees in pearls round my neck.'

'I knew before I came,' William said. 'Jessica, has the British Resident spoken to you?'

'Not more than two words. I have a feeling he's appalled by the situation.'

'He is. I called to see him yesterday and he invited me to stay the night. He's very, very worried that, after marrying a European wife, Kesri has now taken a European mistress.'

'Has he sent you here to talk me into giving Kesri up? I say, William, it's just like *Traviata*. Imagine you as an emissary of the Raj. Are you getting paid?'

William took me by the shoulders and tried to make me face him, but I kept my head turned away so that he should not see my angry tears.

'I promised no more than that I would see you and talk to you,' he said steadily. 'Of course, as I suspected, the situation is far more complex than it seems on the surface. I understand why you've taken this step. I sympathise with you.'

'But you don't like it.'

'How could I?'

'It's not going to be permanent,' I said, admitting something I had known from the start. 'When Antoinette comes back Kesri will drop me. I know it's wrong, William, but what further harm can it do me? I'm a divorced – or nearly divorced – woman with one lover behind me already. My reputation has suffered to the extent that taking another lover can hardly make it worse, unless you think that living with an Indian, even a Maharajah, is more sinful than committing adultery with an Englishman.'

'It'll do more harm to Kesri than it will to you.'

'How could it? Kesri has had dozens of women.'

'His people don't like it. They think he's moving away from them. The Resident is afraid of a demonstration against you.'

I was shaken to realise that I had totally disregarded the teeming thousands of Kesri's subjects. Indeed, I had not realised that they would know about me. Silly of me. Everyone knows everything in India.

'I've done nothing to harm then,' I said uncertainly.

'And nothing to help them.'

'Kesri is giving his profits to a hospital.'

'The rumour in the city is that for every *lakh* of rupees he's given to charity he's spent a *crore* on his British mistress.'

'That's ridiculous! He's given me this necklace . . .' I touched the pearls at my neck '. . . some opals and, of course, I draw a salary for my acting. It's true he's promised to set up a company to continue film-making, but with any luck that will soon finance itself. William, I need that film company. How am I to manage if I can't earn?'

'I know. If Kesri sets up this company and keeps out

237

of the actual business of making films himself and, above all, if he is seen to have returned to his wife, however unsuitable she may be, then the damage may be limited.'

'It seems hard that he can't be allowed to follow a career at which he happens to be extremely good.'

'Kesri has had a career ever since he was ten years old and the old Maharajah finally admitted that he would never have a male child,' William said gently. 'He was brought up to be the ruler, the father of his people. He was married to the *maharajkumari* so that their children could descend from the old line. At first he was popular, but the European influence has been too strong. He has turned away from the duties he should be performing and the people no longer have access to him. He must get out amongst them again and to do that he has to spend the greater part of his time in Bhuredar.'

'We must finish this one film,' I pleaded. 'Just *The Warrior Queen*, William. After that, quite honestly, I don't care what happens to Kesri.'

'That's a terrible admission.'

'I'm sleeping with him for money. That's what we do, we concubines. Once I've made my pile I'll pack up and go.'

When William took hold of me again he gripped me so hard I thought he was going to shake me. Instead, he pulled me towards him and I collapsed against his shoulder and cried the hurt, angry tears I had been trying to suppress.

'Why didn't you come to me?' he said. 'I would have helped you.'

'I know. I just couldn't bring myself to ask. Self-help, that's my motto, and now look where it's landed me. What can I do, William?'

After much searching William managed to produce a slightly crumpled handkerchief so that I could mop myself up.

'I'll talk to the Resident,' he promised. 'And I'll try to spread some counter-rumours in the city.'

'Can you?'

'I had some success in that line during the war. I don't suppose I've completely lost my touch.'

I was momentarily diverted. 'William, what did you do . . .'

'Ssh.' He touched my lips with one long finger. 'Go and wash your face and make yourself look beautiful again. Kesri mustn't suspect I've been bullying you or he'll throw me out.'

'I don't see much of Kesri during the *Dassera*,' I said.

I hoped I didn't sound as forlorn as I felt. Not even to William – especially not to William – was I prepared to admit how badly I was missing Kesri's attentions.

The *Dassera* came to an end on the tenth day with a most magnificent procession. They brought out the State elephants, all three of them, and painted them with elaborate scrolls. I watched from a vantage point over the ramp which led down to the city as they set out for the final ceremonies at the temple.

Kesri rode in a gold *howdah* on the back of the largest elephant. He was wearing a red and gold brocade coat and white satin jodhpurs with red satin slippers on his feet. His turban was of gold tissue decorated with a *sarpech* shaped like a feather and glowing with rubies and pearls set in gold. Round his neck was the famous Bhuredar diamond necklace. Each separate stone was worth a fortune and there were five strands to the necklace. He looked remote and alien, not at all like the Kesri who refused to speak anything but English with me and who, I thought, was interested in nothing but film-making and sex.

He was surrounded by a crowd of servants in gold, blue and white and by soldiers in gorgeous uniforms carrying an array of weapons which were to be taken to the temple for the *shashtra puja*, the worship which in the past had preceded the autumn fighting. There was one sword which dated back to the days of the warrior queen, but which was considered so sacred that not even Kesri would allow it to be photographed. For the film a replica had been made, using fake stones and gilded metal for the splendid handle and the ornate scabbard. I saw the original now,

239

for the first time, borne in the procession by the hereditary sword-bearer, who as far as I could make out, performed no other function and was kept in the Palace to carry out this ritual once a year.

The music for the procession was loud and discordant and the colours were so vivid that they made my head swim. Kesri and his elephants were winding their way down the slope and there was nothing left to see but the tail-end of hangers-on shuffling in the wake of the main cavalcade. I turned away. By this time tomorrow Kesri would be released from his vow of celibacy and presumably would turn to me once more. In the meantime, I had all too much time to think about what William had said to me.

He had worried me. For the first time it occurred to me that the people who had gathered round to watch the scenes we had shot on sites around the city of Arangapore had been curiously quiet, not at all like the jostling chatterers we had attracted in Bombay. Was it a hostile silence, and was their hostility directed at me?

I would have done better not to have spoken of my disquiet to Kesri, but it was so much on my mind that I told him about it almost as soon as we were together again. He was not pleased.

'Kindly do not get yourself involved in political matters,' he ordered.

'It's not political,' I protested.

'Yes, it is. It's an attempt by the British Resident to interfere in my personal life. The British government didn't like my marriage to Antoinette and they put every possible obstacle in my way. Did you know that if she has a child he will not be allowed to be my heir?'

'You already have an heir.'

Kesri dismissed that with an impatient wave of his hand. 'If I had *not* got two sons already then Antoinette's son would not be allowed to inherit.'

'You wouldn't ever try to disinherit Rukmini's two boys, would you?' I asked with misgiving.

'Of course not.' For once I had really shocked Kesri.

240

'They were bred especially for the purpose of ensuring the succession. It would be unthinkable to make any other arrangement.'

He looked at me sideways and added softly. 'Neither would I favour any son you might give me, although I would make sure he was maintained in comfort.'

'That wasn't in my mind,' I said.

'No? Perhaps not while you are not pregnant, but keep it in mind in case it should happen. There is nothing to be hoped for but a small pension.'

The sort of thing my grandfather had arranged for my grandmother. With that sour thought in my mind I was not responsive when Kesri held out his hand and said, 'Come. I am hungry for you, my jewel. Do you not wish for me?'

I unloosed the end of my sari and let it drop to my waist, but I was still sufficiently worried to say, 'If your people are really against me, will they make trouble when we resume filming?'

'Certainly not. They know I would be angry with them. As I shall be angry with you if you keep me waiting much longer.'

He was only half joking. He was already undressed and wearing only a loose silk robe tied at the waist with a twisted cord. He could scarcely bear to wait while I removed my tight-fitting bodice and unwound the rest of my sari before he tossed off the robe and pulled me on to the bed.

'Ah, that's good!' he said, wrapping his arms and legs around me and straining me to him as if he would swallow me up. 'I am in a hurry this time, my delight, but afterwards you shall have all the pleasure I can devise for you.'

Our lovemaking was so protracted that we fell asleep without eating. It was three o'clock in the morning when Kesri woke up, felt hungry and sent for food. There was a curtain surrounding the bed, like an English fourposter, and this was drawn to hide my nakedness as the servants padded into the room with the dishes he had commanded. I lay, half asleep, and thought about the cooks who had

241

been awakened, the fires which had been relit, the bearers and waiters turned out of bed, and all to satisfy the appetite of their amorous ruler.

'May I have some?' I asked, peering out from behind my curtain.

'Don't come to the table or it will all be contaminated and I'll have to send it away,' Kesri said. 'See, I'll put a little of everything on this dish and put it on the floor and you can take it from there.'

'Is thy servant a dog?' I asked, but Kesri missed the reference and thought I was joking.

I took the food he allowed me and sat on the bed, crosslegged and naked, to eat it, reflecting on the oddity of a man who had plunged into my body like a diver looking for pearls, but who would not allow my hand to defile his food.

'When you lie with me are you doing an unclean thing?' I asked curiously.

'There are many ways of looking at it,' he answered evasively. 'To the orthodox, yes, I suppose I am. On the other hand, the warrior is allowed his pleasures.'

I chuckled over that, but it was not fair to laugh because Kesri had fought in the war against Germany, and fought gallantly. Dominic had told me that. The thought of Dominic went through me with such pain that I had to close my eyes and clench my hand round the bed curtain. How he would have enjoyed this feast in the middle of the night. Every time I went to bed with Kesri I betrayed his memory. He was getting further away from me. I was losing him.

It would never do to allow Kesri to guess what I was thinking. I wiped my plate clean with a piece of *naan* bread and put it back on the floor, then I went into the bathroom to clean myself up.

'Stay there until I tell you the coast is clear,' Kesri ordered and I waited obediently while the servants cleared away the empty dishes, growing a little chilly with my feet on the marble floor. It was not yet November and the weather was comparatively cool. A cockroach scuttled across the floor and I flicked at it with the end of the towel, too inured to the sight of these creatures to wonder at it even in a palace. By the time Kesri called me back I was sleepy and cross and I was glad that he wanted to do nothing more than sleep the rest of the night away.

We started filming again the next day. The crew must have noticed that their leading lady was somewhat heavy-eyed, but I put all the energy I could muster into the scenes where I marshalled my troops in my husband's absence, learnt of his death and decided to carry on fighting for the sake of my infant son.

'The son was a well-grown youth of fourteen at the time and ought to have been encouraged to take up arms himself instead of leaving it to his mother,' William said – but that would have destroyed our touching story. I found it difficult to look William in the face after the night I had spent with Kesri, but he was as calm and friendly as ever, and his advice on the battle scenes was invaluable.

I took him on one side during a break and asked, 'Am I imagining it, or have the people who are looking on warmed towards me since I was last acting my heart out in front of them?'

'They've learnt that Rukmini was your friend. They were devoted to her and anyone she liked can't be all bad.'

'That's your doing?'

'And yours. When you visited the Palace as a guest you took the trouble to go and see her at the Lake Palace.'

I remembered that visit and Rukmini looking sad and ill. I remembered, too, the talk I had had with Lady Cynthia on the way back.

In despair, I said to William, 'Even in the middle of all this I still find myself missing Dominic.'

'Careful, my dear. You can't give way now. There's some very good tea being brewed back here. Come and have a cup.'

'Kesri won't eat with me,' I said as I took the cup.

'You find that inconsistent? Yes, of course. I can only

243

repeat what I said before, that your liaison with him would be better brought to an end.'

'As soon as this film is over. As soon as I'm sure that my future is secure.'

I was called back to the set, an old ruined temple which had been cleaned up and which provided an excellent background for a charming scene with my film son, a roly-poly child of three who was enchanted by his brocade coat and miniature sword. My heart hungered for the baby I had left in Bombay, so that my gesture as I went down on my knees and hugged him was not acting at all.

'We've done well,' Kesri announced. 'Jasmina, your scenes were excellent. I can hardly wait to see the rushes. We should finish on schedule.'

He liked to talk like that, using expressions – 'on schedule', 'rushes' – he had picked up from the American film industry. And in front of the rest of the cast he always called me Jasmina.

Kesri still had every intention of having the film ready for the Prince of Wales's visit and time was running short. We hurried through the final days, rushing from one site to another, improvising as we went, while William threw up his hands in horror and abandoned any attempt to make us conform to historical fact.

'Are you pleased with the way it's gone?' I asked Kesri after we had finished the last day's filming.

'Very pleased. But it will be my last film.' He did not sound as regretful as I would have expected.

'Must you give it up?' I asked.

'I think so, yes. It has been most enjoyable and I've proved that I can if I wish be as professional as an ordinary man, but there's a lot of boredom also and there are many other things I want to do. I shall learn to fly, I think. That is the transport of the future, Jessica. Just think of the time that would be saved if I could fly my own aeroplane to Delhi or Bombay.'

'Your train is very comfortable.'

'But slow. I'm already in touch with an aeronautical

company in England and I hope to arrange for them to send me out an aeroplane and an instructor.'

So that was to be the next craze. Films were over.

'You still mean to finance a company to make movies?' I asked, cautiously, because I was afraid that if I pushed too hard he might say no.

'Yes, yes. It will be a service for the people and provide employment as well as entertainment.'

'If the films are successful they'll also make you a great deal of money,' I said.

'That's not important.'

'Am I still to be your star?'

'That will be for the new director to decide. Times are changing. It may be possible to find an Indian actress to share the limelight with you.' With a smile he took my hand and pulled me towards him. 'You are still my star here, in this room where we have shared so much pleasure. Have I made you happy, Jasmina?'

'Yes,' I said steadily, and it was true, up to a point.

'Good. I have a present for you.'

'A final present?'

'By no means. Why do you say that?'

'Because Antoinette will be back very shortly.'

'In four days' time. I am to travel to Bombay to meet her from the ship in my slow, slow train and I will take you with me.'

'I'll travel to Bombay with you, but after that we must part.'

I expected him to agree with me, even to be grateful for being given such an easy way out of our affair, but it seemed Kesri had other ideas.

'Naturally I must give my attention to my wife on her return, but there will be many occasions when I shall be in Bombay on my own and you can come to me then.'

'As your part-time whore? No, Kesri, I'm not prepared to do that. When we leave here our affair will be finished.'

He looked amazed and when he spoke it was with the haughtiness of a man who was accustomed to having every wish fulfilled. 'It's not for you to decide when you will leave me.'

'Why not? I'm a free agent. I've shared your bed with, yes, I agree, mutual pleasure, but my future doesn't lie in becoming one of your dependents. I have to make my own life. This is the time when, for both our sakes, we should part. I could grow too accustomed to the luxury you provide and begin to take it for granted and you . . . you have to think of your other duties and your subjects.'

'That's not you talking, it's your stupid British Resident.'

'Since he got William to explain how the people felt about me I've seen for myself that they don't like me being your mistress. William has coaxed some of them to take a more lenient view of me, but the prejudice is too widespread to be cured completely.'

'I'm extremely displeased that William should have interfered. He had no right to do the Resident's dirty work for him.'

'I took it better from William than from anyone else. Be reasonable, Kesri. Antoinette will be upset and jealous when she hears about me – and you know she will hear. Far better for you to be able to say that it's all over.'

He did not reply to that and it seemed that I had struck the right note. I descended to coaxing him out of his sulks. 'Are you too cross with me to give me my present?'

He tossed the jeweller's box down on the table. 'Your wages,' he said. 'Since that's the way you look on what we've done together.'

He had chosen another magnificent necklace for me, sapphires set in diamonds. I suppose if I had been as highminded as I was pretending I would have refused to take it, but Kesri was right, I looked on these perks as my wages, over and above what I earned by acting in his films.

Very slowly I began to undress, while Kesri sat in his chair and watched me with sullen eyes. Then I put the blazing necklace round my neck and held out my arms.

'Let me thank you,' I said.

He liked me like that, naked except for the jewellery he bestowed on me. I knew he would not refuse me. He was rougher with me than he usually was, angry because he still wanted me and I was getting away from him, but I thought that by the morning we had been reconciled and he was resigned to losing me.

I found out how wrong I was on the train going back to Bombay. I was lolling on one of the plush settees reflecting how truly I had spoken when I had said I could easily grow accustomed to this level of comfort and Kesri was looking through a sheaf of papers.

'This will interest you,' he said.

He handed over a formal-looking document and I sat up with a jerk as I realised that what he had given me was a contract between myself and a company called Arangapore Pictures to make a film within the next year, the title to be decided later. The salary was only slightly more than I had received for *The Warrior Queen*, but what interested me was that it gave me an assurance of income and employment for at least one more year.

'If you like, you can sign it here and now,' Kesri said.

'I'm not happy about the salary. *The Warrior Queen* is sure to be a great success. I'm entitled to recognition of my part in that.'

'What price do you put on your services, Jasmina?'

'I'm looking for a fifty per cent increase.'

'I'm not a haggler,' Kesri said. 'But I think that's a little high. Could we compromise on thirty per cent?'

I could see he did not like this mercenary talk so I thought it would be diplomatic to close with that offer and it was written into the contract by Kesri's secretary. I signed the document and the secretary witnessed my signature.

'I hope it won't take long to find a story,' I said.

'I've been looking into the family history again and I've found just what we need. Here, you can read the outline.'

I read the brief synopsis through and then turned back to the beginning and read it again to make sure I had understood it. When I looked up Kesri was smiling in a

247

way that was not altogether pleasant and I understood then that this was his revenge for my rejection of him.

Trying to conceal my dismay, I said, 'The main part is that of the *nautch* girl.'

'Exactly.'

'You expect me to play that role?'

'Of course.'

'She's a very unsympathetic character.'

'Dramatic. Think what a chance it will be for you to act.'

'That's true, but all the same I don't like it.'

The two women I had portrayed so far had been high-class and virtuous. The fact that they had also been shown as beautiful and seductive was by the way and a bonus for the audience. This new role was that of a scheming dancing girl who enslaved a young ruler and came near to ruining him before she met a suspiciously timely death and good triumphed.

'You must have a few redeeming features written into the character, otherwise the audience will hate her,' I protested.

'They'll enjoy hating her, especially if she is played by you – an Anglo-Indian.'

That really niggled me. 'I won't do it.'

It was Kesri's moment of triumph and he made the most of it. 'Examine your contract, my dear Jasmina. You have agreed to work for the new company and you lay yourself wide open to paying compensation if you let us down.'

There was no need to look at the contract. I knew when he called me 'Jasmina' in that sneering way that there was no way out. As far as I was concerned that finished Kesri. While I believed that he had some feeling for me and was sorry our affair was coming to an end I felt regretful and quite tender towards him, but if he was prepared to take such a petty revenge then I had done with him.

We parted with smiling courtesy on the platform at Bombay and the only consolation I had was that William was with me.

248

'Something's wrong?' he asked.

'I've parted with Kesri and he's resentful. He wants me to make a picture I don't like. I'm determined to get out of it even though my contract seems unbreakable.'

'He's been a little cool towards me, too. Does he know I spoke to you about making a break?'

'I'm afraid he does. I'm sorry, William. I hope it won't turn him against you.'

'It's of no importance. Shall I see you home?'

'That would be nice. I'd love you to see Jane.' My worries melted away and I was full of anticipation. 'She must have grown while I've been away. I'm longing to see her.'

The small bungalow I had rented was not in a fashionable part of town and we had a long drive to get to it. For some reason passing the familiar landmarks reminded me of Edmond.

'Do you know, I don't actually know whether I'm divorced or not,' I said.

'Would you like me to enquire on your behalf?'

'Oh, William, would you? What a blessing you are.' I took his hand and gave it a grateful squeeze and we sat like that, hand in hand, until the bungalow was reached.

'My humble abode,' I said flippantly.

'As good, if not better, than the one you grew up in.'

'Trust you to remind me of that! You're right, of course. My standards are higher than they were then. Look, look! Maria has brought the baby out to meet me.'

I jumped out of the taxi and ran up the three wooden steps to the verandah, leaving William to pay and unload my luggage.

'Maria, is she well? Has she been good?'

'Baba is very well.'

I took Jane in my arms. She looked up at me suspiciously and then the corners of her mouth turned down. 'She's forgotten me. It's your Auntie Jess, Janie. You remember your old auntie, don't you?'

It was no use. Jane's short memory did not include these unfamiliar arms and she opened her mouth to bawl. I treated it lightly, but did feel slightly dismayed. If I continued my film career I was going to have to spend periods away from her and I did not want to return as a stranger every time.

'As she grows older she'll remember you better,' William said.

'She's not doing herself justice at the moment, but you can see how beautiful she is, can't you?' I asked.

'A truly remarkable baby,' William agreed, but I could see he was amused by my fervour.

Reluctantly, I handed Jane back to the *ayah* and her squalls subsided.

'Come in, William. Shall we have some tea?' Inside the house I looked round in dismay. 'Isn't it disheartening the way things are neglected when one isn't around to supervise? Oh dear, I sound like a real *memsahib*! But they knew I'd be home one day this week. You'd think someone would have had the foresight to give the place a clean before I arrived.'

There was a film of dust over everything. The bearer had not even had the initiative to throw away the dead flowers which had withered in a vase on the sideboard. I could have screamed with vexation and once William was out of the way I would have some sharp words to say. Not that it would do any good. Everyone would blame everyone else, there would be an orgy of cleaning and, as long as I was there to impose my rigorous standards, my small staff would give me eager, willing service.

'A little dust is no hardship to someone who has been digging in the desert,' William said in his gentle way.

He stayed for about half an hour and after he had gone I went through the rooms like a whirlwind. It was a couple of days before I was satisfied, but after that I had time to sit around and think. I was making quite a lot of money out of *The Warrior Queen*. On top of that I had Kesri's jewels which I could sell if necessary and obviously they would fetch a great deal of money. Could I afford to retire? Come to that, did I want to retire?

As one quiet day succeeded another I realised how much I was missing the interest of the career I had adopted. I wanted the excitement and satisfaction of earning my living doing something I was good at. Even if my jewels were worth hundreds of thousands of rupees, as they probably were, enough to pay for Jane's education and keep us in modest circumstances for years to come, I would still not be satisfied with sitting at home doing nothing.

CHAPTER THIRTEEN

For weeks before the Prince of Wales's arrival in India the streets of Bombay were plastered with posters telling the people to boycott the visit, while advertisements in the newspapers suggested everyone should stay indoors and treat 17 November as a day of national mourning. I felt sufficiently interested to go and watch him disembark and I rather hoped that the campaign would mean I could do it in comparative comfort, but the crowds were as great as if there had been no effort to persuade people to stay away.

The Prince was smaller than I imagined, very boyish-looking and slight. He had smiles and waves for the crowds and I think everyone was surprised by their enthusiasm. Once he had driven off I turned away, satisfied to have seen the heir to the throne. If everything went well I might actually be presented to him when *The Warrior Queen* was screened.

I took a Victoria to get home, but as we crossed the city we began to travel more and more slowly. I had expected congestion near the route of the Prince's procession, but this was something different. Small groups of people came running out of the back streets, looking over their shoulders, and I could hear shouting. I asked my driver what was going on.

'There is a demonstration, *memsahib*,' he said.

As we turned off the main road the shouts became more distinct. Above the confused shouting one voice declaimed 'Mahatma Ghandi!' and a crashing chorus responded '*Ki jai!*' I wondered whether Hari Chand was somewhere out there orchestrating the protest. Damn him, he would have been better employed making provision for the child he had fathered. That thought made me impatient and I urged the driver to push forward.

'Very difficult, *memsahib*,' he said apologetically.

Of course he was right. It was almost impossible to push a way through the mob of people, half of them wanting to join the protest against the Prince's visit and the other half trying to get away from it.

We turned a corner and found ourselves in the middle of a fight between demonstrators and the police. *Lathis* were flailing and I saw a man stagger and fall with blood streaming from his forehead. There was a different sound coming from the crowd now, a deep, angry roar. Even the lethargic horse between the shafts of the Victoria began to shift restlessly. I had a horrible vision of him rearing up and smashing down with his hoofs on the people milling all round, in which case I would certainly be thrown out and probably massacred.

It was impossible to go forward, but I looked over my shoulder and saw that we might be able to go back the way we had come. There was no room to turn, but the driver got out and went to his horse's head and succeeded in persuading him to back up. At the next corner we were able to turn into a comparatively quiet street. Behind me I could still hear the dreadful sound of a mob howling for blood and in front of me was the procession route where Indians had thrown themselves down in an excess of loyalty to kiss the dust over which the wheels of the Prince's car had passed.

By making a long detour the Victoria driver managed to get me home. The fare he asked was excessive, but for once I did not argue about it; I was too glad to arrive in one piece.

The film was premièred in Bombay early in the New Year. I was glad to have it to look forward to because Christmas had been trying. The baby was too young to be interested and although she was a delight and the joy of my life she chose the Christmas holiday to have a colicky attack which terrified me. Fortunately, by the first night of *The Warrior Queen* she had recovered and I was able to give my full mind to it.

It was a resounding success. The spectacle was superb and the acting was not too bad, either. I was surprised sometimes, seeing myself on the screen, how well I managed to convey emotion by merely thinking about it. Of course, it would have helped if we had been able to speak; because of this lack the acting had to be broader than it would have been on the stage. All the same, I was not displeased with the finished result.

Kesri was too astute to shut me out of the celebrations, but it was William who escorted me to the cinema that night and because of this I chose to wear Western evening dress, a lovely flowing gown of blue chiffon, and round my neck, with a certain amount of defiance, the sapphire necklace Kesri had given me.

Antoinette was there, very blonde and beautiful. Visiting Europe had evidently agreed with her. She had got back her svelte figure and she looked lovelier than ever. Kesri could hardly keep his eyes off her, which was a relief to me.

She greeted me smilingly at the party after the film and congratulated me on my performance. She was wearing new jewellery, too.

'I'm delighted to see you back,' I said. 'What a marvellous emerald.'

Antoinette touched the enormous jewel at her throat. 'Kesri's "welcome home" present,' she said. 'He knows I like emeralds.'

Her eyes dwelt for a moment on the sapphires round my own neck, but she had the sense not to say anything. 'I hope our people made you comfortable while you were at Arangapore?' she asked.

'Very comfortable.'

I thought of the riotous nights I had spent with Kesri and perhaps my smile had a hint of unworthy triumph because her own smile faded and she turned away more abruptly than was quite polite.

I stepped back, almost into the arms of a small man who was standing close behind me.

'Miss Jasmina, I've been trying to get a word with you. Say, how do I address you? Is "Miss Jasmina" right?'

'Plain Jasmina is what I'm called. Or, if you want to be really formal, Miss Bullen. My real first name is Jessica.'

'Jessica's a Jewish name. Are you Jewish?'

'I'm a bit of a mixture, but I've never heard of any Jewish blood,' I answered.

'I'm Sol Hannabakker, from the States.'

His head was on a level with my shoulder and although I am tall for a woman, that made him very short for a man. He was nearly bald, with a beak of a nose and snapping black eyes.

'I've heard of you,' I said.

'Then you'll know I'm in films, too, and you'll guess why I'm interested in you. You're good in this film we've seen tonight, but you could do better, much better, a British girl like you. Indian films – yeah, great market, but limited to this country. I could make you into a world name. Are you under contract?'

I could hardly contain my excitement, but I tried to seem cool. 'I am, but I don't like the next film that's proposed for me and I'd like to get out of it.'

'Mm, might be difficult. Still, the way they churn out films here you'd probably be free in maybe three, four months' time?'

'Yes . . . provided it's not known that I have another offer in hand. They might slow things down to keep me.'

I meant Kesri, of course. He would certainly not like to think I was escaping to Hollywood.

'They play it rough here, too, do they? Right, Miss Bullen . . . Jessica . . . we'll keep our cards close to our chest. In the meantime, can we meet and talk?'

I met Sol Hannabakker the next morning for coffee at his hotel. Naturally I took great care with my appearance.

'You've got the looks,' he said. 'Sultry, but with a touch

of class. You can act, too, which ain't all that common. I've got a great story lined up about a gal called Theodora who rose up to be an Empress in olden times in Constantinople. I'm not making any promises, mind, but that's the part I've been thinking of for you.'

Another concubine. Oh well, to get to Hollywood I'd play anything.

'Before I threw up everything here I'd want a definite promise of a starring role in an American picture,' I said.

'A business head, too! Sure, sure. I wouldn't go to the expense of transporting you unless I meant to use you. Did you bring your present contract along?'

'I did, but I don't think there's any doubt that I'm tied down to make at least one film with Arangapore pictures.'

'I'll get a legal man to look it over. Like I said, it's no great shakes if you do have to make a stumer here. No one's going to see it.'

I thought of the hundreds of thousands, possibly even millions of Indians who would certainly see it, but I said nothing.

We parted with great friendliness. I liked the little man and it seemed he liked me, too. All my difficulties looked like coming to an end. And not only mine. If I could get Jane to America it would be a break with both her English and her Indian inheritance. A new life for both of us and surely there, in the land of the free, she would be able to grow up in a multi-racial society where a darker tinge to her skin would go unremarked. I could work and bring her up, educate her and see her safely launched in life. For me, too, it would be a fresh start. I could leave behind the mess I had made of my life and perhaps find a different kind of happiness. I felt more than hopeful, I was over the moon.

I was only slightly aggrieved to discover that I would not be in the party invited to meet His Royal Highness the Prince of Wales when he visited Arangapore in February, even though he was to be entertained one evening with a showing of my film. Thinking it over, I realised that my presence would be an embarrassment, if not to

Kesri, who had no shame, then to Antoinette and to the British Resident. The Prince was going to Bhuredar both to play polo with Kesri, who had played in teams with him in England, and to lay the foundation stone of the Hospital for Women which was being built to honour Rukmini's memory. He would be doing it in the presence of Maharani number two, who had already supplanted number one before she died. To have added a recent mistress would have made the situation a trifle too piquant.

The Prince's arrival in Bombay in November had been filmed in colour and that really interested me.

'*The Warrior Queen* would have been truly spectacular in colour,' I said to Sol Hannabakker.

'It'll come. There are technical difficulties to be overcome and, of course, expense. What'll arrive first will be talking pictures. You've got a real nice speaking voice, Jessica. That's one of the things that makes me keen on you. We'll maybe have to tone it down a bit, make you sound less British, but if you work with a voice coach there'll be no difficulty about turning you into a talking actress.'

Sol's time in India was drawing to a close. He would soon be leaving for Palestine.

'Jerusalem! I have to see Jerusalem. You know why? Because my old mother'd never forgive me if I didn't, that's why. India? You can have it. Egypt? Just a lotta sand. She's praying every day for me to get to Jerusalem.'

As far as breaking my contract with Kesri's company was concerned, he was not hopeful. 'Make the picture, girl. Make it and forget about it. If you were a big star already maybe we'd try and break the contract. For an unknown – and you are unknown outside in the big world – my company don't want to take on the expense.'

He would send for me, he promised that. All expenses paid, first-class treatment, a luxury voyage from one side of the world to the other.

'Just one thing, kinda personal,' Sol said. 'What's your marital status, Jessica?'

'I'm divorced.' Was I? I was not really sure. Still, it must be close.

'Adultery?'

'Yes.'

'So where's the other man?'

'Dead.'

Sol's expression cleared. 'That's good,' he said.

'Not to me.'

'No, honey, I guess not, but it makes things a whole lot easier from my point of view. Any other boyfriends?'

'No.'

'Sure? Better tell me the truth.'

I hesitated and then I told him. 'I had a brief fling with the Maharajah.'

'That figures,' Sol said, taking it in his stride. 'D'you mean it's over?'

'I wouldn't go on with it after his wife returned.'

'That's real moral of you,' he said. 'I guess we don't have any problems. Everyone's been divorced once. I have myself. No need to hide it. I've been figuring on presenting you as a woman of the world. A failed marriage along the way is something we can admit.'

I checked with William after that to see whether he had any news about the divorce.

'I've seen Edmond,' he admitted. 'He took great exception to my enquiry and wouldn't answer any questions. The only thing I can think of is to go to the Law Courts and look up the records. I'm sorry, Jessica, I feel I've let you down.'

'Please don't worry. I can employ a lawyer to enquire, can't I?'

'It might be the best thing to do. It was a mistake to approach Edmond. He's very bitter.'

That was something I preferred not to think about. Hurriedly, I began to tell William about my new prospects. 'Isn't it wonderful?' I concluded.

He was not as delighted as I expected. 'America? Well . . . yes, of course . . . you must be very excited.'

'Be pleased for me, William. It's the most splendid opportunity.'

'Yes, of course,' he said again.

'For Jane, too. I can bring her up there without worrying about her background. I don't know anything about California, except sunshine and oranges, but it sounds marvellous.'

'Marvellous,' William agreed, beginning to sound like an echo. 'It's a long way away.'

'When I'm rich and famous I'll fetch you out to visit me,' I promised.

'You're rich and famous already,' William said quietly.

'Not really. Yes, I've made a certain amount of money and I do get recognised in the street sometimes, but it's a very parochial sort of fame. I need to build on that. You must admit that being a film star in Hollywood is rather different from being one in Bombay, where the film industry has barely got off the ground.'

'Yes, indeed. Obviously you're doing well for yourself. Congratulations. Will it make you happy, do you think?'

'Oh, surely! I'll have everything I want. Work, money, a position in the world – and Jane to bring up and love. It's a pity she's asleep just now. She gets prettier every day and every inch an Arkady. Those blue, blue eyes, just like her father's . . .'

'Her mother's, you mean.'

'Yes . . . yes, of course. A slip of the tongue.'

'Was it?' William looked at me for a long time before he said, 'Don't do it, Jessica.'

'Do what?'

'Pretend that Jane is Dominic's child. Yours and Dominic's.'

'I don't . . .' I said, but then I stopped because it was no use lying to William. 'If only she had been! I can't help wishing . . . I love her so much.'

'What about the other sort of love?'

'I've finished with that. Tick it off, William: I've had respectable married love – and didn't think much of it. I've had wonderful romantic love, and sometimes I

259

wonder whether we could have maintained that intensity. I've had commercial love with a man who knew all the tricks. I've got it all out of my system.'

'How old are you? Twenty-four? Rather young to write off a side of life most people find important until the end of their lives.'

'You seem to manage,' I retorted.

'Oh, me . . . I have a regrettable habit of loving the wrong woman.'

I thought of Rukmini and was sad. Did that tenuous affair still have such a hold on him?

'I can't say I like the American plan,' William went on, 'but of course, you're right – it could be a great opportunity for you.'

'It'll be ages, yet,' I pointed out, feeling anxious because he was getting up to go. 'I'll see you often while you're in Bombay?'

'Of course.'

William had hardly gone and I was still feeling worried about his lack of enthusiasm for my new life, and cross with myself for giving away my fantasy about Jane, when I had another visitor who drove every other thought out of my mind – Edmond.

I was on the verandah, lingering after watching William drive away and there was no possibility of escape.

'This is a surprise,' I said as he came up the steps.

'An unwelcome one, I'm sure. You sent your half-caste cousin to ask whether the divorce had gone through. I thought I'd come and tell you the situation myself.'

He was looking heavier and more red in the face. Not very healthy, I thought. He ought to go home to England. He did sit down, but he refused my offer of tea or a drink.

'You've been making quite a name for yourself,' he said.

'I've been fortunate enough to find a profession to follow.'

'You always were a play actress. You fooled me long enough.' He sat looking at me with a curious, baffled expression and I waited, knowing that silence would goad him into telling me what I wanted to know. 'About the divorce – no, it's not been heard yet, but it should come up in the next Court session.'

'It's taken longer than I expected,' I said.

'It's a complicated business, divorcing your wife for adultery with a man who's died. I had to be seen by the hotel servants so that they could say I'm *not* the man who stayed in Agra with you. You didn't know it, but they came to look you over, too, to make sure the identification is all in order.'

The thought of those unknown eyes peering at me for such a reason made me grimace in distaste.

'Don't look like that,' Edmond said sharply. 'You've suffered nothing compared with what I've been through, having to parade myself in front of those sly brutes, being told about them seeing you in bed with Dominic, about the state of the sheets . . .'

'No!' I was on my feet shouting a protest. 'Stop it, Edmond. I won't have it. I won't listen.'

'I had to listen.'

That was why he had come, of course. To get rid of some of the humiliation he had endured by passing it on to me. What Edmond didn't realise, was not capable of realising, was that he was defiling something that to me was a sacred memory. My lovely time with Dominic, made to seem sordid.

'Edmond, I loved Dominic with all my heart and soul. What we did together was beautiful. Nothing can take that away from me, certainly nothing you can say. Please go. You've done what you came to do and I've learnt what I wanted to know. There's no reason why we should ever meet again.'

I had seen Edmond cry before, but this time he was so repugnant to me that I could offer no comfort. He sat on my sofa with his head bowed and his hands between his knees and the tears ran down his grotesque red face.

'I've seen both your bloody films,' he said. 'I've seen the way you flaunted yourself. You know it all, don't you?

261

How many men have you given yourself to? How many besides namby-pamby Dominic?'

'Dominic was the love of my life,' I said steadily. 'I'll never love anyone else.'

I prayed that Edmond had not heard any gossip about my affair with Kesri. Apparently he hadn't because he said nothing about it.

I found the whisky and poured some out for him. He waved it away, but I insisted. 'Don't be silly, Edmond. Drink it and pull yourself together.'

'I've made a fool of myself again.'

'You've been through a very nasty experience and naturally it's made you emotional. What can I say, except that I'm sorry for my part in it.'

'Everyone knows.'

'You should go back to England.'

'I'm going. I might even leave Arkady & Pershore altogether. You've ruined my career as well as everything else. Even so . . .' He took a long swig of the whisky and then he muttered, 'If you'll come back to me, I'll call off the divorce.'

I thought I must have misheard him, but he raised his head and looked me in the face and I saw that he meant what he said. 'I told you I'd seen your films. That's not the half of it. I sat through the first damned thing six times and I've been to the new one twice. I can't keep away. There'll never be another woman for me. I've tried and it doesn't work. Come back to me.'

I was too stupefied to think of anything sensible to say.

'We only have to start living together again and the divorce can be forgotten,' Edmond urged. 'I offered before and you turned me down, but think, Jessica. How long can you go on making these tinpot films? I'm suggesting a fresh start, in England, away from this damned climate and the corruption, the filth. Come back and I'll forgive everything and be a loving husband to you.'

The thought of Edmond being a loving husband to me made me shudder and this time, although I shrank from his suffering, I had an answer ready. 'I'm going to

America – I've had an offer from Hollywood. It's no use, Edmond. There's no future for us, not together. Forget me. Go home to England and find a nice little girl who'll love you as you deserve.'

'I've told you, it's no good!' he shouted at me. 'Not with any other woman, only with you. Watching those bloody films . . . damn you, it's the only time I've felt like a man since you left me. You've got to come back. I can't bear it.'

'It's a temporary thing,' I murmured uncertainly, understanding him at last. 'Emotional stress . . . you should see a doctor. Edmond, I can't help you. You must go.'

There was an air of violence about him which frightened me. I needed help. I wanted William back. What I got was Sol Hannabakker.

'Can I come in?' he asked. 'I never know where the bell is for these Indian houses.' His shrewd little eyes looked from one to another of us. He knew, of course, that he had broken in on a scene.

Edmond, predictably, chose to be offensive. 'Is this the latest?' he asked. 'What is he, a dirty little Yid? I suppose he's the one who's taking you to Hollywood?'

'Edmond, you must go,' I said with all the firmness I could muster.

'On your way, pal,' Sol said. 'You'll find a taxi waiting for me outside. Get in it and make yourself scarce. The lady don't want you around.'

I thought Edmond was going to hit him, but there was another interruption: Maria walked in with Jane in her arms. It certainly stopped Edmond in his tracks, and Sol looked taken aback, too. Maria excused herself afterwards by saying she thought Dr Bullen was still with me and she knew I liked him to see *baba*. My guess was she had heard raised voices and was curious to know what was going on.

'Well, now, what have we here?' Sol asked.

I was in a quandary. I wanted to tell Sol about Jane,

though not to reveal her parentage, but I was not at all anxious for Edmond to know anything about her.

'Is she yours?' Sol asked.

'I'm taking care of her,' I said.

'A temporary arrangement?'

'No.' I took a deep breath and plunged in. 'When I go to America I want to take Jane with me and, if possible, her *ayah*, too.'

The way Sol fell silent felt ominous to me, but I had to turn my attention to Edmond. I had a wild hope that in spite of my denial he might take it for granted that the child was mine and go away in disgust, but he had recovered from his outburst and I saw his accountant's mind checking over dates and probabilities.

'Take the baby away,' I ordered Maria.

'Just a minute.' To my fury Edmond moved closer and peered into Jane's face and that undiscriminating infant chose to be in a good mood and chortled up at him as if Edmond were a favourite uncle. 'She's quite dark,' he remarked. 'Which makes her eyes all the more striking.'

He spoke directly to Maria. 'Is Miss Bullen her mother?'

Maria glanced at me but got no guidance from my wooden expression, so she told the truth. 'Oh, no, sir. Our *baba* belongs to the lady who went back to England.'

One of the men believed her, the other did not.

'How very interesting,' Edmond said softly. He glanced at me, almost smiling, and I hated him for his air of triumph. 'Is there no end to your services for that family?'

'Jane is my adopted daughter,' I said flatly. 'That's all you need to know, Edmond. Now, will you please go?'

He went and I got rid of Maria and Jane and turned to Sol.

'You did oughta have told me about the baby, girl,' he said. 'I thought you were clear of entanglements.'

'I'm not her mother.'

'Aw, c'mon, honey! Who're you fooling? She's your living image with those blue, blue eyes.'

'You heard what our nurse said.'

264

'Sure, and I saw the way she looked at you first to make sure she got her lines right. I'm disappointed in you, Jessica.'

'Sol, I'm telling you the truth.'

'It's your story and if you want to stick to it, that's fine. What I'm saying is there's no way I can import you into Hollywood with a half-caste babe in tow. Her father was Indian, I take it?'

'Yes.'

'But not your Maharajah?'

'No.'

'It starts to sound kind of sordid, Jessica. Trouble is, we've had too many scandals in the film business and people are getting tired of them.'

'I can prove I've never borne a child. I'll have a medical examination, if necessary.'

'Yeah . . . that'd be pretty conclusive, if the doctor was above suspicion, but if we ever had to go to those lengths the scandal'd be out in the open and just as damaging as if it was true.'

'So I can't win either way? What do I have to do to convince you, and everyone else, that Jane is merely a baby who needed looking after and I've taken responsibility for her?'

'It may be true, and your offer of a doctor's report shakes me, but anyone who sees you together is going to take it for granted you're mother and daughter. The only thing you can do is leave her behind in India. On those terms I might – mind you, I say I might – stick to my offer.'

'I can't desert her.'

'You could set up a fund, place her with a family, leave instructions about the way she's to be brought up.'

I thought about it. A child without parents, without the love that I felt for her. A child without identity and without the reassurance that someone who knew the truth about her birth could give her. A child of obvious mixed parentage, growing up to be accepted neither by the

265

British nor the Indian people. A vulnerable little girl who had already been discarded by her true mother.

Sol was losing patience. 'What about her father? Doesn't he have any say in what happens to the girl?'

For one shameful moment I allowed myself to think about making Hari Chand responsible for his daughter. How would Jane be brought up if I did? His family, I remembered, were farmers. Hari would give his daughter to his mother and Jane would be reared in an Indian village, not in abject poverty because I would provide money for her upbringing, but if I were not on the spot how could I be sure it was properly used? Could I be sure she would be treated with affection, the natural, easy affection Indians showed towards children – an unwanted girl child, without caste because of her mixed blood, and an unwelcome reminder of the shame of the educated son who was agitating for Home Rule instead of repaying his parents? Unless I laid down very strict rules – and how could I do that from America? – she would work in the fields, she would be married off young, perhaps for the sake of her dowry, and she would bear her children with little medical help.

I saw her growing up, blue eyed and beautiful – for surely she would be that – but ignorant of her background. I had raged against the limitations of my life, but there had been choices open to me which would never be available to Jane if she were reared as a Hindu girl.

That was the moment when it came to me that I was irretrievably English. Dadda had always insisted on it, Mumma had taken it for granted, but because I had been born in India and loved it I had reservations. I had exaggerated the pull of my drop of Indian blood. William had challenged me on it once and I had admitted that I would not like to lead the life of an Indian woman. Neither could I condemn Jane to it and it was the fact that I used the word 'condemn' in thinking about it that betrayed the depth of my prejudice. I believed that the life I could offer Jane was better than she would get with her Indian

266

relatives and there was no way I could free myself of that belief.

'It's impossible for Jane to go to her father,' I said to Sol. 'I have to keep her with me. If I can't bring her to America than I won't come.'

'You were the one who said it, Jessica, and I guess that's the way it's going to work out. I'm sorry because I could see a great future for you, but there's one lesson you have to learn before you're ready for Supertown Films, and that is that Supertown knows best. Sure, you think you're doing the right thing for the girl. You've got a great heart. We can't afford to have a heart, not when it comes to the good name of our stars. Leave the kid in India and we'll cover up for you.'

'No.'

'That's your final word?'

'Absolutely.'

Sol sighed. 'You're an obstinate young woman, Jessica. It grieves me to see you throwing your future away. If you ever fetch up in Hollywood without ties, get in touch with me and I'll maybe do something for you. If you've got a little brown baby in your luggage, then forget it. I'm going to say goodbye to you now, and don't think I'll be coming back, because I won't.'

I think he expected me to weaken, but I took the hand he held out to me and shook it in silence. I was beyond speaking, too shattered by the loss of my bright dream to do more than watch as Sol stomped away, muttering in annoyance because Edmond had done what he had ordered and taken his taxi.

CHAPTER FOURTEEN

I made the *nautch* girl film and I hated every minute of it. Not only did I dislike the story and the character I was playing, I also discovered the difference between being directed by a Maharajah with a flair for the job, dilettante though he might be, and taking orders from an underling who called himself a professional but whose only experience came from working under Kesri on the first two films. The man was forever querying his own decisions and where Kesri had known instinctively when a take was right this new man always had to have just one more, just one more, until we were stale and exhausted. And, of course, Kesri only had to give an order and it was carried out. There was no one now with that authority, and this led to endless delays and recriminations.

I stuck it out to the end, knowing that I had no choice, but I was thankful when it was in the can and I could stop going to the studio every day. That was one thing we did have now, a proper studio. No more improvising round picturesque tombs: the Bombay film industry was growing up.

Another sign of greater sophistication was that there was a second actress in the film. There had been a queue of applicants for the part, whereas in the past it had been difficult to find a girl willing to show her face on the screen. The one who was chosen was a pretty little thing, very timid at first, but she soon learnt that I was no longer the favourite I had been and was clever enough to see that there was a chance to supplant me.

I was sick to the heart at the thought of my lost chance to go to America. My only consolation was that Jane continued to thrive and I told myself every day that she needed me.

William was still in Bombay and I took it for granted

that he continued to lodge in Kesri's house, but when I spoke of it one day he told me he had moved.

'I'm a little out of patience with Kesri,' he said. 'I decided I'd rather be independent.'

'He's doing what everyone wanted, living with his wife and attending to business,' I pointed out.

'It was cruel of him to avenge himself on you by pushing you into this distasteful film. You're looking very tired, Jess.'

'I'm so exhausted I feel as if I could die of it,' I admitted, shifting my shoulders uneasily inside a thin cotton blouse that was already wet through in the humid heat.

'Take a holiday.'

'I might go away for the whole of the rains. The film won't be shown until the autumn so I won't be needed for publicity.'

'Any plans for a new picture?'

'No. I think I'm going to be dropped.'

'I see. Don't look so despondent, Jessica. Another door will open.'

'Will it? I seem to be forever going through fresh doors and finding nothing on the other side.'

'You really must be tired. It's not like you to be so downhearted.'

'Losing the chance to go to Hollywood was a crippling disappointment,' I admitted.

'You don't regret your decision?'

'I couldn't desert Jane, but I resent having to make such a choice. I can't help thinking "if only . . ." and that's not fair when I really love her dearly and wouldn't be without her. She's probably the only child I'll ever have.'

'I wouldn't take bets on that,' William said.

'Oh, Billy-boy, nobody loves me except you!' I meant no harm. With the careless affection I had always shown him I put my arms round William and hugged him tight.

I was surprised when I looked up and saw that William was frowning. Very firmly, he put me away from him. 'I do wish you'd stop treating me as if I were some sort of eunuch,' he said.

I could hardly have been more surprised if one of William's stone carvings had reproved me.

'I'm fond of you,' I said uncertainly.

'That's nice to know, but you're too much in the habit of looking on me as a tame cat, to be stroked and petted.' With a mixture of exasperation and amusement he looked down into my bemused face, then he took me in his arms and kissed me. 'That's just to show you that I'm a man like any other,' he said when he stepped back and let me go.

' "And wild for to hold though you seem tame",' I said when I had got my breath back.

'Quoting Sir Thomas Wyatt sounds clever, but your teachers should have skipped the Elizabethan poets and taught you about human relationships. Now, let's be businesslike. If you're going away for two or three months will you let me rent this house from you?'

'No, of course I won't,' I said, still trying to get over my surprise. 'I'll be delighted if you'll come and look after the place. I wouldn't dream of taking rent from you.'

'Thank you. Let me know when it'll be convenient for me to move in and, of course, if I can help with your arrangements for going away just let me know.'

We looked at one another for a moment, William with that quirk to his mouth that I knew meant that he was laughing at me inside, and then quite spontaneously we kissed again, with all the warmth of our long affection. When we parted we were both smiling.

If William had wanted to raise my spirits he had certainly succeeded. After he had gone I felt curiously light-hearted, quite giggly. William! Well! Dear old William. He was quite right, I had got into the habit of leaning on him when I wanted comfort. I would be more careful in future. At least, I would unless I decided I'd like him to kiss me again. After all, it had been rather nice. I found myself making sounds like a soda syphon at the recollection. Dear William.

*

I spent three months in Ootacamund, living very quietly. I hardly mixed with the British community. I toyed with the idea of passing myself off as an ordinary wife, or perhaps a widow with a young child, but my face had become too well known and once it was realised that I was the film star, Jasmina, there were too many question marks hanging over me to make me socially acceptable. Jane's presence was a puzzle, too. Of course it was taken for granted that she was my child and although I always said if anyone asked that she was adopted, I could see that I was not believed.

Jane was adorable. She had begun to toddle, staggering towards me on unsteady feet, her face alight with laughter, and she was making noises which I was sure I only failed to understand because neither Maria nor I was sure which language she was trying to speak. She was plump and firm and her black hair curled all over her head even without Maria's devoted combing round her fingers. She was my constant companion during the day, but the evenings were emptier than I liked. The truth was, I was lonely. I wanted a companion. Someone like William, who would enter into my pleasure in our lovely surroundings, go for longer walks than Jane's little legs could support, someone who would talk to me. It was not that I was specially hankering after William, but I wanted someone like him. Even another woman would have done.

So although I benefited from my holiday I was not sorry to return to Bombay, not until I got there. Then I realised that I was still alone. There was a letter waiting for me from William regretting that he had not been able to wait for my return, but had had to leave two days earlier. He had gone to Taxilia, right up in the foothills of the Himalayas. All that long way away. I had so much looked forward to telling him all about my time in Ooty.

Some time soon I was going to have to think about my future, but I put it off until after the first showing of the new film, due in about a month's time. There was an ominous silence from the director; none of the fuss and spoiling I had received after I had made the previous two films, and I missed it.

It was the end of the rains and the temperature was pleasant, warm and dry enough for me to sit out on the verandah and have afternoon tea, just like any other English *memsahib*. It was a welcome break when a visitor arrived, even though the name on the business card he sent in meant nothing to me. A solicitor, it seemed, and from London, too.

'Show Mr Petrie in, Ali, and bring some fresh tea.'

Mr Petrie was a thin, middle-aged man with grey hair and spectacles and I had certainly never set eyes on him before.

'Thank you for seeing me, Mrs . . . ah, Miss . . .'

'Miss Bullen. As a professional actress I've reverted to my maiden name.'

'Quite. Perhaps I should begin by explaining that I act for Mr Steven Arkady.'

'I see,' I said, not seeing at all. 'You will have some tea, won't you?'

'It will be most welcome. I must also tell you that Mr Matthew Arkady died some six weeks ago.'

'I'm sorry,' I said mechanically. I tried to concentrate on pouring out the tea, but my mind had gone back to England and that hard, forthright old man who had been my grandfather.

'It could, I suppose, be called a happy release,' Mr Petrie said, taking the cup I handed him. 'He was sadly disabled.'

He was taking his time about coming to the point. For a moment I played with the idea that dear old Grandad had come up trumps at the end and left me his entire fortune, but it was a passing fantasy. I knew Matthew Arkady would never have done anything so out of character.

'I am aware of your – er, relationship,' Mr Petrie said.

'My father was his illegitimate son.'

'Quite. No provision was made for you in Mr Arkady's will . . .'

272

'I didn't expect anything.'

'Nevertheless, Mr Steven Arkady has it in mind to provide you with a certain sum of money . . .'

That really did surprise me. To the best of my recollection I had never set eyes on Dominic's father. Perhaps it was really Lady Cynthia who had made this gesture, in which case her attitude towards me must have softened since our parting.

I hoped Mr Petrie was going to tell me how much I could expect, but instead he fidgeted in his chair and said, 'I must now turn to a matter of some delicacy. You have a child in your keeping?'

I nodded, but the question had jolted me. So the Arkadys knew about Jane. How much did they know? And how had they found out?

'By what name is she known?' he went on.

'Jane Harold.'

'Ah, yes, good. Her true parentage is known to my client.'

I was not going to be trapped like that. If Steven Arkady really knew about Patricia's baby then this wily little lawyer was going to have to spell it out before I said another word, and so I told him.

'Your caution is commendable, Miss Bullen. Very well, her mother is Miss Patricia Arkady and her father a young Indian lawyer called Hari Chand.'

'Patricia owned up?'

The answer I got was oblique, but I understood it. 'Your former husband, Mr Edmond Fardale, is now in England.'

'Edmond! I might have known.'

'He told Mr Arkady of the existence of the child and his suspicions about the mother although, of course, he knew nothing about the father.'

I could hardly speak for the bitterness that welled up in me. It was me Edmond had been striking at when he had produced his choice bit of gossip.

'Just as well he's in England,' I said. 'I could kill him. So I suppose they taxed poor Patricia with it – not that I have a great deal of sympathy with her after the way she ran off and left me to take responsibility for Jane – and her father thinks it's necessary to pay me hush money. It makes me angry, Mr Petrie. If I'd meant to cash in on what I know I'd have done it before now.'

'You misunderstand my client's motives.'

'I bet I don't! How much is he offering?'

'I'm instructed to pay you ten thousand pounds.'

'Not bad. I'll take it, but you can tell Mr Steven Arkady that the whole amount will be put aside for Jane's benefit. I might have to break into it to pay for her education, I can't tell at the moment, but if not then it'll be waiting for her when she grows up.'

Mr Petrie took his time before he spoke again. I had the impression that I had surprised him, and not altogether pleasantly. 'That isn't what's proposed,' he said at last. 'The child is to be removed from your care.'

That has not occurred to me. To me it seemed obvious that the Arkadys were lucky to have me taking care of Patricia's little by-blow and I thought they must know it. The ten thousand pounds I looked upon as an acknowledgement of what I was doing for them and the baby – not, as it now seemed, a payment for giving her up.

'They can't do that,' I protested. 'I've looked after Jane ever since she was born. She belongs to me more than she does to her own mother. I love her and I want to go on caring for her.'

Mr Petrie was looking really worried. 'I must admit that wasn't taken into account,' he said. 'Mr Arkady thought you'd be glad to be relieved of the responsibility.'

'No! I want to keep her. I've already made considerable sacrifices in order to keep her. Mr Petrie, you must go back to Mr Arkady and tell him how I feel. I'll adopt Jane properly. I'd like to do that. I won't want his money. I can earn enough for both of us.' I spoke feverishly, urging him to accept what I said, because I could see from his unyielding face that he was not convinced.

'I'm sorry, all the arrangements are made,' he said. 'An

English nanny travelled out from England with me and I shall call here with her tomorrow to collect the child.'

'Don't keep talking about "the child"! Her name is Jane, she's over a year old and she's a *person*.'

'I'm sorry,' he said again, which got us no further forward.

I had a sudden inspiration. 'I won't give her up without her proper mother's consent.'

Mr Petrie felt in his breast pocket. Damn all legal minds. He had a letter for me from Patricia:

Dear Jessica, The game's up. I don't suppose you'll be sorry. Mother has promised the baby will be loved and cherished and all that so you can hand her over with a clear conscience. I'm to wipe the slate clean and marry the dook's son and my little mistake will grow up never knowing what a fool of a mother she had. Sorry, sorry, sorry – what more can I say? Patricia.

'I'd like that letter destroyed immediately,' Mr Petrie said.

'Are you afraid I'll blackmail the future duchess? Here, you do it. I simply can't take it in. Patricia getting married . . .'

'Following the death of her brother, and now the death of her grandfather, Miss Patricia is the sole heir to the Arkady fortune,' Mr Petrie said.

'And the future duke is prepared to overlook past indiscretions for the sake of the cash? Or doesn't he know?'

'The matter has been fully discussed by all interested parties . . .'

'Oh, I like that! It sounds so businesslike. Aren't I an interested party? Isn't Jane? Not that she can talk, but I know what she'd say if she could.' I heard myself choke and turned my head away, unwilling to admit to the weakness of tears.

Mr Petrie went on doggedly, 'It was agreed that if the marriage went ahead the matter could be kept safely inside the family. Provided, of course, that you keep silence.'

'Have I said anything up till now? Of course I'll hold

my tongue. Jane can easily pass as my daughter. In fact, most people already think she is. Let me adopt her.'

'You've been too closely associated with the Arkady family and, no matter what you may say, the truth might be discovered, as it was by Mr Fardale. Besides . . . forgive me, Miss Bullen, but there are areas of your life which make it undesirable for you to become the little girl's adoptive mother.'

If I was choking now it was with anger. That was Lady Cynthia speaking – and Edmond. He had opened his mouth to some effect, I could tell that. 'What about my ex-husband?' I demanded. 'Aren't you afraid *he'll* talk?'

'Mr Fardale has decided to emigrate to Canada.'

'And how much are the Arkadys paying him?'

Mr Petrie answered me unwillingly, but he did answer. 'Ten thousand pounds, the same as you.'

'That's the going rate for a high-class family secret, is it? It's no use, Mr Petrie. I won't give Jane up.'

In my agitation I got up and began pacing up and down the verandah while the lawyer watched me with worried eyes. 'Please sit down, Miss Bullen,' he said at last. 'I must admit that from what I was told before I left England I didn't expect this interview to be so painful.'

'Jane is as dear to me as if I'd borne her myself.'

I did as he asked and sat down again and he said, with a gentleness he had not previously shown, 'Then you must want the best possible life for her.'

'Of course. With me.'

'Not necessarily. You're a divorced woman, earning a somewhat precarious living in a difficult profession . . .'

I thought of the fortune in jewels lodged in the Bank, but of course that was not something I could admit to Mr Petrie.

'Hardly precarious,' I said. 'I've made three pictures in rapid succession and no doubt I'll make many more.'

'Will you? Without the backing of your lover, the Maharajah?'

I suppose, in the circles in which the Arkadys moved, that gossip was bound to reach them, but it was really hitting below the belt and it made me wince. 'I can make my way with my own talent,' I said. 'I've already had a very good offer from Hollywood.'

'You should take it. Go to America, Miss Bullen, and leave me to place little Jane in a suitable family.'

'Where?'

He knew he was hurting me by his reply and again he spoke gently, 'It's better for you not to know that.'

I could still not believe it. 'You mean I'm *never* to see her again?'

His silence answered me. 'It will be better,' he said.

'For whom? Me? You're wrong about that. I'll eat my heart out, not knowing where she is or how she's being cared for. And Jane will miss me. To all intents and purposes I'm her mother. She certainly doesn't know the difference.'

'She's young enough to forget.'

The idea of Jane forgetting me had me on my feet again protesting wildly. 'No, no, no! She's all I've got. I've lost so much! Please, please, Mr Petrie, go back to England, tell them I'm the ideal person to look after Jane, tell them I love her. No one will ever love her as much as I do. I am the best person to take care of her, I am!'

For once the legal man was shaken. 'This is dreadful,' he said. 'I never dreamed . . . My dear, pull yourself together. Let's consider the realities of the situation. My clients will never allow you to keep the child and they have the right to decide her future. It was discussed and all parties agreed that she must be adopted completely anonymously.'

'Adopted? Someone else is going to adopt her?'

'A very worthy couple who will have no idea of her origins.'

'She's half-Indian. Do they know that?'

'Yes. They don't consider it a bar.'

'I'll appeal to her father!' That was a wild idea because I doubted whether I could find Hari Chand, let alone persuade him to intervene.

'My dear, he has no rights over her,' Mr Petrie said. 'I

understand his name doesn't even appear on her birth certificate.'

'You know everything,' I said. I was feeling as weary as if I had just completed a day's filming. The sight of the empty tea cups on the table made me nauseous. I rang the bell and gestured for Ali to take the tray away. It was not much, but it gave me a minute or two to think.

There was nothing to be gained by arguing with Mr Petrie. He had his instructions and he would carry them out, blinded to the plain justice of the situation by his deference to the great families he served. I would have to act for myself.

'Please go now,' I said. 'I'm too upset to talk any more.'

'You do understand that I shall return tomorrow with the nanny and take Jane away?'

'Oh, yes, I understand that.'

Except, of course, that I had no intention of being there when he arrived. Where could I go? That was the question that exercised my mind as I said goodbye to Mr Petrie. Out of Bombay, obviously, and as quickly as possible. Not to Delhi and not to one of the hill stations. *Where else?*

It was Maria who supplied the solution. She appeared leading Jane by the hand. 'Missy *baba* come to say goodnight,' she said.

Jane let go of her hand, staggered over to my chair, and climbed on my lap. With my arms round her plump little body and her wet kisses on my cheek how could I contemplate letting her go?

'When you came to Bombay, Maria, did you travel by train?' I asked.

'Oh, no *memsahib*. All people from Goa come to Bombay by ship.'

That was the answer. If Mr Petrie made enquiries he would ask at the railway stations. He would never think of me going anywhere by sea. I would take Jane to visit her *ayah*'s home, the Portuguese enclave of Goa, and with any luck the British authorities would not be able to reach me.

It was already too late to visit the shipping offices that evening, but I spent the time packing and making plans with Maria, who was delighted by the idea of visiting her family and only slightly reproachful about being given no time to buy presents to take home.

Mr Petrie had said vaguely that he would call again 'in the afternoon', so I was waiting outside Shepherd's offices in Frere Street when they opened the next morning to try to book passages on one of the ships which the Bombay Steam Navigation Company ran daily to Goa. As I had feared, I was too late to get accommodation on that day's noon sailing, but I managed to secure a cabin which I could share with Maria and the baby for the one night the journey would take on a ship leaving at the same time the following day.

Paying for the tickets took all the money I had so I went to the Bank and drew out more and also withdrew one of my splendid necklaces, which I hoped to sell in Goa. I took the opal one. Opals had the reputation of being unlucky and certainly I had not been having much luck lately so it might be as well to be rid of it.

Time was getting on. I was desperate to get home and remove Jane and Maria. We would have to go to an hotel for one night, somewhere obscure near the port where Mr Petrie was not likely to find us. Our luggage was ready. All I had to do was to pick the two of them up and disappear.

I was over-confident, of course. I thought I had been speedy and clever, but Mr Petrie must have guessed when I caved in so suddenly that I did not really mean to hand over Jane. When I ran up the steps to the verandah Maria came out to meet me, her face creased with anxiety, her hands writhing together in distress.

'*Mem, mem*, man came! Took Jane *baba* away.'

I went round all the larger hotels until I found the one where Mr Petrie had been staying. He had already checked out.

'Mr Petrie is sailing today,' I was told.

I went to the docks and begged, stormed and pleaded to be allowed to board the ship which was about to sail for England.

'Time and tide wait for no man, *memsahib*,' the cheerful Indian official told me. 'I am very sorry, but unless you are a passenger you cannot pass.'

I took off the opal necklace I was wearing round my neck for safety and held it out to him. 'I'll give you this to let me through.'

His eyes nearly popped out of his head. He even glanced over his shoulder, but it was already too late. There was a long blast on the ship's siren, a dreadful, mournful sound, and she began to move away from the quayside. I had lost Jane.

I was a fool, an utter fool, to have displayed a necklace of opals and diamonds on the quayside, but I was too frantic to be sensible. As I turned away, defeated, I stuffed it into my handbag. I hardly knew what I was doing or where I was going. I was aware of a scattering of Europeans, waving goodbye to the departing ship, and a lot of Indians, the porters, the dockers, the quayside hangers on, just a lot of dark, anonymous faces, all staring at this *memsahib* who was either mad or drunk, or possibly both.

I felt that I was being jostled, then there was a sharp blow in the middle of my back and my handbag was wrenched away from my arm. I staggered and clutched at the nearest support, a white-robed Parsi, who looked round in indignation until he saw that I had been robbed. He lifted his umbrella in the air and shouted. I was doubled up, trying to get my breath back. When I straightened up I saw a confused melée of people, all fighting to get at a thin, very dark boy – one of the Koli fishermen, I thought – with a tousled mass of dark hair and wearing nothing but a white loincloth.

My handbag was borne back to me by the very Indian

to whom I had offered the necklace. He was smiling triumphantly and, of course, looking expectant.

'The police have the man, *memsahib*,' he said. 'But it was I – I, Bhagwan Das, who captured him.'

'Thank you, thank you, you will be rewarded,' I said. 'Please, I must sit down.'

A seat was found for me and several of the British, seeing one of their own kind in trouble, came over to me.

'Pretty smart work, nabbing the chap like that,' one of them said. 'There's a policeman waiting to have a word with you as soon as you feel up to it.'

'I'm all right,' I said. 'Look, I've got my bag back and there's no harm done. Tell them to let the wretched boy go.'

'Oh, I say, we can't have that! An Englishwoman attacked and robbed in broad daylight! It's a scandal. He'll have to be punished.'

Unfortunately, the police took the same view. A robbery had been committed, the robber had been caught and he must be put on trial in order to discourage the rest of his kind. They were somewhat taken aback when they saw the necklace I had been carrying.

'It was very dangerous thing to do,' I was told.

'Yes, I've been foolish,' I said, but my mind was only half with them, the other half was sailing out of the harbour, following a small, black-haired girl with blue eyes.

My triumphant Indian official added the final unwelcome touch. 'If you please, I think I am recognising you, *memsahib*,' he said. 'You are giving your name as Miss Jessica Bullen, but I think you are Jasmina, the famous film star.' I had to admit it. 'I am seeing both your films. Very good, very good. I await with much anticipation the showing of the next one.'

I tried to smile at him. A fine time to meet one of my fans. 'Would you be very kind and see if you can find me a taxi?' I said.

He went off, full of importance at being involved in saving a film star from robbery. The police removed their prisoner and I turned down several offers of an escort

281

home from the well-meaning Englishmen. I scrabbled in my bag, looking for an adequate reward for Bhagwan Das, and my fingers found the tickets for the passage to Goa on which I had pinned such hopes. I was tempted to tear them up, but I did not. If Maria wanted a free visit to her family then she could have it. After all, I had no use now for a children's *ayah*.

I think the reward I handed over was adequate. My Indian friend protested that he had done no more than his duty, but his highminded resistance disappeared when I insisted, as I knew I was expected to.

'Perhaps also you will give me a commendation in writing?' he asked hopefully.

I promised to write to his superiors and we parted with great friendliness. I doubt whether he did much work for the rest of the day since his top priority was more likely to be to round up as many of his friends as possible to tell them about his adventure.

As for me, I went home, dismissed a tearful Maria, paid her a month's wages and sent her off to Goa. I could hardly wait to get her out of the house, even though I liked her; she reminded me too much of what I had lost.

I lay dry-eyed and wakeful for most of the night. I had given my heart to another woman's child and now I was paying for that mistake. I doubted whether I would ever see her again. Wealth and influence had closed ranks to defeat me. Little Jane would be brought up by strangers, never knowing that her mother had become a duchess and quite forgetting the kind arms of her first dark-skinned nurse and 'Auntie Jess' who had played with her and sung her the songs of her own childhood.

The frustrated robbery had seemed of such small account compared to the loss of Jane that I was wholly taken aback to discover it reported in full in *The Times of India* and *The Bombay Gazette*. There were even pictures, one of Bhagwan Das, beaming proudly, a publicity still from *The Warrior Queen* and one I would have given a lot to suppress, a photograph of me escorted by Kesri in which I was wearing the opal necklace. To my disgust I was described as 'the Anglo-Indian film star and close friend of His Highness the Maharajah of Bhuredar'. Anyone could read between the lines and decide what that meant.

The recollection of the skinny torso and terrified eyes of my robber haunted me. I asked to be kept informed of when he was to appear in Court because I wanted to go along and put in a plea for mercy for him. We all expected that he would plead guilty and take the punishment that was handed out. Instead, to everyone's surprise, he not only pleaded Not Guilty, but he was represented in Court by a lawyer.

This made it a much more formal affair and I had to go along to give evidence. As soon as I saw the lawyer defending the thief I understood why he had taken the case. It was Hari Chand.

CHAPTER FIFTEEN

In the end Hari Chand's defence probably did his client more harm than good because the way he dealt with me in Court made it impossible for me to ask for leniency for the wretched youngster.

The evidence I had to give was simple enough since I had no doubt at all that the man in the dock was the one who had snatched my handbag.

I had given my name as Jessica Bullen, but that was not good enough for Hari Chand.

'Is your name not in actual fact, Jessica Fardale – Mrs Fardale, the wife of Edmond Fardale?'

'I prefer to use my maiden name.'

'Why is that?'

'I am divorced.'

I had no solicitor of my own in Court. Why should I? I had not expected to defend myself. I sensed that the man acting for the police was uneasy, but at that point he did not intervene.

'Have you any other names?'

'In my acting career I'm also known as Jasmina.'

'Ah, yes, Jasmina, the well-known film actress, star of *The Story of Princess Sushila*, *The Warrior Queen* and . . . what is the name of your latest epic?'

'*Dancing Destruction.*'

'We have not yet had the pleasure of viewing that performance. All these films were made by your friend, the Maharajah of Bhuredar?'

'He directed the first two films and set up the company which produced the third.'

The judge was getting tired of this line of questioning and interrupted to ask Hari Chand to get to the point. Hari turned to the contents of my handbag.

'My purse, my chequebook, keys, a powder compact, some . . . travel documents and a necklace,' I said.

'How much money was there in the purse?'

'About five hundred rupees.'

'Describe the necklace, if you please.'

'It was an opal and diamond necklace.'

'Of considerable value?'

'Yes.'

'Why were you carrying it?'

'I had taken it out of the Bank because I was planning to sell it.' To keep his daughter and bring her up, because I loved her, as I did not love her father at that moment.

'Did you have a sentimental attachment to the necklace? Was it perhaps a gift from your husband? Or from the Maharajah of Bhuredar?'

The police lawyer exploded at that and the judge sided with him. There was a lot of spluttering about 'total irrelevance' and Hari had to sit down without an answer to his question, but he looked satisfied, as if he had made the point he was after.

I thought that would be the end of it, but there was still one more unpleasantness to come when the man who had captured the thief was induced by Hari to reveal that I had offered the necklace to him.

'For what purpose?' Hari asked, sounding as incredulous as if he did not already know the answer.

'The *memsahib* wished to board the ship which was about to sail.'

'She tried to bribe you?'

Bhagwan Das looked uncomfortable. 'She wished very much to go on board the ship,' he repeated.

'Did you form the opinion that the necklace was worth a great deal of money?'

'Oh, yes, sir, a very, very precious necklace, worth many *lakhs* of rupees.'

'It would be interesting to know why Mrs Fardale . . . Miss Bullen . . . Jasmina . . . was so anxious to visit that ship.'

'We're not here to speculate about that,' the judge interrupted. 'Unless your line of questioning is relevant to the defence of your client I suggest you discontinue it.'

Hari Chand made the best use he could of what had been revealed: his client was a poor man, near to starving, and I was a rich, careless woman who had flaunted a fabulous necklace in front of him, a necklace whose value meant so little to me that I had offered it as a bribe to a dockyard official merely to be allowed to go up a gang-plank. If the temptation of theft had been irresistible to a hungry man with a family to support, who could blame him?

The boy was found Guilty, of course, and sent to prison. The sentence was not heavy so perhaps Hari had achieved something, but I would have pleaded for no sentence at all if I had not feared to make the situation still worse by getting up and speaking.

Outside the courtroom I came in for a lot of sympathy I could have done without.

'Damned impertinence,' the police inspector said. 'I'm sorry you were let in for that, Miss Bullen.'

'It's of no importance,' I said wearily. 'Not much point in complaining, is there, when nothing that was said is untrue? Tell me, is it all right if I talk to Hari Chand now that the case is over?'

'I wouldn't advise it. He's one of those Home Rule chaps, you know. That's why he had it in for you. My advice is to keep out of his way. He's not likely to apologise.'

'That's not what I want. We knew one another well at one time and I have some news about . . . about a mutual friend I'd like to pass on to him.'

I could see that my past friendship with Hari Chand did me no good at all in the Inspector's eyes. I wondered what he would think if he looked up the records and discovered that Hari and I had once been picked up by the police together. The idea amused me, so that I was almost smiling when Hari came to join me.

He was older and thinner and his manner was more defensive than it had been when I last saw him. He looked

286

at me with suspicion, ready to be offended if I reproached him with his tactics in Court.

I plunged straight into what I wanted to say to him. 'The reason I was chasing after that ship was because your daughter was on board. The Arkadys have removed her to England and plan to have her adopted into an unknown family.'

'That seems to me a most reasonable thing to do.'

'I wanted to keep her. She was as dear to me as my own daughter would have been.'

'You had no right to retain her against the wishes of her mother.'

'How I do dislike the legal mind,' I said. 'It was the Arkadys' solicitor who snatched Jane away before I had a chance to take her off to Goa as I'd planned. That's why I was carrying the necklace, so as to have something to sell when we got there.'

'You couldn't expect the great Arkady family to allow a child of their house to be reared on the proceeds of prostitution.'

'Damn you, Hari, that's a wicked thing to say. I worked hard on the films I made. It's true that Kesri gave me that necklace, but it was *not* because I'd slept with him.'

That was a bit of prevarication, because I had always known the necklace was payment in advance, but it did wipe the smug look off Hari's face for a few minutes.

'If I traced Jane and tried to get her back, would you give me your support? No, not money, I don't mean that, but would you say that as her father you'd prefer me to bring her up?'

'Certainly not. I'm glad to hear she's been removed to England. To me she's nothing but an encumbrance, a reminder of my shame.'

'Shame . . . ?'

The face he turned on me was contorted with rage and grief. 'I defiled myself by lying with a member of the race I am sworn to fight. To have my weakness exposed by the existence of a child . . . to be constantly reminded that I could not resist a fleshly urge even though I *knew*

287

I would regret it . . . no! I'm glad the child has gone away. Let her be brought up in England and never know her father was a humble Indian barrister.'

'Humble is one thing you're not,' I said. 'You're so damn sure you're right you'll go to any lengths to make a point against the British, even to the extent of raking over the muckheap of my life. You shouldn't have exposed me like that in Court . . .'

He shrugged, looking sulky but completely unconvinced.

'You said that silly boy had a wife and family,' I said. 'Was that true?'

'Of course. He has a wife and a child. The wife is only fifteen years of age.'

'If I give you some money will you see that they're helped while he's inside? Without anyone knowing that it's come from me, of course.'

For a moment I thought Hari would refuse, but in the end he accepted the cash I tipped out of my bag, reluctantly and with a bad grace, but he did take it.

'Difficult, isn't it, to accept favours from people we dislike?' I said sympathetically.

'You understand me too well,' he said and his grim expression lightened a little.

'You and Patricia . . .' I said.

'Don't ask.'

'Did you love her?'

'Not in the silly, romantic way you have in mind. For a time I was dazzled. She was so ardent – not for me, but for the cause in which I thought we both believed. Sharing the same lodgings, drawn together so closely, it seemed natural for us to live as man and wife. We were a pair of fools. And then, quite suddenly, she changed.'

'The baby brought her back to reality.'

'Perhaps that is so. She asked me to marry her, but on the conditions she suggested it was impossible. She wanted us to go back to England and me to practise at the Bar in London.'

'With her family connections you might have done very well.'

'I couldn't desert India. And I could hardly take Patricia back to my village to live like a Hindu wife with my mother and father. We had to part.'

'You deserted Patricia – completely. Did she mean less to you than Independence for India?' I should have expected the answer I got.

'Yes.' You can't argue with a man as singleminded as that. I would have left him, but he stopped me. 'When your latest film is shown will you be going to Bhuredar?' he asked.

'Probably not. It's not set in Bhuredar like *The Warrior Queen*, so I doubt whether there'll be any special showing of it in Arangapore.'

'That's good. I've heard that there's a lot of resentment in the State because of your involvement with their Maharajah.'

'That's all over. I'm yesterday's girlfriend.' I was surprised that Hari should have news of what was said about me as far away as Bhuredar and said as much.

'Word gets around,' he said. 'I have no great feeling of friendship for you, but you are a surprising person in many ways and I would not wish any harm to come to you. Stay away from Bhuredar.'

The only good thing about the prosecution was that it gave me something to think about. Once the hearing was over I was indeed alone. All I had to look forward to was the first night of a film I regretted making. The new director was taking a long time to get it ready for screening, far longer than Kesri, with his instinctive flair, had done, but at last the date of the first night was announced.

My name was still one that drew the crowds and it gave me a certain thrill to see it up in lights, but this première was nothing like the first, or even the second when I had had William's support. We still aped the trappings of a Hollywood opening: a limousine was sent to collect me and the flash bulbs flared as I arrived at the cinema. I smiled all round as if I hadn't a care in the world, but I was very conscious that this was a second-rate affair. Kesri had not bothered to put in an appearance and the occasion had none of the social kudos his presence would have conferred.

It would have been foolish to wear the opals in public, but I had taken the pearls out of the Bank and they looked well with the sophisticated black lace gown I had chosen. I spent a lot on that dress. Why not? I no longer had a motive for hoarding my money.

The film was quite horrible, but it was obviously going to be a box-office success. The little Indian actress who took the virtuous role could not, in fact, act, but she looked very appealing and everyone seemed to like her.

The director made an announcement afterwards. 'Our next epic picture is already in preparation.' I sat up. That was news to me. 'It will be one of a series of films to be based on our great saga, the *Ramayana*, and the part of Sita will be played by the latest star in our galaxy – Gayatri Bera.'

Naturally I was the first to congratulate her. 'I can't tell you what a joy it is to me that this wonderful classic should be performed by a truly Indian actress,' I said, loud enough for any listening reporters to hear.

I was pleased when one of them pressed forward and asked, 'What are your own plans?'

'I've had an offer from Hollywood and I expect to leave as soon as I've settled my affairs here.'

I wrote to Sol Hannabakker the next day telling him I was free of my previous commitments and could travel to Hollywood whenever he liked.

The weeks went by and I received no reply from Sol Hannabakker. Possibly my letter had gone astray, or he might be filming on location, but I had a nasty flat feeling that he had written me off and could not be bothered to tell me so.

Christmas came and I had a complaining letter from Mumma. Edmond's father had taken our divorce hard and he was not pleased that his son had emigrated to Canada. I gathered from Mumma that they were united in blaming that on me, with some justice, I suppose. She wanted to know whether I meant to stay in India or return to England. The answer was neither, if I could help it, but I had almost lost hope of escaping to America unless I went independently and risked being rejected by the film industry over there.

William, as usual, sent me an enchanting present: a Moghul miniature of a hunting scene, full of tiny beasts and flowers. I hung it near my bed where I could see all the exquisite details every day in the clear morning light.

He remembered my birthday in February too, which was unusual, but this time he only sent greetings and a scrawled note asking, *Are you going to Arangapore for the opening of the Rukmini Singh Hospital? I've been invited and as my work is coming to an end here I think I'll try to attend.'*

I had heard nothing and suspected that I was being shut out, just as I was when the foundation stone was laid. It was a real pleasure when the invitation arrived two days later. Somewhere at the back of my mind I had a vague recollection of Hari Chand's warning against visiting Bhuredar, but that had been months ago and I had not taken it seriously even then. Certainly I meant to go. After all, Rukmini had been a very dear friend. And William would be there. Perhaps if I talked to William he would help me to reach a decision about the rest of my life.

There was no private compartment this time when I went to Arangapore and I had to pay my own fare. All the same, I travelled in some style, in a first-class compartment, with my own bearer and maid to look after me. I had company, too, since in India even the most reserved Englishman would talk to a fellow European. Early on in my journey I met a charming couple, he a newly-appointed District Officer and she a history graduate with a keen interest in the antiquities of India. When I mentioned William's name her face lit up. She plied me with questions and I replied as best I could, amused that in this company his fame outstripped mine.

I told William about it when we met in Arangapore. We were neither of us staying in the Palace, but in one of the princely guesthouses. Probably Kesri meant me to see that as a snub, but in fact I was a great deal more comfortable in the guesthouse than in the grand apartments in the fortress Palace.

'The nice woman I met on the train nearly swooned when I told her you were my cousin,' I said. 'For two pins she would have deserted her husband and got off the train with me to come and meet you. I told her you'd written a book and she wanted to know when it would be out and who was publishing it. I was terribly ashamed when I had to tell her I didn't know.'

'The Cambridge University Press and it should be out in August if we can get one or two difficulties about illustrations sorted out.'

'You're a tremendous swell in your world, aren't you?'

'My dear Jessica! I'm moderately well-known amongst a few specialists. Let's keep it in proportion.'

'I don't think you're as modest as you pretend. You're actually looking quite pleased.'

William shook his head, but he went on smiling.

'Talking to people like the ones I met on the train made me realise how cut off I've been in recent months,' I said. 'Not that I was ever on visiting terms with the Indian Civil Service . . .'

'The "heaven born".'

'Precisely. If I'd let it out that I was not the nicely behaved young Englishwomen they believed, but the slightly suspect film star with a smidgin of native blood they would probably have frozen me out.'

'Not necessarily. Times are changing and even the "heaven born" are more tolerant than they used to be. You should have told them who you were. They might have been enthralled.'

'I didn't dare risk it. I liked them too much. They were my sort of people – the kind who *do* things. When I was a Company wife I got on better with the husbands than the wives and it wasn't a sex thing – well, not entirely – but because I was more interested in their jobs than in problems with the servants or whether the next boat from England would bring some decent hats.'

And that brought me neatly to what I really wanted to talk to William about. 'What am I to do with myself? I've almost lost hope of an invitation to go to Hollywood.'

William settled down to consider the question in that satisfying way he had of giving his whole mind to a problem. 'Where do you want to live? India?'

'No. I thought I did, you know. I thought I belonged here, but I don't. I don't seem to belong anywhere.'

'That leaves the whole world open for you.'

I smiled at him shakily. 'You make it sound like an adventure.'

'Why not? Do you want to go on acting?'

'I'm not sure about that, either. If I'd been free to take up Sol Hannabakker's offer when he first made it then I might have plunged into Hollywood and enjoyed it, but now . . . I have to admit I've gone lukewarm about it.'

'Your dance-girl film is showing here in the town. Did you know?'

'Ugh! I saw the posters as we drove in from the station. That was the film that really put me off a career in the cinema and it also showed me that I wasn't truly an actress because if I had been I would have welcomed the chance of playing such a strong part.'

William was looking thoughtful. When he eventually spoke I was surprised. 'What you really like is business and organisation,' he said. 'Arkady & Pershore lost an asset when they let you go.'

'My grandfather said he could have made something of me if I'd been a boy,' I remembered.

'Yes . . . it's a pity he didn't see that your being a woman could have made you no less valuable to him.'

I was more cynical than he was. 'Come off it, William!

There was no way he could promote his own grand-daughter – his illegitimate son's child – to a high-up post in the family firm. I was always doomed to be one of the typists.'

'What about marriage? You told me once you wouldn't venture into it again. Do you still feel the same?'

I took my time to answer that because I was no longer as sure as I had been about making my way in the world alone. 'I've been very lonely since Jane was taken away from me. No companionship, no work, no friends. It's a dismal life, William.'

'You must be careful not to drift into another unsatisfactory relationship just as a way of escape.'

'How horribly true. You don't have a very high opinion of my good sense, do you, William?'

'Not when it comes to choosing men,' he agreed.

We got nowhere and yet I went up to bed that night feeling cheered. At least for the next few days I would have companionship, both from William and from the other people accommodated in the guest-house, who were mostly doctors and nurses about to be employed in the new hospital.

They knew who I was all right and I was amused to discover that they were awestruck at being under the same roof as a real live film star.

'Your work is far more worthwhile than anything I've ever done,' I protested.

'Not in terms of money,' one of the nurses commented and there was a general laugh.

'But you've had to study for years and you help people.'

'You entertain them.'

'I wiggle my hips and roll my eyes or else I strike a pose and look noble. It's harder work than people outside the studio realise, but the rewards are out of all proportion. In your company I feel ashamed.'

'So when do you start training to be a midwife?' someone asked.

That was not a profession I felt drawn to either, or I might have joined Patricia in nursing during the war.

Wednesday had been chosen as an auspicious day to open the hospital. Having triumphed by getting the Prince of Wales to lay the foundation stone, Kesri had decided to do the opening ceremony himself. As usual he laid everything on in style. We were collected by the Palace limousines and taken to the site. I had hoped Kesri would have the elephants out, but he had decided it was too modern an occasion for that. He and Antoinette came in an open horsedrawn carriage escorted by his splendid lancers on matching bay horses. There were pennants attached to the lances, streaming out behind as the horses trotted by. Kesri wore dark blue and silver with a few tasteful diamonds. He was looking very handsome and very pleased with himself. For a moment I was fiercely jealous of Antoinette, resplendent in rose pink and gold, and then I told myself not to be a fool. I had been nothing but a plaything to Kesri and I ought to be glad to be free of him.

All the same, when he looked towards our seats and caught my eye I tilted my chin and smiled. I had chosen to be very subdued in a loose cream silk dress with a big black hat. Quite the lady and not at all like the wriggling *nautch* girl displayed on those regrettable posters in the city, but Kesri had seen me in that role not only on film, but in more intimate circumstances, and when he looked at me he remembered and I saw him remember.

The ceremony went ahead, a mixture of East and West. The priests chanted, lit little fires and burnt incense, Kesri did *puja* and then, when that side had been attended to, he cut a ribbon with a pair of golden scissors and declared the Rukmini Singh Hospital open.

As yet there were no patients, since the presence of so many visitors would have been distressing to the women for whom the hospital had been built. We toured the empty building and admired the long, airy rooms, the labour ward, the operating theatre, beautifully appointed with all the latest instruments.

'How pleased Rukmini would be,' I said to William. 'She was devoted to her people.'

'I hope the people are equally pleased,' William said drily. 'There's a lot of opposition to Western-style medicine. In some ways Bhuredar is very backward.'

'Surely the women will come for treatment?'

'Eventually, but it may be slow work to persuade them. If only this could have been done in Rukmini's lifetime. She would have won them over.'

There was a great feast laid on in the grounds of the hospital after the opening ceremony. Kesri and Antoinette and their important guests retired to a silk tent. We lesser invitees were herded together in another marquee, which turned out to be a mistake.

William went out to talk to some men he had spotted who had helped him when he had been excavating his old ruins. He came back looking worried. 'There's a stupid rumour going round that we've been served beef,' he said. 'I've said very loudly that of course it's nonsense and I've asked my friends to contradict it, but there's a nasty feeling in the air.'

It might all have blown over if Kesri had not indulged one of his whims by leaving his tent to come in search of me. William and I were standing outside the marquee, mainly because William was insistent that we should leave as soon as Kesri and Antoinette made a move.

Kesri came padding up like a predatory tiger. Was it imagination or did I feel William stiffen?

'Well, Jessica?' Kesri demanded.

'A splendid occasion, Your Highness,' I replied politely. 'The hospital will be a great blessing to the women of Bhuredar. Her late Highness would have been pleased.'

'You're very formal all of a sudden,' Kesri said. 'Hello, William. Glad you could come.' He turned back to me. 'Sorry you have to be put up in the guest-house. There's rather a crowd at the Palace, but most of them will be leaving tomorrow. Come and spend a few days with me quietly before you go back to Bombay.'

I was wearing the pearls. It was a piece of bravado on my part and I knew I would have done better to leave them behind, but they were mine, damn it, and they

296

looked very well with my cream silk gown. As he spoke, Kesri took hold of one of the long strands and stood swinging it in his hand.

It was far too intimate a gesture to be made in public, coming from a reigning prince to a European woman. I could almost feel the spontaneous intake of breath from a thousand throats as it was noticed.

'I'm leaving for Bombay first thing in the morning,' I said.

'Change your mind,'

'No.'

With his eyes fixed on my face and his fingers still fondling the pearls Kesri said, 'Antoinette has engagements in Delhi for the next week.'

'All the more reason for me to go.'

Kesri shrugged and turned away. I knew that moody look. Someone was going to come in for a nasty show of temper if he was crossed again . . . Even as the thought went through my mind a man darted out of the crowd with a garland in his hand and attempted to put it round Kesri's neck. Not even pausing in his impatient stride Kesri pushed him away and the man stumbled and fell. Again I heard that collective intake of breath.

I felt William take hold of my elbow and draw me back. 'There could be trouble,' he said.

'That he should dare to speak to me like that in front of you,' I said, almost choking.

'Never mind that. We're leaving, now, even if we have to walk.'

It was mid-afternoon and the heat was intense. The vivid colours favoured by Kesri's subjects – vermilion, scarlet and maroon, yellow, royal blue and emerald green – dazzled in front of my eyes. The smell of the sticky rice and vegetable curry which had been served to them was heavy in the air. Through the thin silk of my dress I could feel William's fingers clamped to my arm.

We made slow progress through the people hunkered down on the grass. I saw their faces upturned towards us, but they expressed nothing, not even curiosity, until someone said, 'Jasmina . . . Jasmina . . .' I heard the sound go through the crowd like the rustle of wind through a cornfield. They began standing up to get a better look at me.

'Smile,' William said.

Like royalty, I bent my head from side to side distributing smiles, not really seeing any of them.

We had almost reached the place where the motor cars had been left, still moving slowly and followed now by a knot of curious people, when a man sprang out of the crowd immediately in front of us.

He was wearing nothing but a tiny apron over his genitals. His body was smeared with ash, his long hair was unkempt and his eyes were red with the *bhang* he had been smoking. In his hand he brandished a long pole with a three-pronged fork on top.

He danced in front of us, chanting a song of denunciation of the foreign whore who had led the ruler of the State away from his religion and the care of his people. I felt more indignant than frightened. Considering the brevity of my affair with Kesri, not to mention the amount of money I had helped him to make which he had spent on his new hospital, I thought it was pretty unfair, and if the *sadhu* had been in a more reasonable state, instead of being driven out of his mind by drugs, I would have stopped and argued with him.

The *sadhu* jabbed at me with his trident and William spoke sharply, commanding him to step back. He did give way, but now all the people round us were on their feet, crowding closer for a view of this woman the holy man had condemned.

William spoke soothingly, cracking a joke, and I saw a few smiles. Reassured, I stepped forward boldly, even though I could still hear the hostile murmurs outside the circle William had been able to influence.

Just short of the gleaming row of Palace limousines a few little native carts had been drawn up and the emaciated horses were cropping the sparse blades of grass which had straggled up through the baked red earth. A man sprang up on to one of the carts and began shouting and pointing at me.

'What is he saying?' I asked William because I could not believe I had understood it properly.

'That what the *sadhu* said was true. You're a wicked woman who poisoned the Maharani and led the Maharajah astray,' William said grimly. 'He knows because he saw your story at the cinema.'

'But that's the *nautch* girl film. He can't believe it was *true*?'

'These are simple people.'

The man was fairly dancing in the cart with rage. Startled, the little horse flung up its head and backed. The man was thrown to the ground, the horse continued to back and the wheels of the cart went over the man's legs with a sickening crunch.

'William, how awful! We can't leave him. Surely there's something we can do to help?'

'Once I've got you safely into a car I'll come back,' William said.

There was an anguished shriek from a woman who threw herself on top of the man. When she found he was still alive she half-raised herself and looked round, straight at me, and raising her arm, pointed at the one she blamed for this misfortune. A young man who had run forward with her followed the direction of her accusing finger. I saw the naked hatred in his eyes one second before he snatched a knife from his waistband and sprang on me.

I was in pain, terrible pain. There was blood all over the cream silk of my dress. I wanted to lie down, but William wouldn't let me. He picked me up, which hurt even more, and carried me through a throng of parakeet people, hostile, avid with curiosity, frightened . . . all the faces blurred and I lost consciousness.

CHAPTER SIXTEEN

'If you have to get yourself knifed it's very clever to do it outside a brand new hospital with a team of doctors and nurses eager to start work,' William said. 'They were queuing up for the honour of putting in the next stitch.'

He was sitting by my bedside with my right hand resting in his. I was too weak to do more than give him a very small smile. My other arm seemed to have been immobilised and all my left side was strapped up. I tried to move and stopped as pain shot through me.

'I . . . hurt,' I said with difficulty.

'Yes, my darling, you were quite badly injured, but you're going to get better. You mustn't talk.'

I closed my eyes and a series of pictures flitted across my closed lids. As I remembered what had happened my eyes flew open again. 'The man . . .' I said.

'The one who hurt you? Don't worry about him.'

'No . . . other man . . . with cart . . . his legs.'

William's grip on my hand tightened for a moment. 'He's been treated, too. His legs were broken and badly bruised, but he will heal – as you will.'

'Hospital . . . for women,' I pointed out.

'They took him in. Now you must stop talking or I shan't be allowed to visit you again.'

'You've been here . . . all the time,' I said.

'I didn't think you were conscious.'

'I . . . felt you.'

William bent over and brushed my forehead with his lips. 'Rest now,' he whispered.

The nurse came in and gave me something to drink and I drifted into an uneasy sleep, disturbed by dreams and by pain whenever I moved.

Three days later when the pain had been replaced by

discomfort and even I could sense that I was on the mend, I made an interesting discovery.

'How are we feeling today?' my nurse asked. She was Eurasian, a roly-poly girl with a cheerful smile and a bright manner I tried not to find irritating.

'Much better,' I said. 'As weak as a kitten, though.'

'That's not surprising, considering the amount of blood you lost. My word, you were lucky that Dr Bullen had the same blood group as you. We weren't ready for emergencies and we had nothing to give you.'

'William gave me his blood?'

'Indeed he did. As I say, you were lucky.'

I tackled William about it that afternoon.

'That's right,' he said. 'My life's blood. Behave yourself or I'll ask for it back.'

He was trying to make me smile because he sensed that I was troubled, but I had too much on my mind to be diverted. 'Why do they hate me?' I asked.

'They are simple people,' William said, as I remembered him saying once before.

'I felt – I still feel – nothing but goodwill towards them.'

'The man on the cart identified you with the *nautch* girl in that film you so much disliked. That may seem foolish to you, but it was real to him.'

'I don't suppose the *sadhu* had seen the film.'

'I'm suspicious about that *sadhu* and so, I may say, are the police. He disappeared very conveniently when you were attacked. We think he was sent here to make trouble and you were a convenient scapegoat.'

I tried to work that out, frowning until William's fingers stroked away the lines between my brows.

'I don't see it,' I said. 'What's to be gained by stirring up trouble in an independent State?'

'In the distant past the British might have been to blame. A State which has been destabilised is easily taken over. Nowadays . . . well, there are many other political interests besides those who simply want Home Rule. Kesri has made himself vulnerable by his foolish marriage, by his Western ideas, his film-making and even, I'm afraid,

301

his involvement with you. The loss of Rukmini was a blow to the people, too.'

'If Kesri went . . .'

'His son is still a child. He could perhaps be manipulated as Kesri, with all his weaknesses, cannot.'

'So . . . not entirely my fault?'

'You were merely a tool; picked up, dropped and damaged in the process, poor dear.'

I began to feel a little easier in my mind; not entirely satisfied, but not as bewildered as I had been. 'Kesri sent me flowers,' I said.

'So I see.' William turned his head to look at the vast basket of exotic blooms which stood on a table by the window.

'There was a package, too,' I said. 'I couldn't open it with one hand and I didn't want the nurse to do it. Would you . . . ?'

William undid the small parcel and handed me a square box. That I could open for myself. Inside was a magnificent diamond brooch in the shape of another basket of flowers and a small card with the message: *Get well soon*.

'More jewellery,' I said. 'You'd better take care of it, William.'

The only comment William made was, 'I've got your pearls, too.'

'Where is Kesri?'

'He decided it would be expedient to go to Delhi with Antoinette.'

'I must be gone from here before he comes back.'

'That's all arranged. As soon as you're strong enough I'm taking you to Kashmir.'

'Kashmir? What about your work?'

'There's a site near Srinagar I want to explore. I've been waiting for a suitable opportunity.'

'You make it sound quite plausible.'

William laughed and got up to go. 'It happens to be true.'

'I'll be in your way.'

'Nonsense! I'll probably find a job for you. I've always wanted a secretary.'

'I'm highly trained and very expensive.'

'Food and drink and a tent over your head, that's all I'm offering. Take it or leave it.'

'Camping?'

'Yes, my pampered plant. That's why you've got to be quite well before we leave.'

It was another two weeks before I was judged fit enough to leave with William. I stayed in the hospital all that time and as soon as I was able to walk about I spent a lot of time going round the wards, talking to the women who had been admitted since the opening, encouraging them and, I hope, giving them better heart in their misfortunes, not to mention making them think better of me.

I began to realise that there had been a dimension missing in my understanding of India. I was a big-city person and this was almost my first contact with the people who scratched a living from the unrewarding soil. These women, worn out in their thirties by toil and incessant childbearing, accepted the additional burden of bad health with a stoicism which meant that too often they came for treatment far too late. It was education that was needed, I could see that, then there would be a greater willingness to accept advice early in an illness, instead of a mistrust of modern scientific medical practice until after everything else had been tried.

Most of the women were content to pass their days in hospital doing nothing, probably for the first time in their lives, but some occupied themselves with little handlooms or embroidery on coarse cotton. The best of the designs had a vigorous boldness and I bought a few things, glad of the chance to give them a little money.

By the time I was fit to travel I had managed to make several friends. I was touched by the group of doctors, nurses and patients who clustered in the porch of the hospital to say goodbye when I left.

'I'm taking you to Rawalpindi by train,' William said. 'After that we'll travel by road. I'm told there's a metalled road all the way to Srinagar now and motor cars run over it, but I'll sort that out in Rawalpindi. It's a bit early in the season and if there's been a landslip on the road a *tonga* can be manhandled over it where a car could only turn back.'

It sounded rather more adventurous than I had anticipated, but William seemed to know all about it so I left it to him.

The long train journey to Rawalpindi exhausted me and I was glad that William had taken rooms at the Imperial Hotel for three nights. He said it was to give him time to make our travel arrangements and for me to buy some more sensible clothes than I had taken to Bhuredar, but I saw him looking at me surreptitiously and the depth of his anxiety made me realise how close I had been to losing my life.

'It's to be a *tonga* for us,' William announced. 'I've looked at the available motor cars and I wouldn't trust them to run me to the nearest bazaar let alone over a mountain pass. I say, that's a fetching outfit.'

Myself, I did not find the khaki drill divided skirt and cotton shirt I had bought particularly seductive, but William seemed to approve so I pirouetted to display my new wardrobe and laughed at the memory of the silks I had recently worn.

We set out the next day in a *tonga* for William and me and an *ekka* following behind for our luggage and his bearer, my own servants having been sent back to Bombay from Arangapore.

I think William was worried about the effect on me of jolting along in a horse-drawn carriage and he had taken rooms for us in the hotel at Murree, a journey of only about forty miles. I protested that I could have gone on, but William was adamant that we were doing the journey in easy stages.

It was a long drop down to the Jhelum Valley the next day. The scenery was splendid, especially where we could see the snow still lingering on the mountains, but there was bad news for us when we reached Kohala.

'There's been a landslip between Dulai and Domel,' William told me. 'This is what I was afraid of when I heard there'd been heavy rainfall recently. A team of labourers has been working to clear the road since yesterday, but no one has yet come through from the other side. Perhaps we should wait another day before attempting it.'

'What would you do if you were alone?'

'Try to get through.'

'Then that's what we'll do.'

When I saw the road cut into the face of the cliff beyond Dulai I wondered whether perhaps I had been foolhardy, but William was heartened by the sight of a string of pack ponies advancing towards us. He leaned down from the *tonga* to speak to the men leading the first pony.

'Sounds all right,' he said. 'You won't mind walking a few yards, will you?'

'What's that noise?'

'You'll see in a minute. The Nansook River comes out of a deep gorge just ahead of us and joins the Jhelum.'

I did indeed see. Swollen by melting snow and the recent rains the Nansook roared out of the rock face and I shuddered at the swirling chaos of water as the two rivers met.

We drove through a small tunnel and met the landslip on the other side. William got out and went to confer with the leader of the gang working on the shifting ground.

'He says there's always trouble here and their judgement is that we could drive over it,' he reported. 'I don't think we'll take that risk, but we will go on.'

With William's hand holding mine I climbed and slithered over the untrustworthy ground, then William went back to help the *tonga* driver lead his horse over the bad patch. It was not too difficult, but I was not sorry to feel more solid earth under my feet.

'We'll push on to the Garhi *dak* bungalow,' William said. 'I hope you took my advice about bringing a few essentials with you because if the *ekka* doesn't catch up

305

with us you'll have to manage without your luggage tonight.'

Once again we had only travelled about fifty miles, but I had stopped arguing with William about our pace and the *dak* bungalow at Garhi had great charm. We shared it with a couple of sportsmen intending to strike out into the hills. We turned out the next morning to watch them crossing the rope bridge across the Jhelum.

'It makes me feel quite sick,' I said to William. 'You're not expecting me to do anything like that, I hope?'

'A lot of people hate that bridge,' William admitted. 'Our way lies across the plain.'

'Thank goodness for that. Where are we making for today?'

'Rampur – about another fifty miles.'

'I could go further, I'm sure I could.'

'I'd like to take a trip to visit an ancient temple at Buniar, which will take a bit of time. You don't mind, do you?'

'It'll relieve my conscience. I'm sure I'm taking up too much of your time.'

'We're only taking four nights on the road instead of the usual three.'

In fact, I was glad when our slow progress allowed the *ekka* to catch up with us and I could wear a clean blouse for dinner that night at our next *dak* bungalow.

We arrived in Srinagar on the fifth day of our journey.

'I want to visit the Shankaracharya Temple, which is on a hill just to the east of Srinagar, so for the first few days we'll stay on a houseboat on Lake Dal,' William said. 'It's still a little early in the year for visiting Kashmir. The flowers will be lovely, but it may be chilly.'

'Dadda used to talk about a holiday in Kashmir, but we could never afford it.'

'You'll find it quite different from the India you know.'

He was right about that. Just as the people of Kesri's State of Bhuredar were distinct from the mixed population I had known in Bombay, so the Kashmiri people were different again. They were mostly Moslems, of course, and many of the women were shrouded from head to foot in the black *chador*, while the men wore layers of loose garments over trousers tied at the ankle and on their heads what looked like a crocheted skull-cap.

The houses fascinated me, towering wooden structures wider at the top than the bottom, as if at any moment they must topple into the water. The balconies and latticed windows were decorated with elaborate carving. Darting over the water there were long, flat boats, mere shells, propelled by men – and even children – sitting on the prow and using a single paddle.

'They're called *shikaras* and we have to take one to get to our houseboat,' William said.

The *shikara* we took had cushions and an awning and a grinning boatman called Nazim. To me it seemed that we were exceedingly low in the water, but Nazim skimmed his boat across the lake with the ease of generations of inherited skill.

The houseboat was a revelation, as elaborately carved as the houses and nearly as roomy. We had three bedrooms and a bathroom, a dining room and a sitting room, and an upper deck where we could sit out and admire the view.

'Foreigners aren't allowed to buy land in Kashmir,' William explained. 'But, of course, a lovely place demands to be visited and so the British started building and hiring these boats. You can't keep the British out.'

'Where's the kitchen?'

'On a floating island at the back. Just as well, I think, because these wooden boats must be highly inflammable.'

The houseboat was furnished with old-fashioned comfort, very heavy and ornate.

'It's so odd to be sitting in a boat at a walnut dining table which must seat at least eight,' I said.

'Weird, isn't it? Come up on deck and look at the sunset over the lake.'

The light was magical as we leaned on the rail and watched the sun go down. We could see the shoreline and the mountains against the evening sky. From somewhere

in the distance came the call to prayer, long drawn out
and haunting.

'I feel most peculiar,' I said. 'As if I've just come out
of a chrysalis and my wings aren't dry yet. The past looks
like a dream from which I've woken up. Do you think
it's the effect of nearly dying?'

'Possibly. For a few minutes we thought we'd lost you,
but you rallied and fought back.'

'With the aid of your good red blood.' I turned and
saw a building on top of a hill, outlined by the golden
rays of the setting sun. 'Is that your temple?' I asked
William.

'That's the one. I'll be walking up and down that hill
for the next three days. I don't think it'll take me longer
than that to see what I want.'

'It's a temple, not a mosque?'

'Yes – Hindu, not Moslem. The present building dates
back to the eighth century, but the site originated in about
200 BC, when Ashoka's son Jalauka built a temple there.'

'You know so much.'

'Even you must have heard of Ashoka?'

'He was a great Indian King and he put up lots of
pillars with laws and things inscribed on them.'

'That's one way of describing him,' William agreed with
amusement. 'He ruled over a vast empire and he was
converted to Buddhism, which was exported from India
to the Far East, but then died out where it originated. He
must have been a remarkable man. If I had a choice I
think I'd rather meet Ashoka than Alexander himself.'

'Did they live at the same time?'

'No, when Alexander marched into India it was Ashoka's grandfather, Candragupta Maurya, who fought
against him. Ashoka lived from around 269 to 232 BC.'

'So long ago and yet you talk as if you read about them
in last week's newspaper.'

William laughed. 'It's more difficult than that,' he said.

For the next three days William disappeared at first
light. I lay in bed a little longer, listening to the water
lapping against the side of the boat as his *shikara* pushed

away. I had a leisurely breakfast and then when I felt ready for it I took to the water with Nazim and drifted round the waterways. The wind was cool, but Nazim provided me with a quilted coverlet and with that tucked round me I was warm enough to enjoy the sights.

We saw the floating markets, the artificial islands where vegetables were grown, the shops on the waterside, the lotus plants spread over the water. My resistance to the pedlars who pursued us was a disappointment to Nazim, who could have looked for a rake-off from any sales to me, but I shook my head at all the offers of woodcarving, papier-mâché, metalwork and jewellery. I even resisted the wonderful carpets. I wanted nothing but this gentle meandering around the backwaters.

'I'm beginning to get a glimmering of an idea of what I might do next,' I said to William.

'That's good.' He waited, but I was not ready to tell him any more and so he went on. 'I want to investigate a site about twenty miles away and I need to be on the spot. It's taken two years to get permission to do a dig and I'm only being allowed a few weeks, so there's no time to waste.'

'I thought you'd invented an excuse to bring me here to recuperate.'

'How very egotistical of you,' William said with his gentle smile. 'You will come with me to my dig, won't you? Conditions won't be too rough, I promise you.'

I agreed, of course, though I was none too sure what I was letting myself in for. Still, William had done this before and he knew how to organise it.

'We can go by boat as far as the Shalimar Bagh,' he said. 'After that there's a short trek, but I'll arrange a pony for you.'

I was amused by all this anxiety for me. My wounds had healed and I was feeling fit and, after all my inactivity, slightly restless. I was more than ready to take off into the wilds and I told William so.

'Not that wild,' he said. 'You can be back in Srinagar within a day if you find you can't bear it.'

For all that, I noticed that he was well stocked up with supplies and it took three pack ponies as well as the rough-coated little beast I rode to transport everything we needed up the hillside from the lake.

We ambled through the pine trees, following an almost invisible track, until we came to a large flat site where some trees had been felled.

'Good,' William said. 'I asked for some preparation to be done and for once it looks as if someone listened to what I said. This is where we'll camp, to get the benefit of shelter from the trees, and over there is where I'll make my first trench.'

William and I had three tents, one each for sleeping and another which William described as our sitting-dining-writing room. A few steps out from the trees and the view was spectacular, but one had to be careful not to tumble down the hillside or to slip into the stream which cascaded over a rock on its way to feed the lake.

'Not for drinking without boiling, even though it looks clean,' William said. 'But it's perfectly all right for washing. We can use it as a shower bath. I'll take it in the evening because I'll be mucky then and you can have it in the morning.'

'Thanks very much. I get the chance to break the ice!'

The splash and murmur of the water made a background to the noises of our camp, that and an occasional sighing sound from the tops of the trees high above.

We fell into a routine and the days began to slip by. I was woken each morning by the sound of William calling to the workmen, some of whom came up from the lakeside every day. I heard them talking and laughing and the chink and clatter of dishes as William had his breakfast, then the sounds died away and Abdul, who was Nizam's cousin, brought me a cup of tea. As soon as I had drunk it I crawled out of my sleeping bag, seized my towel and soap and went off for a shiveringly cold wash in the stream. By the time I was back and dressed Abdul had breakfast ready. It was usually eggs in some form or other – William would not have been so insensitive as to bring bacon into the camp, even if it were available – with toast and more tea.

After that the day was mine. The curious thing was I never seemed to be bored. If I felt energetic I could walk to the nearest of the Moghul gardens, the Shalimar Bagh, and wander up and down the terraces. The almond trees were blossoming, pink and white, and the hillside was studded with spring flowers, small starry narcissi and daffodils, bluebells and more varieties of iris than I could count. If I thought of it the day before I could tell Abdul and he would get one of the workmen to pass word to Nizam and he would come with the *shikara* to take me on the lake.

I only once went as far as Srinagar and that was because William asked me to go and see if there was any mail for him.

'And for you, too,' he said. 'I asked for your letters to be forwarded.'

As it turned out, there was more for me than for him and of some importance.

It was evening before I returned and the light was fading. William had washed and changed and was sitting by the charcoal brazier with a drink in his hand.

'I was hoping a search party wasn't going to be necessary, because I'm feeling much too lazy,' he said. 'You found your way all right?'

'Of course! Nizam guided me every step of the way.'

'And you're not too tired?'

'Certainly not. Stop treating me like an invalid.'

'If you'd seen yourself lying on that hospital bed drained of blood you'd fuss, too,' he retorted. 'Any letters?'

'Quite a bundle. Only two of you, but five for me. A couple of bills, which will have to wait until I get back to Bombay, one from Mumma – rather more forgiving than the last one she wrote to me – mostly about Patricia's wedding.'

'A big event?'

'The wedding of the year. Mumma has sent me the newspaper account. St George's, Hanover Square, yards

311

of white satin, antique lace veil, eight bridesmaids, royalty present and a honeymoon in the South of France.'

'Try not to be bitter.'

'How can I help it? I still ache for Jane. I ought to have been allowed to keep her. Oh, curses, I meant to be so good and not say anything more about it. Can I have a drink?'

'I'm sorry, I should have given you one straight away. That's what living in the wilds does for your manners.'

I blew my nose and took the whisky and soda William held out to me. His own two letters lay on the table unopened. They looked very official and important. One of them had a crest of a Cambridge College on the flap of the envelope. Presumably they were about his work, but it seemed that he was not going to open them.

'Do you want to know my other news?' I asked. 'Edmond has written to say our divorce has been made absolute and he's getting married again.'

'Quick work.'

'Yes, I hope he's not rushing into it and making another mistake.'

'Why did he write? He didn't have to let you know.'

'So that he could crow over me and say, "Look, you haven't messed up my life; someone else loves me." Poor Edmond, I wish I could feel more kindly towards him because I know I treated him badly.'

There was no reply to that from William. 'Blow you, William,' I said. 'Any other man would say "Oh, no, you didn't" or "It wasn't your fault".'

'But you did and it was,' William said calmly. 'You married a man who had no sort of insight into other people's feelings and you ran rings round him. I can't believe you were ever in love with him. If I'd been in England I would have forbidden the banns.'

'I was in a terrible mix up,' I tried to excuse myself. 'I'd given up Dominic and I could see no hope of a career, just dreary drudgery. Edmond had never wavered in his desire to marry me and, of course, he was coming out to India . . .'

312

'That was the lure that drew you. Wrongly, Jessica. You should leave India.'

'I know. I've known ever since Patricia had her affair with Hari and I was shocked to the point of being sickened. Feeling like that, how can I regard myself as a citizen of this country? I was disgusted with myself and my blind, unthinking prejudice. I hope I'm cured – I ought to be, considering my own affair with Kesri – but I no longer feel at home here. It may be the place where I was born, but it's not my country.'

'You'll go back to England?'

I twisted the last of my letters in my hand. 'I'll have to think about that. This letter has been waiting for me for weeks in Bombay. It's from Sol Hannabakker to say that there's still an opening for me in Hollywood if I'd like to get myself out there. I don't know what to do.'

'I'm the last person to advise you. Do you want to go on acting in films?'

'Not particularly.' I puzzled over it. 'It's most peculiar. Everything to do with that time has faded into the background. I can hardly believe I was audacious enough to put myself up on the screen and pretend to act. It doesn't seem real. Do you think it's your blood circulating round my veins that's turning me into a different person?'

William threw back his head and laughed. 'I think you need your dinner. Come and eat. And let me know when you've made up your mind about Hollywood.'

It was all very well for William to say 'make up your mind', but I was quite incapable of deciding what to do. Did I really want to go to Hollywood? No, not particularly. What did I want to do? I didn't know. It was a wonderful opportunity. I might like it when I got there – I might even be a great success and make a fortune. The thought left me cold. Where was my ambition? Where was my determination to make a place for myself in the world? Quite dead, as far as I could tell. It was most peculiar, and it left me thoroughly dissatisfied. William had told me once when I was down that another door would open. Well, here was a door, wide open and welcoming, and I had no inclination at all to go through it. Suddenly I was no longer content with my lazy days. 'Find me something to do,' I demanded.

'If you want to be helpful you can take charge of the small finds. They have to be carefully washed and numbered and always, *always* put back in the box from which you took them. I don't know the men I'm working with here well enough to trust them and I once had a terrible experience with a helper who hadn't been properly trained; he took all the finds from the different strata and happily tipped them into one wash bowl.'

'Was it an absolute disaster?'

'Fortunately there was other evidence to fall back on, but it was a blow.'

It might have been a tedious job, but I could always look up from what I was doing and watch what was going on as the men dug and sifted. William was forever jumping down into the trench and propping his measuring stick against the sides to take photographs or make drawings. Sometimes he would be down there on his knees for hours, scraping away at something he wanted to free from the soil.

'Come and help,' he called to me one day. 'This will interest you more than those little bits of stone.'

I abandoned my bowl of water and ancient toothbrush and went to join him. The outline of a leg, bent at the knee, could already be seen.

'Is it a statue?' I asked.

'That's right. Probably a Buddha. Here, take this trowel and work on the right side while I deal with the left.'

I copied the infinite care with which he scraped away at the surrounding soil and other details began to emerge. 'It's not stone, is it?' I asked.

'Probably bronze.'

'Not gold?'

'I hope not. Gold finds are a nuisance, they lead to robbers. Come on, time to take a break.'

'We can't leave it now,' I protested.

'You're hooked,' William said. 'Try to stand up, then you'll see why I think you should take a break.'

As I straightened I realised that my neck and shoulders were aching and my knees would scarcely hold me up.

'Let's see if Abdul has got some tea for us,' William said, taking hold of my arm to support me.

'My throat is full of dust,' I admitted.

We had our tea, but I could hardly wait to get back to the trench. Before we broke for dinner that night we had freed the statue. It was about eighteen inches high, a seated figure, with one foot on the ground and the other leg bent to rest on the seat. The figure leaned slightly to the right with the elbow of its right arm resting on the bent thigh.

'Very nice,' William said.

'It's lovely, so graceful. Is it a Buddha, like you said?'

'It's a Bodhisattva Padmapani and I'm fascinated to find it here.'

'How old is it?'

'Eighth, possibly seventh century. But I'm convinced this site is far, far older than that. What is interesting is the evidence that it went on being used not just for hundreds, but for thousands of years.'

We had a small celebration that evening, after we had cleaned ourselves up. I washed my hair and had to join William with it still spread out over my shoulders.

'I've half a mind to cut it off,' I said as I accepted the drink he handed me.

'If you go on with your film career perhaps they'll want you with long hair.'

'I've almost made up my mind to turn that offer down. I want . . . something different.'

I paused because I thought William was going to speak, but he said nothing and I went on, 'What I really must think about is what I'm going to do with all that jewellery Kesri gave me. I'd dearly like to parcel it up and send it back to him.'

'It would be a satisfaction to you, but would it benefit anyone else?'

'Not really, Kesri would be angry and, surprisingly enough, I think he would be hurt. I accepted the baubles readily enough and he had no reason to think I wasn't pleased with them. On the other hand, I could never bring myself to wear them again.'

'Not much point in keeping them in the Bank.'

'That's what I think. Perhaps I should sell them and give the proceeds to charity.'

'I've been turning another idea over in my mind ever since you first asked for my advice. Have you ever thought of becoming a merchant, Jessica?'

'How extraordinary that you should say that!' I felt quite lit up with excitement because William and I had been thinking along the same lines. 'It's been at the back of my mind ever since I drifted round the backwaters of Srinagar and looked at all the pretty things the pedlars tried to sell me. Could I, do you think, import in sufficient quantity to set up a little shop in England?'

'With your talent for bargaining I should think you'd do well, but what I had in mind was more far-reaching than that. Do you remember telling me about buying the embroidery the women were doing in hospital? How about encouraging village industries?'

'If I could supply them with better materials . . . show them the sort of thing I could sell . . . William, that's a brilliant idea!'

'It would need a lot of organising. You'd have to come to India at least once a year and take some weeks to visit the workshops.'

'It would be a joy to feel I haven't absolutely severed my link with India. I'm really excited about it.'

'I think you'd have to keep out of Bhuredar. It would be more tactful to confine your efforts to British India.'

'Yes, that's true. "British India" – we've got a nerve, haven't we, calling it that?'

'I think so. More and more I'm coming round to the idea of leaving India.'

316

'But your work!'

'There are other fields. I've been offered the curatorship of an important museum in England, together with the chance of directing an excavation in Persia. One of those letters you brought for me the other day was the formal offer, which I've been expecting, and the other was a personal letter from the outgoing curator urging me to accept.'

'And will you?'

'Logically I ought to snap it up. I've been working very happily for several years under Sir John Marshall, but this would be an opportunity to run my own project.'

'So what makes you hesitate?'

'There are . . . other considerations,' William said.

I ran my hand through my hair to see if it was dry and William leaned forward and took a long tress in his hand. 'It's very beautiful,' he said.

I smiled at his serious expression and William gave an odd little grimace and let the handful of hair fall back on my shoulder.

I opted out of the more strenuous digging the next day and went back to my small finds. William seemed preoccupied, but I understood that now. He must be thinking very seriously about his future.

The days were warmer than when we had first started. The chilly wind which had blown through the trees had left us and the sky was a clear blue. By the middle of the afternoon I was able to discard the woolly sweater in which I normally worked. Even in the shade of the trees it was too warm for that.

I paused with my hands in the muddy water, feeling in the murk for a small piece of carved stone I knew was there. Idly, not thinking of anything in particular, I watched William as he talked to one of the workmen. He stood on the edge of his excavation, quite still but full of contained energy, intent on what he was explaining. He was wearing a loose cotton shirt with the neck open and the sleeves rolled up above his elbows, and crumpled cotton trousers, with native sandals on his feet. His head was bare and his dark hair was ruffled. His spare, taut figure had a curious elegance, silhouetted against the sky. As he turned away the workman made some remark and William flung up his hand, acknowledging a joke. Suddenly I was aware of him as I had never been before.

I saw, as if for the first time, the strength and vigour of his body, the long bones, the fine planes of his face, the texture of his skin, the way his ears were set against his skull and the way his hair lay at the nape of his neck. I saw the way he walked with balanced ease over the rough ground and I thought that was the word to describe William – balanced. A man at home with himself, firm in his integrity. A man to love.

In that moment my life changed. It had been coming on for a long time. Now that my eyes were open I could see that. *I loved William.* This was not the exasperated affection which was all I had managed to feel for Edmond, nor the white-hot intensity of my love for Dominic; it was not the guilty sensuality I had shared with Kesri. This was love – not being in love, but love, authentic and enduring.

I must have been a strangely silent companion that evening. I kept glancing at William and looking away again, struck by wonder and shyness. He was the same as he had always been and yet so different. He was my world and I had no idea how it had happened. Or, indeed, what I was going to do about it.

'We both seem to have lost our tongues,' William remarked.

'You've got things on your mind and so have I,' I said. 'Do you think I can settle in England, William?'

'I like to think you can,' William said. He looked at me with frowning intentness as if trying to fathom my mind. 'Are you changing your mind about your trading project?'

'Possibly. I've begun to see . . . difficulties.'

'Want to talk it over?'

I shook my head. There was nothing I wanted to say to William except that I loved him.

I spent an almost sleepless night. Again and again the same question came into my mind: if Dadda had not died and I had stayed in India, would William and I have turned to one another? He had always been fond of me and I had always looked up to him. How differently my life might have turned out if I had not left for England when I was fifteen. Looking back at the scrawny, self-opinionated youngster I had been then I felt affection and disbelief. I had been so sure that I knew best, both for myself and for everyone else. I was not so self-confident now, in spite of my wider experience.

I loved William. That was an unalterable fact. Without him my life would be so diminished that I could hardly bear to think about it. I wanted to share everything with him. If that was not possible then the idea of marketing Indian crafts in England, coming and going in the country that had been ours, in touch with William but not part of his life, was too painful to face.

The alternative was to go to Hollywood after all and try to make a successful career for myself, but that success no longer seemed particularly desirable. It had a tawdry feel to it. I had no illusions about the kind of film Sol had in mind for me. Not for me the respect given to a serious actor: I was to be a symbol of glamour and sex. I could see it a little too clearly for comfort – money and acclaim and plenty of men, but none of them a man like William, whose children I would be willing to bear. I knew myself too well now to believe that I could live without a man in my life. There would be other Kesris and with each one I would feel my self-respect slip a notch lower.

The only way out of that downward spiral that I could see was to fight for what I really wanted. William was free and he was fond of me. He had called me his darling and he had kissed me once. I had never been quite sure how to interpret that episode, but it did seem to show that William was attracted to me, though he might not love me in the way I had discovered that I loved him.

319

Looking at myself dispassionately I saw a beautiful young woman, slightly shopsoiled perhaps, but William was a large-minded man and he would not hold my past against me. I was reasonably intelligent and I had already begun to share some of his interests. I was capable of developing an independent existence, running my own project to help Indian villagers, and I thought William would approve of that. I could give him the family I believed he must want.

By the morning I had decided to ask William to marry me. If he turned me down I would sell my jewels and give the money to charity and then put half the world between us and go to Hollywood.

I was a nervous wreck the next day. It was all very well in the lonely small hours of the night to make a momentous decision, it was something else to put it into practice in daylight. I avoided William as much as I could. In fact, I behaved so oddly that he asked me if I was feeling quite well.

'Oh, yes . . . yes,' I said airily. 'William, this evening I must talk to you.' I blurted it out because I knew that given half an excuse I would go back on what I had decided, I was in such a state of nerves about it.

'It's time we talked,' William agreed.

All the same, we exchanged nothing but the lightest chit-chat while we were eating that night. The light had faded and we had lit the lamp before William said, 'We've both got things to say. Do you want to go first?'

'Perhaps what you want to say might change my mind about what I want to say.'

'And vice versa. One of us has to start.' He looked at me with that amused smile that had suddenly started making my heart twist in knots. 'I think it had better be me,' he said. 'I've decided to accept the job in England.'

'I thought you would and I'm glad. I'm sure it's the right thing for you.'

'And you – are you really having doubts about the Indian trading project?'

'I'm keeping Hollywood in reserve in case . . . in case

what I really want doesn't happen.' This was my chance. It was now or never. I gulped and blurted out, 'William, you'll need someone to look after you in England. Servants are difficult to come by since the war and you aren't used to running a house. What about me?'

I took a quick look at him and saw surprise, worry and something that looked strangely like anger all reflected in his face in quick succession. 'Are you suggesting yourself as my housekeeper?'

'No, we'd have to get married.'

William stood up, pushing back his chair with such force that it fell over. He took a few steps away from the table and stood with his back to me, looking out over the dimming view towards the lake. Obviously I had said completely the wrong thing, but I was not going to let him get away without a fight. I went to join him.

'You're fond of me,' I pointed out. 'And there isn't anyone else, is there?'

'There's never been anyone else since you came back to India and I saw you in Bombay,' William said without looking at me.

I was still grappling with that when he turned and took both my hands in his, holding them so tightly that the bones felt crushed.

'My dear, you've been married once to a man who loved you more than you loved him. Could you endure that a second time? I'm tempted to say yes, yes! Give me what I want more than anything in the world! But I love you too much to let you walk into what may seem to you like a trap.'

'You love me?' I whispered.

'Of course I do! Think, Jessica, think. I've worked damned hard at seeming uninterested, but you must have had some inkling of the way I felt.'

I shook my head, not because I disbelieved him, but to try to clear my chaotic thoughts so that I could begin to make sense. Before I could speak William had pulled me towards him, more roughly than I think he intended, and set his mouth to mine.

321

This was my language. All I could think of as I clung to him was that this was the way I could show William how much I loved him. Once he had begun to kiss me he was not easily satisfied and I was certainly not going to let him go until he showed signs of stopping.

At last his lips reluctantly moved away from mine, but he still held me close. With his face nuzzled in against the side of my neck he said, 'Oh, God, Jessica! What am I going to do?'

I could feel a smile tugging at the corners of my mouth. Judging by the state of his body poor William was in a very bad way indeed, and it seemed that he was still in need of reassurance.

'I love you,' I said softly, but very clearly. 'I love you as much as you love me and possibly more. As to what you can do about it, goodness William, you don't need me to tell you, do you?'

He lifted his head and looked at me, quite dazed. 'You love me?'

'I've only known since four o'clock yesterday afternoon so it still feels very strange, but I knew I'd got to make some attempt to join my life to yours or I'd be lost forever. I decided I'd better ask you to marry me.'

William looked at me, a long, fixed stare, and then he said in an unsteady voice, 'I accept.'

We began to laugh, uncertainly at first and then helplessly, holding one another up in our joy and relief.

'Four o'clock yesterday afternoon,' William said. 'What did I do at that particular moment to make you fall in love so satisfactorily, my darling?'

'Nothing. You just stood there and suddenly the whole world turned upside down.'

'The same thing happened to me when I saw you in that flat in Bombay. You flew towards me and when I'd disentangled myself I looked down and saw the girl I'd always wanted and she was married to another man.'

'William . . . how awful! I never suspected, not for one minute.'

We moved towards one of the trees that had been cut

322

down and sat on the fallen trunk with our arms round one another. We kissed again and it was a revelation. Chaotic thoughts of Edmond and Dominic and Kesri tumbled about in my mind, but this was William and it was different and unbelievably sweet.

'Goodness, what will the servants think,' I said, trying to be sensible.

'Abdul will be relieved. He's been having doubts about my manhood. I hope I misunderstood him, but I think he was giving me hints about aphrodisiacs the other day.'

'I don't think that'll be necessary.'

'Hardly. My self-control has already been strained to its limits. You're the most exciting, desirable woman I've ever known and I love you, love you, love you – perhaps above all for your beautiful generosity. Who else would come round from a stabbing and start worrying about the injuries suffered by her attacker's father?'

'I never expected to be loved for my moral qualities,' I said, deeply gratified. 'We've been good companions, haven't we? We mustn't lose that.'

'It's the most satisfactory thing in the world, to love and be loved by someone who is also your best friend.'

'Yes,' I said, really struck. 'That's something I've never had before. I . . . I think I ought to speak, just this once, about the other men I've known.'

'If that's what you want to do.'

'Edmond . . . you know about poor Edmond. I married him without really loving him and nothing he did made me feel any better towards him.'

'I could see you weren't suited and it didn't make it any easier to go away and leave you with him.'

I brushed my lips against his forehead and went on, 'Dominic – I really loved Dominic, both before and after I married Edmond. It was an intensely physical relationship. I've tried to tell myself that it was strong enough to have endured, but sometimes I wonder. I wasn't a good Company wife – would I have got on any better with the Army? We had one week in fairyland. One week. Even now I don't think I could bear to go and see the Taj Mahal with anyone else.'

'I'm not jealous, if that's what you're worried about. You're clearsighted enough to know that your time with Dominic had very little to do with real life. Keep your lovely memory. What we've got to learn to do is to live with one another in the world with all its problems and annoyances. Darling, have you really been having second thoughts about going on with your acting career? Because, if so, I'm sure we can work something out. You could go off and make films and I could console myself with a dig.'

'Is that what you'd really like?'

'No, I'm selfish enough to want you with me all the time, but you did make quite a name for yourself and if you want to build on it I'll grit my teeth and bear it.'

'I don't altogether like the name I made for myself. No, I don't want to make any more films. I was keeping Hollywood in reserve in case you turned me down. I think I will want an outside interest. I'm sorry, but that's the way I am.'

'And that's the way I like you. I'm sure we can work up the connection with Indian craftsmen.'

'Bless you. But, of course, what I want more than anything else is a family. Would you like children?'

'Very much. Your children.'

'Oh, dear, you're making me cry.' I rubbed my hand across my eyes and went on resolutely with the recital of my past sins. William didn't require it, I knew that, but I wanted to get it out of the way, once and for all.

'Kesri – what can I say about Kesri? I went to bed with him because it was one of the conditions of being employed.'

'And enjoyed it,' William said calmly.

'Oh, heck, I was hoping to avoid having to admit that. Don't look at me. I feel ashamed.'

'I'd much rather you admitted to a bit of hotblooded lust than to a cold, joyless prostitution. Kesri, I imagine, is highly educated in the art of pleasing women?'

'He knows all about it,' I admitted.

'Ah, well, with a bit of goodwill on both sides, and a lot of love, I dare say we'll manage all right, you and I.'

We looked at one another with amused complicity.

'So . . .' I said.

'So . . . your tent or mine?'

'Oh, William, those camp beds!'

I began to laugh helplessly as his arms closed round me. William's mouth felt for mine and we exchanged one more kiss. When I opened my eyes I saw that the moon had risen. As we walked with our arms round one another the short distance to my tent, I could see far below us the glint of water through the trees. Lifting my head I saw the moonlight on the distant mountains, shining white.

England would be different, and strange to both of us. It would be difficult to settle, but we would be together. Never mind the pleasures and palaces through which I had roamed . . . I had found the place where I was meant to be. I was with William. *I had come home.*